Copyright © MARTIN KNOX 2019
First published by Zeus Publications 2019
http://www.zeus-publications.com
P.O. Box 2554
Burleigh M.D.C.
QLD 4220
Australia.

A catalogue record for this book
is available from the National
Library of Australia

ISBN: 978-1-920699-57-4

Martin Knox Books

Available from Amazon in Australia, USA, UK and Canada

The Grass is Always Browner (2011)
Love Straddle (2014)
Presumed Dead (2018)
$hort of Love (2019)
Time is Gold (2020)
Animal Farm 2 (2021)
Turkeys not Bees (2022)
Brisbane River Anti-Memoir (2023)
The Camel, The Lion and The Child (2024)
Energy Lessons (2024)
Nanny State (2024)
New Climate War is Real (2025)
Facets of Femininity (2025)
Philosophical Harvest (2025)

Dedication

I dedicate this book to
my family: Zoe, Tessa, Amani, Uly and Dorian

Contents

PROLOGUE

It is July 2006.

As Tom's plane climbed away from Calgary, a gong sounded to unfasten seat belts. He reclined in first class. He had a mental technique for enjoying travel in planes: he imagined he was a pupating insect, like a silkworm in its cocoon, in suspended animation. He had all he needed to be comfortable: adjustable seats, footrests, air vents, lights, video, audio and a button to summon a flight attendant. He could metamorphose and emerge ready to face different conditions at his destination.

Cocooned, he could reflect and update his understanding of past events that had caused him to make this journey. If he had known earlier what he knew now, he would have sought closure many years ago.

Here is the story of the relationships and events causing him to be flying from Calgary to London, including feelings he should have anticipated, but had ignored until they were problems.

They had started while he was living at home on Priory Farm, Yorkshire, many years earlier.

CHAPTER 1
DISCOVERING GIRLS

Competition for university entrance was fierce. His school's study regimen was gruelling, with little extra-curricular social contact and no opportunities to meet girls. His main recreation was interschool rugby. He sometimes captained the forwards, announcing the plays that the eight would execute.

The spectre of a nuclear catastrophe overhung his teenage years. Tom was apprehensive. Like several of his classmates, he was appalled by injustices adults imposed on their world. In his view adults were complacent and derelict in failing to halt the Cold War, which was escalating. Most of the adults he encountered were bigoted, narrow-minded, ignorant and lacking in understanding of adolescents. He resented his powerlessness. One night, standing under the stars, his mind spoke to the universe, dedicating his life to bringing freedom and happiness to youths and children everywhere.

The land of Priory Farm had most of its area planted to wheat, with 1000 sheep and several hundred beef cattle in lots. His father employed half a dozen local farm workers but for the family the workload didn't cease after hours. Males were on duty to care for livestock 24/7. Females cared for the men and sick animals. Tom helped at weekends but his school work was higher priority. Holidays were rare and time for recreation was taken when the weather was too foul to work outside. Family outings and picnics were sometimes held in the rain.

Tom's presence in the farming community was tenuous. He was a social misfit, although some of the local girls regarded him as exotic. He read an illicit copy of *Lady Chatterley's Lover* and discovered how sexual relations were conducted within struggles of loyalty between the sexes and classes. When he was in final year at school, a conclave of Church of England parsons arranged for boys in the sixth form to consider boy-girl relationships with their counterparts from the girls' grammar school. When asked to discuss how emotions could affect sexual relations, Tom and his classmates were ill-prepared and too shy to speak. The instruction was abstract and incomprehensible and the ensuing discussion monosyllabic. His mother upbraided the school principal for exposing Tom to this topic without parental permission.

'You have no right to put these notions into his head,' she said. 'He is more interested in Chemistry.'

When this was told in the staffroom, Tom was nicknamed 'Chemistry' Archer by the teachers, embarrassing him.

Tom made friends with girl students on the bus to and from school. When it was crowded a girl would sit on his lap, where his intrepid organ would make its presence felt. When he stood up, he kept his hand in his trousers' pocket to hide the tent.

At parties in the village hall he danced pelvis to pelvis with buxom Sharon Wright. Her seraphic smiles encouraged him to hold her close and she let him press against her. In the darkness outside, they discovered French kissing.

Tom's attention was usually on one or other of the local girls. He was thirsting for sexual involvement at a time of maternal prohibition. He would ride on his horse past his latest heart-throb's home, lacking courage to knock on the door but hoping to glimpse her. Or he would arrange to meet her in a mossy glade of a local wood, where they would hold hands and kiss.

When his radio played The Beatles' number 'I Want to Hold Your Hand', an ocean of intimacy beckoned. He kissed his sister's Dutch pen-friend in a dinghy rocking on the farm pond. At Christmas, he groped girls under duffle coats in the darkness of the backs of Land Rovers that carried carol singers from farm to farm.

Furtive embracing did not much appeal to the girls. They wanted their relationship to be respectable and open to public scrutiny, the exact opposite of Tom's interest in casual sex.

Tom imagined he was missing out on never-to-be-repeated opportunities for fun. His life was being taken from him. When he saw a bonsai tree in a garden shop, he self-identified with its stunted growth. Whenever he declared an interest in a girl, his mother objected. She could find no good in anyone. A girl would be unacceptable because of undesirable religion, ethnicity, family history, health inheritance or deficient property ownership, economic prospects, social class or community standing. In short, her ruling was that no girl was good enough for Tom, nor allowed to be trialled by him.

He became friends with a girl who lived up the road and travelled on the bus. When he sought permission to go to a movie with her, his mother was adamant.

'Certainly not. She is working class, not our type. Her father went insane once; he might still be crazy now and madness runs in their family. You will not have anything to do with her. You don't need a girl now. That will come later. If you don't get on with your school work, you'll have to leave school and be a mechanic.'

His mother's prejudices and bigoted over-control were crushing. Leaving home couldn't come soon enough.

In his final year at school, Tom took the advice of his Chemistry teacher and applied to several universities to study petroleum engineering. When he went for an interview at Liverpool University of Technology, he liked the ambiance and was delighted to be offered enrolment, conditional on getting high grades in his exams.

Two months later his 'A-Level' results were out. He received As and Bs and his place at LUT was secured. He leapt for joy. Release of pressure from years of delayed gratification made his head spin. He began to smile and people noticed.

'When are you leaving?'

'Next month.'

'Lucky you. You've got it made.'

CHAPTER 2
GOING UP

Tom's ascension within the rigid social hierarchy of the Dales was sensational.

A few days before Tom would go away to university, Lord St Tanby, Priory Farm's landlord, invited him to afternoon tea at Wortham House, an unheard-of honour for a tenant farmer's son. He was nervous as he cycled between the gamekeepers' cottages and along the sweeping drive, through the Great Park with its deer and peacocks, past the laurel hedges of the maze, to climb the balustraded steps and tug on the brass bell-pull of the great Elizabethan country house. He was received by the sole remaining servant and led into a sumptuous drawing room where Lord St Tanby, an elderly bachelor, was taking tea before a blazing log fire with his two spinster sisters.

It was rumoured locally that the three had never married because they were so wealthy they could never trust a lover not to be a gold digger.

'Aristocrats are a separate species,' Tom had read in a political pamphlet. 'They don't breed fertile offspring with lower-class people, at least not openly. They are in-bred, with their gene pool declining. Disabilities and speech impediments are frequent.'

Lord St Tanby was a bumbling, kindly man, well-liked within the world he owned, which was everything within a radius of 10 kilometres, including scores of tenanted farms and half a dozen two-pub, one-church villages that William the Conqueror awarded to his ancestor.

'Ah, Tom! I'm glad you could come,' he said genially and introduced him to his sisters. They poured him a cup of tea and questioned him about his schooling. They wanted to know how the university application process worked and what subjects he would be studying.

The Right Honourable Lord St Tanby had been Chief Whip for the Conservatives in the House of Lords. He eyed Tom with suspicion, as if he might be a potentially dangerous mutant. Education of the masses at university, as proposed by Labour, could disempower his kind.

'Hmm, engineering,' said his lordship. 'I suppose we do need engineers. Liverpool is just the sort of place that needs them. I went to Cambridge myself. Not much engineering there, by Jove. Mostly hot air, what?' he laughed hollowly. 'Your parents must be proud of you. Now, what do you think about the election? Are you for MacMillan's lot? I mean, what do you think about this new, er, chap, Harold, er, Wilson?'

'I like Mr Wilson,' Tom said, unaware of the significance to his hosts of Wilson's threat to dispossess the aristocracy with inheritance and wealth taxes. Had he realised, discretion might have been the better part of valour, for Tom's reply startled his lordship and he slopped tea into his saucer, while his sisters shook their heads despondently.

'Really? And why do you like him?' Lord St Tanby looked over his glasses at Tom in astonishment, as if Tom's endorsement heralded an apocalypse.

'Labour would increase the number of students at university,' Tom said, naively parroting radical opinion. 'It would level society. A coal miner's son could study alongside the son of an earl. People would understand each other better.'

'Really?' Lord St Tanby was sceptical.

Tom nodded. That was the end of the conversation. They shook hands, St Tanby wished him well and rang for the servant to show him out.

CHAPTER 3
LEAVING HOME

He took a nostalgic turn around the market square of Wortham in his old Volkswagen beetle, an ancient 'pretzel' model, with a split rear window. Fighting men armed with pikes and hay picks had gathered here on the cobblestones to resist marauders from the north and east. His eyes cherished the uniformity of the houses, regimented shoulder to shoulder for shelter and warmth. Men were setting up pens for the annual sheep fair. There were stalls where women would sell foods. It was an environment that afforded few luxuries but he knew he would miss his community of hardy Dales people.

He passed between narrow walls, crossed a humpback bridge and drove up Nidderdale to begin a new life. The road intertwined with the river, rippling between banks where tall oak, birch, sycamore, horse chestnut and ash trees stood like sentinels. Cultivated fields alternated with rectangular patches of woodland. He knew these covers well, from walking through them in a line of beaters, putting pheasants to flight towards the guns of their landlord's shooting parties. There were crows' nests on the leafless furthermost branches, too slender to hold the weight of any except the lightest of boys, when they climbed up and stole eggs, as he had done.

The road climbed on up the dale between sheep pastures, a patchwork of emerald fields draped across the bottom of the glaciated valley, turned up at the sides to meet the moor reaching down from above and quilted by sunken dry-stone walls.

Sunlight broke through here and there, adding patches of pale purple heather, soft brown bracken and light greens of cotton grass, bilberry, heath and mosses, grazed by sheep trailing lambs. Soon shepherds would bring them down for the winter, to the in-bye fields where there was grass and hay in barns.

He ascended towards the pass through rough grazing, where wisps of mist oozed down the hillsides from the peaks. The road went under a vast rail bridge, a procession of soaring brickwork arches. He emerged with a greener land before him and in the distance, a glimpse of Liverpool where he would start his new life.

He turned on Radio Luxembourg and listened to the Beatles' number 'Ticket to Ride' as he jinked down the hair-pinned road, yelling: 'She ought to think right. She ought to do right by me. He is going away and he don't care'.

'Nothing can stop me now,' he thought.

FIRST YEAR

CHAPTER 4
MARATHON MAN

Eighty-two fresher students, all males, filled the lecture theatre. This inaugural lecture announced commencement of a contest.

'We won't have room for all of you next year,' said the course convenor. 'Those of you with low marks, the bottom 10%, will have your enrolment cancelled at the end of this year.'

Tom liked competition. He had the ability to shut out the world and give his attention to one thing at a time, not letting feelings and emotions get in the way.

Engineering was what he liked doing best. He had spent his school holidays at home building racing carts, tree houses, rafts, dams, waterwheels, hydroelectric generators, siege catapults and flying foxes. He had modified farm machinery, converted a street car into a go-kart and made chemical explosions. He had a thirst for technology and used every opportunity to learn as much as he could.

His task was not merely to pass. He wanted First Class honours. Top marks would win a good job, high salary and attract exciting females. He wanted to be an oil tycoon, pilot his own plane, ski, sail, scuba dive, live in a penthouse and drive a fast car. To do these things he had to distinguish himself.

Imagining the task ahead, Tom had an epiphany that he was lined up with the other freshers at the start of a three-year academic marathon.

'How can I finish in first place?' Tom asked a friend who was an endurance runner.

'How will they assess you?'

'Finals exams.'

'You must establish superiority early, keep up with the leading bunch, conserve energy and sprint into the lead during Finals,' he said.

None of them had studied engineering before. Tom's A-Level grades were above average but not outstanding. He knew little of the others' abilities.

'I would have done better at school if I hadn't hated it so much,' he thought. *'I can top this class if I put in enough effort.'*

They set off tightly bunched at a blistering pace. It was difficult to pick the frontrunners, because some hung back to conserve energy. He recorded opponents' traits that might indicate high potential: assiduous note-taking; high-quantity library borrowing; interaction with lecturers outside class. He tried to establish mutuality with the better students in conversation and by sharing answers to assignments with them. The high-flyers were reticent. Those who reciprocated were mediocre. He persevered and people started coming to him for help with their work.

He ratcheted up his effort until he was fully loaded. The pain limiting him was cerebral not muscular. It hurt to pore over abstract theories for hour upon hour with his body screaming for recreation, but he became habituated and even enjoyed the work.

He whistled The Beatles' song 'Baby You Can Drive My Car, yes I'm going to be a star'. He loved being a university student, living away from home beyond his mother's control. He worked as hard as he could. When the others went to the Students' Union bar, he studied. When they went to parties, he studied some more. He allowed himself one night off per week. He accepted he was going to miss out on a lot of fun, but he could catch up on that after he finished.

He thrived in a strict routine. He studied 14 hours a day, six days a week and watched peers lose motivation, reduce their effort and drop out. He shared a room with Sean, a student from Manchester who was soon out of his depth.

'I thought engineering was designing things, not fooking maths,' Sean grumbled.

Sean induced his own demise by writing his lecture notes on toilet paper, the old hard type, in biro. When he tried to revise from a pile of sheets that leaned against the bedroom wall, it toppled over. He tried to sort the unnumbered pages into order, without success.

'Fook it!' Sean threw his notes into the air, where they drifted down like snowflakes into a valueless heap.

'Ah'll git a job,' he said. 'I'm nah coot aht fur stoodyin'.'

A few days later Sean went home to Manchester and didn't come back.

Studying suited Tom fine. He was in the leading group and looked for ways to improve his efficiency for the long haul ahead. He eased off a little, to everyone's relief.

CHAPTER 5
THE VALUE OF LOVE AND MARRIAGE

Thousands of healthy young men and women, aged between 18 and 25, crowded into LUT's buildings all day, every day. Learning was only one of pursuits possible. Coupling into heterosexual monogamous pairs was popular. Sometimes the attachments became permanent.

He was intrigued how students paired off. Not every student wanted permanent commitment to a partner and explored temporary relationships. A male could meet a partner the way termite drones did, landing from the mating flight and coupling with the nearest queen. More often, liaisons began with serendipitous meetings, but Tom found many students selected their partners systematically by observing informal social hierarchies. After reading an academic article: 'The Economics of Love and Marriage', Tom became aware that many students at LUT were active in a notional 'love market', where love trysts were struck between needy 'buyers' and willing 'sellers', according to personal worth. Relative values of each male and female were speculated on within the social community of the university, depending on their attributes, circumstances and social successes.

Females competed informally for male attention. Each wanted to display her own high value to attract a high-value male. They vied with their peers for social pre-eminence in attention from high-status males, who rated highest a girl with qualities of beauty, personality and wealth. Their interest established a social hierarchy of female value, like a squash ladder.

Attributes and possessions determined who could pair with whom. Top girls paired off with men they rated highest up a ladder of male value, depending on attributes of wealth, socialism, social connections, sports cars, physical strength and beauty. There was a surplus of males and inexperienced fresher men like Tom were not rated high enough up the ladder for university girls to be interested.

The most desirable female paired off with the male highest up the male ladder, allowing a little flexibility for personal preferences. The second most desirable female would gladly accept the most desirable male but when he was already taken, she settled for the second most desirable, again with a little leeway. Girls with the least man-pulling ability, near the bottom, found matches with low-ranking males. The process continued until the least desirable males remained untaken and had to chase skirt off-campus, or spend their time in the bar playing darts with other males.

It didn't matter how much a man wanted an intelligent and beautiful partner, or how many things he was willing to give up or provide for her, he had no chance if a more highly rated male was available. Competition was all-or-nothing; if a male had half the attraction of his competitor, the result was he lost and the winner took all.

Beauty was the medium women preferred to reveal in match-making, because those without means but having looks could attract a more desirable man by suppressing revelation of their lack of wealth.

The hiding of wealth was not in the interests of less wealthy people. The notion of romantic love exclusive of material consideration was copied from fiction stories that pandered to populism. A couple's consideration of the balance of their wealth was deemed unromantic, as if a better match should result by hiding it.

Social conventions hid from view the material dimension in love matches, protecting wealthy and poor people. The rich insulated themselves from competition by hiding their wealth, except from each other and were accustomed to wealth being a criterion in matches.

For ordinary people, 'pairing off' was a fraught business, in which a partner's possessions were concealed. Young lovers' experience of wealth was limited and they were ill-equipped to negotiate material terms. They deemed irrelevant financial resources, property and inheritances, not just because these were 'unromantic', but because many people who heard wedding bells were imbued with meritocratic and egalitarian urges. They thought marriage would level their contributions. Unless they had experience of the intrigues, subterfuges and perils of deception normal in commerce and politics, young lovers went like lambs to the slaughter, leaving material matters until later. Unfortunately, a naïve lover could become exploited, or an exploiter.

'The financial dimension should be out in the open,' Tom thought.

Tom saw little prospect of a match with a university girl until his second year. He figured he would be better off spending his first year developing personal attributes the girls would value once he was in the running. Instead of spending his time at extra-curricular activities such as debating, which had kudos but required much time, he hit the academic straps. A trajectory to a First-Class degree could score a classy chick in second year. High achievement wasn't everything but it could go a long way with girls.

By chance, halfway through the year, he met an attractive first-year girl, Bridget.

CHAPTER 6
BRIDGET

They studied side by side and began dating. It was Tom's first relationship and affirmed that at least one female could want him and her interest in him seemed to be increasing. His affection for her was growing too. The Beatles' song 'She Loves You' seemed to speak to him alone. Bridget required a permanent commitment before having sex, but Tom wasn't ready to settle down just yet. He wanted to explore a range of girls. His and Bridget's lodgings were far apart, their landladies were strict and sex was not possible.

Towards the end of first year Bridget started planning for them to live together in second year, but Tom shrank from the prospect.

'I'm not sure Bridget is the one,' he thought. *'My choice is forever. I don't want to get stuck.'*

She wasn't the one. Tom imagined living with Bridget would be too sedate. They would rent a sensible dwelling, lead a sensible home life, take sensible holidays, apply for a sensible mortgage, invest in sensible superannuation and have sensible babies.

He wanted adventures, especially sleeping around. Commitment to Bridget would mean staying sober, leaving parties early, ugly pregnancy, noisy babies, whinging children, outings to shopping centres, family gatherings, conformance, predictability and having to plod on the treadmill of a career to pay for his family's normalised consumption. His life would be over before it had started.

Tom's amygdala wanted emotional challenge, not settling down. He would be clipped like a nestling's wings before it had flown. He was acutely aware he was a virgin. He had flying to do.

He would decide what to do with Bridget before the end of the year. Her blushes reminded him too much of his mother's face, flushed with self-righteousness. When Bridget told him she ironed her hair to remove natural curls, he was amazed that an intelligent woman could be so influenced by arbitrary fashion. He was fond of Bridget but he was not ready to commit to a life of hair ironing.

Staying with Bridget would trade off relief from his anxiety about being a virgin for anxiety about his loss of freedom. He would have to be 30, in another 10 years, before he could consider a permanent relationship. Before then he had a lot of living to do, like James Bond. The chances were he would get a shag with some girl soon. He did not like Bridget enough to spend the rest of his life with her. Because it might be difficult to uncouple, he would be better off not to hitch up. He decided to break up with her. To minimise her hurt, the separation had to be decisive and quick, like ripping off a bandaid.

'Goodbye, Bridget,' he said. 'You are a wonderful person. I met you 10 years too early.'

He wanted to be kind and have her think the deficiency was his, so he didn't tell her she was not his type.

'How can you be so unfeeling?' she said.

He did have feelings but not the ones she wanted.

Her unhappy face seemed to pop up around the university for weeks afterward, but there was no way back. She took up with his former friend Wyatt. Tom had little in common with either of them and forgot them both.

Free from Bridget, he reverted to the company of his classmates, who by now had formed into social groups. One group was from northeast England, its talk strongly accented. Foreigners were in other groups. There were Iraqis, Iranians, Continentals and Colonials. Others played snooker in the Students' Union together, instead of going to lectures.

Tom became friendly with a middle-middle-class group, dominated by ex-public schoolboys from 'county' professional homes in the southeast. They played rugby and cricket, driving their sports cars in rallies at weekends.

'Tom, as you don't have a sports car, you can time us crossing the finish line.'

After the race no-one offered him a lift to the pub and he realised he didn't 'fit in' with them.

He fell in with several provincial lower-middle-class grammar school types like himself. His Yorkshire identity amused them as much as it embarrassed him. They made him say, 'Eee, lad, tha'll zoon be olt'nuff t'go down't pit.' It meant: 'Well, boy, you will soon be old enough to go underground mining.' Repeating the words was boring and he tried to hide his regional identity. If he could acquire language and a manner that was urbane and cosmopolitan, he would be better able to obtain a girl likely to embrace the new sexual freedom he had heard about.

CHAPTER 7
GIRL

He scanned the crowded coffee lounge in the Students' Union for a familiar face. He had been preoccupied all year with studying and seldom came here. Socialising was not his scene but he needed a new girlfriend. He felt geeky and awkward.

Groups lounged in arm chairs and chatted, or sat cross-legged on the floor, with onlookers standing around. Students with coffee mugs cruised looking for girls, or for friends, or for a space to stand and watch the action. He didn't see anyone he knew. These students had been forging friendships while he had been busy studying,.

'Next year I will try to make some friends,' he thought.

Ceiling speakers pumped out 'Help' by The Beatles but it was drowned out by the hubbub. At the far end of the room, he spied though a pall of smoke a group sprawled over the furniture. They were so casual, fashionable and confident that they had to be third years from well-off homes. An exceptionally good-looking girl was at the centre of the group.

Tom focused on her as he sipped his coffee. She was like the glittering centrepiece in a diadem, reflecting light to and from lesser settings. She was absorbed and yet aloof, possibly a little bored. She spoke quietly with sincerity and good humour. He wanted to hear her talk and he shoved through the crowd towards her, apologising to those he pushed aside.

As he got closer he saw she was a magnet holding her group together. She sat back in a maroon silk blouse, her breasts bulging under a pattern of bunches of shiny red cherries with dark green leaves. Tight blue jeans encased long slim legs and maroon knee-length leather boots. She was smoking a cigarette delicately, with straight fingers, blowing smoke upwards in a narrow jet.

From time to time, she uncrossed her legs and leaned forward to tap ash into a tray on the table. She was talking with several of the males. Her posture was self-conscious, knowing she was being watched. A woman who has the attention of males attracts other males.

He stood to one side, where he could see her face. She looked across at him and he returned her gaze, giving her a wry smile. She smiled back coolly with brilliant green eyes and looked away. She was breathtakingly beautiful. Her long thick hair, the colour of old copper, was tied high in a ponytail that swung as she talked. Her hands, wrists and arms were slender. She wore a classic Cartier watch in gold, presumably an heirloom. Around the other wrist was a chunky gold bangle, with no join that he could see and was probably solid. There was a gold loop swinging by a chain from a stud in her earlobe. The jewellery she wore was worth more than most students' total possessions.

When she turned, her face was almond-shaped and fair, with a light sprinkling of freckles across the centre. Her eyes were playful and up for adventure. Her nose was narrow, straight, and finely chiselled, with the end upturned away from her sensual mouth. A smile habitually played on her full lips. It was the face of an aesthete, accustomed to refined living.

The others turned to listen to her. He heard her say 'Smith' and 'Wilson' in a melodic BBC voice above the noise. He guessed she had gone to a posh private school. She seemed to be talking about the Unilateral Declaration of Independence threatened for Rhodesia.

'What will Smith do when, um, Harold arrives in Rhodesia?' she asked in a lull in the uproar, looking around at her companions for an answer.

'It will escalate,' said someone. 'Smith will stand up to him.'

She shook her head, her ponytail jiggling. 'No. Smith will make some piddling concession so Wilson can save face, like promising to have an election at some vague time in the future. Wilson will claim he has won a back-down and will go home.'

Tom had been following the situation with some Rhodesian students. He was impressed by her handle on it.

'She's right,' he interrupted loudly, over the top of a student who was speaking. They all looked at Tom. He had shown support for their leader and they would allow him in.

'Harold is most interested in getting re-elected,' Tom said. 'Getting justice for black Rhodesians won't win him many votes over here.'

The group was silent as they listened.

'If he sends the troops in against Smith, British settlers in Africa will be rooted. They will be out of Africa. Voters with relatives in Africa will hate Wilson. African mining companies will go against him. No . . . Wilson will pull out and leave Ian Smith to crush the movement Labour encouraged last year in the name of democracy. He will desert the blacks. It's a hypocritical double-cross.'

He stopped. The girl looked at Tom thoughtfully. He knelt and sat cross-legged on the carpet near her and nodded to the student sitting on her left, an engineer in second year. After his outspokenness, Tom felt threatened by the silence. When the buzz of conversation resumed, he knew his intrusion had been accepted. She turned and spoke to the student beside her. Tom tried to lip-read his response and recognised some words: engineer, nerd, girlfriend, finished. She was getting the low-down on him and Bridget. He resented being labelled a nerd, as if he lacked social adroitness, which was manipulation he despised. The informant was probably a socialite.

Another student said that because Rhodesia depended on the UK's mineral markets, Wilson should adopt economic sanctions. It made good sense but the girl was not interested. He supposed that even the most stringent trade embargo could not mitigate her condemnation of Wilson for his treachery.

She was aware of him looking at her. Her smile lingered as she feigned interest in others' conversations, threw back her head and combed her hair with her fingers. Her display worked on him — he was entranced. He wondered what subject she studied.

'She is too alive to her surroundings to be a lawyer,' he thought. 'Lawyers are intuitive and judgemental thinkers. This girl is different. She is a feeler rather than a thinker and a juggler of decisions. She could be an art student or maybe in education.'

After half an hour, everyone got up and went off to lectures. She passed by him politely, with a smile, wafting a scent of wild flowers. Her bare arm brushed against his and his hairs sprang erect, tingling. His heart pounded jubilantly as he hurried to his lecture. As he strode along, he whistled through his teeth, 'Help me get my feet back on the ground'.

He had a goal and his studies could take second place for a while.

He knew he wanted her.

CHAPTER 8
MIMETIC DESIRE

I returned the following day. Trying to be social, I scanned the crowded coffee lounge for a familiar face. I had seldom come here as a fresher, because I had spent my time studying. Socialising was not my scene, but at the end of the previous year I had finished with Bridget, and needed a new girlfriend. I felt geeky and awkward.

At the far end of the room sprawled a casual group, fashionable and confident, third years from well-off families. The good-looking girl ornamented the group. I focussed on her as I sipped my coffee. She seemed to be holding court, the centre of attention, at once absorbed and yet aloof, seeming a little bored. Her head swung her ponytail. Sincerity and good humour alternated with scepticism and ridicule. I wanted to hear the talk and tried to get closer. I pushed through the crowd towards her, apologising repeatedly.

From time to time, she uncrosses her legs and leans forward to tap ash into an ashtray on the table. She is talking, discussing something with her group. Her posture is self-conscious, and I can see she is making an effort to be heard amid the uproar. She seems to have a personal interest in the topic. She shows a curious mixture of strength and vulnerability. I hear her say 'Smith' and 'Wilson' in a melodic BBC voice. She seems to be talking about the threat of Rhodesia's Unilateral Declaration of Independence, ridiculing Wilson's weak stand against Smith's white racism. I guess she went to a posh private school and is studying law.

I stood to one side, where I could watch her. She looked up at me and I returned her gaze, putting on my happy face. She smiled back with brilliant green eyes and looked away. She was breathtakingly beautiful and used to admiring stares. Her long thick hair was the colour of old copper, tied high at the back of her head and swung as she talked. She had slender hands, wrists and arms. On one wrist, she wore a classic gold Cartier watch, presumably an heirloom. On the other is a plain gold bracelet, a solid gold bangle, by the absence of a join mark. She wore jewellery worth more than most students' total possessions. Her ear was white and fragile like a seashell, with a light gold circle swinging by a chain from a stud in the lobe.

When she turned, her face was almond-shaped and fair, with a light sprinkling of freckles across the centre. Her nose was narrow, straight, and finely chiselled, with the end upturned away from a sensual mouth. A smile plays on her full lips. It is the face of an aesthete, someone with a passion for refined experiences. Her eyes were playful, up for adventure. I got an impression of kindness, intelligence and fun.

'What do you think Smith will do when, um, Harold arrives in Rhodesia?' she asked. I was too far away to join in this conversation. She seemed accustomed to speaking in public on issues and has ideals.

'The situation will escalate, Vicki,' a student said.

A pretty name, I think. She shakes her head, ponytail jiggling. 'No. Smith will make some piddling concession, so that Wilson can save face, like promising to have an election. Wilson will claim it is, ah, a back-down.'

'Vicki's right,' I interrupted loudly, over the top of a student replying to her. He was surprised and fell silent. Vicki turned her head and looked me up and down. I continue, 'Harold is most interested in getting re-elected. Justice for black Rhodesians won't get many votes.' Everyone looks at me. The group falls silent as they strain to listen. 'As Vicki said, Wilson will desert the blacks, pulling out and leaving Ian Smith to crush the movement that Labour has encouraged up to now. It's a double-cross.'

Vicki nods at me thoughtfully. I kneel down and sit cross-legged on the carpet beside her. When I speak in a group, the silence afterwards always hurts and I feel rejected. It is a test of my intelligence and the buzz of conversation resumes.

Then another in the group starts rebutting my argument, stating that because Rhodesia depends on our mineral markets, economic sanctions would be successful and that is the way Wilson will go. It makes good sense and I learn from it. I have already achieved what I wanted. I have made a favourable impression on Vicki and the group. I have guessed correctly that they are not Labour stalwarts and my attack on Wilson is acceptable.

I watch Vicki's eyes and I try to imagine being her, aware of her deep beauty and unique features. Dark green irises nestle quietly but alert in her pure white sclera beneath long copper eyelashes. Her eyes retract as brow and cheeks come together in deep smiles that crinkle at her temples.

She is totally alive to her surroundings, feeling others' emotions and moods, giving her mind to understanding, rather than pronouncing judgements, her awareness composed rather than fearful. She is her own person in every way. Her friends return her smiles. I had heard that *'A woman who gets male group attention is attractive to individual males.'* I was not the only male who desired her. According to philosopher Girard, my desire for her could originate from their attraction to her. I am a victim of mimetic desire for her, taken from the others.

I studied my desire for her. It was third person desire from her other admirers and I had caught it. Their desire was covert, intensely embarrassing and they wouldn't admit to it. The power dynamics made them miserable. I was too new to the group to enter into any rivalries over her. The others wanted to reduce the conflict.

She was aware I was watching her by her lingering small smile, her feigned interest in others' conversations and the way she combed her hair through her fingers. I feel myself falling under her spell. She had infected me with desire to be with her. I wonder what subject she studies. She was too alive to her surroundings to be a lawyer. She could be an art student or maybe in education.

After half an hour, everyone got up and went off to lectures. Vicki passed me by politely, with an encouraging smile, as if she wanted to meet me, but I was too shy to say anything. She left an odour of wild flowers. Where her bare arm brushes against mine, my hairs spring erect and my skin tingled. Her acknowledgement had my heart pounding jubilantly in my chest as I hurried to my lecture. Suddenly, my whole world had changed. As I strode along, I whistled through my teeth a Beatles song: 'Help me get my feet back on the ground'.

I had a goal and my studies could take second place for a while.

My desire for Vicki is more than I can remember with any other girl.

In the days following, Vicki is often with her group, older male students, law students. Group members affect tiredness or perhaps boredom and make cynical remarks or laconic jokes. They laugh at each other and call each other by nicknames, lolling on the furniture, putting up their feet and striking poses, having a great time. I can't get close to her. I think of going boldly up to her but dismiss the idea because she seems so sophisticated, while I am so naïve.

I feel out of my class. I have never before thought about a girl's social class, at least not consciously. Vicki and her group seem to be sophisticated and middle class, but it could be superficial. I can imagine myself as one of them next year. I feel the equal of Vicki on the inside, where it counts.

I wanted to meet Vicki socially. The Students' Union holds dances on Saturday nights, called 'hops', with music by popular bands. I looked for her in vain. There were plenty of girls who lived and worked in the city. They teetered around in groups on high-heeled platform-soled shoes, enjoying the music and dancing, hoping to meet the boy of their dreams. Students called these tottering girls 'totty'. I learned to call the hops 'cattle markets'. I learned that Vicki wouldn't come to a hop. She would probably be at a middle-class private party, out on a date, or at home.

On the following Monday, in the Union coffee lounge, when one of her companions vacated a seat, I sat down beside her.

'Hi,' I say. I am self-conscious, trying to hide my Yorkshire accent, saying as little as possible. 'I'm Tom.'

'Hi.' She gives me a perfunctory smile and looks away, disinterested.

I am tall and fair with the straight nose of an aristocrat, school principal or inspector of police, and high cheekbones. I am upright with a distinguished bearing. I have broad shoulders tapering to a slim waist with strong arms, thighs and legs. My movements are deliberate and powerful. I am adept at swimming, skiing and simple dances but awkward at soccer. I am unable to follow even simple routines such as aerobics and yoga.

I am dressed in a brightly coloured shirt and jeans, with large feet wearing desert boots.

I offer her a cigarette. She accepts it and I light it.

'Where are you from?' I ask her.

'Salisbury.'

'Wiltshire?'

'Yes. Not Rhodesia.'

She continues to look away. I suppose male students pester her all the time.

'Are you going to the protest?' I ask in my broad Yorkshire accent. The Students' Union was organising a rally in support of increased government grants to students.

'Maybe.'

'I will be going,' I tell her, 'though it won't make any difference to me. I'm on the minimum grant.'

She looks interested. Her face is soft and mobile but sets in a few expressions that hide what she is thinking.

'You must be rich?'

She sounds middle-middle class. I hide my accent. However, I am proud of where I come from. I have never exchanged more than a few words with a middle class girl from down south before.

'No,' I tell her. 'My parents have a bit of brass and they pay my bills.'

'Good for you,' she says.

'I like your gold things,' I say. I speak carefully with an Oxford accent, as spoken by BBC newsreaders.

'Thanks. They cheer me up.'

'Is something wrong?'

'My father is ill.'

'I'm sorry. Is it serious?'

'Dementia'

'What do your parents do?'

She spokes hesitantly, as if the situation is tentative.

'My mother has, um, chemists' shops. My father has stopped working.'

I deduce she is middle-middle.

'He is in a bad way then?'

'Pretty bad. He doesn't know who I am any more. Look, I have a lecture. I'll see you around.'

She is not a snob. She has come out of her shell and is reaching out to me as an equal.

'See you around. I'm Tom, by the way.'

'You said. I'll remember.'

'Bye, Vicki.'

She smiles and is gone.

I am besotted.

In aiming to win this girl, I know I am an outsider, with odds against me.

CHAPTER 9
LADDERS

Another way to obtain a girl friend at Liverpool University is the informal 'ladder' method. Males and females ascend an imaginary two sided step ladder, which poses ratings of males and females opposite each other. I will try to match Vicki on the ladder. The most attractive single girls are those rated highest by the male students, whereas those with least man-pulling ability are left down near the bottom. Unattached male students are rated according to female attention, getting most attention from girls near the top of the ladder. Fresher males like me are near the bottom. Although the ladders are imaginary, everyone knows who is above them and everyone's ranking.

When the students are all gathered together, males and females stand together in small groups of similar desirability, with their gender. There is a melee as everyone tries to assert their own value.

The final step is when a male and a female of similar desirability are aligned. The most desirable female pairs off with the most desirable male, with a little flexibility for personal preferences. The second most desirable female would gladly accept the most desirable male but when he is already taken she settles for the second most desirable, again with a little flexibility. The process continues until, because there is a surplus of males, the least desirable males remain untaken and have to chase skirt off-campus or spend their time in the bar playing darts or getting drunk. When there is a surplus of unmatched girls or men, they pair for queer social activities.

When one of them perceives the match he or she wants is above her or him, they are guided by the their perception of value from an exchange, trying to be equal. Tom is aware he is below Vicki, who is higher up. He can wait for his value to appreciate or for Vicki's value to fall.

Fresher men like me are not rated high enough up the ladder to pair off with a university girl but we will get our chance in second year. First year relationships generally don't last into second year.

Traditional matching is approximated with many variations. A minority of strange women and bizarre men are matched by high-ranked individuals. Weird pairings disrupt but do not destroy the hierarchies. Availability of The Pill has meant that men are no longer expected to take responsibility for offspring from sexual relations. Consequently, the coupling process is more for instant gratification and ratings are awarded more for fashionable qualities, such as socialism, social connections and sports cars, than for traditional values such as heredity, virginity and family support. I am looking forward to getting a pairing in second year.

I didn't form a pair with any girl in my first attempt.

By my reckoning, the best way to get a classy chick is to get a First Class degree. Instead of spending my time on extra-curricular activities with high kudos, such as debating, I plan to hit the academic straps. I see plenty of other male students who are after the same chicks as me, withdraw from the ladder and pursue their fame in the Students' Union social venues. Who will score best in the end is going to be tested. Already a pattern is emerging.

CHAPTER 10
LONG ODDS

In the days that followed, Tom often went to the coffee lounge wanting to meet the girl but she was always with her group. He watched her with them, as they affected boredom or tiredness, made cynical remarks, told laconic jokes, lolled on the furniture, put up their feet, struck poses, laughed loudly and spent days pursuing a philosophical argument. They were sophisticated and he felt naïve. They were middle-middle class whereas he verged on working class.

It would be easier to talk with her away from her social group. The Students' Union hired popular bands to play at 'hops' on Saturday nights. Single male students went there to pick up 'Totty': these were girls who worked in the city and tottered to the dances on platform-soled shoes, hoping to meet a university boy. Tom looked for her in vain. When an acquaintance denigrated the hop as a 'cattle market', he knew he wouldn't find her there. Vicki would probably be on a date, at a private party, or at home with friends.

He found her in the coffee lounge smoking. When one of her group vacated a chair, he sat down next to her.

'Hi, Vicki,' he said. He was self-conscious, saying as little as possible, trying to hide his Yorkshire accent.

'Hi Tom.' She gave him a perfunctory smile and looked away.

He offered her a cigarette. She accepted and he lit it.

'Where are you from?'

'Salisbury.'

'Wiltshire?'

'Not Rhodesia.'

She looked around as if she was bored.

'Are you going to the grants protest?' he asked.

'Maybe.'

'I'm going,' he told her, 'but it won't make any difference to me. I'm on a minimum grant.'

Government grants were means tested. His father's income was too high to get more than a pittance. Displaying his affluence was a bit obvious but it could interest her.

'You must be rich?' she said.

'No. My father is a good farmer.'

'It must be hard work.'

'Yes. It's large — but there are half a dozen workers.'

'Will you be a farmer?'

'No. I have brothers.'

'What do you study?'

'Petroleum engineering.'

'Will you make a lot of money?'

'I want to. I like your gold things.' He said it carefully, with an Oxford accent, like a BBC newsreader.

'Thanks. They cheer me up.'

'Is something wrong?'

'My father is ill.' She stood up. 'I have to go to a lecture. I'll see you around, Tom.'

She had come out of her shell and was talking to him as an equal.

'See you . . . Vicki.'

She smiled and the girl he had dreamed of was gone.

He was besotted but the odds were long.

CHAPTER 11
PAIRING OFF

His parents paid for him to live in a residential hall in second year — more fun than digs. He moved into Sidmouth Hall with several friends from Commonwealth countries. They were learning to speak BBC English to conceal colonial accents, as he tried to lose his Yorkshire accent and speak like Vicki.

Tom was delighted to discover Vicki had moved next door into Exmouth Hall. She and several of her girlfriends sat with his group in the dining room shared by the halls. He wanted to ask her on a date but would wait until he got to know her better.

The best place to score crumpet was at a party on a Saturday night. When he and his friends weren't invited, they gate-crashed.

'We're friends of Dave,' they said at the door.

There were many Daves.

'Okay. Come in.'

One Saturday night, Tom and Steve ran into Vicki at a party, where she was dancing with her female friends. He was only a little drunk and she seemed pleased to see him.

'Hello, Tom.'

'Hi, er . . . Vicki. Dance?'

'Okay.'

They showed each other their moves. She danced with a bored look on her face, as was customary, but she danced well and he tried not to look awkward. They danced close, to The Beatles' number 'Girl'. Her body fitted his perfectly.

When the music finished, they found they had been born within a few days of each other. They talked about where they came from. She had gone to an exclusive girls' school he had heard of. He doubted that her classmates would be dancing with a grammar school boy like him.

'I didn't see you around last year,' she said. "Did you have a girlfriend?'

'For a while,' he said, 'but we finished at the end of the year.'

'Why did you break up?'

'It didn't work out.'

He hadn't wanted to settle down.

'Did you have a boyfriend last year?' he asked.

'Not really . . . There was someone . . . We broke up.'

They talked about their plans for travel and jobs. She wanted to live in Mexico for a year and then do a research degree. His mind raced, adapting his plans to fit in with hers.

They hugged; her hair smelled clean and her skin of flowers. Her mouth was soft and tasted of sweet apricots. When he delved with his tongue, she twisted her head away.

'No,' she gasped.

They kissed some more. His erection pressed against her and she pushed back. He told his friends to get a ride with someone else and drove Vicki back to Exmouth Hall.

'Can I come in?' he asked her.

'No visitors after 10.'

'I won't be visiting you. I will be escorting you to your room.'

'Nice try,' she laughed. 'No.'

'See you tomorrow, Vicki,' he said with a kiss.

'Thanks for the lift. Good night.'

The next day they 'pashed' in his room. They lay on the bed hugging and kissing. He wrote messages on her back with his finger, for her to interpret.

'T.O.U.C.H.,' she said. 'Touch.'

Her body felt wonderful, with its firm curves and soft recesses. His hands slid down her back, up and under her T-shirt, feeling her shoulder blades, but she stopped him undoing her bra.

'No,' she said.

His hands went on and explored around her taut waist, then her flat belly.

'Oi. Get your finger out,' she said when he toyed with her belly button.

He held her perfect breasts and caressed her nipples.

'That's enough.'

She got up. They kissed as they hung out the window and jeered at police and university officials as they scratched their heads and pondered the lake, into which student pranksters had pushed the warden's car.

'The pigs won't find out who did it,' Tom said. 'We look after our own.'

'Poor things,' she said. 'They must think students are terrible.'

'We are,' he said. 'All except you.'

They kissed as they derided those watching a beer-vomiting race. They kissed also at the halls' formal ball.

Vicki was a lovely positive spirit. She was beautiful. She wore invisible make-up. She peered at flowers, spoke to birds, patted dogs and stroked cats. She was trusting and open with a warm smile, steady eye and a firm handshake. She was mini-skirted with fine-boned legs and hips that swung alluringly when she walked.

They saw each other every day. She declined more kissing and persuaded him to spend time socialising.

'How's your father?' he asked.

'His dementia is getting worse.'

'I'm sorry. Is he in a bad way?'

'Pretty bad. He doesn't know who I am.'

'Is he suffering?'

'Not much.'

'It must be awful for you. Do you go home much?'

'About every three weeks.'

'What do your parents do?'

She spoke hesitantly, as if the situation was tentative. 'My mother is running our chemists' shops.'

'How many shops do you have?'

'About 25 or 30, I think. It's a chain, in the southern counties.'

Tom didn't know the name. He had never before exchanged more than a few words with a middle-class girl from southern England.

'I'm sorry about your father.'

'Thank you.'

They didn't have sex because she didn't want to. All he got was kissing and a painful bulge in the front of his jeans. Her passivity was unnerving. He imagined that for her, making love had to be a mutual endeavour, equal and lasting. He blamed himself for lacking sexual experience that would attract her to have sex with him.

Vicki stopped coming to his room. Although he was attentive, she declined dates with him and he was disappointed. He didn't know what was wrong. She seemed to be looking for someone better and it hurt. She gave him just enough encouragement to keep him on a piece of string.

He became aware they had different interests.

'We don't have to be the same: opposites attract,' he said to her. 'In Jane Austen's books, existence of love between a man and woman was more important than social equivalence in making a match.'

'The magnetic attraction of opposites may not last,' Vicki said. 'A match of like with like is more resilient.'

Tom's social class was unlike hers. His family were tenant farmers, employers who sometimes laboured in the fields. Vicki spoke plummy BBC English, was demure and good-humoured, with an exclusive education. She enjoyed quality music, literature and visual arts. She drove a new car and holidayed on the Continent. She shopped at Selfridges, Debenhams and Waitrose. She had sailed with her father, crewing on their family's yacht. She no longer went to church but took an interest in politics and went to the theatre regularly. He was curious why she was at LUT, because good students with her background could gain entry to study Biology at more prestigious Cambridge or Oxford. He thought her A-level grades might have been too low but he didn't ask her, as it might embarrass her.

He tried to replace his Yorkshire accent with a cosmopolitan identity. He chose the company of middle-class people. He acquired their diction, conversations, colloquialisms, slang and swearing. He learned to mimic a range of regional accents and postures, within which he could lose his own. He soon had a repertoire of comic dialects to set against the neutral speech he was developing. Yorkshire people take pride in straight dealing and blunt talking. He retained this part of his heritage. He was clawing his way up the male social ladder as high as learning and good prospects could take him, to a level where class would not be a barrier with Vicki.

A difficulty was his makeover might be insufficient to overcome the differences. The conventional perception was that a person could not change the social class of their birth.

When he couldn't get a date with Vicki, he pursued other girls openly.

'Vicki can't expect me to pursue her exclusively,' he thought. *'We aren't engaged. She is a southerner, endemically insincere, devious and too reticent to call a spade a spade. Until she shows more interest in me, I'll play the field. Perhaps if I have sex with another girl, Vicki will have sex with me.'*

He redoubled his efforts looking for a girl to have sex with. He believed The Beatles when they sang 'Life is very short and there's no time . . .'

Finding a girl on the social ladder seemed like a better plan than social climbing or studying.

43

SECOND YEAR

CHAPTER 12
LOVE PAIR

One Saturday night, I was gate-crashing parties with our gang when I came across Vicki dancing with her female friends. I was only a little drunk and she seemed pleased to see me.

'Hello, Tom.'

'Dance?'

I had the impression that Vicki would be a subdued and sedate dancer, but was delighted when she began throwing herself into the dances vigorously, like Sue had done in Wales.

I jived with her and danced Rock N'Roll, calypso, reggae, salsa, twist and more. She was magnificent. Onlookers began watching us.

We showed each other our routines with feet, arms and body. She danced mechanically with a bored look on her face, as was the fashion. I tried not to look awkward. For the Beatles' 'Girl', we danced close together. Her body pressed against mine, and I soon become aroused. I close my eyes and imagined we were spinning endlessly in a Viennese waltz, in a magnificent ballroom. She wore a white spreading gown and I was in black tie and tails.

When the music finished, we went into the garden, held each other and talked about ourselves. She was shy and I had to prise out personal information. As I thought, she went to an exclusive girls' school. I doubted that her classmates would go with a boy from a plebeian public grammar school like mine.

I asked her whether she had a boyfriend in first year, but she didn't answer. I took this to mean she had. We talked about our dreams and plans, for travel and jobs. I wanted to be an oil tycoon. Her dreams were of travel and scholarly research. I found myself revising my plans, trying to fit in with hers. Born within a few days of each other, we were two of a kind, both dreamers. Like me, she was introverted and a little nervous in company, forcing joviality with a supercilious grin, fiddling with her hair nervously, cluttering her words under the spotlight of group conversation. Most of all, I liked the way she seemed to understand me, listening to me uncritically.

We hugged and her hair smelled clean and her skin of flowers. Then we kissed. Her mouth was soft and tasted of sweet apricots. I tried to French kiss her but when I delved with my tongue, she twisted her head away.

'No,' she gasped.

We kissed some more and I ground my erection into her pelvis. I felt at a disadvantage about what to do next, as I was a virgin. Perhaps she was, too. In an earlier age she could have been called demure. I managed to get rid of my passengers and drove her back to Exmouth Hall. She didn't ask me in, so I kissed her outside. There was a sign forbidding visitors at night. She seemed friendly; that was all.

'See you tomorrow, Vicki,' I said carefully.

'I expect so, Tom,' she said.

'Goodnight.'

'G'night.'

CHAPTER 13
DESIRING VICKI

I don't know where my desire for Vicki originated. Perhaps it came from envy of her middle class university student friends. I imitated them in mimetic rivalry, desiring to be like them, in pointless competition. It was an ontological sickness that grappled with reality.

'Desire is caught from another, not emerging from within', said philosopher Girard.

I realised that I was pursuing Vicki because she was popular, rather than from my own desire. There was kudos from being with the best-looking girl in second-year. The music was too loud to talk and I didn't find out much about her.

We spent our time together kissing.

Vicki's diffidence had me on my back foot; so I didn't try for a date. I didn't want to have her turn me down. For several weeks after our first kiss, we spend time together having fun. I soon took up with her where I had left off with Bridget, with long kisses and hugs, with the difference that I now had the privacy of 'pashing' with her in my room in hall. We lay on my bed while my hands caressed her back under her top. I wrote finger messages on her silky smooth back, for her to sense and interpret as letters and words.

'What does this say?' I ask her.

'T.O.U.C.H,' she says.

Her body is wonderful, with firm curves and soft recesses. She lets me go so far and then stops me.

We kissed as we hung out the windows and jeered in unison at pranksters, as officials tried to maintain order, for example, when the police came to find out who put the warden's car in the lake. We kissed during food fights in the kitchen. We kissed when our gang created a disease hoax and quarantined everyone. We kissed as we watched a beer-vomiting race. And we kissed at the formal ball.

She is lovely, a positive spirit. She looks at flowers, speaks to birds, strokes cats and pats dogs. She smiles wryly at strangers, with a suggestion of naughtiness. But when you meet her, she is trusting and open, looks levelly, shakes hands firmly, holds eye contact. She is gentle and graceful, with fine-boned legs, long skirts and hips that swing alluringly; she wears soft materials and pastel colours. On some matters such as cruelty to children and animals, she displays a campaigner's zeal and will brook no compromise.

I am delighted to find she is neither vain nor precious. She is beautiful without make-up and wears it invisibly. She is intelligent and insightful and can read my emotions like a book.

After kissing to get to know her, there is kissing to build up trust, and then kissing to undress her. Kissing and a painful bulge in the front of my jeans is all I get. I don't try to shag her, because I am too inexperienced. I don't take the lead because I don't have her support. I have always found myself unable to make love to a passive woman, for then it is just sex. Love has to be a shared experience, equal and lasting.

We see each other every day. To my consternation she wants to spend more and more time with her group, socialising. I blame myself for lack of sexual experience to keep her interested. It is the same with my conversation but I learn to tease out her deep thoughts. They are critical and incisive. I have never known anyone as intelligent and I learn so much from her about people, their motives and their deceptions. We go to the movies together with our group and she holds my hand. When I ask, she explains who is who, because in a complex plot, I forget who characters are.

When she takes on too much, which is often, she tends to neglect those closest to her. Her inertia, her tendency to keep doing what she is already doing, is large. Her days are filled with activities and routines she has engaged in for many years and has scheduled forward in her mind. She lacks flexibility to vary her schedule to deal with new and emerging needs. She fits me in, but it costs her a big effort to be flexible.

Unlike me, she is gregarious and hangs out in groups. Whereas some girls speak to draw attention to themselves, Vicki speaks for effect, quietly in measured tones, occasionally with explicit reflection. She is disorganised and untidy but makes an effort occasionally to create an ambitious event, such as a theme party, with others' support.

I am very happy. I am doing well in my course, and I have Vicki who is wonderful. I have surprised myself that I have as my girlfriend the prettiest girl on campus. Since I first saw her in the Students' Union coffee lounge, she has been at the centre of my life. I have gone full circle from wanting independence when I was with Bridget, to waiting for Vicki to settle down with me.

Our relationship doesn't settle down and it doesn't seem to be going anywhere. Vicki is transactional and the transactions become spasmodic. Vicki no longer comes to my room. Empathy is not my forté, but I have the idea that Vicki won't have sex with me because I am a virgin. It is a Catch-22 situation. Vicki will not put out until I have experienced a commitment and I will not make a commitment until Vicki has put out. It is a standoff.

CHAPTER 14
TOWN GIRL

Girls were a distraction. In first year, his appetite for female company had been sated by Bridget, when he had ploughed through assignments day after day, producing high-quality output. Now in second year, he was finding it difficult to settle into the work and deduced he needed a steady female companion.

He framed his need as casual sex rather than love. The irony of his predicament was that he couldn't get any sex until he had had some. He figured that to be successful with university girls, he had to have lost his virginity. He didn't know any girl who could verify this. To broach this topic with a university girl could make him a laughing stock.

Tom imagined that girls would become more promiscuous with the advent of easy access to The Pill, but he was without evidence. Contrary to his expectations, girls were becoming more discriminating and demanding love rather than sex.

'A girl wants a man who will commit to settling down,' Lisa told him. She and Larry had become inseparable. 'Do you think you'll ever want to settle down with a steady girlfriend, Tom?'

'Getting hitched won't be on my agenda until I'm 30.'

'Could there be a girl who changes your mind?'

'I doubt it. She would have to be special!'

'Would you like to meet my friend Barbara?'

Lisa gave him a phone number and he called and made a date.

I complained about my frustration with Vicki to Larry. Lisa was there.

'What do you want from a girl? A life partnership?' Larry asked.

'No,' I said.

'A girl wants a man who will commit to settling down,' Lisa told me. She and Larry had become inseparable. 'Do you think you'll ever want to settle down with a steady girlfriend, Tom?'

'No. Getting hitched won't be on my agenda until I'm thirty.'

'Could there be a girl who changes your mind?'

'I doubt it. She would have to be special!'

'Would you like to meet my friend Barbara?' Lisa asked.

I hesitated for a moment, wondering how Vicki would react in competition with Barbara. But Vicki hadn't shown much interest in me for weeks. A problem is that the customs of her class lead her to expect that a guy should pursue her exclusively, whereas at home we do not expect a guy and a girl to become exclusive until they are engaged. To have an exclusive relationship with Vicki, I was prepared to get engaged and looked for an opportunity to obtain rights over her. But this had been the situation with Vicki for months. I wasn't getting anywhere. I was used to finding my girlfriends myself but I hadn't been successful for some time and it was time to move on.

'Okay,' I told Lisa doubtfully.

Lisa gave me a phone number and I called and made a date.

Later that week my battered old car pulled up in front of a tidy detached house in a suburb near the university. I knocked at the front door.

'I'm Barbara.' She held out a fine hand.

'Tom. Pleased to meet you.'

Her hand was delicate. I opened a car door for her. She was slim and rather angular with a shy face that came alive when she smiled.

We went to a pub and talked over drinks. She was intelligent but under-confident and l liked her. She worked as a secretary.

'My grades weren't good enough to go to university,' she said sadly.

I was embarrassed that my own success had probably been unfair.

'Why weren't your grades higher?' I asked.

'I didn't try hard enough. There was no encouragement. No-one expected me to go to university.'

'Girls are treated unfairly,' I said. 'Perhaps you will be a big success at something else.'

'I'm trying. Do you think I'm dumb because I don't go to university?'

I didn't, but the difference in our activities was difficult to ignore. I spent most of my time studying, while Barbara worked office hours and then spent her time with nothing to show for it. I didn't meet her friends and I seemed to exist in a separate compartment of her life where our interaction revolved around having sex.

It was an arrangement that suited me well, but it was not my idea of a trade in a market for love. Commodification of love could arouse suspicion that the intent was for men and women to exploit each other.

Later that week, my battered old car pulled up in front of a tidy detached house in a suburb near the university. He knocked at the front door.

'I'm Barbara.' She held out a fine hand.

'Tom. Pleased to meet you.'

Her hand was delicate. He opened a car door for her. She was slim and rather angular with a shy face that came alive when she smiled.

'Car, meet Barbara. Barbara, meet car.'

'Do engineers believe machines are alive?'

'Yes. They like them and care for them.'

'Like in 'Zen and the Art of Motorcycle Maintenance'?'

'Exactly! Pirsig's passion for his motorbike was both rational and romantic at the same time.'

'Your car is hardly romantic.'

'You've only just met it. The romance may not happen overnight, but it will happen.'

They both laughed. She was intelligent but under-confident and he liked her. They went to a pub and talked over drinks. She worked as a dental assistant.

'My grades weren't good enough to go to university,' she said sadly.

Tom was embarrassed that his own success had probably been unfair.

'Why weren't your grades higher?'

'I didn't try hard enough. There was no encouragement. No-one expected me to go to university.'

'Girls are treated unfairly. Perhaps you will be a big success at something else.'

'I'm trying. Do you think I'm dumb because I don't go to university?'

'No. Many important skills can't be learned at university. I imagine your scheduling of appointments takes skill. One day the skills of a dental receptionist will be rated as valuable as a dentist's and she will be able to drive a Porsche.'

Barbara was gracious, thoughtful and pleasant company. She didn't talk much and only about straightforward matters.

'Who was your last girlfriend?' she asked.

'A girl called Vicki.'

'Are you still seeing her?' Barbara asked.

'Not for some time.'

When he pulled up outside her house to drop her off, they kissed hungrily.

'Is that romantic enough for you?' he asked.

He ran his hands over her body. She was skinny like Twiggy, with some delightful curves. She was a better prospect for sex than Vicki. They arranged to see each other again in a few days' time. It seemed like his drought was about to break.

Perhaps Barbara wanted from him what a prudish fiancé would not provide. She might be a liberated girl who wanted sex for the same reason as Tom. He would keep himself for Vicki.

He was surprised when she asked him in to meet her parents. Her father was a solicitor. He poured him a malt whisky. This was not in Tom's plan.

'Do you like engineering?' asked her father.

'Most of it. I'm not keen on complex numbers or sewage treatment plants.'

Her mother interrogated him with penetrating questions about his family. She seemed like a bottle wasp stinging a spider with anaesthetic, to store him alive in her larder for her offspring to eat later. His free life would be suspended and he would eventually be consumed.

Their interest in his permanent involvement with their daughter did not match the casual relationship he intended. When he was with her, he did most of the talking. He told her about difficulties with his studies and his ambition to be an oil tycoon. She listened but had no comments or insights and eventually he stopped telling her what he was doing. Most of the time they didn't talk.

When a girl attracted him, it was lust speaking rather than a relationship plan. It was quite usual for both young men and young women to have a bit on the side before they became engaged. The tradition in the country was that men could philander discretely. Women's liberation was encouraging women to assert rights that many men, including Tom, were unaware of.

He wondered if Vicki knew he was seeing someone regularly. She was a frequent visitor at Larry's flat.

'You won't tell Vicki about Barbara, will you?' he said to Larry.

'If you double-time Vicki, that's up to you. She's a good friend, but I won't say anything.'

A few days later he was escorting Barbara to his room, when they ran into Vicki in the foyer. She looked through him and walked on.

'She may be put off by seeing me with Barbara, but I will not skulk around trying to conceal her,' he thought. *'When I have done with Barbara, I'll be able to get back with Vicki.'*

CHAPTER 15
PROTOSEX

Whereas virginity in a girl is attractive, Tom's was an impediment and distorted his interaction with females. His sexuality had not yet been established and he felt alone in his predicament. No man he knew talked about his virginity, even as a joke. Those initiated did not remember how they had felt before. Drivers who have licences forget the apprehension a learner experiences before he or she takes the wheel.

When he met a female, a voice inside him asked: '*Is this the one who will have sex with me?*' He knew what he wanted. If she refused no-strings sex within a reasonable time, he would finish with her and try another.

When Barbara hinted at wanting a permanent relationship, he asserted he was looking no further ahead than the end of the course, in just over a year's time, when anything was possible. Although he was desperate for sex, he did not pressure her, or make a commitment he would have to honour. There was a sexual revolution in progress and the media showed celebrities jumping into bed together in droves. If he could get Barbara to jump in with him, he would be a free agent.

For most of the year he had taken it easy but he swotted intently for second-year exams. It was time to distinguish himself. He studied for long hours all week and saw Barbara on one evening at the weekend.

'If we don't do it soon, I am going to explode,' he said to her.
'It's a big deal for me too.'
'We will have to be careful.'
'*She must not become pregnant,*' he thought.
'Mmmm,' she kissed him, without concern.

He wanted to have sex with Barbara without making any commitment. There seemed no point in delaying a deed that he had waited for so long, as there were no other candidates. He listened to The Who sing 'Substitute' and hoped that sex with Barbara would pave the way to a sexual relationship with Vicki.

Before the end of second year, in two months' time, he had to lose his virginity and establish a satisfying sexual relationship with a reliable girl so that he could get away to a flying start in Finals' year studies.

'How can I get sex with a girl without strings?' he asked a friend who studied psychology.

'A method proposed by Jacques Lacan, a French psychoanalyst, is for the man to persuade the girl that the absence of sexual relations is an obstacle of his own making. The girl will try to overcome it, absolving him of responsibility.'

Tom tried it on Barbara.

'If we have sex, it wouldn't be fair to you,' he said. 'I might take a job overseas and then where would we be?'

'Could I come too?'

'It might not be possible. I could be away at drilling camps for months on end. You could be stuck somewhere, all by yourself.'

'I wouldn't mind.'

'So you would be okay without me?'

'If I have to, yes. But it may be better if I stay here where I have a job, family and friends.'

'Then it would not be unfair to have sex while we can?'

'It would be unfair not to.'

'Are you on The Pill?'

'No.'

'Why not?'

'I haven't needed to be.'

At a party, after some smoochy dancing, he borrowed a bedroom.

He had a condom in his wallet. He had been carrying it since the lower sixth and it had embossed a circle in the soft leather. The mark embarrassed him because it advertised the years of frustration he had suffered. He dreaded being questioned about it and kept it well hidden.

It took some time to get going. Fortunately, he found some Vaseline in a drawer and took a chance that it would not weaken the rubber.

He began to enjoy himself. But nothing could prepare him for what happened next. Without warning, he teetered on the brink of ecstasy before plunging into the delight of an orgasmic snowdrift. He gave his body and mind over to instinct, for an interval somewhere between a few precious seconds and eternity, during which time he was sure he was immortal. No words could express the joy he felt.

Barbara was quiet.

'More?' he asked her.

'No. It was lovely.'

'Did you have an orgasm?'

'I don't think so.'

'Have you ever had one?'

'No.'

'Do you mind?'

'No. It was okay.'

'It will be better next time, I promise.'

He took her home around midnight and then went back to bed. He awoke in the early morning with a new glorious world before him and another painful hard-on, as if his member had discovered its vocation. Now that he had experienced the real thing, simulation was possible. For the first time he masturbated to orgasm. He imagined hearing the warning voices of clergy, teachers and parents, but he applied himself to the task in hand with a free conscience until release magically came.

When he went into uni, Richard and Bruce cornered him in the coffee lounge. They sensed a change in him.

'Were you with Barbara last night?' Bruce asked.

Tom nodded and tried to turn away but they thrust their leering faces close to his.

'Tell us what happened.'

He shrugged and grinned self-consciously.

'Did you go all the way this time, Tom?' Bruce said. 'You did, didn't you?'

Tom would neither affirm it nor deny it and was embarrassed.

'Was it good?' Bruce persisted.

He didn't answer and looked at his watch.

'Excuse me, fellas. I have a meeting with my tutor.'

He left.

'What's wrong with those guys,' he thought. *'They must not be able to get laid.'*

He had enacted the final rite of passage into adulthood. Sexual intercourse was supposed to be the ultimate human experience. With that one act he had dispelled his fears that he was doomed to an alternative existence. Even if he died tomorrow, he would have lived somewhat normally. He could resume his pursuit of Vicki with confidence. Nothing could stop him now.

Although Barbara's needs had not been fulfilled, physical passion dominated their relationship. She was content to spend Saturday evenings together, followed by sex at his place. This kept his uppity organ satisfied. He felt empowered and applied himself to his studies with new-found concentration.

'You are putting in some long hours,' said Richard. 'Barbara seems to have settled you down.'

'Regular sex is so good.'

'You are playing with matches. Be careful you don't get burnt.'

'No chance.'

Because she was not on The Pill, he used condoms.

'I hate putting on these things,' he said to Barbara.

'Thank you for doing it.'

'They might not always work. They can overfill.'

'Can you get a larger size?'

But the other types he tried had the same problem. The problem was solved when they got together on Wednesdays too.

He had achieved a milestone, not the millstone he feared. Sex with Barbara had not increased his commitment to her. Barbara had another life she did not share with him. She didn't invite him to any social events. The rut they were in seemed strangely narrow. It did not seem possible that it could lead to a permanent relationship.

'What do you do all week?' Tom asked her.

'I usually go out with friends.'

'Females?'

'Males too.'

'The same ones?'

'Sometimes.'

He couldn't exclude that she had another man. He hoped she did.

'She might not want me to meet her town friends because of the 'town and gown' divide,' he thought. *'She might assume I would not get on with them. Our relationship is for sex not sociality and only temporary.'*

It suited him well.

CHAPTER 16
ASK NO QUESTIONS

Tom told Vicki his plans for the summer.

'Steve and I are going to Montreal. We have vacation jobs at an oil refinery.'

'Angela and I have vac jobs in Boston, doing psychology.'

'Terrific. We'll be heading south from Montreal in the first week of September,' he said. 'Could we visit you?'

'Yes, we'll still be there then. That would be great.'

Because he had had no intimacy with Vicki for some time her invitation surprised and delighted him. Maybe he would be able to get back with her again.

Tom and Steve were waiting for the girls at Boston University, at reception in the Department of Applied Psychology.

It was the summer of '66 and the boys had come to visit the girls at their vacation jobs, after completing their own vacation employment in Montreal.

Tom, in T-shirt and blue jeans, sat with his long legs crossed, looking at a brochure. His face had the open, dark looks of the actor Alan Bates. Steve was holding up a battery record player with a Bob Marley song, as his body reggaed jerkily around the reception area. His face was Nordic, with white skin, high cheekbones and a blond forelock spilling down his forehead. He wore a colourful tropical beach shirt with a cravat at his throat, his short legs in turned-up jeans. When the song finished, he sat down and looked archly down his aquiline hooked nose at Tom.

'Where is your woman, man?' His accent was singsong Jamaican.

Tom looked at his watch. Maybe the girls' jobs had fallen through.

'They are six minutes late. Vicki wrote that they would be here.'

Tom was not used to girls keeping him waiting. By now even his idol, Dr Spock, would be growing impatient.

After five minutes, two girls breezed in, wearing white lab coats.

'Tom!' Vicki said, smiling broadly. 'It's great to see you.'

'Hello, Vicki. It's terrific to see you too. Are you selling ice creams?'

They laughed and hugged. Her clean smell and the firmness of her body were reassuring. Steve hugged petite Angela. The two had started going together only recently.

'I hear you did well in your exams, Tom,' said Vicki. 'Congratulations. You must be pleased with how you went in second year.'

'I didn't get everything I wanted,' he said with a grimace.

'Could you have wanted too much?' she replied, reproving.

Chastised, he looked away without answering. They chatted about jobs and travelling.

'Come and see our lab,' Vicki said. 'We'll show you around the campus later. Bring your stuff.'

They hoisted their packs and followed along corridors to a laboratory, where she introduced them to the supervisor, Brad, in a white coat, with a shock of unruly hair.

'Pleased to meet you — I'm Brad McCarthy.'

'Tom Archer.'

'Steve Morgan.'

'Welcome to the Lie Detection Laboratory. Vicki and Angela have asked me to demonstrate what we do here. Can we show you by testing you?'

'Did you say 'lie detection'?' asked Tom, puzzled. 'What kind of lies?'

Brad shrugged. 'Deception. We investigate methods of interrogating suspects for the FBI and CIA.'

'Crikey. I don't do lies.' Tom turned to Vicki. 'Am I a suspect or something?'

She shook her head. 'No, Tom. It's just a bit of fun.'

They went into a room with chart recorders and headphones, with a window overlooking a room with a chair like a dentist's.

He regarded lying as low behaviour. As a student engineer, he valued true knowledge acquired by honest methods. A lie detector was not a threat and even an asset.

The psychologist continued: 'We will measure your word association responses. When a suspect hears a certain word, for example, the word 'gun', it could connect him with a crime and he may become anxious. His anxiety triggers adrenalin and his heart will beat faster, causing him to sweat more, allowing current to conduct between two electrodes touching his skin. A pen jiggles and draws a squiggle on a rotating chart, called a polygraph. The bigger the lie, the bigger the squiggle. If he has denied having a gun, a squiggle could be evidence of a lie. Other records of heart rate, blood pressure, respiration rate and muscular reflexes can also indicate lying.

'Today we will only have a brief informal test to show how a lie detector works.'

'Is it to interrogate Soviet spies?' Steve asked.

'No comment,' said Brad with a smile.

'How accurate is it?' asked Tom.

'Detection of lies is not completely reliable. For example, a psychopath may be so inured to the facts of a murder that when he is asked about them he does not break out into a tell-tale sweat. On the other hand, a person can be fearful and sweat when he or she is innocent. Lie detector evidence does not have much weight in courts of law these days. It is seldom used to convict anyone but it can be used to extract a confession.'

Tom turned to Vicki. 'I confess: I never lie to you!'

She laughed. 'I know that, Tom.'

'Then why do you want to test me?'

'Our project is to compare a person's true feelings with what they actually say.'

'What if I say I want one thing but prefer something else? Am I lying?'

Vicki looked at him and smiled, as if she knew something he didn't.

'Each situation is different,' she said. 'We want to test your feelings in familiar situations. Will you give it a go, Steve?'

'Go on the lie detector? Sorry but no thank you. Tom will do it — he doesn't mind telling lies.'

'Get fucked, Steve.'

'Steve doesn't want Angela to find out about Margot, his bit on the side,' Tom thought.

'What about you, Tom?'

Tom was infatuated with Vicki but they were not yet a couple. He thought she might be more amenable when she was sure he was besotted with her. He had always dealt with Vicki openly and if he refused she would construe that he was hiding something.

'Okay, I'll do it,' he said. 'My life is an open book.'

'A mystery book,' said Steve.

'Non-fiction.'

'We'll soon see,' said Vicki with a smile.

'You already know all about me, Vicki.'

Vicki and Tom had lived in adjoining halls of residence for six months and had talked almost every day.

'The test is to find out your true feelings,' she said. 'It will be fun.'

Tom was reassured and hoped that Vicki would realise that his affection for her was genuine and she would bond with him.

'I'm ready,' he said.

CHAPTER 17
LIE DETECTOR

'Okay, let's begin,' said Brad. 'Tom, would you sit in the chair.'

Vicki, Angela and Steve watched from the control room through a window. A technician in a tan lab coat adjusted the chair until Tom was comfortable. 'My job is to make sure the tests are done as scientifically as possible,' he said. 'The electrodes measure skin resistance. If you lie, perspiration will reduce skin resistance and be recorded on these charts.'

He smeared gel on electrodes and taped them to Tom's face and scalp. He attached wires and gathered them into a bundle going into the control room. He strapped Tom's arms on to the armrests.

'What are these straps for?' asked Tom.

'If you move the electrodes can be dislodged.'

He put a headset on Tom. Then he and Brad went into the control room too. Tom could see them through the window. They were wearing headsets and looking at him. Brad sat at a table beside a polygraph recorder with a mic.

'Testing,' said Brad, his voice distant. 'Can you hear me, Tom?'

'Yes, I hear you.'

'Would you answer some questions?'

'Okay.'

'Do you own a car?'

'Yes.'

'Do you have a girlfriend?'

Where is this going? Tom thought. *There is Vicki sometimes. Barbara regularly.*

'Yes; I do.'

'What is her name?'

'Vicki.'

'Do you have another girlfriend?'

'Yes.'

'What is her name?'

'Barbara.' It was annoying to have to say it.

'Vicki already knows this,' he thought. *'Why is he wanting me to name Barbara? Vicki has had a hand in these questions.'*

'Do you have a driver's licence?'

'Yes.'

'Have you ever had an erection?'

Tom was taken aback. 'Yes.' He felt foolish and grinned. 'Several.'

'Have you ever masturbated?'

He had never been asked this before. He blushed. His embarrassment would be off-scale if it was being monitored.

'Yes ... but not like in Portnoy's Complaint . . . not into the family liver.'

'Who do you think of when you masturbate, Barbara or Vicki?'

It was a loaded question: he usually thought of a girl; he didn't want to say who. He was not used to talking about his wanking. This wasn't fun.

'It's private and I won't answer.'

He tried to get out of the chair but he was strapped in and couldn't move.

'Let me out,' he demanded.

'In a minute. Would you answer that question? Who do you think of, Barbara or Vicki?'

He hesitated and thought: *'Does it matter if Vicki finds out?'*

'Vicki,' he said.

'Have you ever engaged in sexual activity with another family member?'

There had been some looking and touching with his siblings when he was small that he had never admitted to anyone.

'Yes.'

'Have you ever had sexual intercourse with a girl?'

'Yes.'

He could see the girls' faces watching him from the control room but he was unable to see their expressions.

'How many times have you been to the United States?'

'Twice.'

'How many times have you had sexual intercourse in total?'

Two months ago, he could have said 'none' truthfully. He could see the girls' faces in the control room. They were frowning.

Then they asked him intimate questions over headphones. He was embarrassed and tried to get up, but he couldn't move.

He tried to break the straps on his arms but they were too strong.

'Let me out. This is illegal. I'll sue ...'

'Tom, don't worry,' said Vicki, coming in from the control room. 'We will keep your answers confidential.'

'I don't want to answer any more questions. Let me out.'

The premise of the test was that he had something of import to conceal. It was shameful. He wondered how much Vicki knew about him and Barbara. He had no secrets from Vicki. He hadn't tried to hide his relationship with Barbara from her, but neither had he mentioned it and she probably didn't know they were fucking. Anyway, Vicki knew it was her that he wanted and she would understand that Barbara was for sex only. He hoped she would be okay with it — his relationship with Vicki had not been intense enough to be exclusive.

She went back into the control room.

'Nearly finished, Tom,' said Brad. 'How many times have you had sexual intercourse in total? Never, once, twice, more than twice?'

'Twice.'

'Who with?'

'It's none of your damn business . . . Barbara.'

'Is there any other girl you like more than her?'

Tom hesitated. Was Vicki finding out where she stood with him? Good. She might not believe he genuinely loved her. She would see now that he wasn't lying.

'Yes,' he said. 'Vicki.'

He was weary. He wanted this grilling to be over.

'Who do you feel more possessive about, your girlfriend or Vicki?'

'Vicki.'

'Who would you rather be with, in the future?'

'Vicki.'

'Have you promised to stay with your girlfriend?'

'No.'

'Have you made a plan to finish with your girlfriend?'

'No,' he thought. *'Yes,'* he corrected.

'I will when I get back.'

The plan was in his head: it wasn't a lie.

'Do you love Vicki?'

It wasn't a lie, although right now he was feeling cross with her for setting up this test.

'Yes.'

'On a scale from 1 to 10, how much do you love her?'

His feelings for Vicki were in turmoil. Perhaps true love was like this.

'Ten.'

'Has there ever been a time when you have wanted to have two girlfriends at the same time?'

When Vicki had been unresponsive, he had had dates with other girls.

He hesitated. *'I won't admit it,'* he thought, *'but having two females would be good — the more the merrier.'*

'No.'

He felt his heart lurch and knew his lie would be registered. In the control room, Vicki looked up from the polygraph and frowned.

'Thank you, Tom, that's all,' said Brad.

For 30 minutes the questions had explored his sex life, including his activities with Vicki and other girlfriends, in great detail, which of them he liked most and so on. It included details of what he did by himself. His answers showed he was besotted with Vicki and that was no secret.

The questioning had been intrusive and he resented it. The exposure of his feelings for Vicki had clearly been contrived by her and put him at a disadvantage that was a stumbling block in their relationship. It was a low-point in their relationship so far. He supposed that her asking about his other girlfriends was a test of loyalty and could be grounds for disaffection. He regretted that he had volunteered.

The technician undid the straps and removed the sensors and wires. Tom stood up.

'Thank you for your cooperation,' said Brad.

'Did you get what you wanted?' Tom asked angrily.

'Yes, thank you. You didn't lie until the last question.'

'Big deal. Most guys would prefer to have more than one girl.'

'I agree. Vicki and Angela made up the questions. They wanted to practise using a lie detector in a situation where a couple doubts each other. Tom, you have been an unusually honest subject. You did not try to conceal you had a crush on Vicki and had a sexual relationship with another girl. Males can be motivated by testosterone to have many sexual partners. Denying interest in more than one partner is a common strategy of males to deceive a partner. It is an interesting situation. Goodbye and good luck.'

He turned away and continued writing on the polygraph.

The four of them left the laboratory.

'Vicki, why didn't you ask me about Barbara?' Tom was indignant. 'You know I am crazy about you.'

'So you say.'

'It's true.'

'We will compare your true feelings with what you said.'

'You won't find a difference: I said what I felt.'

'If we have upset you, I apologise. I thought it would be fun.'

'Everything I have done . . . including Barbara . . . has been to get experience . . . for you.'

'Sex is not transitive, like equality in maths. Good sex can't be passed on,' she said, turning away.

Tom said nothing.

'There's a cafeteria along there,' she said, pointing outside. 'Come back at 3 pm when we finish work. We will meet you here and take you on a tour. Then you can come back to our place. We're having a barbecue tonight.'

CHAPTER 18
GOING SOUTH

The next day after his ordeal on the lie detector in Boston, Tom was going south on a Greyhound bus with Steve. They had spent the evening with the girls at a barbecue and slept in sleeping bags on the floor of the games room. The girls had gone to bed early. Tom had been hoping to be with Vicki, but she had been unfriendly. He did not understand why and he felt chagrined. He had lain awake, mulling over her behaviour, concluding that she thought he wasn't good enough for her.

He sat back on the bus and reflected on what had gone wrong.

'When Vicki analyses the polygraph,' he thought, *'she must see that I was telling the truth.'*

The lie detector showed he was honest but revealed he was fucking someone else: Barbara. Vicki might not accept that it was casual and innocent.

He told Steve, 'I should have done what you did: refused to be tested.'

'If I were Vicki, I would have been shocked by how cold-blooded you are. I hadn't realised you were such a sex fiend. Your shenanigans with Barbara will have put her off.'

'Why would that put her off? I was getting experience to apply to her.'

'You used Barbara for sex without remorse. Did you know *'Morally right outcomes do not excuse morally wrong actions'*? I think Vicki is a caring and loving person. She probably believes sex should be for love.'

'It is not as clear-cut as that. I have feelings for Barbara.'

'Well, Vicki will not be a bit impressed. When a girl finds out you are double-timing her, you can lose her.'

'*Shit,*' thought Tom. '*It's obvious. Why did I think Vicki would accept it?*'

He had a lot of learning to do about women. But he wouldn't admit that to Steve.

'It is not as if promiscuity isn't natural,' he said. 'It is common in nature and has a positive role in diversifying the gene pool. Bonobo monkeys have sex regularly with others in their group. It maintains social cohesion and reduces tension. That's cool.'

'Humans are not bonobos,' said Steve. 'Women believe relationships should be monogamous. On the other hand, most men want several females at the same time, with each girl staying loyal — a double standard. In these days of female equality, you are a dinosaur.'

'Monogamy is the dinosaur: it has outgrown its usefulness. If they are going to be equal, women will have to condone plural relationships, as men do.'

'Women don't accept promiscuity.'

'Women should compromise with men, not enforce feminism. Women's Liberation should not crush masculinity.'

Tom was still angry about the lie detector. Vicki had invaded his privacy, found him wanting and rejected him. He felt as though he had been mentally raped. Her derision hurt. His self-image had been scorned. He had been vulnerable and she had hurt him.

'Vicki used Brad's authority to get answers to her insinuating questions,' Tom said bitterly. 'Her ruse was to turn over stones to see if incest, infidelity, homosexuality, promiscuity or any other nasties would crawl out. She didn't have the nerve to ask me herself. She wanted to check me out covertly. How sneaky was that? I am an honourable person and my perception is that in the mating game, she has cheated.'

'I doubt Vicki was playing a game,' said Steve. 'She could be serious.'

'Unless she becomes friendlier, I won't finish with Barbara.'

'Everyone knows you don't play two girls off against each other.'

'I am not playing with anyone,' Tom protested. 'Vicki knows she has it over Barbara.'

'Vicki could be concerned about being made to look foolish or cheap,' Steve said. 'Girls see their relationships from a third-person viewpoint. She might have to explain to her friends what you are doing with Barbara. Your preference for a town girl puts down Vicki's intelligence. She would lose face with her peer group.'

'You mean she is an intellectual snob.'

'She won't compete with Barbara.'

Tom understood. *'How could I have imagined Vicki wouldn't mind that I had fucked Barbara?'*

'What a cock-up!'

Steve got out a book and started reading.

Tom looked out the window at the procession of roadside hoardings. The advertisements targeted vanity. He did not understand why he was so drawn to Vicki and he was uneasy. He had become infatuated with her despite her discouragement. He had heard of Stockholm Syndrome, when hostages become enamoured of their captors. She had captured him on the lie detector and had a hold over him.

The Greyhound driver played the song 'Eleanor Rigby'. The words repeated over and over: 'Ah, look at all the lonely people.' The music grated on him and he felt isolated. Perhaps he should have been more considerate in his relationship with Vicki.

CHAPTER 19
SOCIAL CLASS

Back in Liverpool, Tom reflected that getting Vicki to be his girlfriend was more difficult than he had supposed.

Finding a suitable girl had considerations beyond matching of desire and establishing a relationship. Traditionalists wanted a match of social classes too.

'I was born into farming stock' he thought. 'How can I shed my provincial, rural, farm tenant, lower-middle class identity and be more middle class like Vicki?

Brits tend to classify a person by the way he or she speaks. George Bernhard Shaw, in his play, 'Pygmalion', tested having a lower class girl pass as upper class, after education in speech. Her unfashionable vocabulary and tortured pronunciation were incongruous. Education was said to be a great leveller, a better indicator than breeding. A Labour politician said:

'At university, an aristocrat and the son of a coal miner can rub shoulders.'

This was the thesis in DH Lawrence's 'Lady Chatterley's Lover', with an unbridgeable chasm between her upper classness and a well-born but educationally and socially deprived gamekeeper, Mellors, stuck in the working class. They both have birth, brains and intimacy, but the game-keeper's education is rudimentary. It was a tryst between nature and nurture. It seemed idealistic.

For a marriage match, both nature and nurture could be considered. Jane Austen put love above both in 'Pride and Prejudice'. Although education, skills and social connections are ascendant under American influence, heredity nevertheless persisted of great importance in the UK. Whereas in America wealth is a class of its own, in Britain class cannot be bought. 'Old money' is required for entry to the upper class and is often frozen in hereditary assets.

Because 'new' money is more available for luxury cars and yachts, to the impoverished upper class such items are sour grapes, in 'bad taste', bourgeois and vulgar.

Even new money could be acceptable in the UK. Jane Austen wrote 'It is a truth universally acknowledged, that a single man in possession of a good fortune, must be in want of a wife.'

Like most of his peers, he did not possess a good fortune and would have to obtain a wife on the strength of other qualities. Each class has distinct occupations, habitats, ownership, possessions, education, behaviours, languages, customs, recreations and entertainments. The subspecies, 'Farmer', can vary from lower class, at the level of a subsistence farm with a cottage plot and a few animals, to middle class where the owner is the partner operating a food production conglomerate with intensive meat-growing factories and robotic dairying. Somewhere along this spectrum, were tenant farmers like the Archers.

'We are working class,' his mother said, exuding hubris and expecting to be corrected that as an employer of workers, my father could not possibly be working class.

Tenant farmers are somewhere between working and middle class. They do not have the independent income of the professional, military and clergy, nor the investment income of land and property owners. They work for themselves in a secure occupation and this puts them a cut above the wage-earning laboring classes.

Vicki seemed to be middle-middle. She spoke plummy BBC English, was demure and good-humoured and went to a private school for girls. It must have been a school for middle class girls, because she had a wider understanding of cultured life than he did. She drove a new car and holidayed on the Continent, off the beaten track. She shopped at Selfridges, Debenhams and Waitrose, but not with aristocrats and the nouveau riches at Harrods. Vicki used to sail on her father's yacht. She no longer went to church, but took an interest in politics and went to the theatre regularly. He hadn't asked Vicki about her ancestry. If it were high class, she probably wouldn't be at a redbrick uni and would probably be in a job where she would meet high-class males, such as arts, fashion or publishing.

Engineering students in his year often had similar social classes and sometimes joined social groups from places related geographically. One social group of working class students was from northeast England. Middle class students could afford to live in residential halls, whereas working class students lived in digs. Other groups include the Iraqis, the Europeans and the Colonials. A counterculture group hung out in the Union playing snooker instead of going to lectures.

He tried to join a middle-middle class group, dominated by ex-public schoolboys, involved in rugby and cricket-playing, from 'county' professional homes in the southeast. They drove sports cars in rallies at weekends. He had found out they didn't want him.

'Tom, as you don't have a sports car, you can stay and keep time when we cross the finish line.'

They left him stranded when they forgot to tell him which pub they were gathering at.

Next he fell in with several provincial lower middle class grammar school types like himself, led by an impoverished middle-middle class ex-public schoolboy. Our provincial dialects were revealed by our BBC English. His Yorkshire identity amused them as much as it embarrassed him. They made him say, 'Eee lad, tha'll zoon be olt'nuff t'go down't pit' (meaning 'Well, boy, you will soon be old enough to go underground mining').

By the end of the first year, his provincial identity was preventing him from mixing with students he wanted to move into hall with next year. At the start of second year, he decided to redefine myself as middle-middle class. It was a bold plan because one's social class normally doesn't change. However, becoming more like Vicki was highly desirable. Although opposites are sometimes said to attract, it was also said the effect did not last. On the other hand, there is little evidence that couples from different social classes complement each other. Matches of like with like were said to be most resilient. Accordingly, he became middle-middle, like Vicki, deserting his former friends and falling in with Vicki's girlfriends when they started to hang around. As a rural provincial, he was something of a curiosity, but he was not lampooned as he had been in first year.

CHAPTER 20
THE GAME

I felt vulnerable with Vicki and it might be more than our social class difference. I looked in some psychology books that offered advice on gender relations.

In tennis and in contract bridge, you are vulnerable when you are about to win, or lose precariously, as if on a precipice. In dating, being vulnerable was not good, a weak position. Men can seek women based on a deceptive ploys used by a community of secretive pick-up artists (PUAs). 'The Game', a book by Neil Strauss documents tips and tricks to use for finding and picking up women. The book has been disparaged as misogynistic and not relevant to respectable women. It is mentioned here as a curiosity and to embolden men to ignore their own shortcomings and adopt strategies of fringe pick-up artists.

Many men approach women and tell them they're beautiful, whereas PUAs will speak to every woman except the one they want to pick-up. She might feel she has offended him and try to establish contact. A pick up artist could say something to lower the woman's self-esteem, such as remarking her hair looks a bit funny, or she has a piece of fluff on her jacket. By such a put down, called a 'neg', the PUA makes himself more desirable. Invariably the 'negged' girl would try to win approval from the gamester, as if this would cancel the 'neg'.

During the course of his narrative, Neil changes from a shy, timid man and becomes an heroic pick-up artist on a world stage. He is initially insecure and awkward but, through practice, becomes one of the world's top PUAs.

Approaching women in a bar should never be straight on, nor from behind because that's intimidating and scary. Approaching at 45° is appropriate and not too confrontational. After the approach the

PUA can show he has value, by providing the woman he wants with something. He can show her a magic trick, or leave her with the impression that he is knowledgeable and valuable.

What was most intriguing however, was the PUA's manipulation of human psychology and social dynamics to influence the behaviour of the women. These worked like a type of forbidden black magic, using deception and misdirection to persuade women to give their phone numbers (and sometimes much more) to strange, wildly-dressed men they just met in a Los Angeles nightclub.

A great way to break the ice with women is to fake personality assessment, as if by an expert. Women love to talk about themselves and what they want in life.

Independently of Strauss' advice, I have used Briggs Myer Personality Assessment to gain women's interest in four dimensions: intraversion, sensing, thinking and perceiving. Each dimension is binary and there are 16 personality types, all having definite positive attributes.

A different ploy I investigated was to comment on any difference in dilation between a girl's pair of eyes, which I attributed to differences in left brain and right brain thinking, with the eye on the side with most brain activity distended or bloodshot. My method hasn't been published but I have credible evidence of its utility. With the intimacy of expert gazing into eyes, girls will believe an arbitrary personality rating.

Deceptions are easiest in the noise, hype and romance of a night club. Some can be used outside the nightclub. They centre around manipulating assumptions and asserting social dominance over individuals to manipulate them onto paths of their choosing.

Neil describes bizarre tactics, particularly the practice of 'peacocking,' where a man wears the loudest most obnoxious articles of clothing he can find (such as large red cowboy hats and even T-shirts with light up programmable LED messages). He stands out and attracts a mate, not unlike the display by a peacock. A different ploy is to ask a woman to sit in a corner and talk with him, gaining prominence.

Many of these tactics could be used outside the nightclub. They centre around asserting social dominance that manipulates the woman onto paths of their choosing. Some of it gets a little goofy and delves into creepy things like hypnotism, but some of it actually seems plausible and plays off the default settings of our basic tribal mentalities.

Women are wired to find dominant men attractive. A neg makes men more desirable. Nice guys watch from the sidelines as dominant men succeed. Nice guys, like I used to be, finished last.

I quickly discovered that relationships manipulated by these techniques were unsustainable and emotionally hollow. Relationships should be authentic, with self-acceptance as the basis of connection.

CHAPTER 21
ROUGH

His brother Howard's visit to Sidmouth Hall for a weekend was their mother's idea. Tom could hardly refuse, as his parents were paying for his residence there. Howard would drive up with their sister Heather and a rugby friend.

I was delighted when Vicki agreed to keep an eye on Heather at Exmouth Hall.

I waited in my room with her for the visitors to arrive. She looked at her watch.

'They're late. Maybe they're lost,' she said.

'I sent a map with the route marked right into the car park.'

Just then an open-top sports car pulled up outside in an area marked 'No Stopping'.

They went downstairs to meet them. The three had climbed out and were stretching. His brother stood with his beer gut hanging out, scratching his behind.

'Hey, you!' I called down from a window. 'You can't stop there!'

The three looked around, startled.

'Oh, look what we have here,' said his brother, 'a useless student!'

Robert, the rugby friend, stuttered with gusto, 'S-students have got to be s-smartass-sses.'

'This is Heather, Howard and Robert,' I said. 'This is my friend Vicki.'

'Hello, Vicki 'my friend',' said Howard.

'Pleased to m-m—' Robert began.

'That's enough of that,' said Howard. 'We haven't got all day.'

'Don't be rude,' I admonished Howard. 'You are getting worse.'

My brother punched me hard on the upper arm. I winced, the pain making me angry. Howard was arrogant and a bully, showing off to Vicki. His bum crack was visible.

'Keep your fists to yourself, fat bastard,' I said.

It was not an auspicious start. Tom expected Vicki to leave at any moment.

'Let's have a drink,' Howard said. 'Is there a bar in this dump?'

I drove with them to the Ball and Powder, a public house just off campus. There Howard and Robert each downed six pints of the local brew. I drank two while Vicki and Heather each had a Babycham. She was a schoolgirl and in awe of Vicki. It was late Saturday afternoon with sports teams letting off steam. The pub was in an uproar.

As night fell, drunken louts lobbed glass tankards into the passing traffic. Howard and Robert went to join in. There was the smash of a windscreen, a squeal of brakes and a succession of impacts.

'Come on,' I said, heading for the door with Heather and Vicki.

I hoped never to see Howard or Robert again.

We went to the Students' Union where the Spencer Davies Trio were pumping out 'Keep on Running'. The audience was packed shoulder to shoulder and had an excess of male students competing to pair off with town girls. The wooden floor was bouncing like a trampoline. The administration manager announced that the weight exceeded the floor's loading limit and stopped the band. Everyone jammed into another room where 'The Who' were playing songs from their album 'My Generation'.

Howard turned up with Robert. He pushed through the crush, knocking people aside and talked to a girl, who shook her head and backed away. Tom took Vicki to dance with him.

Vicki danced energetically with reserve and elegance. She was an understated person and perhaps that is why I loved her to distraction. Other females tried to be someone they were not, but Vicki was the real thing.

I drew her outside to the verandah, where we could look out across the city lights to the towers of the city centre. She shivered and I wrapped my arms around her bare shoulders. When she turned to say something, I kissed her gently then passionately.

As Tom drove them all back to hall, a horn blared and a car drew alongside. Four male faces glared at them and shouted abuse.

'You cut him up,' said Howard. 'Nice!'

He wound the window down, shook his fist at them and shouted, 'Motherfuckers!'

The strangers pulled across, blocking the road. Howard got out and Robert said, 'F-fight, you c-cunts!'

It was Howard's and Robert's preferred activity. They fought in the road and were more than a match for them. Tom usually declined to fight unless it was necessary. Because Vicki was there, he squared up to their driver and traded a few punches that calmed him down. After a short while, the four yobs got back into their car and drove off.

'That s-showed them!' said Robert.

When they got back to Halls, Vicki asked him about Howard.

'You said he works with your father on the farm. Did he go to university?'

'No. He had to stay on the farm.'

'Is he jealous of you?'

'Of course. He lives with my parents and he would like the freedom I have.'

'What about your sister?'

'She wants to try for university next year.'

'Is Robert her boyfriend?'

'No, she's not allowed to have a boyfriend.'

During that weekend, Vicki helped Tom show his visitors a good time. They were envious of the student lifestyle.

'You've got it made, you jammy bastard,' Howard told Tom. 'Money for nothing; work when you feel like it; hot and cold running chicks. I wouldn't mind getting into some of this quality skirt.'

Howard's boorishness embarrassed Tom and it was a relief when they went home. He thanked Vicki for helping him with them. He regretted that her role as his girlfriend had come to an end.

A few weeks later Vicki told him she had received a letter from Howard. Tom was indignant.

'You didn't want to hear from him, did you?' he asked.

'I won't reply.'

He asked her to go to a movie but she declined. He suspected that she had lost interest in him because of his family and lack of sexual experience. He could make do with another girl and began chasing Annette, who also lived in Exmouth Hall.

'What if Vicki sees you with Annette?' Steve asked him.

'I don't care.'

'She might not like it.'

'Too bad. I've gone without long enough on Vicki's account. Her credit with me has run out.'

CHAPTER 22
LIMITED COMPANY

'I have a friend at Cambridge who can get tickets for the May Ball at St John's College,' said Steve. 'It is a black-tie affair, the apex of their social season. I am driving down with Angela. Would you and Vicki like to come with us?'

'Thank you,' said Tom. 'I'll ask Vicki.'

It was an opportunity to get back with her.

'Would you like to go?'

'I'd love to.'

A few days before the ball Vicki put her hands on his shoulders and looked into his eyes.

'Thanks for asking me, Tom. I would like to drive down with you and Steve, sharing the cost. I'll give you the money for my ticket. I like you but I want to, um, go with Angela. Um, don't take it the wrong way. Okay?'

'Is there a right way?' he thought.

'Okay,' he mumbled, having no choice.

But it wasn't okay. He had little interest in going to a black-tie affair without a partner. His prospects for scoring crumpet were dismal. Angela had lured Steve too and both boys were locked in.

'Maybe they want to pick up Cambridge guys.'

'What a con.'

'Bloody rude.'

Vicki had wanted him to understand something but he only understood her rejection. He felt wronged and tried to imagine what her rebuff meant. University women's conceptions of their roles in relation to males were in turmoil. Vicki could be exercising self-determination and politely setting Tom aside while she tried out other men.

'What's their game?' Steve asked.

'Girls toy with guys' affections. They tease us when they can.'
'It isn't to their credit.'
'It's a turn-off.'

Tom continued trying to get with other Exmouth Hall girls, making no effort to keep his trysts secret, not caring what Vicki would think. He could play hard to get too.

He started seeing Linda, a lithe first-year doll studying Drama and Dance. Before that there had been Annette, an elegant bird from American Samoa. He spent joyous times in bed with them but without coitus. He made no effort to conceal these affairs from Vicki. He hadn't cheated on her — they were not in an exclusive relationship. He was getting experience to take their relationship further. If Vicki wanted him to pursue her monogamously, she should be more responsive to him.

Steve had been playing the field, too.

'We are taking chances,' he said. 'Girls talk to each other.'

'I only date other girls when Vicki turns me down. Surely she doesn't expect me to wait around for her?'

'She probably does.'

'No way. This is the age of Free Love.'

'Not free at all. Girls are calling the shots now.'

On the day of the ball, Steve drove with Tom in the front, the girls in the back. The boys were disappointed in not having partners and there was little talk.

They arrived and handed in their overcoats. The ball was in ancient college buildings and spilled over into a handful of marquees on the quadrangle lawns. The cloisters were lit by the soft light of candles and lanterns.

The two girls were stunning with tied-back hair and long gowns. Vicki was wearing a long glittery figure-hugging sheath, with bare shoulders. They threaded their way through the crowd of St John's College students in formal attire, who greeted their friends exuberantly.

'We will meet you here at 4 am,' said Vicki.

'That's in six hours.'

'Bye.'

They disappeared into the throng, leaving them rejected and feeling dejected.

There were dance floors with trad, jazz, folk, steel band, pop and swing music. The opportunity was wasted because there were no girls without partners.

They drank at the bars but found little to talk about. There was a cold buffet of venison, pheasant, caviar, oysters, lobster and smoked salmon. The desserts were gateaux, crème brûlée, tiramisu and cheesecakes. Tom and Steve ate without appetite.

They didn't see Vicki and Angela and time dragged interminably. 'Day Tripper' seemed to play endlessly. By about 1 am they were ready to leave.

'How can we fill three hours?' Tom asked.

'We could find somewhere to lie down,' said Steve.

'The girls could turn up any time.'

'Too bad if they can't find us.'

They lay on settees in a lounge. Tom got up periodically to check for the girls but they didn't return until dawn. They were alone and didn't say what they had been doing or whether they had met any men. As they rode back to Liverpool, they were silent or asleep.

Tom was not able to talk about his feelings. He wanted to ask Vicki why she had snubbed him. Although she had apologised, she had not explained. He inferred that she had hoped to meet a stranger with a better pedigree. Like most students at redbrick universities, he resented the better facilities, entitlement and elite lifestyles at Cambridge colleges. Vicki's rejection was like a slap. He was not used to being stymied. No Wortham girl would have deserted him at a May Ball.

'That's the end of that,' Tom said to Steve. 'I wish I knew what the problem was.'

'Vicki likes you, funnily enough,' said Steve. 'She may still choose you, if you are patient. Don't you think she is worth waiting for?'

'I need a regular screw without complications.'

'There is no such woman, Tom. Why don't you wait until Vicki wants you?'

'I don't have the time.'

'You are too wrapped up in your work. It will be your undoing.'

'She has been driving me crazy!'

He feared Vicki was a 'hooker' who would keep him on a piece of string, to haul in when she wanted, like a fisher who strikes, driving a barb in deep, so the prey can never escape. It was too manipulative.

'An Australian woman, Germaine Greer, is making the news advising women to keep men waiting,' Tom said to Steve. 'She is bringing consumerism into how women choose men.'

'What would she know?' Steve said. 'I'm not impressed by these flaky uni girls. Town girls who go to work are more reliable. Look at Larry: he is doing okay with Lisa.'

Lisa worked as a business secretary and lived with her parents. She was pretty, intense and insightful.

'Larry is hooked,' Steve said. 'We could be next.'

'I'm not going to settle down until I'm 30.'

'There won't be any females of your age left by then.'

'I could go a young chick.'

'She will be demanding.'

'Females always are, sooner or later.'

'How are you going to find one whose demands you can put off?' Steve asked.

'Girls who are nurses and art students also come to the hops. There are some casual fun types.'

A few weeks later, there was a knock on the door of his room. It was Vicki.

'Tom, are you doing anything this evening?'

It was a breakthrough that Vicki wanted him for something.

'I'm seeing Linda. Why?'

He need not have mentioned her and rearranged his date. But he was still smarting from the way Vicki had stood him up at the ball.

Linda lived in Exmouth Hall with Vicki. She would realise that there was more in his life than waiting at her beck and call.

'Never mind. It was just an idea.'

'Another time?'

'I'll let you know.'

When days and weeks passed and he was unable to connect with her, he knew that something was keeping them apart but he didn't know what, unless it was his inexperience.

CHAPTER 23
CONDITIONAL LOVE

Girls came to Tom's room and they kissed and fondled. He wanted to gain experience for winning Vicki, but these hall girls wouldn't go all the way. He was soon chasing so many girls he was getting muddled. A love revolution was underway and he was frantic to share in the spoils.

He heard on his radio The Beatles' song 'Love You Too', with sitar and tabla. The monotonic Hindustani strains evoked the eternal sexual mystery. Girls were in no hurry to have sex with him and they wouldn't let him rush them into it. When he pretended he wanted to settle down, they would lie on his bed with him, he would hold their breasts and try to get his hand into their pants.

The closest he could get to intercourse was a 'dry fuck': lying on top in his clothes. His thrusts and bangs sometimes resulted in a sticky ejaculation in his pants. It prevented 'blue rocks', an excruciating pain in his testes and an unpleasant mess when it went cold.

His prurience became known to Exmouth Hall girls and he lost credibility. He had to go to other halls further afield to find girlfriends.

There was a knock on his door one afternoon. He was surprised to see Vicki. She could see behind him, on his bed, a halls girl. She flushed and turned to leave.

'Oh, sorry, Tom. I'll see you later.'

'Vicki, I—' But she was gone.

He bumped into her in the dining room later and asked her on a date, but she shook her head.

'Tom, all you care about is sex.'

She was not wrong. He knew he should be more aware of girls' feelings and genuine with them. Each girl had her own special magic and all were kind, sincere and distrustful of men. They were tolerant of his country manners but he was on a different page with sex: he wasn't able to get them to take off their jeans.

He saw Vicki almost every day and although they sometimes spoke, it was only briefly. He asked her out regularly and she always turned him down. Without having any other explanation, he concluded that it was his sexual inexperience that was the problem. His failure to have a relationship with her worried him. He was still a virgin and it dragged him down, like a ball and chain.

He realised that sexual intercourse with Vicki would be conditional upon prior love, which would take time to establish. News stories reported that a sex binge called Free Love had spread from America. He supposed women created in him two needs, one for love and the other for sex. For love he wanted Vicki and he would keep looking for another girl for casual sex.

CHAPTER 24
SHE WON'T SEE ME

A week later, he carried his evening meal over to join Vicki and her girlfriends in the dining room. They smiled politely and continued their talk. When the others departed, he was alone with Vicki for the first time since before the May Ball. She lit a cigarette and sipped her coffee.

'I have been playing The Beatles,' he said.

'Which one?'

'Rubber Soul'. What do you think of 'You Won't See Me'?'

'I love it. Why?'

'It could be me,' he said, his voice hurt.

'Won't your girl see you?'

'No; you won't, will you, Vicki?'

'I'm not your girl.'

'It's not for want of me trying!'

'There's trying and there's trying. Paul McCartney doesn't go about it in the right way. Did you see the story in *The Guardian* about him and Jane Asher?'

'No,' he said. 'Are they fighting again?'

She rolled her eyes. 'Of course. Jane won't wait around for him the way Cynthia waits for Lennon. The men go off recording all day and leave her. It's hard for her to get a look-in.'

'Jane is in a different class to Paul,' he replied, blowing smoke. 'Jane's middle-class Willesden and he's working-class Liverpool.'

'Willesden middle phooey,' replied Vicki. 'Asher's other place is an exclusive Marylebone address. Paul's gone up in the world.'

'Jane has class, I agree. Is that a reason for her not to hang with Cynthia?'

'Jane has a job. Middle-class women want to have a career,' said Vicki, stubbing out her cigarette. 'Tell me, do you think Paul is smart, Tom?'

He wondered what she was getting at.

'Very,' he said. 'He's always first into the studio and he works hard. Do you think he is smart?'

'Not when it comes to understanding Jane.'

He got her drift: understanding a woman required special intelligence.

'Art is seldom compatible with fidelity,' he said.

'Are you suggesting that artists are only capable of casual relationships?'

'Paul and Jane are hardly casual,' he said.

'Rumour has it Paul doesn't often sleep alone.'

'Artists have traditionally tended to stay single,' he said. 'Living separately gives both of them freedom.'

'Cheating won't help them get together.'

'They aren't married, so how can it be cheating?' he said.

'I'll bet Jane doesn't see it like that. If he is having one-night stands, you can't blame her for staying in Bristol.'

'For him, having girls is like brushing his teeth.'

Vicki was pensive. 'The thing is, Jane has to make a stand for her career. She represents the hopes and ambitions of all those English women whose brains and skills have atrophied under their husbands' thumbs. She wants independence within marriage, without cheating. She has monogamous sex as a principle.'

'Her career may not be compatible with his.'

'You seem to be on Paul's side. It is a gender power contest and the lines are drawn,' Vicki said hotly.

'No,' he said patiently. 'I am on the side of the one who is least able to compromise.'

'Paul?'

'Yes. The band rely on him. Jane could take leave from the stage and go back later. He needs her to be with him right now. His lyrics tell it all: 'I'm looking through you, and you're not there!' He is indignant about her going off: Jane is deserting him when he needs her. Every day at the top is an ordeal for him.'

'He is the one at fault!' Vicki said. 'He is so unfair claiming she is letting him down. Millions of women are counting on Jane to resist him and do what she wants.'

'Is she their champion?'

'Yes,' said Vicki. 'If Jane will say no to McCartney, then all women can defy their lesser men.'

'Jane is unlike those women.'

'Stronger, you mean?'

'I feel sorry for him,' Tom said. 'It is amazing that McCartney, who has never had a woman turn him down in his whole life, now has Jane telling him to get lost.'

'So you think Jane should give in to him?'

'Paul sings 'I'll get you in the end, yes I will, oh yeah!''

'But Lennon sings 'Nowhere Man. Isn't he a bit like you?''

'But I do have a point of view – and I am going places,' Tom said.

'Your career is everything to you, isn't it? What about me? I want to have a career too.'

'Why not?'

'It's a new idea for a woman to have a career,' Vicki said. 'Men like Paul aren't used to sharing.'

'They say love will find a way. Let's take in a movie.'

'Not just now, Tom. I have to study.'

They hugged and parted. He didn't know what to do with Vicki. But he had a date with Barbara he could look forward to.

CHAPTER 25
YEAR END

Second year came to an end and their exam results were posted.

'How did you go, Tom?' Vicki asked.

'I was top in the engineering subjects.'

'Well done. You worked for it.'

'Thanks,' he said. 'How did you get on with your biology?'

'I failed.'

'I'm sorry. Why didn't you do more study?'

'I wasn't interested. I am going to change over to counselling.'

'Why counselling?'

'We did a unit of psychology. It's what I want to do.'

'Discovering what you want is good.'

'It will take another three years.'

'You'll be good at counselling,' he said. 'It is your natural demeanour.'

'Thanks.'

92

THIRD YEAR

CHAPTER 26
SOCIAL CLASS DIFFERENCES

Vicki and I were still friends but the love affair when we first met had fizzled. To my chagrin. There had been several times when I thought we would get together but it hadn't happened. Vicki had snubbed me, by going with me to a ball but spending the evening flirting with locals and I was hurt. I felt I was the wrong social class for her. In the UK, social class is established by what school you went to, by old money and by breeding. I had learned to fake them. I got no pleasure from misleading superficial enquirers and felt no guilt in that enterprise. But she had not accepted me.

I had adopted a new social class which morphed into Vicki's. To make my social identity more acceptable, first I distanced myself from my family and former class peers by absenting myself from their company. I learned to speak Oxford English, deserting my Somerset lowlands garble, which advertised my uncouth lack of intelligence and culture.

I tried to climb up to Vicki's class by acquiring her speech, conversation, colloquialisms, slang, swearing, values, attitudes, materials, locales, experiences and media interests. I learned to mimic a range of regional accents and postures, within which I could hide my Somerset accent. I soon had a repertoire of comic dialects that I used to showcase the neutral speech I was developing. I could conceal my new identity with Somerset, Yorkshire, London, Devon and Texan accents.

Imitating Vicki's bourgeois BBC English was difficult and dangerous if I was found out. Working class lingo revealed I was a prole.

I admired Vicki so much, I would happily end my search for love and sex in a relationship with her. However, I realized that it would take some time to develop a relationship and that early sex with her was unlikely, whatever commitment I made. The major obstacle between Vicki and me could be our different customs for exclusive relationships, which I didn't understand. If I pursued another girl, I would do so openly. Yorkshire people take pride in straight dealing and straight talking, at the risk of bluntness and terseness. A Wortham girl would never have deserted me at the May Ball in Cambridge the way Vicki did.

By contrast, we find southerners insincere, devious and reticent to call a spade a spade. I fear that Vicki may be a 'prick teaser' who enjoys keeping me, as well other guys, on a piece of string, to haul us in when she wants us. I didn't have time for that and would sniff around for a girl who was more accommodating.

Bright, adventurous and beautiful, Vicki stands very high in my female hierarchy. I am making it my business to claw my way up the male ladder as high as hard work can get me. Without class as a barrier between us, she was my ideal match.

CHAPTER 27
COMMODITY MARKETS

I was infatuated with, but frustrated by, Vicki. The supposed pairing off between gender hierarchies wasn't working for me. Vicki seemed to be higher up than I could ever reach and I was disillusioned. The uncertainty and emotional cost was more than I could afford.

'Ladder matching couples is superficial, corruptible and unreliable,' I thought. 'There has to be a better way to find a partner.'

I was interested in methods for matching buyers and sellers where prices varied in time with supply and demand. I was writing an assignment on the commodification of crude oil. It seemed likely a global oil futures market would be established soon.

'What is good for trading crude oil, might possibly be good for trading love,' I thought.

I wondered if a commodity market could trade love prospects as commodities. There was demand, supply, substitution and matching of buyers and sellers. Men and women could have wider choices than under the system prevailing at LUT, with its ranking of males and females and pairing off from the top.

'Oils ain't oils,' was the objection of suppliers of the best quality crude oils used for gasoline.

'We can crack anything,' was the mantra of refinery engineers who bought low quality oils cheaply.

'You get what you pay for,' was the credo of brokers who arranged trades. For the first time in history, oil was being dealt with as a commodity, a tradable product. I was convinced by my study that trading of futures in oil would stabilise prices and enable suppliers and refiners to get on with their work without oil supply uncertainty. Perhaps love could be traded between buyers and sellers.

'Love matches at present lack the rigour that could be obtained if love was dealt with as a commodity. Traditional matching is inferior. Girls ain't girls.'

A woman would have full rights of self-determination and would give her consent to a relationship before any trade took place.

'If love was a commodity, I could do a trade and get on with my work,' I thought.

Trading in love would have to protect women from exploitation, benefitting them without any possibility of harm. I knew that money in love transactions could arouse fear of sexual slavery and human trafficking. Sexual slavery and trafficking in women were illegal. It was unlawful to abduct, hold captive, apply force to, sexually assault, exploit sexually, bigamise, or psychologically harm any person.

Trading in a love market would be by mutual consent. I felt sure I could devise market regulations that would prevent non-consensual trading, in the same way that deception, fraud, theft and other hazards were prevented in oil trading. I was determined to turn my experience into a love market.

Compared with the ladder matching method, a love market would allow everyone to participate and would not depend on social appraisal and covert ratings of arbitrary value by an 'in crowd'. Buyers and sellers needed to be aware of many exchanges occurring and be able to value offers realistically.

I was convinced a well-organised love market could attract speculators and improve love matching. It would replace complex and inequitable negotiations between men and women with structured exchange such as between wheat growers and millers about quality. The presence of speculators would stabilise the market and benefit everyone.

A person seeking a love partner could want a match immediately, or search carefully online until they eventually found someone to meet their needs. A person's attractiveness could increase or decrease with age, experience and presentation skills. Their wants could change and so the finding of a partner required diligence and luck. The love market had to prevent deception and abuse.

'To advertise my new method I can get drama students to put on a spoof ridiculing current matching difficulties,' I thought. 'First I need to develop the terms of agreement.'

I talked with a LUT researcher who was trialling a computer dating service but there was little transparency and no role for speculators. Genuine lovers insisted on transparency. The love market, as it existed in computer dating, was not transparent. Buyers and sellers were self-promoting, not explicitly declaring their assets and often intending to deceive. This was a make-believe world and could result in fraud, exploitation, emotional hurt and disappointment.

I lacked practical commodity market experience. I could not start a love-trading enterprise until I had more experience and could demonstrate a relationship with a female with whom I had traded love successfully. My relationship with Barbara had love but seemed incomplete because she seemed reticent to offer herself in a trade with another man. She stuck to me and I could see that finishing with her was a problem I would have to solve soon.

Unable to secure love with Vicki, I had a love relationship with Barbara.

CHAPTER 28
COMMODITY SPECULATION

A computer dating service started at the university and I was curious whether I could start a dating system that would match men and women as efficiently as buyers and sellers of oil were finding each other on the commodity exchange.

I met Wilbur, an American researcher at LUT, who paid for his sports car and skiing holidays with his profits from speculating on commodities.

'When commodities compete, how does that work?' I asked him.

'You mean when they are substitutes for each other?'

'Yes.'

'A buyer gets various offers,' Wilbur said.

'Different prices for the same thing?'

'Similar things. He would look for the cheapest offer.'

'Like a sailor with a girl in every port?' I said.

'The quality of a commodity can vary. A sailor would be selective.'

'Would their prices differ?'

'The prices of substitutes would vary with quality.'

'Also with supply and demand?' I asked.

'Yes. There would be more girls in some ports than in others.'

'Prices might be lower where there is poverty, I suppose,' I said.

'Markets are never perfect. Prices he would pay in different ports would relate to prices of substitutes.'

'So prices for commodities are always relative?'

'Yes. My experience is with grains: wheat, barley, oats — that sort of thing,' said Wilbur. 'The prices are relative because they can substitute for each other.'

'Do the different grains have steady prices?'

'They do from week to week but not from year to year,' Wilbur said. 'Grain trades involve physical supplies and demands.'

'Love can get pretty physical,' I said, pretending experience.

'Love has an emotional component too,' he said.

'I suppose hungry people get emotional about grains,' I said.

'The demand for grains is for future delivery from storage. Love is more spontaneous and immediate.'

'Not always,' I replied. 'There can be a waiting time until delivery, called engagement.'

'Hmm. I suppose a love commitment could be like a 'future',' Wilbur said.

'Could I make an investment to trade a girl like a commodity?'

'You can't be serious!'

'I am. Why not?'

'What a hoot! You will be in big trouble when the girl finds out. Every girl thinks she is unique, with a mystical quality that Mister Right will appreciate when she finds him.'

'Isn't each grain shipment unique?'

'Yes — the price is adjusted for quality,' said Wilbur. 'Grains have price adjustments for high and low quality. But it is not the same as valuing a girl's unique quality. There is no formula for adjusting a girl's price. Dating services are paid for by both men and women, each wanting to connect with a person they could have affection for during correspondence or in a meeting. The problem is that people exaggerate, lie and try to put one over on other applicants. I'm not saying it won't be possible to trade a girl as a commodity, but that each buyer would appreciate each girl differently, not as a predictable commodity.'

'Trades could be individuated.'

'Exactly,' said Wilbur. 'Would you like to see how commodity trading works by investing in a grains straddle? You will see that commodity trades are individuated, but the adjustments to prices are universal and honest, preventing disappointment. The economic dimension is the most important and final. Agreement is reached at a certain price.'

'I doubt a girl could be traded like that. Price could come first, with adjustment later.'

'That would be different. You would have to try it and see. I have an awesome prospect in grain trading for you. You are sure to double your money. Are you interested?'

'That sounds great. What is it?'

'It's a spread. I'll explain.'

CHAPTER 29
SPREADS

Wilbur thought that the love market I was proposing could be unethical. He helped me to understand how it could work.

'What do you mean by 'a spread?'' I asked.

'A spread is between two different commodities, often called an inter-commodity spread. It involves taking simultaneous long and short positions in the futures markets of two related commodities. This approach aims to profit from changes in the price difference (spread) between the two commodities, rather than their absolute price levels.'

'Could I have a spread on girls?'

'What girls?' he asked.

'Two types: girl graduates and girl secretaries.'

'Vickis and Barbaras? If they were wheat and barley, you might buy wheat expecting it to increase and sell barley expecting it to fall. You would have protection and profit from the difference. The trader buys (goes long) in a contract in one commodity and sells (goes short) in a contract on a related commodity at the same time and for the same delivery month. Profit or loss depends on how the price difference, or spread, changes—not on price changes for either commodity alone.'

'How much profit??'

'You would deposit three thousand dollars minimum for each trade. Imagine three thousand dollars is the cost of buying a railcar of wheat and you can spend an equal amount of money buying a railcar of barley to cover the short you would sell. A deposit of $6000 for the spread.'

'$6000 is a lot of money compared with the cost of my room in hall, which is $100 dollars per week. I could borrow it until

September from my father's overdraft account. I'll have to pay it back by September when my father pays the rent for the farm.

'No worries. By then you will have made a large profit.'

'How sure are you?'

'It's a cinch. Wheat and barley prices have never been as close as they are now. When the gap widens back to normal, you will profit big-time. These trades will be made at a margin of 5%, meaning your profits and losses on nominal amounts will be multiplied by 20.'

'Who is putting up the 95%?'

'The broker, for a fee,' Wilbur said. 'Delivery is not until the end of September. That's why they call it a 'future'. If grain crops are destroyed by bad weather in Russia, the USA or Canada, the wheat price will increase and offset your extra cost of buying scarce barley if its price increases too. You will be protected.'

'What if wheat falls?'

'Barley's price is likely to fall too and your short will protect you.'

'Am I exposed to the difference between the two commodities, with a spread between them.'

'Exactly. Sometimes the gap isn't normal and you can lose.'

'How can a gap be normal?' I asked.

'When it narrows to the usual gap again.'

'Yes. The gap between wheat and barley is narrower today than at any time in the past twenty years — without good reason. If a new animal feed technology had been invented that favours substitution of barley, the gap could narrow permanently – but it hasn't. I have searched grain industry literature and news articles but can't find any mention of such a discovery. The market must be in error, an aberration. I have stumbled on it by accident. No-one else has realised it yet. Prices must correct before long and then we will profit.'

'Are you saying I can't lose?' I said.

'It is an ideal investment,' said Wilbur. 'A spread controls against internal risks like the weather and protects against external risks, like innovation.'

'Excellent. I'll be in it.'

Wilbur introduced me to his broker and I transferred $6000, $3000 of it for wheat at 380 dollars per tonne and $3000 for a short on barley at 275 dollars per tonne.

That afternoon the broker left a message for me to call him.

'Margin call,' he said. 'Your wheat is down to $370 per tonne but barley has gone up, to $280 per tonne. What are you going to do?'

I bit my lip.

'Holy shit. This wasn't supposed to happen. Wheat was supposed to go up and barley was supposed to go down, widening the gap. But the opposite is happening. What's going on?'

'Nothing new,' he said. 'Just normal trading.'

I hope Wilbur knows what he is doing,' I thought.

'How much have I lost?' I asked.

'You are down $10/tonne on wheat and you will have to pay $5 more per tonne on your barley short.

'How much altogether?'

'You have 3000 tonnes of wheat, so that loss is $30,000. You will have to pay an additional $5 per tonne for 3000 tonnes of barley, or $15,000. All together you are down $45,000 and your deposit of $6,000 won't cover it. Deposits on spreads are at a margin of 5%, amounting to 20 times your deposit of $6,000 = $120,000. Your deposit is enough at present.

'I'll hold position and hope the trend turns around,' I said. I did not feel at all comfortable with so much money at stake.

The following morning the broker phoned again.

'Margin call. The gap has continued to narrow,' he said. 'Your deposit is gone. Will you put in another $6000?'

'Barley is going up faster than wheat is coming down. The gap is narrowing. I can't afford to hold both.'

'Then break a leg.'

'Which one?'

'Keep the wheat, hoping it will go up.'

'And the barley?'

'I'll close it. It's up $5 per tonne for 3000 tonnes, or $15,000.'

'You'll have to pay the full cost of the barley, $825,000 as it will be outside a spread and not on margin,' said Wilbur. 'I would hate to be exposed like you, with a short of $825,000 on barley. If you keep it, at settlement date, if there has been a shortage of barley, a weather event, or demand from the malthouses, come September you might not be able to buy it for love or money. Then you could lose your shirt. You would be wise to take your loss now.'

'I'll take my loss of $15,000 on the barley with my deposit of $6,000. I'll write you a cheque for $9,000. I wasn't expecting this and it hurts.'

I closed the barley future and transferred $9,000 to the broker to cover my loss.

'You still have the wheat and if you don't find a buyer, in September you will have to take delivery,' he said. 'If there has been a glut, you could receive several railway wagons filled with wheat that no-one wants, paying transport and storage, losing most of the $3,000 you paid. I wouldn't be able to sleep at night. You had better pray the price starts going up, due to bad weather, crop failure or wheat disease, in America, China or Russia.'

'Why did you expose me to this?'

'My prediction said you couldn't lose.'

'Your prediction was shit.'

'My prediction was okay,' said Wilbur. 'Shit happens.'

For the next three weeks, I anxiously studied world weather reports and wheat price trends. I was relieved when the September wheat price increased. A week before the end of term I sold it at a profit of $10,000. With my loss of $15,000 on the barley, my overall loss was $5,000. I would have to borrow it somehow. My father would notice the trading in his account. He never gambled himself and he would not like my profligacy.

I was desperate.

I asked Wilbur 'Would you lend me $5,000 until the end of the year?'

'I would like to, but I am in a hole too,' Wilbur said. 'I am hanging on to get the quitters' money.'

'My money!'

'To profit you have to stay in the game. Your wheat could come good.'

My barley short had taken up more than my initial deposit and was closed. My long on wheat had held its own for several days now.

'It might recover,' I said hopefully.

'It's a risky business,' said Wilbur. 'That's why my money is all tied up. Sorry Tom.'

'That's okay. I'll get a loan from someone else.'

There were a couple of people I could try before I sold my car.

'The theory is sound,' I thought. 'Too bad the commodities didn't do what they were supposed to. The prices went against the odds. If the deal was in girls, there would be a good chance of coming out ahead.'

In a love straddle, I would be transacting the commodity love, not as a subjugator of women but as a speculator. Women and men would consent to be matched, with their consent. They would benefit from opportunities to enter a love match by participation in a larger market. Love is necessarily tenuous and temporary but within a love market, exchange could be more secure. By commodifying love, the vagaries of love trading, such as fraud and bigamy, could be greatly reduced or even eliminated. I would try it, pioneering selling Vicki short in a love trade.

CHAPTER 30
GIRLS SPREAD

When I could see the potential of investment in a spread, I became very keen to try it out with a girl.

I found Wilbur in the coffee bar and told him that Richard might pay to get access to Vicki.

'I have seen how grains are bought and sold as commodities. People use the market to supply them with what they need and to make a profit when they have something to sell,' I said. 'Could people who want a partner, or who want to finish with a partner, search in a love market? There could be a trading floor, or an online display, or an app, offering exchanges.'

'It satirises love matching,' said Wilbur. 'Love is monetized, demeaning and ridicules the romantic element. It's too dangerous. I'd stick to grains. Love between a man and a woman is supposed to be a unique match, not like a miller with a recipe to purchase a future trainload of grain.'

'But love is a trade, isn't it?'

'Yes, of a type,' Wilbur said. 'Males and females exchange their values.'

'Do they balance?'

'It is difficult to calculate, but balancing is an ideal, yes.'

'Why?'

'If one side does most of the taking, the giver could be resentful,' said Wilbur.

'Because the other is taking unfairly?'

'Yes. However, a fair exchange in love is not always possible.'

'Coupledom does have agreement though,' said Tom.

They looked around at other students in the bar, mostly couples intent on each other.

'Couples negotiate relationships: that is their main intercourse,' Tom said.

'A love match would exchange more than material value,' said Wilbur. 'The couple would agree to devote their interests, skills and wealth to each other.'

'Like with a dowry?'

'Wider than that. A bride can supply a dowry as part of the price a man is demanding for his commitment,' said Wilbur. 'He would get her loyalty, income, possessions, beauty, personality and her 'chemistry'. She could have many features he would value. Different men would rate wants variously, depending on the woman.'

'Not to mention access to her reproductive organs and maternal caring,' I said.

'The matters for negotiation could be extensive,' said Wilbur.

'Her wants would differ from a man's,' I said.

'What do you suppose a woman would want from a man?' Wilbur asked.

'Access to his affection, physique, character, income, prospects, material assets, sperm and money,' said Tom. 'There could be many things. Ideally contributions of the woman and the man would balance.'

'That seems unlikely.'

'They can fine tune by negotiating what they will exchange.'

'Including certain rights to each other.'

'No woman will consent to give up her rights to a man,' said Wilbur, shocked. 'A man can't own a woman.'

'No, she can't be repossessed like a chattel. The trade is not about rights of possession but what each will voluntarily bring to a mutually respectful union.'

CHAPTER 31
VULNERABLE LOVE

'Could you lend me $5000 until the end of the week?' I asked Larry.

'Shit. What have you done?'

I told him about the grains straddle and unexpected result.

'Archer, you are a bloody fool!'

'It seemed quite safe.'

'So did the South Sea Company. I can only lend you $500. Lisa and I are getting married and we need every bean.'

'Thanks — five hundred would help. I'll try the others first. I may take you up on it.'

'Ask Richard. He's rolling in it.'

Richard was in the kitchen making a bacon butty.

'Richard, I need to borrow $5000 by the end of the week.'

'Have you tried everyone else?'

'I have borrowed against my father's overdraft account, but I need to repay it urgently.'

'Let's get this right,' Richard said. 'You have grabbed a piece of your old man's credit and now you want me to save your ass by giving you some of mine. Am I a sucker, or what?'

'It isn't exactly like that. I had some bad luck. Shit happens.'

'Let me think about it. Ask me tomorrow.'

The next day Richard came into my room where I was studying.

'Tom, I can get the money for you, but there is a condition.'

'What?'

'You would have to stop chasing Vicki. I want her.'

I was surprised but pleased. I might have suggested it in return for a loan. I knew Richard wanted her but I didn't think he stood a chance. She hadn't shown much interest in him so far. I had nothing to lose and money to gain by conceding his suitor position, which was virtually defunct. Was it possible Richard's prospects with Vicki were as good as he imagined?

'A love match is more than an economic transaction. Love is for keeps,' I said.

'Finding a partner with the skills you want seems straightforward,' said Wilbur.

'Economics is only one of several possible dimensions of the exchange,' I said. 'They can have as much emotion and psychological involvement as they want. It is up to them how economic and material they get. Negotiations can take several years.'

'Sometimes love is everything,' said Wilbur. 'Couples commit to love each other and haggle later about things they will share.'

'It's not usual to talk about money and possessions, is it?' I asked.

'Negotiating material considerations before the wedding could be unacceptable in some social circles,' Wilbur said. 'It could seem to revive historical practices that overrode a woman's right to self-determination.'

'There is no fear of that,' I said. 'This is progressive: she can choose a partner or stay single. There would be a legal contract, not unlike a prenuptial agreement.'

'Prenups are about reserving assets, not about trading them,' said Wilbur.

'Isn't a pre-nup a trade? It reserves the minimum price each would pay.'

'Not really,' Wilbur said. 'A prenup agreement is about what is yours, what is hers and what each of you will take away if you separate.'

'Same thing,' I said. 'If a man pulled out and took back his interest in a female, wouldn't that be like selling her?'

'If she consented.'

'What if he wasn't in a relationship with her — could he sell her short?' asked Tom.

'Of course, supposing he could find a buyer who she will consent to accept,' Wilbur said doubtfully. 'He would have to get her back, or get another girl like her, to deliver on settlement day.'

CHAPTER 32
CONSENT

In a class-free interval, he had coffee with Steve. He told him about his agreement with Richard. Steve was astonished.

'Selling your girlfriend is a joke, isn't it?'

'No. I'm serious. I will sell Vicki to Richard for $5000 for delivery before July 31st.'

'But you don't possess Vicki.'

'I will by then, even if I have to pay more for her.'

'Vicki can't be sold and bought like a thing.'

'I agree. She can refuse.'

'Refuse what?'

'To partner the buyer.'

'Why would she give her consent?'

'She could want to be with me. It's entirely voluntary.'

'It foregrounds money, when it should be offstage.'

'Financing of the deal would be offstage, between Richard and me. This is not a misogynistic scheme to exploit a sex slave. She already knows him and can choose to accept him or not, on her own terms. In fact, she is more likely to get the guy she wants than if she leaves it to chance.'

'Why do you want to sell her?'

'I can't afford her and I need the money.'

'$5000 compensates me for getting a hold on Vicki in the future and denying demands of other men who could want her.'

'$5000 isn't much of a price for a woman like Vicki, when you think about her asset value. It's far less than the value of her earning potential, cost of her education and her property value. Richard is getting off lightly.'

'I agree, but I couldn't ask him for more.'

'Why not?'

'He has to go to his parents for the money. If she is too expensive, they might balk.'

'Could you get the money by selling Barbara?'

'I need her until after finals, when I will set her up with another engineering student. If I get a First, Barbara will get kudos. An ambitious man will value a woman who has been with someone successful like me.'

'You really are up yourself, aren't you? An ex-Tom girl would in fact be stigmatised.'

'On the contrary, she would have had a successful relationship and be able to use her experience to attract another partner. If a man wants her, but lacks the means, I could forego my brokerage.'

'It's a scam! You are a rake!'

'How so?'

'A rake speculates in casual love. He commits to a girl and when he has made a profit, he reneges on the deal. A rake never intends to transfer his assets, but she cannot detect the difference between his offer and that of a genuine buyer. His honour is in tatters and she loses social standing.'

'You are trying to get Vicki by delaying your move on her until you have finished your studies and have a job lined up. You are trying to keep Richard away from her by getting him to pay for exclusive access to her and encouraging him to make his pitch early. It is a scam.

'Relationships often don't have total commitment at the start. Barbara can leave me, or Richard, or anyone, whenever she wants.'

'She might think she can reform you.'

'It is not necessary.'

'No other woman would ever want to go near you again.'

'Don't be so sure. Women like independent men. They don't want a spaniel. I will be able to command a high price.'

'You may be intelligent, but you are socially obnoxious and your ideas about how to bond with girls are crap,' said Steve.

'I haven't noticed you dripping with blondes. Vicki is at the top of the girls' ladder because she is popular with guys. She can command a very high price in commitments, obligations and conditions. For a guy she wants, she can lower her price.'

'For someone as weird as you, her price would be 'Not For Sale',' Steve said.

'What do you mean 'weird'?'

'You don't seem to have emotions, Tom. A guy and a gal commit to each other a bit at a time, so they can pull out without losing face, without being relegated down their gender hierarchies. A girl doesn't wear a price tag visible to all-comers, or reveal any price at all.'

'The prices are hidden from view,' Tom said. 'Vicki's 'price' sums up her conditions for entering into an exclusive relationship. Her demands now are more than I can provide. But when I have graduated and am in a good job, her price could be within reach.'

'Tom, you are playing with bloody fire!' Steve said. 'You are trying to resolve issues of love, loyalty and morality by an economic strategy.'

'Correct. She is a bad buy at her current price. I can get her for less later.'

'If you get lucky,' said Steve.

'Love is risky. You have to put yourself out there.'

'Rather you than me.'

'Where's your sense of adventure? This could be fun,' I said. 'Try it yourself with Angela and Margot.'

Stephen shook his head. 'It's all a prank to you, isn't it? Women will despise you. Some men will too.'

I sensed that Steve was envious of the deal I had created. He didn't have a deal with a girl.

CHAPTER 33
COMMODIFYING LOVE

Steve's arguments about the emotionality of love dismayed me. I wanted to benefit women. Commodifying love would bring transparency to relationships that could be flawed. Those who would object most would be unable to negotiate a match, because they were impecunious or pretending to have assets. A love market would thwart inequitable relationships and would be just.

My method offered men a way to secure a partner in the future when they could not secure a relationship now. They would receive from another suitor a payment to stand aside until a time when they can make their best offer. A templated contract agreement like mine could prompt them to form a liaison with a girl of their dreams.

Nor was a spread unjust when it allowed substitution of partners.

'It is not different to what happens when a lover has a bit on the side,' I said, 'except that instead of the two relationships being concurrent, they would be serial and more respectable.'

'You are bucking tradition,' said Steve. 'It's like with any social innovation; people won't understand it at first.'

'There is nothing illegal.'

'They will imagine this scheme could expose them to new dangers and not want a bar of it. The law may not be enough to protect them.'

'How can they be suspicious of a scheme that requires mutual consent?' I said. 'It has none of the compulsion of a 'shot-gun wedding.'

'Women will oppose you.'

'When they see it working, they'll welcome it.'

'Are you going to short sell Vicki?'

'Yes. I can't afford her now. I may be able to after exams. She will be free to choose between Richard or me, or someone else, or no-one at all. I am creating opportunities for her. Commodification will emancipate her.'

'You are a cold-hearted, selfish and cynical bastard,' said Steve. 'You will deserve it if both women tell you to go to hell! How will you explain this to Vicki?'

'I won't. She hasn't been taking much interest in me lately.'

'On settlement day she will discover you sold her out and there will be hell to pay.'

'I will help Richard to make his pitch and cover any extra costs he has,' I said. 'If Vicki won't consent, I'll pitch to her. She doesn't need to know my deal with Richard fell through.'

'If she did, she would feel manipulated.'

'She won't know,' I said. 'Few people are privy to how their partner has chosen them. They may never know who else was in the running.'

'You are breaking too many rules, Tom,' said Steve. 'Commodifying Vicki will expose her to more suitors she does not want, conceal her individuality and prevent her finding a partner of her own choice. Her relationships will be monetized, reducing her choices.'

'I have to stop Vicki disrupting my work. She has upset me several times. By commodifying her I can deal with her at arm's length and get on with my study. I know it is a long shot, but it could work. It won't do any harm and it will pay off my debt.'

Later, Steve put his head into Tom's room and quoted Shakespeare's Julius Caesar:

'Yond Cassius has a lean and hungry look;
He thinks too much; such men are dangerous.'

'Nothing ventured, nothing gained,' he replied, smiling wryly.
'It will be a miracle if you bring it off,' Steve said. 'What a hoot!'

CHAPTER 34
DELIVERY CONTRACT

Later I met Richard to play tennis at the uni. I showed Richard the agreement I proposed.

'This is our agreement about Vicki,' I said. 'Would you sign it, please.'

Richard read it carefully.

Agreement

'I Tom Archer (The Seller) agree to sell short a love relationship with Vicki Hillstone (The Commodity) to Richard Armitage (The Buyer) with delivery at Flat 6, Byron Estate, Ennerton, Liverpool by July 31st, 1967 (Settlement Day) with her consent. The Buyer agrees to pay The Seller 5000 dollars on the condition that The Seller avoids all amorous contact with The Commodity before Settlement Day. If, lacking her consent, The Commodity is not delivered to the Buyer, nor an acceptable substitute provided, the Seller's obligation under this contract will have been fulfilled.

Signed Seller:

____

Tom Archer

Signed Buyer:

____

Richard Armitage

Agreement Date: November 16th 1966
STRICTLY CONFIDENTIAL

Richard finished reading. 'Why does it have to be in writing?'

'We would forget.'

'It's not that fucking serious.'

It fucking is,' I said. 'I am concerned that Vicki could find out about it and misunderstand. If you blab I will tell her you paid me 5000 bucks for her.'

'It was your idea,' said Richard.

I said to him: 'Okay, here's the deal you agreed to. If you sign this, You will pay me $5000 and I will be honour bound to stay away from Vicki until July 31st. She can go to you or not when she wants. If she doesn't go to you, then she can go to me if she wants.

'After July 31st.'

'That's right. Imagine that I have sold you Vicki for delivery by July 31st. I may be able to come up with another girl graduate for you. I am trying to sell Barbara as a girl secretary, if you're interested.

'Vicki could choose you, me or another man, or no-one at all. She could self-own without any male interest in her — a position a liberated girl like Vicki could prefer.'

'It's risky but it seems okay,' said Richard. 'What I hear you saying is you won't make any moves on her before July 31st.

'What is Vicki supposed to do?'

'She can do whatever she wants.'

'What will you be doing with Barbara, Tom? Do you have a deal with her?'

'Not as a part of our deal. I could place her with some well-off engineering student who wants a girlfriend who has shown she is able to partner a hard-working engineering student.'

Richard laughed.

'Would Barbara agree to that?'

'Necessity is the mother of consent.'

'You bastard.'

'So we have a deal?' I asked.

He hesitated.

'Okay,' said Richard. 'I'll get your money.'

'Neither of us will look real good. I won't say anything.'

'No. Nor will I.'

'Do you have the cash?'
He handed it over. I counted the money.
'Sign.'
Richard signed. Tom handed him a copy of the contract and a receipt.
'It's all good,' he told himself. *'My relationship with Vicki will be at arm's length until July, when I will buy her, or a substitute, for delivery to Richard, with her consent.'*
He thought of the song: 'I wanna hold your hand' and sang quietly: *'I'll get you in the end.'*

'Deuce,' Tom said. 'Even with me out of the running, you still look bad. You won't have an advantage for long.'
'I'm saving your bacon, Archer. You should be grateful.'
They played the point.
'Advantage server.'
'Vicki is fortunate that you will be off her case,' said Richard. 'A girl shouldn't have to put up with a control freak like you.'
'Fuck you Armitage. At least I have gone after her fairly, without having to pay off the competition.'
Tom served and won.
'Game.'
The signing of the contract meant Tom would no longer be distracted by Vicki's antics. It was a relief. He could forget about her, until at the end of the year when he had a degree and a job. There would be fewer students around, demand for her would be reduced and her price would be lower. He might be able to afford her.
To implement the straddle while expressing interest in getting together with her later, he would withdraw from her. It was a tricky message and he wanted to deliver it personally. He tried to meet with her but she rudely put him off. He would not try again. She could infer that she was on his back burner.
'Maybe she'll be more tender if she simmers for a while,' he thought.

CHAPTER 35
FLING

One Saturday morning, Roger gave me a message that Vicki was having a party at her place that evening and I was invited.

'Why didn't she ask me herself?' I thought.

Because I had an agreement with Richard not to chase Vicki, I did not reply to the invitation and went on a date with Barbara.

On the following morning, I was studying at home when Roger dropped in.

'Hey, Tom, Richard screwed Vicki last night,' he said. 'He spent the night with her after the party.'

'Whaaat?' I could hardly believe it. Richard had taken delivery of Vicki months earlier than I expected, indeed I hadn't expected it to happen at all, though there was nothing written in the contract to prevent it. It was an oversight.

'I thought she was your girl?' said Roger.

It was an epithet that was music to my ears. I hadn't heard this lately and wondered if Roger was trying to cause trouble.

'Not anymore,' I said ruefully. 'This is the end.'

I had to sit down. Room and furniture rocked as my heart pumped adrenalin for a fight with Richard. He had gone behind my back. I tried to think what it meant for my relationship with Vicki. It could be over. A heavy curtain of grief descended.

'I sold my rights in Vicki to him,' I thought. *'We agreed he would wait until after July 31st.'*

Realistically, I couldn't expect to have my short cake and eat it, but I had never expected her to accept Richard. I had imagined he would try to get together with her after Finals.

With her rejection, my evaluation of myself plummeted.

'I won't get her now,' I thought gloomily. *'Vicki, why did you do this to me?'*

My chagrin primed me to hit back. When Richard came in, I confronted him.

'Did you fuck Vicki last night?'

Richard sighed, nodding gravely, looking away. 'Yeh.'

'Was she a virgin?'

He shook his head. 'No. There was a guy in Spain, when she was with her family on holiday.'

My intuition was that Richard was telling the truth. I wondered if I should fight him. I did not see that a punch-up would achieve anything, even if I won.

Richard didn't apologize. I had renounced my claim to Vicki when I sold her to him and took up with Barbara. But the code of honour that one should respect a mate's relationship still applied. Richard's going with Vicki was bad form.

I recalled Oscar Wilde's words: *'A good friend will always stab you in the front.'*

'Why do you think she did it?' I asked Steve despondently when he dropped in.

'You told me you had cut her adrift,' he said. 'She was free to find another guy. What did you expect? Didn't you have a deal with Richard about her?'

'Richard wasn't supposed to get her until after July 31st. The bastard broke our rules.'

'Why would he do that?'

'She probably put him up to it. Going with a flat mate's girl without asking is hostile. Perhaps she got wind of our deal and wanted a fling with Richard to drive a wedge between me and Richard, destroying our friendship.'

'Maybe you had hurt her. Did she know why you dropped her?'

'I was going to tell her but she was so avoiding me, I didn't get to talk to her...'

'Well, you botched it,' Steve said. 'I warned you.'

'Richard ratted on me. Going with a mate's girl is a foul.'

'Did Richard know you still wanted Vicki?'

'I agreed to stay away from her until the end of July, when he could try for her.'

'So why shouldn't he try for her before?' Steve asked.

'We had a verbal agreement. Not everything was written down.'

'Richard wouldn't want to wait. What about Vicki?'

'She didn't know about our agreement. If she had she wouldn't like us manipulating her.'

'That's true. What will you do now?'

'I'll try to forget. I'll keep on studying as if nothing has happened. What else can I do?'

'You could forgive them.'

'I can't ignore how they have dissed me.'

'Richard's agreement to stay away from her wasn't written down. Vicki would hardly respect you if she knew you had sold her.'

'She might have gone with Richard to demonstrate she could do what she liked.'

'That's most likely,' I said. 'Why would Vicki want me, when I have delayed our relationship and been beaten to the scoring line by Richard?'

CHAPTER 36
OUTMANOUVRED

When Richard and Vicki didn't stay together, I expected Richard to ask me to return the $5,000 he had paid for access to her until the end of the course, July 31st. Now he had taken delivery early, I was under no obligation to return his money and I could take up with her earlier, if she wanted. But Vicki showed no interest in me. Her tryst with Richard had intruded into my prospects with her and couldn't be ignored. But what to do?

I still had a spread, with a short on Vicki and a long on Barbara. I could profit from the narrowing gap of the spread, if Vicki's price was increasing and Barbara's decreasing. But the fling was evidence that the gap was widening and I was losing. Fortunately I had not been able to place the spread, because my love commodity was experimental, so I didn't lose any money.

I had been outmanoeuvred and I beat myself up. When Vicki and Richard's tryst did not develop into a relationship, her rejection and Richard's disrespect rankled and my hurt eased a little. My short had been closed. My interest in Vicki was ended, unless I made a new bid for her, but it was unlikely to succeed. I grieved for what I had lost, like death of a friend.

'Was she merely inconsiderate or did she deliberate her malice towards me?'

CHAPTER 37
RETALIATION

I was not going to take it lying down. My urge to punch Richard subsided and I focussed on exacting revenge less dramatically, by withdrawing from helping him with our studies. Richard was going for a First Class degree too.

The work had stepped up to a higher level of difficulty.

'What did you get for the assignment?' Richard asked me.

'A.'

'I got B. I thought we had the same solution. Did you go on and do more work?'

'I can't remember.'

'Can I have a look?' asked Richard.

'No. Get fucked.'

I wanted no part in normalising his achievement.

Slowly and inexorably I pursued my revenge. I was one of the leaders whose work was passed around and copied, but now I kept my answers to myself and handed them in without showing Richard, who struggled to keep up.

After Easter, the class rounded the home turn with only Finals ahead. Our studies required long hours of hard work. I was fortunate to have Barbara to relax me. When I picked her up for our weekly date, my head would be spinning with formulae, unable to do small talk. Gradually, she brought me back to earth and restored me for the gruelling week ahead.

My feelings for Vicki were ambivalent. She had shot herself in the foot, disqualifying herself from my attention. I wondered what I had done to deserve her cavalier and hurtful rejection. Her fling with Richard had spurned my feelings. Her motives were puzzling. I had regarded her as a gazelle, a dainty shy herbivore, but now she seemed more like a secretive, sleek and dangerous feline who had mauled me badly. Despite my wounds, I still wanted her. If she would apologise, our friendship could recover.

I took Barbara on dates to country pubs. She drank Babycham and we ate wholesome inn fare. We strolled along country lanes in the local hills and then sped back to my bed. She had me drive her home in the middle of the night to sneak into her parents' home like a teenager, as if what we had been doing was illicit. Our relationship was convenient. It brought me emotional security and the stability I needed to devote myself to study.

Initially I harboured ill feelings for both Richard and Vicki. It was too late to undo their actions but I got satisfaction from cutting off contact with them. This inconvenienced Richard, but there was nothing with Vicki that I could withdraw from. I had not achieved any part of the outcome I had wanted. I was not proud of my retaliation against Richard and I realized that I had botched my short sale of Vicki rather than being a victim of Richard's greed.

The outcome was that I was nowhere with Vicki, despite all my efforts to present myself acceptably at the appropriate time. Vicky continued to be cold and distant with me. The tension between Richard and me weakened and as the end of my course neared the incident diminished in significance and Vicki was just another student experimenting with relationships.

PART 6

FORCED WITHDRAWAL

CHAPTER 38
TRIAL BY CONSCIENCE

Tom remained in Liverpool to attend the graduation ceremony.

'My government has greatly increased the number graduating today,' said PM Harold Wilson in his address.

When Tom walked up onto the stage, the PM shook his hand and gave him a scroll.

'Congratulations, Tom.'

'Thank you, Prime Minister,' said Tom. 'May I ask you a question, please?'

'Go ahead.'

'Will you prevent North Sea oil from being exported?'

Wilson was taken aback.

'Is there a problem?'

'It would be used up too quickly and Britain wouldn't benefit as much.'

'We can't have our cake and eat it too,' Wilson said. 'We need the export revenue to strengthen the pound.'

'It will weaken when the oil is gone and we have to import oil,' Tom said. 'We need to keep it to get the most value.'

'That is too far ahead to worry about.'

'Won't you consider limiting exports?'

'We have considered it but it is not necessary. Thank you for your ideas. What have you been studying?'

'Petroleum engineering.'

'Do you have a job to go to?'

'Yes — but only until the petroleum runs out.'

Wilson grimaced, not sure if Tom was joking. He shook his hand and turned away to the next graduate. Tom returned to his seat.

'What did you talk about?' Steve asked him.

'I asked him to stop North Sea oil being exported.'

'What did he say?'

'Export would be good.'

'He's a politician. What did you expect?'

'His job is to lead the country forward, not to sell off the farm.'

'Do you really expect oil to become scarce?'

'Yes and so should you. Petroleum is the lifeblood of the world economy and it is running out.'

'You had better find some more of it then.'

After the ceremony, they posed in a group, threw their mortar boards in the air and leapt gleefully about in their gowns, while their families and friends took photos. His father was happy and proud of Tom's achievement. He had left school at 14 to labour in the fields. Tom was grateful to his parents for enabling him to escape to a world of opportunity.

With his way cleared to leave Liverpool, he went for a last movie outing with their gang. As they emerged from the theatre, he remembered that Barbara would be back from holiday. He had to call her and finish with her. He couldn't put it off any longer. He steeled himself and called from a telephone box.

'Hello.' It was her flat voice.

'Hi, Barbara. Sorry I didn't call earlier — I have been busy.'

He was not sorry.

'I'm pregnant.'

'What?'

'I'm pregnant.'

He was shocked.

'How do I know it's mine?'

'What do you mean?'

'It can't be mine!'

He had always been careful to use a condom. To establish his paternity, she had to refute his denial.

'I never want to speak to you again!' She hung up.

Her timid behaviour on the phone fuelled his suspicion that she had been impregnated on holiday in Majorca. She was counting on him to trust her and assume paternity. Why should he? She had been trying covertly to get his commitment for months and this seemed like more of the same. He had wanted to finish with her but not like this. Others would view him as behaving badly.

It was the worst thing that had ever happened to him and he fought down his panic. He left the phone booth, stunned.

'Something has come up,' he told the others. 'I'll see you later.'

He did not regret his denial. The burden of proof lay with her. A court would consider evidence from both sides, an ugly proceeding. She could plainly see what common sense should have told her all along: he was never going to marry her. He had simply been using her for sex. He was the archetypal philanderer and she should have recognised that. Was she so stupid?

'Why don't you go on The Pill?' he had asked her several times. She had evaded answering. It was a smoking gun. He could assume she was secretly trying to get pregnant.

Could she have conceived while she was in Spain? Yes, there had been time. It was possible she had contrived to have sex with a stranger while on holiday, intending to become pregnant and trap him before he went away, assuming he would do the honourable thing and enlist as the father.

Faced with a choice of dishonour or possibly being deceived, his heart thumped with the adrenalin of fear. There was no time to freeze, no-one to fight and nowhere to take flight to. He walked for several kilometres back to his flat, turning it over in his mind.

There was no way back: he had burned his bridges. His denial had soured their relationship. Nor would they ever be able to parent successfully with this legacy of antipathy between them. As he walked, he pondered whether there was anything he could do. It would be heartless to propose an abortion and it could be misinterpreted as an admission of liability.

On the High Street, he ran into Steve. He told him everything. Steve listened and Tom calmed down. The weight became bearable.

'Think it through carefully before you decide anything,' Steve said.

'It's too late for that,' Tom said. 'Barbara and I are finished.'

Tom decided to go home to the farm. He wouldn't get any sympathy but he could lie low for a couple of weeks until he left to go overseas. He packed his things. He waited overnight, expecting to hear from Barbara's former school friends, Lisa and Margot, in support of her claim that he was the father. When they did not contact him, he was certain that Barbara had set him up and his heart hardened. There was no reason for him to stay any longer.

Vicki drove past and waved. He was glad she didn't stop. He was too ashamed to face her. Whether he was the father or not, he was dishonoured, disgraced.

He left without saying goodbye. Barbara did not have his address but she could get it from Tom's friends. He hoped she would not contact him.

CHAPTER 39
CLIFFHANGER

At home, he did not mention Barbara to his parents, brothers or sisters. He had never spoken of her to them and he didn't reveal his predicament now.

A few days later, when he came in from work on the farm, his mother yelled at him.

'You ought to be ashamed of yourself!'

Barbara's mother had phoned, threatening to have a maintenance order served on Tom and prevent him from emigrating.

'It can't be mine,' he said.

'Nonsense. It must be yours.'

Although she had predicted such a paternity claim in her warnings to him about girls who would use pregnancy to trap boys, his mother was obdurate, it was his. He told his version of events.

'She hasn't faced me yet,' he said. 'She told me she was pregnant over the phone. No friend of hers has come forward to back her up. I've never been to a social event with her friends. She could have another boyfriend. She was in Spain on holiday when she conceived, at a resort where casual sex between strangers was commonplace. I overheard her talking with Margot about the men they had been with on holiday.'

'I don't believe it. Men like you are a menace, leading innocent girls up the garden path.'

His mother's venom was hurtful and he was mortified when she used his example to warn his sisters of the falsity of men.

His father's concern was Tom had disrespected his betters. 'A solicitor's daughter! Tsk, tsk!'

Tom tried to take an objective view. Barbara's claim was weak. She had left it to be inferred from their association that he must be the father: she had not denied it could be someone else or that she had partnered another male.

During the month when she became pregnant, it was unlikely but conceivable a small amount of semen could have escaped a condom, during the ovulation window and had reached her Fallopian tubes. The chance of this causing conception was tiny.

'It is very unlikely that I caused her to be pregnant,' he said.

His mother knew little of the conception process or of condoms and disregarded his analysis.

'It must have been you,' she said.

Tom was in a quandary, as he faced either being shackled by an unwanted marriage or by dishonour. If he ran, he would be a coward in his own eyes, leaving a girl in the lurch. It clashed with his self-concept as a man who treated women kindly. Would Vicki ever have him back?

On the other hand, he couldn't imagine living with Barbara. He knew next to nothing about her. What would they do together, besides caring for the baby and having sex? Did she have home-making skills? She had never cooked him a meal. She had never been with him when he got up in the morning, or seen him shave. They had never spent a whole night together, nor even a whole day. They had never gone anywhere together more than an hour's drive away. Would she be able to cope with living with him, without family or friends, in the harsh climate of Western Canada? Would she be a good mother? What interests did she have? What did she care about? What did she want? A good marriage was not possible after this shallow and conflicted start.

He couldn't be a good father with the child's paternity in doubt. DNA testing was years away. If the child was physically dissimilar, it would remind him always of possible infidelity and dishonesty. Using pregnancy to trap a person into an unwanted partnership was low. The psychological consequences for the child of him staying unhappily with Barbara could be worse than if he left her to raise it alone.

By accepting Barbara's dismissal, he believed he was doing what was best in the long term. He couldn't live with a woman he suspected of manipulation and duplicity. She deserved more love than he would ever have for her. He had denied being the father and she would never love him.

He did not know the rules by which they might assign paternity to him. He knew no-one who could explain what this would entail. In his mind he suffered remorse and denied responsibility simultaneously. His paternity was like Schrodinger's Cat, existing ambivalently both dead and alive at the same time, like a foetus being considered for abortion.

His mind kept churning the options and the future seemed dismal. He began to consider another option.

He asked his father for work on the farm and was assigned to drive a tractor pulling a haymaking machine from dawn to dusk. The field had thorn hedges on three sides with the fourth overlooking a river. An unfenced cliff dropped down vertically 30 metres to a boulder-filled riverbed. When feral dogs drove them over, sheep had been killed.

He steered around the hayfield, raking together a long row for the baler to engorge. Bitter that he was being blamed unfairly, he drove close to the abyss, not caring about a landslide. His radio earphones played The Beatles' 'A Day in the Life' with the words: 'He blew his mind out in a car.'

Driving across a headland towards the cliff, he was aware that if he didn't turn away, he would launch into space. Falling onto the rocks would kill him and he would be free of Barbara. His parents and siblings would believe he had dozed off.

There didn't seem to be much reason to head away from the cliff. He watched seagulls ride the wind as they followed the swathing machine, diving for insects. Life was tenuous and all living things were destined to die eventually. Better to die than to live with the shame of deserting a child or marrying a woman he didn't trust.

The seagulls screamed: 'Die!' and the sound blew away in the buffeting wind.

The tractor gears ground noisily and inexorably forwards. It was a couple of hundred metres to the cliff. There was no middle way.

Ambivalence would only aggravate the hurt. Separation had to be quick, clean and as painless as possible.

His ears were assailed by the clatter of explosions in the engine, cams hitting rods, rods lifting valves and big end bearings bouncing. He was just a cog with a job to do to keep the whole thing working smoothly; too much was being demanded of him.

It was about 100 metres to the cliff. All his senses sharpened. He sensed the moment in vivid detail. There were skylarks pirouetting crazily overhead, the liquorice stink of hot diesel, the sweet odour of the hay, the sun warming his back, the bouncing of the hard metal seat and the wrenching of the steering wheel against his hands. It was surreal.

He was 40 metres from going over the cliff.

He thought of the foetus. By what right could he cause it to be killed? It was a right exercised by a victorious lion when he killed his predecessor's cubs. It was a right exercised by a kangaroo when in a drought she discarded a joey from her pouch. It was a right exercised by parent birds when in a famine they ceased to regurgitate food into the gaping maw of the weakest chick. It was a right that humans exercised when they terminated an unwanted pregnancy, declining to accept responsibility for an offspring and preventing inferior care by others.

Twenty-five metres from the cliff he relaxed his grip on the steering wheel, ready to go straight over. The tractor would drop, smash, bounce and roll over him. He would be killed and his pain would cease.

But his father would regret not having been there for him and blame himself. Tom's gravestone would cast a shadow over the remainder of his life.

There were only seconds left before his wheels would reach the abyss. It would be too cruel to his father. He loved his father too much.

He yanked the steering wheel hard around and continued along parallel to the cliff top. Far below, the river thundered between boulders. He would live on and if they demonstrated his liability, he would accept responsibility.

A week later Barbara's father wrote that she would have a termination. It was a civil letter, without recrimination, requesting he pay half. Tom sent the money and thanked him for arranging it, adding that he was sorry. He didn't add that the initial wrongs were that he had wanted to use her and that she had allowed herself to be used. He had gone out with her in default of Vicki. He hardly knew her, even after a year together. He hoped she would have a happy life.

He waited with impatience to embark for Canada. When the day arrived, he left home, gave his sisters a kiss on the cheek, hugged his mother and promised to write. His father and Roger took him to the ship and saw him off. His father's eyes were moist as he shook his hand.

Tugs pushed the liner away from Prince's Dock, breaking the streamers that were his last connection with the land of his birth. Tom felt a weight lifting off him. He didn't know when he would return, if ever. He was going away to make a fresh start.

CHAPTER 40
CELIBATE REACTION

The great ship slid slowly down the Mersey towards the Irish Sea. Tom stood on the foredeck, braced against the wind. He was 21 and on his way to join the exploration department of Canada's largest oil company, Canoil.

When he arrived in Calgary a month later, Larry and Lisa were already there. He hadn't seen them since their wedding reception in Liverpool. They invited him to stay in their first married home, a rented apartment. Together they explored their new territory.

Tom was apprehensive that Lisa would blame him for her friend Barbara's pregnancy, but she never mentioned her. If he was the father, wouldn't Lisa remonstrate?

Barbara's father wrote to him, reporting that she had aborted and was recovering satisfactorily. He hoped that she would be able to make a fresh start. The tragedy reduced Tom's interest in all girls and it was a year before he resumed dating.

His thoughts were often with Vicki in Liverpool.

Canoil's engineering orientation programme began at its headquarters in downtown Calgary, with Tom and 15 other graduate recruits. He worked three-month stints at several different oilfields until they assigned him to a tar sands project at the all-male Tundra township in remote northern Alberta.

He received a letter from Richard.

#4 South Court,
Park Estate
Mersey Avenue,
Liverpool

21/04/68

Dear Tom,
Chuffed to get your letter. Bruce and I are working all hours. Jozef has your room and is entertaining a series of fresher girls. I am envious of your skiing as I didn't go this year and worked through the Christmas and Easter holidays. Doc Bishop still wears that old suit for thermodynamics lectures, with the sleeves held on by threads. There is a girl fresher in Engineering this year; it will never be the same again, thank God.
Vicki is working hard at Counselling. She has had several boyfriends but they haven't lasted for long. Angela has also switched over to Counselling and they are still living together.
Dave Klein is Union President and Tony Benwood is Chairman of Deb Soc. Jozef ran for President but the socialists gave him a hard time in hustings. Tits Patricia is still around and both are doing well.
Yours studiously,
Richard

Strangely, after all they had been through, he trusted Richard. It seemed too late for deception and animosity. It had taken Richard all final term to recover from his nervous breakdown and he had not been well enough to sit the exams. Now he was repeating final year. With Tom gone, he was acquitting himself with aplomb and on track to secure First Class honours. Richard's undoing had been his competitiveness and in Tom's absence he was succeeding.

He received a terse postcard from his brother Howard who was travelling in Mexico. He had not heard from him for two years. Howard wrote only when he wanted something. He was coming to stay but didn't say when he would arrive. Tom wanted to reply that he couldn't put him up, but there was no return address.

When spring break-up made the roads passable again, Tom drove to Calgary for weekends, where he partied, skied, learned to fly and played rugby. He met females and soon relinquished celibacy.

He wrote to Vicki, hoping she would be envious of his lifestyle. If he could entice her to visit him, they could renew their fractured relationship.

c/o Canoil Ltd
Tundra Oil Project
Bear River Township
Alberta
Canada

28/04/68
Dear Vicki,

I hope you are enjoying Counselling and are managing okay without me.

Richard tells me you are working hard. Good for you. Also, that Angela is with you. So you are with some old friends. I wonder who is new.

I am living in a caravan and driving a carload of oil people through the snow to and from work at a tar extraction plant. Spring break-up is underway and the road is slush and ridged ice. The other evening it was so cold the LPG froze in its bottle and our trailer was without heating. I would have had to snuggle up to the other two guys, but they held a flame-thrower on the frozen gas bottle, while I cowered under the table.

I would sure like to warm my hands on you, which is what the Choctaw Indians say when they mean, 'I am missing you'. I want to find out all about the new Vicki while still having some unfinished business with the previous one. I want to explain my sudden departure from Liverpool under difficult circumstances.

How about making me a visit after Easter? We could drive to the Rockies on a skiing trip. You need have no fear of wolves, moose, elk, grizzlies, mountain lions, wolverines, racoons, skunks and other varmints. Critters will stay clear if you urinate on trees around the camp perimeter before turning in. I could help you with this.

We can trap our own food. Next season I will run a trap line with a sled and a team of huskies. There are tourist eateries in Banff where the traditional fare of the Choctaws is a short stack of pancakes with clotted cream and maple syrup.

I had better do some work now. While I have been writing, some oil has run away. I will lead a posse to slip past it and, damn it, sometimes work interrupts my leisure.

With love,
Unrequitedly yours,
Tom

He hadn't expected to get any reply and when she wrote that she was coming to ski with him in the Rocky Mountains, he was surprised and delighted. He would pick her up at the airport in Calgary, to go on to Banff for a week of skiing. It seemed perfect.

PART 7

CHOICES

CHAPTER 41
RUTTED RENEWAL

There was a knock at the door of James' and Hayley's house. His older brother Howard was there, with an inch of stubble, a dark tan and a backpack. Tom had given him this contact address in Calgary. He hadn't seen him for two years and he had not missed him at all. Howard punched his shoulder, temporarily disabling his arm and pushed his way inside.

'I'll sleep on the settee,' he said.

'Leave your pack by the door. I have to ask if you can stay.'

James and Hayley were out.

'O nice,' he said as if he was a victim of Tom's inhospitality.

James and Hayley allowed Howard to stay for the night.

Tom would pick up Vicki from the airport to go skiing the next day. He was caught in a dilemma: should he leave him at the YMCA or take him skiing?

'I'll ask Vicki if you can come with us.'

Howard had met Vicki on his visit to Liverpool two years earlier, when she was Tom's girlfriend.

'Vicki likes me. No problem,' Howard said.

'She likes hyenas too.'

'Do you have any skiing stuff I can borrow to wear?' Howard asked James.

'Sorry,' James replied. 'We need our gear — we are going skiing too.'

Tom had warned James about Howard's grasping nature. He would be able to hire equipment at the resort.

Next day, he waited in the arrival lounge at Calgary airport for Vicki to arrive.

He could hardly believe she was coming. He doubted she had come all this way unless she was interested in a relationship with him.

When she came through, she was even more stunning than he remembered.

'It is great to see you,' he told her.

'You too.'

Her magic happened to him all over again.

Vicki was okay with Howard joining their skiing holiday.

'You can come with us,' he told Howard.

'Good,' he said.

Tom was under no illusion that Howard intended the holiday to be good for him but he wasn't so sure his participation would be good for Vicki and himself. He had looked forward to being alone with her and mending their bridges. He wanted to warn Howard that his relationship with Vicki was fragile, but he would not understand. Tom said nothing, hoping that Howard would have the good sense to leave them alone together.

They set off westwards in his station wagon to the Rocky Mountains. Vicki sat in the back, reading a book and couldn't be induced to talk.

'Is it because Howard is here, or do we have an issue?' he thought.

He wanted to tell Vicki the reason he left Liverpool without saying goodbye was Barbara's pregnancy, but he didn't want Howard to hear about it or the abortion.

'We would be safer if you went faster,' Howard said.

There was a thick layer of ice over the road, making bends precarious.

'We could slip off the road,' said Tom.

'We couldn't come off this road if we tried. The ruts in the ice would hold us on.'

It was a theory Tom had heard before and disbelieved.

After about two hours, when they were in the desolate foothills, he moved off the crown of the road for an oncoming truck and plunged head on into an embankment of snow heaped up to head height by a mechanical snow thrower. The hood popped up and they were thrown forward against their seatbelts as steam hissed out in a cloud from the ruptured cooling system.

'Holy shit!' Howard exclaimed.

'Are you okay?' Tom asked Vicki.

'Yes.'

'Did you lose your place?'

She did not reply.

The car was not drivable. It soon cooled down inside and they were shivering. When they thought they would freeze, a vehicle going the other way stopped. The driver offered to take Vicki and Howard on to the resort, while Tom waited for a recovery truck.

'I'll see you at the Excelsior,' he said. 'Tell them my name and check in.'

Vicki and Howard took their bags and went.

Fifteen minutes later, prominences on Tom's face and tips of his ears were throbbing and freezing. He was careful not to scratch them in case bits rubbed off. By the time a tow truck arrived from the garage, he was shaking uncontrollably. He sat in the warm cab as the truck winched the wagon back onto the road and up onto the trailer. He went with it back to the garage and arranged to collect it in a week's time. There was a bus coming through shortly and he waited in the cafeteria. He hoped Howard was not bothering Vicki.

His bus ride into the Rocky Mountains was overhung by spectacular pink peaks, with shadows from scudding clouds scuttling along the valley floor.

When he reached the ski resort, he found Vicki and Howard sitting in the hotel bar. Howard was surrounded by empty beer glasses and Vicki was reading her book. He could not get her to talk and mistrusted her book as the possible cause of her truculence.

'What does Sartre write about?' he asked her.

'We make our lives from choices we take, by reasoning within ourselves.'

'Not by following tradition blindly?'

'Exactly. It is our will and our actions that count,' she said.

'We are responsible for ourselves?'

'Yes.'

'What should we expect from others?' Tom asked her.

'They should engage with our whole selves, not just the bits of us they like,' she said.

'Because we have integrity?'

'Yes and we should accept the flaws in others,' Vicki said.

He wanted to find out what had happened between her and Richard after the party. He was waiting for her to apologise. Her treachery with the lie detector had made him mistrustful. The Beatles' song 'Hey Jude' prompted him to let her into his heart but her withdrawal from him now was discouraging.

In his mind, he ran through possible conversation starters.

'I forgive you.'

'I have finished with Barbara.'

'Can we make a fresh start?'

'I love you.'

He couldn't say them with Howard there.

She went back to her taciturn reading and he couldn't get her to talk again.

Her reticence was hurtful. The reconciliation he had been looking forward to wasn't happening. It was as if she had feelings that were causing her to withdraw from him. Her ability to communicate seemed paralysed, weighed down by sadness or loss.

'How's your mother?' he asked her.

'The same.'

'Why don't you try one of the black runs?' he said to Howard. 'I want to talk with Vicki alone.'

'No, I'd rather ski together. Why don't we all try a black run?'

'You go first.'

'Let's go together.'

Howard couldn't be persuaded to leave them alone. Tom stayed behind with Vicki on the slope and Howard climbed back to them. When Tom took Vicki for coffee, Howard went too.

Tom couldn't understand why Vicki had cut herself off from him. In the year since they had last seen each other, a lot had happened. It had been unkind of him to turn his back on her for Barbara and then go away to Canada without saying goodbye. He wanted to explain what had happened but it was too painful to get started.

His journey with Vicki had not led where he expected. The way she had intruded into his privacy with the lie detector was like being stalked by a predator. It had driven a wedge between them. He had contracted her to go to Richard, imagining she would never consent and amazed when she slept with him immediately after. Her fling had in one fell blow torn up his relationship with her and with Richard. It was hostile and had hurt him badly.

'Hell hath no fury like a woman scorned,' he thought. *'My going with Barbara and shorting of her may have antagonised her. She may have come to Canada now to bury the hatchet. But we haven't been able to do that — yet.'*

Her fling had caused him astronomic jealousy, which she could have intended. Richard had been mauled and had become seriously ill. All three of them had been injured and the hurt was continuing. Although a year had passed, Vicki's wounds could have festered. Tom's scar tissue lacked flexibility and prevented him getting closer. He wanted to, but was too wary of her to try.

She had burned her bridges with him but their roads still led towards each other. A way might eventuate to cross the gulf between them and restore their relationship. For their wounds to heal, they had to catch up their understanding of the events that had traumatised them.

CHAPTER 42
CHASED DESCENT

Tom wanted to talk with Vicki alone, to try and resolve their differences. Howard was always in the way, following Vicki around. He stayed with them on the slopes all day. In the lodge, he bragged about prejudices, cynicism and inhumanity. Tom regretted having invited him to join them.

'Two is company and three is a crowd,' he thought.

After eating, they drank and danced themselves to a standstill in the noisy bar. Howard confounded Tom's relations with Vicki by trying to hit on her. She seemed complicit, disrespecting Tom. Disappointed in her, Tom went to bed early.

On their last day, Howard and Vicki were on the ski lift in a chair in front of Tom. Howard put his arm around her. Tom realised he had to assert himself or lose his self-respect. When they got off, he deliberately tracked across Howard's skis and put his shoulder into him, knocking him over.

'Bastard,' Howard said. 'What was that for?'

'Interfering,' Tom said. 'You have been getting between me and Vicki.'

Vicki was there but made no comment.

'Fuck you,' Howard said as he struggled to his feet and lunged for him. 'She's not interested in you. I'll trash you, crazy boy!'

'You'll have to catch me first,' Tom said and took off down a trail leading to the steep giant slalom run.

Over his shoulder, he saw Howard charging after him on his skis, 50 metres behind, exactly as he had planned. Tom crouched low, head down, bum up, poles under his arms and went fast. He descended the mogul slope threading the quickest possible route, the way water would flow down, weaving a path between the icy mounds, his knees absorbing shocks.

He was a good skier, a bit out of practice. Quite soon Tom felt the pain of over-exertion in his thighs and knew that if he did not rest he would lose control. When he looked back, Howard was gaining, now 30 metres behind. He crossed the piste and sped off along a track into the forest. Howard was close behind and would soon catch him, knock him over and trample him under his skis. He went fast around a sharp turn and took off over a 10-metre-high cliff.

Tom had practiced jumping down from it the previous day. Behind him, Howard was going too fast to stop and toppled over the edge. He dropped vertically onto rocks at the base, bounced and rolled down the scree slope in a tangle of skis. Tom meanwhile had landed safely in soft snow and climbed back up to him. Howard was unconscious with his legs at odd angles. Tom put him in the recovery position.

Vicki arrived. 'You planned this, didn't you?' she said.

He nodded. She said nothing, as if she disapproved of unmitigated sibling rivalry. She went down the mountain to summon ski patrollers to bring him down on a 'crash wagon' sleigh. They spent the rest of the morning getting Howard into Banff hospital. He had broken both legs and six ribs.

Vicki spoke to Tom curtly: 'I want to go by bus to Calgary, to the airport.'

She wouldn't let him drive her.

'Stay here and take care of Howard.'

He waited with her for the bus to depart from Banff. It was the first time they had been alone together on this trip.

'Pity Howard turned up when he did,' Tom said. 'We never even caught up with each other.'

'I think your mind was already made up,' she replied.

'I was waiting to hear your side.'

'About what?'

'You and Richard.'

'Nothing happened.'

He could hardly believe it. Roger had been sure she was in a fling with Richard. Who should he believe?

'I wish I had known,' he said.

'So do I,' she replied.

She wouldn't talk, as if the time for that was past. He couldn't think of anything to say. The issue was the disdain she had shown him. True, his short had postponed his interest in her, but two wrongs did not make a right.

As she got onto the bus, he tried to kiss her but she gave him a quick hug and turned away.

'I'll write,' he said.

'Yes, keep in touch,' she said without enthusiasm and climbed on without so much as a backward glance.

'If she disapproves of my revenge on Richard and Howard,' he thought, *'she should recognise her duplicity was pivotal in both conflicts. My injury from her fling with Richard, a year ago, has kept me waiting for her to express remorse. But nothing had happened with Richard, except she gave Roger and me reason to think it had. She is a troublemaker and provoked me to retribution.'*

After she had gone, Tom grieved for the opportunity he had lost. He heard his own sadness in The Beatles' song 'Yesterday'.

He stayed with Howard for a couple of days but they didn't speak to each other. He returned to work in Edmonton. Canoil transferred him to Calgary where he rented an apartment with another engineer. After three weeks, an ambulance brought Howard there on crutches. He was pathetic and Tom talked with him, helping him recover. A month later he was in rude good health and obtained labouring work on a high-rise construction site. His accident had not subdued his tendency to get into fights with other workers.

After a week, he was dismissed.

'My standards are too high for them,' he bragged. 'They couldn't build a sandcastle.'

'Not with you around,' Tom said.

Howard found other work but they fired him for fighting.

He was an unwelcome guest at Tom's place. Bullied by Howard, his flatmate moved out. Howard was rough with girls and Tom kept him away from them by shutting down his own love-life. He demanded Howard pay him rent. He was relieved when their parents sent for Howard to return to help on the farm in England.

PART 8

BREAKING FREE

CHAPTER 43
PICK-UP ARTIST

When Howard had gone, Tom took his mind off Vicki by going on a sex binge. At the rugby club, in a bar, or at parties, he would operate with one or two male friends, moving in on a small group of girls, trying to get at least a telephone number. He developed his pick-up technique by trial and error.

He learned to be well-dressed, attentive and courteous. He pretended interest in girls' accomplishments and interests. He played The Beatles' 'Hello, Goodbye' on the jukebox or entertained them with exaggerated foreign accents. He introduced them to his music, or to photography, or to literature, or art, or philosophy, sometimes under the influence of marijuana.

His most successful pick-up ploy was to diagnose a girl's stress or depression from the bilateral symmetry of her eyes. He would tell a girl she had a slight asymmetry between her eyes.

She would be nonplussed by his negativity, being used to having guys tell her how beautiful she was. She would infer that she had offended him and her reflex would be to chat and win him over. He would explain the theory of left and right brain hemispheres coordinating logic and creativity respectively, on opposite sides of the body.

If her left eye was shrunken or dull, he would ask if she had some internal issue causing her right-hand brain to withdraw from its creative role. She would reveal personal difficulties she was having. He would gaze into her eyes and they would bond. It was not a scientific theory but it was a good way for him to meet girls.

A different strategy was to assess a girl's personality as one of 16 possible types by Myers Briggs assessment. He would question her on the four major dimensions.

'Susan, you are an E because you are extroverted; an S because you observe with your senses rather than by intuiting; an F because you go by your feelings rather than by thinking; and a P because you perceive situations rather than making snap judgements.'

'Your type is ESFP, known for generosity,' he would say. 'Are you kind to people at home or at work?'

His predictions could never be tested. She would be amazed by his insight. She would trust him and develop a rapport.

The next step was to get her to have sex with him. She had to feel loved and in control. He nurtured this with attention and by giving her choices. The options he offered all led eventually into a bed. His machinations had to be concealed, because most females regarded partner manipulation as their province.

'My pick-up technique is no more dishonest than the methods advertisers use to get people to try a new product,' he thought. *'In commerce, the caution: 'caveat emptor' is observed. Men and women know to beware each other. My dating is not at all predatory and is motivated by genuine desire for romance.'*

Another approach was to take over the talk in a group, occupy others' spaces and move into the best physical position from which to dominate. Girls liked an 'alpha' male who respected their femininity and independence, controlling other males present.

He had retained his hippy persona, with respect for and gentleness with women. He was living in the moment, with his natural self and intentions transparent.

When he was picking up or on a date, he sometimes missed Vicki. Thoughts of her would intrude and spoil his fun. He kept a part of himself for her.

CHAPTER 44
UNCONVENTIONAL CHOICE

Later, that summer, Richard wrote to him that Vicki had a new boyfriend, William. He was an engineering student from Bigeria, an African country. His skin was black, unusual at LUT. Like Vicki, he was involved in campus politics.

Tom imagined Vicki introducing William to her conservative English family, who would be puzzled by her choice of a partner of different ethnicity and culture. Vicki was not a demonstrative person and this partner would put her in the public eye. Did her unconventional choice indicate she had become rebellious?

Tom concluded that Vicki must be very fond of William. He hoped they wouldn't last long together and afterwards he would be able to revive their relationship. He wrote to Vicki a soliloquy.

'Like moles, our lives are solitary, our souls always out of sight of others, our workings invisible except when, in the dead of night, we surface to meet a mate. Urgently, we search our old tunnels, looking for intersections with another, a soul mate. Sometimes we hear another's soft footfalls in the distance but when we get there, we find nothing – it is only an echo from the past. Blind from birth, we touch, hear, smell and taste each other, discovering empathy and building trust. After mating frenziedly and briefly, we return to solitude. We communicate our imaginings to our children, as a part of the lore and traditions of our kind.'

Vicki didn't reply and then he heard from Richard that she and William were an item. After the assassinations of Martin Luther King and Robert Kennedy, racial tension had spread to the UK. Jimi Hendrix's guitar screamed defiance at white society.

A hundred years before, Liverpool was the number one slave port in Europe, transhipping slaves captured in Bigeria and other African countries to the US. In 1792, 40,000 slaves were transported by Liverpool vessels to the plantations of America and the West Indies. For the next 60 years, each year between 40 and 110 ships sailed from Liverpool, laden with slaves penned like cattle, many dying cruel deaths before reaching America. Slavery had been abolished in the UK in 1833 but continued in the USA until 1865. A Liverpool actor lamented: 'Every brick in this infernal town is cemented with African blood.'

The horror that had been Liverpool was only a little older than living memory. Tom wondered how Vicki could entrust herself to someone whose ancestors had been enslaved by hers. Might not William seek retribution from her for the awful injustices his people had suffered at the hands of her countrymen? Would he let her down when she was most vulnerable? Or was this concern merely Tom's racist jealousy of William?

CHAPTER 45
WILD SOWING

Tom worked for three years and saved his money. He took lessons in Spanish and prepared to travel for a year in Central and South America, before returning to the UK to do a PhD.

His work colleagues asked: 'Why are you leaving Canada?'

'To travel.'

He was too polite to reply that his lifestyle in Calgary lacked culture, was too materialistic and too crass. His rugby club arranged a farewell party to honour him. Ignoring his protests, they followed the club's tradition and engaged a stripper for him to fuck with everyone watching.

In the basement of someone's house the club members crowded around him, pushing him towards her.

'Come on, show us your style, Tom.'

'No, sorry. I can't do it with people watching.'

'Feeling a bit shy, are we?' said the nude girl with pompoms, unzipping his fly and holding him.

'I just can't do it. Okay?'

'We can go in a bedroom,' she said. 'It will be private and nice; I promise.'

When he couldn't be persuaded to fulfil his obligation, the onlookers were disappointed.

'Faggot,' someone said.

Another player substituted for him, pumping her vigorously on the concrete floor. From upstairs Tom heard his shout of triumph as he came, followed by applause.

The old and new worlds were in conflict and Tom secretly redefined himself. He adopted hippy values, which included respect for women, love and peace. His work colleagues, his housemates and his rugby club friends were sceptical of the youth revolution that radiated from California but he felt it summoning him to migrate south.

He packed his things, despatched a trunk to his family in the UK, finished work on a Friday and drove east the next day.

CHAPTER 46
HIPPY LOVE

He drove east across Canada in his station wagon, giving rides to Americans dodging the Vietnam draft. He had metamorphosed from a short-back-and-sides engineer, in a business suit and tie, into a bearded long-haired hippy adorned in love beads, feathers, flowers and bells. He shared spliffs with his passengers and listened to the radio playing Dylan, The Beatles, Hendrix and Joplin.

Being hip attracted friends wherever he went. He wore old blue jeans, long unkempt hair, sunglasses, a bandana and leather boots with medium heels. He learned to greet by touching knuckles and gave the 'V' sign for peace to authority figures such as police. When something was good he said: 'Ace, man', 'Groovy', 'Far out', 'Too much' or 'Let it all hang out, babe.' If something was bad he said: 'Crap, man.' If something was both good and bad, like an addictive drug, it was: 'Shit, man.' If it was difficult to understand, it was: 'Heavy, man,' and if this was because he was intoxicated, it was: 'Fucked, man.' He tried never to behave like a 'Straight' or a 'Shithead'.

Hippy values of universal peace and love required certain behaviours. Feelings and emotions replaced his engineer's objectivity. Working for 'the man' was repressive: he shed his work ethic and put his profession aside. He would go back to it later. As he drove south, he stayed with Peace Corps volunteers. They shared accommodation, food, marijuana, LSD and sex freely in urban communes growing in cities throughout Central America.

He spent a couple of months driving around Mexico, smoking Acapulco Gold almost every day. His passengers were an extroverted couple from Melbourne, movie actors. Their colourful bandanas, ponchos and sandals attracted attention. They were the nucleus of a group of gringos who trespassed to go where they wanted and thieved from food stores for ideological reasons. They were a sensation with young Mexicans, who imagined that a worldwide revolution started by Che Guevara and John Lennon had arrived. Large crowds gathered chanting 'Che' or 'Peace', until they were dispersed by police.

The Gold stimulated Tom to try and keep the sun from setting, as he drove towards it along a highway going westward, following it down around the curvature of the earth. The circumference of the earth is 25,000 miles and turns once in 24 hours, so he calculated his speed had to be a bit more than 1000 miles per hour. He was unable to achieve that speed because staying on the road, when he had been smoking 'Gold', took all his concentration at walking pace. He snailed along with his passengers convulsed with laughter.

He received a letter poste restante at Acapulco from Richard. He said William had finished his course and had gone home to Bigeria without Vicki, because her white skin was unacceptable for a black politician's wife. The irony delighted Tom. He thought that by the time he got back to England she would be recovered from William and he would be able to get her back.

Richard reported that Vicki had started working as a professional counsellor at a hospital. He wrote her a postcard.

Acapulco
June 14th, 1969

Dear Counsellor Vicki,
Congratulations on your graduation.
I hope your new job is going okay.
They will soon realise and appreciate your smarts.
Mexico is amazing. I am on the grass at the beach.
The waves are high too.
Wish you were here.
Love
Tom

PS Would you like to live in a commune?
PPS Please write to Poste Restante, San Salvador, ASAP as I should be down there in a month or two.

PART 9

COMMUNES

CHAPTER 47
LIVING TOGETHER

When he had lived in Calgary, Tom shared a house with 10 single men, kindred spirits, who employed a part-time housekeeper to cook and clean for them. Living in a group was practical and fun. Later when he was travelling it was his Holy Grail to find a commune where he and Vicki could live together.

He visited a remnant of the New Australia Commune in Paraguay, founded in 1892 by William Lane, a prophet of anarchical communism. The Paraguayan Government wanted to repopulate after the Great War of 1864-1870, in which Paraguay was utterly defeated and nine out of ten males died. They gave Lane 75,000 hectares to start an agrarian commune. In 1891 after the shearers' strike was broken, he brought from Australia a shipload of 220 socialists, mainly males.

'I expect the local women made them welcome,' said Jill, his travelling companion.

'Lane forbade the Australian men from consorting with Guarani women,' Tom said, reading from a handbook. 'He had with him his wife and three sons. The commune failed because the single men were dissatisfied without women. They deserted Lane's leadership and turned for comfort to the Guarani women and rum. In 1899, Lane quit and went to New Zealand.'

At Cosme, where the utopian colony had started, they met Gabriella, a sociologist and descendant of a New Australia communist.

'The fundamental problem they had was achieving egalitarianism,' she said. 'Some people would not do their work.'

'How can work be divided fairly in a commune?' asked Tom.

'They have to share,' she said, reading from a book. 'A commune is defined as an intentional community of people living together, sharing common interests. To live together they must share material things.'

'How can they share?' he asked.

'There has to be mutuality.'

'What mutual interests can they have?'

'Socialism isn't enough,' said Gabriella. 'Lane's commune lacked cohesion. It's not unusual. Socialist communities, some large and whole nations, may have failed for the same reason. Successful communes develop social cohesion from emotional bonding, such as religious cults, or missions, cooperatives, artisan groups, or growers and users of hallucinogenic drugs.'

'Would you allow couples to join your commune, Tom?' asked Jill.

He wanted to be with Vicki but not with other couples.

'No. Couples compete, especially if there are children,' he said. 'Polygamy might be better.'

'How would it be better?'

'Promiscuity brings social cohesion in groups of bonobos. It probably would in a human group too.'

'It's too hot here for frequent sex,' said Jill. 'Monogamy would be cooler.'

Tom and Jill overheated in Paraguay. They farewelled Gabriela and flew back to Quito, with its lower temperatures at higher altitude.

'A commune has to be comfortable,' said Tom.

CHAPTER 48
POLYGAMY

In Guayaquil, Tom boarded an Ecuadorean Navy ship for its monthly patrol of the Galapagos Islands. It could accommodate 40 tourists. He met Vanessa, Genevieve, Estelle and Stacey, hippies from the United States attired in bandanas, beads and bell-bottoms. Vanessa was tantalising in a bikini, but because the men's and women's hammocks were in separate parts of the ship, Tom saw less of her than he wanted. Together on shore excursions, they ogled the wildlife very closely. Wild animals had suffered little human contact and were unafraid. Charles Darwin had been able to study unprecedented detail of the beaks of fearless finches.

After two celibate weeks at sea, when they returned to the mainland, Tom was ready to explode. He wanted to consummate his friendship with Vanessa and, if possible, the other girls too. When they booked into a hotel in Lima, he suggested they get one large room. The other girls seemed interested, but Vanessa objected.

'Tom and I need privacy.'

'We don't have anything to hide,' Tom said.

'I am not doing group sex,' Vanessa said.

'It could be fun,' said Genevieve. 'If Tom is up to it.'

Estelle and Stacey giggled.

Vanessa thought for a moment. 'Not tonight; I want Tom to myself. How about group sex tomorrow night, okay?'

It was agreed. Vanessa and Tom went to a room, leaving the other three together, with Genevieve in a single bed and Estelle with Stacey in a double.

The arrangement may not have been equitable, in some way unknown to Tom, for next day Genevieve left to fly back to the USA. Four of them set off by bus for Cuzco, to go to the Incan ruins at Machu Picchu. Estelle met Jarl, a Dane, and the two took a separate room. Vanessa, Stacey and Tom were in a room with a very large bed. Stacey was in the middle and Tom caressed her while she intertwined with Vanessa. He brought Stacey to orgasm at the same time as she induced a climax in the narcissistic Vanessa. She was even noisier than the night before with him.

Tom fell asleep but awoke and heard the two girls talking. He got out of bed, went around and climbed in on the other side, with Stacey in the middle. He and Stacey interlocked legs like two pairs of scissors, while she stimulated her friend Vanessa.

Someone would surprise the other two with their urgency and they would all become aroused. Multi-mating was as enjoyable as he had dreamed it would be. Tom loved women and found their different qualities fascinating. He tried to scratch the itch of his love for Vicki with Stacey and Vanessa. The composite of the two girls' qualities went further towards satisfying his appetite for sex than any one girl ever had.

After three nights together, in the morning Vanessa asked him, 'How do you feel about me now? How would you be if there were just the two of us?'

'I like you very much,' he said. 'We could be alone; but what about Stacey?'

'You don't get it, do you? Have we bonded at all?'

'Oh, I see. Yes, big time.'

'Emotional bonds?' she asked.

'Yes.'

'Like love?'

He knew that when a girl served with the L word, the best return was to dissemble.

'Yes,' he said. 'I'm almost sure.'

'I'm not completely sure,' she said.

'Is that because you are not sure you have feelings or because you don't know whether your feelings are love?' he said.

'Of course I have feelings,' she said. 'I am not a herd animal. Sometimes I think all you care about is multi-mating.'

Usually, he liked her. He could feign affection but doubted she would be convinced.

'That is so untrue,' he said. 'Let's continue this conversation later.'

The advantage of polygamy for him was his women would be rostered for his personal attention if they behaved well. There was less chance of him being womanless. He went to find Stacey.

CHAPTER 49
LOVE IN RUINS

Tom had researched Machu Picchu at a library in Lima. The deserted empire was discovered in 1911. The ruins were at a remote and easily defended mountain location with temples and horticultural terraces. The stone walls had survived because the blocks had dished faces and were held in position when earthquakes shook the walls.

The site was abandoned after the Incan king leapt to his death from a high place, shortly before the Spanish conquistadors found the site deserted in 1532 when they arrived in Peru. Disappearance of the entire population was a mystery. For every male skeleton discovered, there were 80 females. Parthenogenesis, or virgin birth without males, has been extremely rare in humans, although common in over 100 species of reptiles, fish and birds. It was unlikely that the population could have been sustained without males, even by the method supposed for Jesus' conception.

The Incans were peaceful and without enemies. The community was believed to have been a sex cult led by a handful of priests who brought maidens from all over the Incan empire to be their servants. Few males were needed and boys were disposed of by infanticide.

They wound their way up the steep road in a bus to the historic site. When they got out, Tom led them away from the tourist route along a little-used path up the mountainside.

'Where are we going?' asked Vanessa.

'I have a hunch we can find a quiet place to camp out.'

They came to a sign: *Entrado Prohibido*.

'They are trying to keep out people who speak Spanish,' Tom said. 'We're okay.'

They continued along a narrow precipitous track. After a two-hour trek, the overgrown path reached a hilltop with ruins like those at Machu Picchu. They took off their clothes and lay on their ponchos, stark naked in the sun, with a breathtaking view over a precipitous gorge. Presently, Vanessa, Stacey and Tom made love. Tom imagined he could hear the rhythms of a husky cantata played on breathy pan pipes by Quechuan Indians. Estelle and Jarl had started together nearby but soon came over and joined in with them. It was sublime.

Tom succumbed to his atavistic alpha male desire to promote his genes, by mating with all the females. He tried to attract Estelle into his harem, while keeping Vanessa and Stacey away from Jarl. Polygamy was hard work and he had to allow Jarl in for multi-mating.

'Peace, man,' he said to Jarl when he tried to take Estelle back. 'Make like a bonobo.'

They read, talked and made love in their condor's eyrie perched high above a verdant valley that receded into the distance like the nave of an immense cathedral, sided by a procession of gothic arches rearing steeply from the floor on both sides. Tom thought he could hear the thin air pulsating with Mozart's 'Requiem' played exuberantly on a pipe organ, with throbs and trills, as the light fled and shadows stole down the aisle, until with one crashing chord that reverberated the silence, the condor folded her wings and darkness settled over them.

For three days they stayed on a drugless sex-filled high, basking in the warm sun and clinging together at night under their ponchos. They took water from a stream but had nothing to eat. Eventually they dressed and walked down to get food. The girls went back to Lima to fly back to the USA. Tom went on alone to Brazil.

CHAPTER 50
ERMELO

At Rio de Janeiro Yacht Club, Tom put his backpack aboard the 20-metre ketch *Ermelo* to work his passage to the Caribbean, with three men from South Africa, two from the UK who had sailed in her from Cape Town and a Brazilian girl who had joined the crew with him.

At a sundowner in the cockpit, the captain-owner tried to berth the girl in his cabin against her wishes. Tom led the others in opposition and she moved into the sail locker.

The skipper was angry with Tom.

'Just remember whose ship this is,' he said.

'Aye, aye, skipper.'

The next morning, they hoisted the sails and set off. It was Tom's first experience of offshore sailing and it was a baptism by fire. A storm struck as they left Rio, as a monstrous wind flung them across the South Atlantic towards Africa and they lashed the helmsman to the binnacle, as waves crashed over them. After three days the wind dropped, they hauled in the sea anchor and headed in the opposite direction. Without coastal radio for navigation, they only had a sextant and a skipper without experience of how to use it. They were lost.

They headed west, blithely ploughing the empty ocean with blustering winds abeam. Tom and his buddy on the midnight to 8 am watch marvelled at the Milky Way, spread like a glowing canopy overhead. Pinpoints of luminescent microfauna gleamed in profusion in their wake.

One afternoon the lookout yelled, 'Land ahoy!' It turned out to be Recife in northeast Brazil. They rowed in the tender to the yacht club to celebrate their survival. That afternoon they were drunk, paddling back to *Ermelo*, low in the water with supplies, when the dinghy capsized. They were a kilometre from shore, halfway to the boat, swimming through bobbing cans, beer bottles and floating food.

'I can't swim!' said the girl.

With her body over his and her arms around his neck, Tom backstroked as he followed the others towards land. They came to a large oil slick along the shore. He was too exhausted to swim around it and they were coated from head to toe in brown filth. At the club, they cleaned up with diesel under the scorching sun. That evening Tom collapsed with heatstroke.

Two days later he was still semi-conscious in his hammock, when he heard the captain say: 'We can put the hippy over the side.'

Tom regretted their earlier confrontation and tried to appear recovered. When they reached Barbados he was well enough to fly home to the UK.

On arrival, he telephoned Vicki. He had last seen her during their abortive holiday in the Rockies two years previously. He had written several times during his travels and received a couple of letters from her. He had heard from Richard that she had several guys since William but not for long. He was disappointed when she wouldn't see him.

'I don't have time,' she said.

Despite heatstroke, Tom had enjoyed his experience at sea on *Ermelo*. His travel had changed him from self-interest to caring for disadvantaged people. He had the idea to start a sailing commune and Vicki could join him to help disaster victims. He was confident that she would join him in a sailing commune because she was adventurous and she had enjoyed sailing with her father.

Soon after returning to the UK, Richard returned to him his copy of their contract and a note.

> *Welcome back, Tom. I guess I won't be able to collect on this now. So you can have her, if you can get her.*
> *Good luck,*
> *Richard.*

Tom had repaid his father, which had been his main aim. His short on Vicki was void because she had not accepted being delivered to Richard and she was now self-owned. He could reacquire her for himself if he could afford her.

CHAPTER 51
ABODE OF LOVE

As a child, Tom interpreted the spectre of nuclear annihilation as evidence of universal malign adult intent. It was incomprehensible that the world could be in such an awful state as the Cold War except by a malignancy that had infected adults. As a teenager he had pledged his life to bringing freedom and happiness to children everywhere. So far he had not been able to do much. Now his ambition flowered trying to found a commune that would sail to disaster areas and rescue child victims.

On his travels in Latin America, he had experienced several places where there was poverty and malnutrition. He was aware that the value of his camera exceeded the local average personal annual income, generating envy, resentment, vulnerability and setting him apart. He was uncomfortable in his superior position and was glad to finish his overland travels at Rio. His experience of poverty interested him in communism, socialism and living in a collective, despite American opposition in Vietnam.

In the UK, there was news of tsunami disasters in Asia. He watched video reports of destroyed communities with young children uncared for and hungry on the streets. He wanted to help. He imagined a sailing vessel could anchor nearby, bringing hospital care to child victims.

A shipboard commune could have its members bonded by their caring mission.

He needed a crew. An all-male crew could become unruly unless it had an outcome goal, such as winning a sailing race. Because his humanitarian mission lacked such a goal, for harmony aboard he decided on a female crew.

When he visited Vicki, she was living in her hometown, Salisbury. She had obtained a graduate teaching diploma and was working in her profession of counsellor at a high school.

They went together to Salisbury Cathedral, a huge Gothic building with flying buttresses and a delicate spire.

'This is the finest building in all England,' he said reverently.

'I agree.'

Their eyes drank in the perfect repetition of the massive symmetry. They went inside through the ornate Gothic doors and along the nave towards the distant altar. His eyes were drawn from the tunnel of columns and arches on both sides, up to the triforium, with the clerestory arches supporting the magnificent vaulted ceiling.

'How can it have been constructed with such uniformity and precision?' he asked, emotion choking his words.

'People can do anything,' said Vicki, 'if they want it badly enough.'

'When they have a mission?'

'Yes.'

They looked at a stained-glass window of a saint with reverent eyes uplifted.

'If we shared a mission, we could do great things together,' he said, musing.

'What mission?'

'It is just a vague idea at present. I'll tell you as soon as I can.'

'What if I don't agree?' Vicki said.

'We could agree to disagree.'

'Would you be able to compromise?'

'Yes, for the mission to succeed.'

'I doubt you have a mission I would want to join in,' Vicki said.

'Please keep an open mind. I'll tell you about it as soon as I can.'

They went back to Vicki's place. Tom stayed another day and returned to Liverpool.

Tom had commenced research for a PhD in Management. He was investigating an organisation design for governments to end the Cold

War. The sailing mission diverted his attention away: Vicki was a higher priority.

He decided to recruit a crew of 20 women. He would be the only male in a commune called 'Mission Figurehead'. He had adopted a potent icon for a sailing ship, a woman with naked breasts carved in wood, to placate the gods of the sea and ensure a safe voyage.

Tom heard of a commune called 'Agapemone', or Abode of Love, a cult that operated for over 80 years until the 1930s in Somerset, with a large group of females under a flamboyant male leader: Henry Prince. He left the Church of England in 1843, when he was 32, claiming that the Holy Ghost had taken up residence in his body.

The sect proclaimed the imminent second coming of Jesus. Henry Prince travelled in a gilt carriage with a team of four and outriders, from London to his cult's headquarters in Spaxton, attracting female followers along the way. The cult was sustained by lonely young spinsters and middle-aged women from the rich upper class, who were looking for excitement. They gained entry to the cult by liquefying their assets and paying the money into Prince's bank account.

He moved into the luxurious 20-room residence he had built in 1846. He was the only male and pursued sacred sexual rituals in religious ceremonies with his favourite women. Ten years later there were more than 200 people living there to attend to his various needs, most of them female, many his children.

Tom planned Mission Figurehead to be a catamaran 40 metres long to be built in Liverpool at a cost of £3,000,000 shared between the crew equally. It would accommodate 20 women in luxury, plus a 20-bed hospital and an orphanage. Women could afford a share by selling or mortgaging their property.

CHAPTER 52
ATTRACTING FOLLOWERS

Tom copied Henry Prince and recruited moneyed women. A sociology research acquaintance extracted from a database a list of addresses of upper- and middle-class households in Liverpool with single or separated women between 25 and 50 years. He invited them to a banquet at an exclusive hotel.

He had parked his rented white Ferrari conspicuously outside. He appeared to have means and have a purpose higher than grabbing their money. As each woman arrived, she received a brochure 'Mission Figurehead'. It had an artist's impression of a schooner sailing into a glorious sunset, below a banner headline that asked: 'Will This Be Your New Home?' There was a festive ambiance with vases of calla lilies, decorative lighting and a grand piano played by a nightclub pianist. Tom wore a claret velvet suit and a garland of purple flowers.

They enjoyed a sumptuous dinner. When the uniformed waiters had served dessert and topped up the champagne glasses, Tom stood up and surveyed the dining room. It was good to be in such select company, with the prospect of paying his bills from subscription money taken that evening. He straightened his bow tie and undid his jacket to reveal his tartan waistcoat. Prince had been flamboyant.

When their attention turned to him, he spoke with quiet self-assurance.

'Good evening, ladies. Welcome to Mission Figurehead. I am Tom Archer. I am a spiritual adventurer and our project is called Mission Figurehead. Our ship will sail the seven seas to natural disasters. We will rescue children and help restore their lives, applying the skills you have and those you will learn. Our ship will be an orphanage that will take care of infants and young children who might otherwise perish. We will return them to their communities

when they can be properly cared for, or we will arrange adoption in accordance with their governments' requirements.

'Mission Figurehead will be run by an all-female crew under my captaincy. My role will be limited to orienting our mission. Women will run the hospital and orphanage and sail the ship.

'I need women of age 25 to 50 to share in the cost of a ship with high standards of safety and luxury, We need women with relevant skills who are prepared to learn from others and work in teams. Women work together better without men.

'If you are interested, give me your name and contacts. I will interview you and take you out for a day in my sloop to get to know you and for you to find out how you would like living under sail. If your application is successful, financial details are explained in the brochure. You would be able to sell your share and leave at any time.

'This is an opportunity for you to make a difference. Now we will drink a toast to ourselves. Please be upstanding and raise your glasses. To Mission Figurehead, Good Deeds and Good Luck to those who sail in her.'

His words were repeated by the company.

'God Save The Queen.
'Thank you all for coming. Enjoy the rest of the evening.'

The occasion became social.

'Would the yacht be safe in an earthquake, tsunami or cyclone?' a woman asked him.

'Yes,' he said. 'She will be designed to survive a cyclone. Several weeks could pass before we arrive and immediate danger would have passed. Provision of shelter and relief of disease, hunger and thirst could be wanted for months afterwards.'

Several women transferred the subscription cost of £150,000 into his bank and he settled his account with the hotel. He took his plans for the vessel to a Merseyside shipwright, who began a detailed design.

Applicants were eager to try sailing with him and he looked around for a small boat to buy.

He would soon be ready to ask Vicki to join Mission Figurehead. It would be a radical change for her but she liked yachting. He would ask her on a sailing holiday with him and hope to re-establish trust.

CHAPTER 53
MATE TEST

With the last of his savings, he bought *Minetta,* a two-berth sloop. He asked Vicki to cruise with him to the Isle of Man for a week during her school's summer holiday. To his delight she agreed.

Vicki drove up to Liverpool and brought her gear aboard *Minetta* at the marina. They cast off and sailed down the Mersey shipping channel. She wore a nautical striped T-shirt, deck shoes and the briefest of shorts, barely containing her perfect butt. In the small cockpit, when he brushed against her, the hairs on his arms and legs sprang erect, as if every cell in his body was enamoured.

Hours later, they were out of sight of land when the wind changed and the sails flapped and jerked. Without warning, a strong gust from a different direction knocked *Minetta* flat. The mast went under and the sails filled with water, preventing the hull from self-righting. Water poured in over the gunwales as he and Vicki crawled over the lifelines to the far end of the keel, trying to use their combined weight to lever the yacht back to vertical. Their knees bled with cuts from barnacles. Slowly the mast and sails emerged from under the sea. When they broke free from the surface, she righted and they tumbled inboard. Waves rolled in over the gunwales and filled *Minetta,* with only a few inches of freeboard remaining.

'We have to bail her out before she goes down,' Tom said, gasping.

'Don't you have flotation?' asked Vicki, alarmed.

'The hull is fibreglass but the keel is lead. If we bail we might be able to save her. Come on.'

They bucketed water out from the cockpit, she rose a little and waves stopped coming in. Tom swam through the hatchway down into the cabin where food, clothes and flares rafted near the roof. The radio was underwater.

'Put this on,' he said, handing Vicki a lifejacket.

They resumed scooping water over the side. By the time it was down to the cockpit seats, they were exhausted. They sat dispiritedly and took stock of their situation. With visibility through the mist at under a kilometre, their patch of ocean was empty. The wind was blowing steadily over the stern from starboard and *Minetta* limped along with wet misshapen sails. Sluggishly she came back on course.

'How much further is it?' Vicki asked between breaths.

'We're about one third of the way – about 10 more hours.'

'Can we go back?'

'The motor is stuffed. It could take hours to get it started.'

Vicki looked around grimly. The mist was closing in.

'Are you sure you can find the island?'

Tom hesitated. The Isle had some high ground and on a clear day it was visible from 10 miles away. By the time they would get there, it would be dark. A lighthouse and light buoys would lead them into the harbour.

'The course we are on will take us there,' he said.

He could see by her worried face that she was not convinced.

'What do you think?' he asked.

'Could we go aground?'

'The island's coast is steep and rocky. The depth finder is not working but we could swing a lead weight on a rope.'

'By the time it feels the bottom, we could be on the rocks,' she said.

'We can get a fix from the lighthouse.'

They both knew one beacon could not triangulate and fix a location. She gave him a smile. Tom had glossed over the difficulties of navigating in strange waters in the dark but there was an element of uncertainty in sailing that Vicki understood. Something would turn up. It did not daunt her that they would spend the night on *Minetta,* with their bedding soaked. She was a sailor and knew that inconveniences had to be tolerated.

'Okay,' she said. 'I'm going to finish the bailing.'

She was an ideal crew, an extension of himself and they worked as a team. They got out as much of the water as they could. Vicki took the helm while Tom removed the cylinder head from the motor, dried it and reassembled it. It took him an hour. He hesitated before pulling the starting rope.

'Wish me luck,' he said.

'Hope to die.'

On the third pull, the motor coughed into life.

He shouted above the din, 'Want to go back to Liverpool?'

'No way! This is fun.'

He loved her with every fibre of his being. Life with Vicki was one long adventure.

'She must realise that we are good together,' he thought.

The wind picked up, he stopped the motor and there was only the soft gurgle of water under the hull. After three hours they sighted the lighthouse and guided by a soggy chart, motored into the harbour. As night fell they tied up to a bollard on the quay.

'Thanks,' he said, giving her a hug. 'You were awesome.'

'You were pretty good yourself, skipper.'

They hung out their bedding to dry. A friendly yachtie lent them sleeping bags. Tom's chilli con carne was cold but they ate it hungrily and turned in.

They spent a couple of days exploring the island. They purchased a small radio and on the return voyage they sang along with The Beatles' 'Oh, Darling'.

'I would never do her harm but she didn't need me anymore and I nearly broke down and cried.'

The distance between them had reduced, but they were still on eggshells with each other. He didn't update her that the reason he had left Liverpool and gone to Canada, without saying goodbye, was Barbara's pregnancy. Although it had been a year, Vicki might not be sympathetic.

Back in Liverpool, they parted with a hug and she set off to drive back to Salisbury. He would not tell her about Mission Figurehead until the ship was built. Vicki would take some convincing but she had gone to Canada and skied with him and he was counting on her adventurous nature to bring her aboard and into a relationship with him.

CHAPTER 54
DIRE STRAITS

Many of the women applicants went for a day-sail with Tom in *Minetta*, to check their aptitudes for sailing. These outings sometimes lasted overnight.

Those who were interested paid their deposits. When 20 had paid, the shipyard laid the keel and the shareholders celebrated with a champagne party. A reporter from the local newspaper interviewed Tom and wrote a story.

WOMEN'S MISSION OF MERCY TO SAIL TO DISASTERS

Twenty Liverpool women will give up their homes and jobs to join Tom Archer, 26, on a yacht, Mission Figurehead, which will sail to rescue children from disasters. The women, who are professionals aged between 25 and 50, will use their skills to help communities recover from volcanoes, earthquakes, tsunamis, cyclones, bushfires and floods. The ship will have a paediatric hospital and an orphanage, staffed by medical, paramedical, nursing and rehabilitation specialists. It will anchor near disaster areas, help find relatives of children and assist families to get back on their feet. Tom Archer, the project founder and skipper, said: 'We are a dedicated team of professionals and will collaborate with local authorities to rescue children, relieve their suffering and care for them until they are safe.'

Tom lived at the shipyard in a six-person tent with some of the crew. He stayed most nights and was seldom alone. The women would become aroused and the passion in the group went beyond his previous enjoyment of sex.

They detailed plans for the ship's construction. The crew would be accommodated in four-person cabins with one double and two single bunks in each. The master's cabin, for himself and Vicki, would have a double bunk. The sleeping arrangements were flexible and sharing with an adjoining cabin was possible. Besides the configuration in which Tom would be with Vicki, it could simulate a Kenyan village compound, with the chief sharing his time between his rostered wives in their huts, arranged in proximal order.

He could sail the ship with as much female company as he wanted and sleep with different groups. It was an established fact that humans, both male and female, enjoy having novel partners for sex. But he wanted to have Vicki share the captaincy with him as his partner.

While he waited for Vicki, he enjoyed polyamory with the women. One would initiate, another do the hard work, another exquisite torture, another provide an emotional counterpoint.

Sometimes he was the indulged one, his body stimulated until his will melted down. At others, he was one of a team coaxing orgasm after orgasm from one or more of the women. At first, he was self-conscious, but he learned to express his wants and affection freely. He had his favourites but attended to the greatest good of the greatest number.

When the keel had been laid, he visited Vicki to tell her about his scheme and invite her to join them.

'I have read about Mission Figurehead in a newspaper,' she said. 'Do you really expect me to give up my job and live on a ship with you?'

'We sailed well together on *Minetta*,' he said. 'I have designed the ship for your pleasure. It would be a wonderful adventure.'

'Who would be the crew?'

He told her about the 20 women.

'How did you recruit them?'

'They came to a recruitment dinner and signed up.'

He didn't mention Henry Prince or taking them out in *Minetta*.

'Did you have sex with any of them?'

'A few,' he lied.

'How many?' Vicki asked.

'Maybe 10. It was expected I would be friendly.'

She thought about this for a moment. Then she exploded.

'Friendly! Even if your morals were acceptable, which they are not, how do you think I would feel being on a boat with 10 women who you have had sex with?'

Tom tried to imagine it but couldn't. 'How would you?' he asked.

Vicki threw up her hands in exasperation and spoke with feigned patience.

'Tom, how would you feel if I invited you to a party with 10 men who I had had sex with?'

That was easier.

'If they had all dumped you, I would be wary of you,' he said. 'But if you had dumped them, I would feel superior. Won't you feel respected, when I have preferred you over 20 women?'

Exasperated, she shrieked and held her head. 'Tom, you are fucking impossible.'

He was dismayed by her rejection but he thought she might be more accepting later. If he had to, he could make do with her alone. In the meantime, he continued living in the tent with the girls and they worked with him to design the ship's interior.

When the hull had been constructed, a local newspaper ran an article.

SHIP LOVE CULT DENIED

Tom Archer, a 26-year-old researcher, is leading Mission Figurehead, a ship that will sail to aid children in disaster areas, crewed by 20 women.

'The ship will be a children's hospital and orphanage,' he said. 'Our mission is to rescue children from the effects of disasters in a ship that will provide effective and efficient transport and self-sufficient accommodation.

'I will lead the mission with an all-female crew who will care for the children and sail the ship. Women have sailed in competition against males and won.

'The group is certainly not a cult,' Mr Archer said. 'My relationship with the women is that they are professionals in a team. Some are affiliated with various religions and some do not have a religion. They all have experience of children. We will provide practical help to communities shocked and suffering after natural disasters.'

The 'cult' label stuck despite his denial, He was pestered by reporters who tried to create a scandal from the unusual gender make-up of the crew. People came to the boatyard and stared at them.

'Perverts!' a woman called out. 'We don't want your type here.'

At night, local thugs climbed the boatyard fence, curious to see what they were doing in the tent, but the lights were off.

Sensation-seeking publicity harmed the project. Tom received letters from crew members, informing him they were pulling out and asking for their money back. Despite his best efforts, there were more leavers than joiners. He postponed construction while he endeavoured to attract more women.

CHAPTER 55
REALITY CHECK

Tom phoned Vicki to try again.

'Vicki, this is the opportunity of a lifetime.'

'I'm perfectly happy doing what I am doing.'

'Your job would be there for you when you get back — or another like it.'

'This mission thing has taken your attention off your PhD. Are you making progress with it? Have you fixed on an idea yet?'

'Several. I don't have an hypothesis yet but I'm getting there.'

'What academic discipline are you following?'

'A synthesis of political economy, psychology, sociology and social psychology.'

'Don't you have to stay within only one?'

'My framework is political economy but I need to bring in the others to explain superpower behaviour.'

'I know from my psychology studies that it could take more experience than you have to identify the superpowers' motives.'

'That's a harsh call. Why do you think I can't do it?'

'To solve the Cold War could take maturity beyond your years. Until the brain of a baby has developed and can coordinate all the skills needed, it cannot walk, no matter how much it tries and practises. International relations is like psychology: it uses abstract theories and requires practical experience to understand.'

'Are you saying the Cold War is too abstract for a 26-year-old to solve?'

'Your sexfest at the marina could be distracting you.'

'It is not a sexfest. The crew is helping design the ship.'

'You could be addicted to sex. Perhaps you are trying to relive the buzz of your first experience, as addicts often do. It's all you seem to care about.'

'It's not like that.'

'Whatever it is, you seem to depend on it. Even if you controlled your sexual urges, you would probably become dependent on something else. You could have a predisposition for addiction.'

'How would I know that?' he said, mollified by her criticism.

'Addicts often have obsessive compulsive personality disorder, with episodes of excessive work, golf, gambling, shopping, bargain hunting, shoplifting, tidiness, hygiene, dieting, exercising, love, anorexia, muscular spasms, or religion.'

'Not me. What about alcohol?'

'Yes, that's common. So are overeating, chocolate, tea, coffee, Coca-Cola, marijuana, cocaine, heroin and petrol sniffing. Even if you bring your sexual activity under control, you might switch to something else to soothe your anxiety.'

'Supposing you are right, is there any way of getting off the roundabout?'

'You can join Alcoholics Anonymous and put your faith in a Higher Power. They have 12 steps that you can follow.'

'But I'm not an alcoholic.'

'Alcoholics Anonymous treat any type of dependency with the same 12-step method.'

'Is there any other way?'

'You may be able to stop by willpower alone.'

'I'm not dependent on sex and can stop whenever I want. We would be in a monogamous relationship. If you come on Mission Figurehead I won't cheat on you.'

Vicki shook her head. 'If I joined, it wouldn't work. You have had sex with too many of them. Tell me, in your mind, is this scheme a sex junket?'

'No. I want you as my partner, in the fullest sense, respecting your integrity the Sartre way. Won't you reconsider?'

'No, Tom. I must go now. Keep in touch.'

He was stung by Vicki's rejection. It was the end of his dream. He had not realised he might be addicted to sex. He would quit the tent and try to revive his relationship with Vicki.

Without his involvement with the women, the project slowly fell apart. A month later, only 10 of the women who had paid remained. Keeping the project afloat was a struggle and it had ceased to be fun.

'To live in a commune together, people must nurture a dream,' he thought. *'Without Vicki, there isn't enough nurturing to continue.'*

He called a meeting of all the participants and presented the facts.

'I recommend we cancel the ship building and wind up the commune,' he said.

They accepted. It was sad because some had sold their homes and resigned from good jobs. Now they looked foolish and would have to re-establish their lives. Tom returned to them the remainder of their money.

It was the end of his plans for communal living. He would have to think of another way to attract Vicki.

CHAPTER 56
SAFE CHOICE

'If I found a way to stop the Cold War,' thought Tom, *'Vicki would be helluva impressed.'*

He had spent a year reading political economy, sociology, psychology and social psychology. The confrontation between East and West was evolving and he was in despair of finding a ready-made theory that would overlie events. The meanings of terms differed between the disciplines and were blurring in his mind. Without a female partner he was unable to focus. He picked up girls for one-night stands but he fell into a black depression, worse than any he had ever experienced. He felt alone and vulnerable.

Superficial sex wouldn't do. He needed a partner to help him cope, someone who would be there for him, come what may. She would love him and he would love her. She would be attractive, intelligent and kind, a lifelong learner. Vicki was his ideal, but time was passing and their relationship wasn't going anywhere.

'Am I crazy about Vicki?' he thought. *'Do other men obsess about the same woman for years without consummation?'*

He had to forget Vicki and move on. He lay on his bed and reviewed entries in his address book.

'Which girl would be best for a long-term commitment?' he thought.

He compared them with Vicki, shortlisting possible marriage partners.

He shared a research room at LUT with Manfred. He told him about his shortlist.

'How can I pick the best one?'

'Weigh up their good and bad points. Choose the one with the highest net good.'

'Gross good would not deduct their bad points, right?'

'Correct. The one with the highest overall total will be best.'

'Some girls have a few big attractions. Others have many smaller ones. The same with their faults. It is impossible to compare.'

'Which girl has the fewest bad points?' asked Manfred.

'Ruth.'

He had met her in Canada. When he was back in the UK and started a PhD, he had thought it would be unfair to keep her waiting three years and stopped writing to her. Perhaps she was still single.

'Could she make you unhappy?'

'I doubt it. I dislike her the least.'

'Good,' said Manfred. 'Avoiding the worst is important. She could be the one.'

He phoned her in South Africa where she lived now.

'Ruth, it's Tom.'

'Hello, Tom! Where are you?'

'Liverpool.'

'It's great to hear from you! How are you?'

'Missing you,' he said. 'How are you?'

'I'm about to move to New Zealand.'

She must not be in a relationship. So far so good.

'Could you go via the UK?'

'It's not exactly en route. It may be possible to change flights. Are you sure you want me to come?'

'Yes, but before we can settle down, I have to finish at uni.'

'How long?'

'Three years.'

'How is your PhD going?'

'I think I can glimpse a solution but I have a lot more to do.'

'What if there isn't a solution?'

'Then I'll keep trying. There is nothing I would rather do. Could you come for a trial?'

'I'll get back to you,' she said.

He thought he might not hear from her again but she called the next day and said she would arrive in the UK in three weeks' time.

While waiting for her to arrive, instead of studying he thought about women. It was the sunset of his womanising: an epochal change to his life was imminent. He felt like a desert plant without water that would flower and then die. He tried to crack on to every good-looking woman he came across and when he didn't succeed, masturbation brought only temporary relief and soreness. He hoped that when Ruth did arrive, he would be able get his mind on to completing the PhD.

He took up with Ruth where he had left off in Canada — in bed. She moved into his flat, in a genteel old house off Ashgrove Road and started in a job as a school health advisor. They split the rent down the middle. He had his research grant money, which wasn't much. She cooked, cleaned and made the bed, enabling him to avoid domestic chores. Women's Liberation had not yet arrived.

'Would you make the bed,' she asked.

'We don't need to make our bed: we have a duvet.'

'It won't take a minute.'

'*I'm not going to waste my time,*' he thought. '*Perhaps she doesn't have enough to do.*'

When he didn't do it, she did.

His work became more ordered and effective. At home, his wishes were respected and he could find his things where he had left them.

'You seem to have it pretty good,' Richard said when he visited.

'Ruth looks after me well,' Tom said. He knew he was using her, but she seemed to like him depending on her. If she didn't like it, she could leave.

Friends came to dinner but he and Ruth weren't invited back. She had a way of killing conversations.

He hardly ever saw Vicki now and he relied on Richard for news of her.

'I saw Vicki at a party a couple of weeks ago. She was with a guy. . . . I think his name was John.'

Tom was jealous but living with Ruth obscured his interest in Vicki. Ruth went to Women's Liberation meetings on several nights each week, dressed in yellow or green overalls, her hair big and frizzy, or tied in bangs. She volunteered at the local family planning centre where women bonded to undermine the capitalist system. They were sure men caused wars and women should take over and bring universal peace.

In October 1973, the Organisation of Petroleum Exporting Countries proclaimed an oil embargo. The price of petrol increased tenfold overnight. The USA led the importers and the USSR sided with the exporters. The Cold War added a new arena in the Middle East. A solution continued to elude Tom.

Tom had heard that the President of the USA, Richard Nixon, would make a talkback appearance on CNN TV and the programme would be networked to the UK. Tom obtained the number, called the station and told his question to a studio assistant.

'Turn off your radio to prevent feedback,' she said. 'Go ahead and put your question.'

'I am Tom Archer in England, Mr President. What price will the USA pay exporting countries for their oil?'

'Thank you for your question, Tom,' said Tricky Dicky. 'The cost of producing oil in most cases is under $1 per barrel, so the old price of $3 per barrel is more than fair.'

'Do you agree that the producers' and consumers' surpluses should be equal?'

'What do you mean?'

'Producers have been getting at least $3 and they are holding out for $5, giving a surplus of $2. If they compromise at $4, each side would get a surplus of $1. That would be fair.'

'No, I don't agree,' said Nixon. 'A price hike to $4 is unacceptable.'

'It would be lower than the $5 per barrel importers have started paying.'

'Why should OPEC get an extra $1 per barrel? Who says the surpluses must be equal? Consumers will pay no more than they have to.'

'$3 per barrel may not be politically sustainable. When oil runs out everywhere except in the Middle East, America will have to pay more than $3 to OPEC, Mr President.'

'Not if we send in our military.'

'We have different concepts of how to trade oil with OPEC, Mr President. I would not consider military sanctions. It is their right to put the price up.'

'When people are trying to corner the market, force is justified. We will work it out fairly, Tom. America will not be dictated to by anyone.'

The host took over and Tom was cut off.

Tom understood the geopolitics of oil but he still had a long way to go to resolve the Cold War. His progress in developing a thesis was slow.

CHAPTER 57
MARRY IN HASTE

When he turned 27, his family pressured him to marry Ruth. He was well under his target age of 30. He had realised that she was not the right woman for him but his married siblings said he had had a pretty good innings.

Tom wasn't sure what love was and doubted he loved Ruth. Nor could he judge Ruth's suitability from his family's reaction to her. He had never introduced a girlfriend to his family before, or ever had any girl wanting to marry him. Their approval seemed absolute, because it lacked any relativity. Maybe this was as good as it got.

His family assumed his reluctance to marry Ruth was weak-willed indecision, when it was his disaffection for marriage in general and to Ruth in particular. He wanted Vicki and wanted to wait for her, preferably with Ruth gone.

His mother and Howard may have meant well and behaved traditionally, but they jackbooted into Tom's life without invitation or qualification. They took it upon themselves to connive with Ruth to transform Tom's cohabitation with Ruth into marriage, that would conform with their narrow morals. Neither his father, two sisters, nor younger brother defended Tom. They had not experienced living together as a couple and were unsure what it meant. They lent their support to the caging of Tom, partly as fulfilment of a romantic ideal and partly from jealousy of Tom's freedom as a single man.

While he was distracted by difficulty with his studies, his mother encouraged Ruth to mount a campaign to get him to marry her.

Ruth had packed her suitcase.

'I'm leaving now,' she said, 'unless we get married.'

'I have to finish my PhD first.'

'I am not going to wait any longer.'

'Why not?'

She didn't answer and he was annoyed that she was renegotiating the terms she had accepted when she moved in. In his mind he ran through the advantages and disadvantages of marrying Ruth. She had agreed that it would be three years before they could settle down but she was trying to renege after a year. Her urgency puzzled him and his intuition was that she wanted a child. His resistance was passive and in a moment of weakness he agreed to marry her.

'Okay, I'll marry you but having a child has to wait until I have finished, as you agreed.'

Ruth stayed. She had trapped him and she was not daunted that he did not love her. Instead of leaving, she manipulated his family to take her side by misinforming them that he would dishonour an agreement to marry her, which was not true.

He thought his relatives might be able to divine if it would be a good match. He trusted they had a wider perspective and would have his best interests at heart. He did not believe then that they would betray him for their own selfish reasons. He learned later that neither his mother nor Howard cared whether he liked Ruth. Because of their twisted interpretation of his tragic relationship with Barbara, they did not respect Tom and sadistically sabotaged his happiness by manipulating a wedding that fulfilled their pride and prejudices.

The demands of studying for a PhD displaced his attention from Ruth's scheming. His mother arranged a date for them to wed in a small chapel near Priory Farm. Friends drove from Liverpool. Vicki came up by herself. He hadn't seen her for months but his mind was on her throughout the ceremony. He was almost paralysed by the folly of the marriage. He lacked courage to call it off and participated minimally. As he echoed the pastor's recitation of vows, Vicki was foremost in his thoughts.

'Why is my mind on Vicki now?' he thought. *'Is she simply the one that got away? Is it unrequited love that attracts me to her? Is her mystery simply that she is unattainable? Am I wanting to climb into her affections, like Mount Everest, simply because she is there?'*

He had rebounded into this marriage when his prospect of partnering Vicki petered out. Her wedding present was a lemon juice extractor as if to remind him their relationship had soured.

When Tom signed the register he was surprised to see that Ruth's birth date was three years before his. She had misled him that their ages were similar. She was 31 and her biological clock was approaching midnight. It was a malicious deception he could never forgive. He realised now she was of the Silent generation whereas Tom and his friends were Boomers, denizens of different worlds with little in common. No wonder invitations from friends to dinner had dried up.

After the wedding, Ruth disdained him. He realised the kind face he had loved was the shop window of her profession as a school health advisor. Her face now was unfriendly. She was exacting retribution for his ending of their correspondence when he returned to the UK. She was slippery and he couldn't trust her. He inferred she cared for him even less than he cared for her.

Ruth had been a dutiful fiancée but she transformed into a wife impelled by feminism and misandry. He was a barely tolerated specimen of the male gender whose role in society she wanted minimised.

'Women can control their own fertility,' she said. 'We are not sexual objects and will no longer be used by men.'

Her interest in him was loveless and selfish: he was merely a means for her to have a child.

'If I don't have a baby soon, it may be too late.'

'Not until my research is done,' he said. 'You agreed.'

'Oh, phooey! What does that matter?'

'Everything. A baby would be a huge distraction.'

'Every day of delay increases the risk that I will be unable to conceive. You should quit uni and get a job.'

Ruth's opinion, concealed until now, was that his research was a waste of time.

'Her treachery and opposition are disloyal,' Tom thought. *'But there is nothing I can do about her.'*

Sensing their discord, friends stayed away. Tom was socially isolated and demoralised. He was having difficulties with his PhD. His research supervisor had encouraged him to browse for ideas in other academic disciplines, despite his lack of experience of their basics.

Tom had devised and trialled, in the town hall of an English provincial city, an algorithm for government planning that could unite the belligerents in the Cold War. Everyday there were news reports that the USA and USSR had added missiles to their arsenals as the conflict escalated. Soviet citizens were trying to escape over the Berlin Wall. The two regimes seemed implacably opposed. Tom read and read, convinced he was making progress.

After two years, his supervisor pulled the rug out from under him.

'I can't help you with this,' he said, abandoning Tom and his ideas without offering constructive criticism or an alternative research topic. 'You're on your own.'

He didn't have a PhD himself and didn't seem to know what Tom had to do to get one. Tom found out he needed external examiners to be appointed, so he could write his thesis within their disciplines and ontologies. His supervisor's desertion left him out on a limb.

As he waited to hear if his grant had been renewed, he was tortured by apprehension. If he didn't get the money, he would have to abandon his PhD. He panicked when he imagined quitting with nothing after three years of hard work, unpaid except for the pittance of a grant.

He sometimes wondered how Vicki was getting on. Richard saw her occasionally and passed on snippets of news. Loyal to Ruth, he didn't contact her. He tried to put her out of his mind but he could not forget his unfulfilled plan to reacquire her interest in him as a partner.

CHAPTER 58
REPENT AT LEISURE

'I'm pregnant,' said Ruth.

At first Tom could not believe it.

'You were on The Pill, weren't you?'

'I stopped.'

'But we agreed: you would not get pregnant until I had finished!'

'I couldn't wait any longer. You were not getting closer.'

It was payback for his leaving her in Canada. Her action conflicted with his plans. Ruth had stopped her contraception with the voracity of a feeding shark. It was at least as harmful to him as the delaying of a baby would be to her. It abrogated their agreement but there was nothing he could do other than accept it without demur.

Her next move commenced immediately.

'We have to buy a place,' she said.

'Why?'

'We could be evicted from here. The baby has to come home to a place we own.'

'We can't afford to own a place.'

'I can get a mortgage.'

'We could be evicted for not keeping up the payments.'

Ignoring his protest, she bought a place, mortgaging her income and demanding he accept liability.

'How will we make payments after you stop work?' he asked her.

'You must get a job,' she said.

'I will when I finish. It won't be long.'

'You have been saying that for over a year.'

Ruth suffered morning sickness. She continued to go to work until a month before the birth was due, then took unpaid maternity leave. The new government did not extend his grant. They had no income to pay the mortgage.

'Why haven't you got a job yet?' she asked him.

'There aren't any part-time jobs.'

'For fuck's sake, quit and get a full-time job,' Ruth said. 'You don't need a piece of paper saying 'PhD'.'

Abandoning his PhD would derail his career plan. His dalliance with academia had not been casual: he had intended it to be the start of a lifelong journey. He would not be able to achieve his ambition. He had slaved for three years for next to nothing.

Tom's predicament compounded. Ruth attended prenatal classes at a health clinic and came home worried about having a disabled baby.

'I am classified as elderly,' she said. 'The birth and child are at risk.'

They had real grounds for concern because babies born to elderly mothers had a higher than normal incidence of a wide range of disabilities. The likelihood of having a disabled child was magnified in her mind because during her training she had done fieldwork with disabled children. She was fearful and anxious, racking Tom's nerves. He was unable to provide practical or emotional support and waves of her anxiety beat against his mental fortitude and eroded his composure.

Her concerns snowballed into panic when she worried she had been infected by German Measles that could cause blindness or deafness in their baby. She harangued Tom with this worry. He knew little of medical matters and was anxious, pumping adrenalin for imagined fights with medics, or for imagining fleeing from a hospital after turning off a life support system to an unsustainable offspring.

The stress loaded him to breaking point. He consumed cigarettes and alcohol in increasing quantity. Anxiety was his constant companion and he lay awake at night worrying.

He had no support from his parents or siblings.

'University research is a waste of time and money,' they said. 'Real problems get solved in the real world. Quit and get a job. Provide for your dependants.'

Although he wanted to leave Ruth, it was unthinkable to do it now while she was pregnant. His thinking was becoming muddled and black.

'I am not succumbing to mental illness,' he thought. *'If I had a predisposition to break down, wouldn't I already have broken down?'*

His uni colleagues warned him to get treatment for stress but he didn't know who to turn to. He had never experienced anything like this before. He would tough it out and think of a way out of his predicament.

The recourse he adopted was to work even longer hours at writing-up his thesis, striving to get done before Ruth stopped work. He worked desperately hard and lay sleepless at night, worrying 24 hours per day.

CHAPTER 59
BIPOLAR EXPEDITION NORTH

Every news report testified to escalation of the arms race. An idea occurred to Tom: could religion be a bridge between communism in the East and capitalism in the West?

'With the same God or a faith in common between the sides, antipathies would be mitigated,' he thought. *'In the East, religion has been suppressed but is still practiced covertly.'*

He lay in bed without sleep, quivering with excitement, elaborating the idea endlessly in his mind. As he tossed and turned, he imagined that frozen ideologies ruled the earth, polarised at the geographic poles. There was planned collectivism in the east and north, opposed by market-oriented individualism in the west and south. He would lead an expedition to bring representatives from the two poles together at a mutually acceptable place, such as Berlin, where détente could result. They could establish a global civilisation to last 1000 years.

After a week without sleep, overloaded and unsupported, his mind was taken over by a paranoid delusion. God had selected him as a messiah to save the world, because he alone understood the ultimate causes conflicting the collectivist East with the individualist West. God had chosen him to end the Cold War.

Vicki had told him during their visit to Salisbury Cathedral that people could do anything they wanted if their purpose was fervent enough. If East and West were devoted with the same beliefs, they could be united.

Obeying the biblical injunction: 'Know thine enemy' he explored the library shelves for an ultimate cause of human communal living. Collectives had evolved from primates that shared the chase and kill. Their communes were nomadic at first then survived in forests by slash and burn agriculture. Each family joined with neighbours in working the land they occupied to grow food for themselves and for less fortunate members of the community. Members helped each other to clear the jungle and build houses. Later, communes became agricultural and then industrial settlements.

Tom hypothesised that collective living was motivated by subscription to a communal destiny. Small collectives migrated north and grew into bands of herders and agriculturalists that were proto-communist societies whose survival depended on the group rather than the individual.

His journey north was an arduous exploration through a jungle of competing ideas. He adopted philosopher Karl Popper's position that all knowledge was uncertain. He began to clear a track through the underbrush of minor academic ideas, to reveal the tall trees of iconic understanding, to fell them by falsification and replace them with more amenable beliefs.

Tom made his way northwards through the open woodlands by keeping the prevailing wind on his left, which was westerly. As the climate became cooler and drier, lichens of controversy grew on the sheltered moist eastern sides of tree trunks.

In the drier savannah, there were agricultural collectives using animal power and machines. On the plains near the Russo-Chinese border, large cooperative farms operated under centralised planning. Here famine held sway. Grain was exported to the capital city under armed guard to prevent theft by hungry local people. Soils were running down, the desert was advancing and the people were demoralised. Their collectivism brought them little joy.

He questioned local people to divulge the archetypal sociological impulse that motivated collective living and communism. He explored the tundra to find if individuals' willpower was reduced by rigours of the climate, with compensating commitment to community. He was surprised to find people had little experience beyond living in a collective and regarded their participation as an individual endeavour.

Tundra people looked after themselves first and each other afterwards. In a collective, an adult was expected to behave in the same way as in an aircraft decompression emergency, putting on their own oxygen mask before helping children with theirs. They sustained themselves first, afterwards their kin. Strangers were helped last, if at all.

Tom had lost his bearings and wandered around aimlessly, unable to get any closer to a collective North Pole. He began to doubt that it existed and he lost contact with reality.

He was found in a cave suffering from hypothermia by a party of indigenous people trekking across the permafrost between research centres, trading artwork for food. They undressed him and put him in a sleeping bag with a naked female, who warmed him up by skin contact. It seemed like a dream and he recovered slowly.

When he was ready to resume his trek, he bartered for supplies.

'What can you exchange with us?' they asked.

'How about some hypotheses?'

'Are they any good?'

'Testable but not yet tested,' he said.

'Easy to test?'

'Easier than Bertrand Russell's hypothesis that there is a teapot in orbit between Jupiter and Earth.'

'Would they be difficult to falsify?'

'Yes. The burden of proof would be yours and intractable. Many would believe anyway, in the same way that people believe God exists.'

'We are supposed to believe in the Communist Party and its plans. Many of us have stopped believing. We will help you because we are all humankind together. We can give you enough food and alcohol for you to walk to the coast, where there are animals you can kill to eat.'

He had expected to find ideals and altruism at the collective pole, but there were none. The group had helped him because he was an atheist and deduced to have kindred genes. The glue of kin group selection was atheistic self-interest, contra collectivism, not idealistic-altruism as he had supposed.

In a moment of epiphany, he realised: *The Holy Grail of collectivism is group self-interest. All humanity is self-interested.*

He rewarded his progress by taking a day off from the library and driving down to see Vicki. They went on another visit to Salisbury Cathedral and paused at the ornate entrance.

'What are you looking at?' she asked him.

Tom's mind was still on his expedition.

'I have a hunch it was built by collective enterprise,' he said.

'I agree. It seems too grandiose for individual ambition,' she said. 'It took generations to build.'

Inside, they admired the massive fluted columns of the nave.

'This is perfection,' Vicki said. 'How did they craft it so meticulously?'

'Fear of retribution?'

'Earthly or divine?'

'Who knows?' said Tom.

'Was it fear or faith?'

'Possibly both at the same time.'

They passed through a stone screen into the choir. Behind the choristers' desks, in an almost hidden corner, she pointed to biblical scenes carved into the wood.

'Who could have motivated and supervised this intricate work?' she asked. 'Why would a carver bother?'

'God supervised here,' said Tom. 'This is the work of a devout master craftsman. In his book *Pillars of the Earth*, Ken Follet described how a cathedral's masonry was carved as a prayer, a supplication without expectation of earthly reward. It wasn't built by a collective: it was built by individual faith. The master mason was inspired by faith and braved hunger, tyranny, insurrection and sectarian conflict.'

'Perhaps the Cathedral, Stonehenge and the Pyramids all express faith in artisan mastery, rather than in collective zeal or religious authority,' said Vicki.

'Exactly. They were created by craftsmen who loved their work.'

'I love my work, so why shouldn't they?'

'I'm convinced.'

'Have you found what you wanted?'

'Yes. Both the USA and USSR respect individuality, but in different ways. Individuals love their work. There's traction in that.'

When he returned to the university he continued to look for achievements by collectives. He pored over books in the library stacks day after day, becoming more and more disoriented. A popular vision that could be a collective goal was the USA's Apollo Mission and moon landing, inspired by the nationalism of John F Kennedy. He had told Americans: 'Ask not what your country can do for you; ask what you can do for your country!' No-one could be ultimately responsible for the achievement of such a huge collective and individuals had to take responsibility. NASA's achievement was motivated by individual self-interest.

'Communism and capitalism have similar aetiologies of self-interest!' he thought. *'A compromise and merger may be possible. If I go to the other pole, I may discover the origin of Western self-interest.'*

He was preparing a plan to go south when Ruth called.

'Tom, I'd like you to come home now,' she said.

'I am not here,' he answered. 'I am on an expedition.'

'What are you doing?' she demanded.

'I am returning from the North Pole.'

'I can't hear you properly. There seems to be interference.'

'It could be the CIA listening,' he thought.

'It must be the Aurora Borealis.'

'Tom! Stop it at once,' she ordered. 'I do not want you getting off on some atmospheric effect. Where are you?'

'In the Arctic. The map coordinates are 121151121. It's a palindrome. Maybe I should head in the opposite direction.'

'You are talking nonsense, Tom. The sooner you quit your damned thesis the sooner you'll have a life.'

The wind blew snowflakes quietly outside and fine snow gathered in drifts, as he thought how to answer this.

'Are you still there?' Ruth asked.

'I'm off the map. I don't know if I'm going backwards or forwards,' he said. 'I'm bogged down in communist propaganda!'

'You aren't getting anywhere. I want you to come home immediately.'

'I'm in the middle of something. I'll be home when I've finished.'

CHAPTER 60
HAYWIRE

Later that day, Tom arrived home, exhausted and manic, unable to disengage his thoughts from his expedition. Lack of sleep was distorting his vision. Ruth was not sympathetic.

'When are you going to get a job?' she asked.

He mooched around in his pyjamas, writing, drinking whisky, dancing and trying to have sex with Ruth, who wanted to sleep.

When he tried to explain his theory to her, she said, 'You are talking gibberish.'

The next morning, Ruth phoned some of his university colleagues.

'Tom is wound up about his work,' she said. 'Could someone come around here and talk with him, please?'

They tried to rescue him but he laughed and pulled them into a rhetorical crevasse. His exuberance and inability to articulate plans worried them. They wanted him to go on holiday and relax.

Because communication with his research supervisor had broken down, Tom requested a meeting with Professor Shapner, his department head. The secretary ushered him into his office.

'How are you getting on?' he asked.

'My research grant has not been renewed,' Tom said.

'How close are you to finishing?'

'I don't know. My supervisor has jumped ship. He has deserted me.'

The professor paused.

'How can I help?' said the professor.

'I would be grateful for your feedback on my ideas, Sir.'

'Where are you up to?' he asked.

Tom handed him a summary of his investigation of collective living.

Professor Shapner read it carefully.

'You are making good progress,' he said. 'You have identified that collectivism originates when individuals who have sustained themselves share a vision.'

'Also, I have found a way to resolve the Cold War,' Tom said. 'If communists and capitalists are unified by religious beliefs in common, hostilities could cease. Could I submit it for a PhD?'

'I am not convinced those governments want unification or would tolerate other religions,' Shapner said. 'When you explore the epistemology of individualism you may discover that all the two sides have in common is mutual hatred.'

'They both have faith in individual self-interest, materialism and enough collectivism to seek peace.'

'We don't get involved with faiths in this department,' he said. 'I am concerned about your health. You have been overworking. My advice is to take a holiday and when you come back write up what you have done for a MPhil. Your research is original and relevant. I look forward to receiving your submission, Mr Archer.'

He turned to the papers on his desk and Tom left.

A MPhil was a lesser degree, a consolation prize and Tom was dismayed. He felt grief for his lost PhD and panic that he had no other plans.

'If I can get good data, Shapner will have to accept my thesis for a PhD,' he thought. *'I must obtain evidence of lifestyles with individual striving, at the South Pole.'*

Tom had been sleepless for five days and had a headache. Ruth persuaded him to lie down and rest. He was intrigued by the fractal pattern of the ceramic floor tiles and planned to tile the hallway walls and ceiling. It would show how international diplomacy depended on voluntarism, such as offering to do the washing-up. He woke Ruth to explain it to her but she was unimpressed.

'I don't understand what you are on about anymore,' she said.

'It's a new paradigm with a vantage point on everything,' Tom told her. 'It is too big to explain in one thesis.'

The next morning, before going to work, Ruth confronted him.

'I want you to come with me to the doctor.'

'There's nothing wrong with me.'

He believed he was in control of the UK Government, of every organisation, of every person and of all their activities, including the play of children outside in the street. He was the Messiah who decided everything for everybody all the time. He had to be on guard, watching the news on TV, his thoughts churning with realisation of the connectedness of everything to everything else.

'We will leave in 10 minutes and walk to the doctor's,' she said.

He thought they were going to base camp. When they arrived at their GP's surgery, Tom wouldn't go inside and they walked home again.

In the afternoon, his sister Heather came with them and they tried again. Tom would not go in, repeating that there was nothing wrong with him. Eventually the two women persuaded him and they all went into a room with an oldish man, their general practitioner.

'How are you today?' he asked Tom.

'I never felt better. How about you?'

The doctor eyed him balefully.

'Who am I?' he asked.

Tom did not answer.

'Who are you?' the doctor asked Tom.

If I say I am the Messiah, he will think I am mad,' Tom thought.

'I have a mission to save the world.'

'How are you going to do that?'

'Why should I tell you?'

'I want to try to help you.'

'I do not need your help. I want to go home.'

'Why do you think I want to help you?'

Tom didn't answer. He was sure the doctor was KGB. They must know about his theory and be trying to 'un-health' him as George Orwell had predicted in his book *1984*.

'You are ill,' he told Tom. 'I want you to take this pill now. It will help you get some sleep.'

'What evidence is there that I am ill?' Tom demanded.

'Your behaviour is abnormal.'

'I am not insane.'

'I would like to do a check-up, take some measurements.'

'Orwell said insanity is not statistical.'

'Take the pill now, Tom,' said the doctor, annoyed.

'It is poison. You are a shaman, a glorified medicine man. Underneath your suit, your body is naked and painted.'

'Tom, this pill will help you.'

'I don't believe you. You are trying to poison me.'

'It is ipecac. It is not poison. It will help you.'

Ruth and Heather persuaded him and he swallowed it.

When he got home, his tongue stuck out involuntarily, like an erection. He was embarrassed and frightened. He had heard that people could swallow their tongues. He could feel his eyes bulging as he gasped for breath. He feared he would asphyxiate. He was convulsed by the desire to vomit and doubled up, gagging. Ruth called an ambulance.

'Jesus never had it half as bad as me,' he thought.

God's heavenly chariot came with two burly angels, psychiatric nurses. They gave him a white garment to put on.

'The other way around,' one said. 'It's a straitjacket. We are tying you up for your own safety. It's standard procedure with mania patients.'

Tom couldn't move his arms. Being tied up in a straitjacket was humiliating. With the klaxon blaring, they sped to hospital. It was a hive of activity. Hundreds of political prisoners shuffled in lines to be processed by the white-coated goons from St Peter's Gate. When it was Tom's turn, he denounced his GP as a poisoner. He was put in a room with chairs around the outside where about a dozen patients shrank.

'I am the only sane person here,' he thought.

He wanted to break the ice.

'You are all mad,' he said.

No-one said anything.

'These people are hopeless,' he thought. An inner voice told him:
'Listen to your feelings.'
He had to get away.

He went out by the back door and fled through the streets, his heart
pounding in his ears. He had been awake for six days and his vision
had objects looming up and others falling away, like looking through
the wrong end of a telescope. His sense of direction gave him only
weak clues about where to go. He sought the help of a lady with a
shopping trolley.
'Can you tell me the way, please?'
'Where to, love?'
'I don't know.'
'Where do you live?'
'I'm not sure. Maybe Ayston.'
'It's a long way. You can get a bus over there, number 162.'
'Thank you.'
He had not been on a bus for years and had forgotten how you
paid. He gave the driver a handful of change from his pocket.
'Where you going, mate?'
'Ayston.'
'High Street?'
'Maybe. Where else can I go?'
'Lochlan Road, Park Road, town hall, swimming pool, library,
Grosvenor Close — take your pick.'
'I don't know.'
'Just moved here, have you?'
'About a year ago.'
'Blimey. Well, I'll let you off at town hall. You can ask there.
That's £1.60.'
'Thank you.'
'Here's your change. You may need it.'
When he got off he was completely lost. He fought down panic.
Two men were further along the street, watching him: CIA. He
walked fast in the opposite direction along the High Street. He didn't
come to anywhere he recognised. He was considering sleeping in a

park when he recognised the town hall and Worthing Street nearby, where he lived.

Tired and footsore he lay on his bed but could not sleep. He had been chosen to be the Messiah to the four billion people who lived on earth. He was exhausted and he took the pills the doctor had given him.

He woke up with his thoughts woolly but placid. The trauma of his psychosis was replaced by medicated numbed thoughtlessness. He sat in the sun in the back garden and watched the cabbages grow. He wanted to be like them: unfolding slowly, in exuberant health, accepting.

He attended the hospital day-care centre for two months, becoming able to chat, play the guitar and sing with the other patients. He concealed his Messiah identity. His higher power would reveal what to do in the fullness of time.

They had diagnosed a disorder between bipolar and schizophrenia. His disciples, Richard, Larry and Vicki, visited him at home. Their coming was like a biblical pageant. Richard was the apostle John, Larry was Matthew and Vicki played Mary Magdalene to his Jesus.

Vicki sat beside him in the garden. She asked what he was experiencing but he was silent. If he talked, the dismal realities of his marriage, his paternity, his PhD, his mortgage, his finances and his employment would be too oppressive.

'Do you hear voices?' Vicki asked him.

He shook his head. Messiahs communicated by thought transference.

'Are you specially chosen?' she asked.

If he denied it, the Higher Power might leave him alone. He shook his head.

'Can you tell me where your thoughts are?'

He said nothing. His rabbit of a mind was hiding in its bolt hole.

'Do you want me to stay?'

He made no reply.

'Well, goodbye, Tom,' Vicki said. 'You are ill and I hope you get better soon. You need to talk about what you are experiencing. The sooner you do that, the sooner you will recover. Remember that I am your friend.'

'Thank you, Vicki.'

'Your thesis idea is important. One day you will complete it.'

He wanted to tell her that he was going to be crucified but he didn't say anything.

'Goodbye, Tom.'

He wondered sadly if he would ever see her again.

The doctors, nurses and friends who visited him said with enthusiasm: 'Tom, you will soon be a father!'

He knew he had to get over his PhD sulk and get a job to support Ruth and the baby. He wanted to complete his research.

CHAPTER 61
BIPOLAR EXPEDITION SOUTH

When they reduced his medication, he was able to concentrate again and returned to the uni to write up his thesis for the degree of Master of Philosophy. He filled notebooks with ideas, diagrams and equations about a religion acceptable to both sides which would resolve the Cold War.

Tom's wheeling thoughts turned to discovering the South Pole of self-interest. Adam Smith was the totemic thinker who had extolled the virtues of a baker, who baked and sold bread for a profit. With his friend Hume, he proposed that seeking profit was better for the community than seeking virtue. Tom wanted his thesis to compare free self-interested individuals with their counterparts in collectives. Which type of society was fairer to its members?

He needed to know the aetiology of the self-interest impulse, in individualism and market capitalism. He holed up in a library carrel and searched in the literature.

Early humans who migrated eastwards from Africa sailed downwind, as suited their more easy-going and group-centred personalities, spreading along coasts through the Orient and China, northwards to Russia, evolving collective societies.

Other Africans and their descendants chose to travel north eventually reaching Europe and Scandinavia, where fairer pigmentation evolved. They forced westwards across the stormy North Atlantic, landing fiercely independent and stoical individuals along the eastern seaboard of the Americas. Wherever this type settled, they evolved frontier economies composed of owner operators with a strong ideal of individual self-interest.

He traced the individualism west and then south to Patagonia. He crossed over the iceberged sea and pack ice to the land, where his dog team dragged the sled through soft snow and boulder fields. He was pursuing effects to their logical causes, supposing self-interest might have a higher cause, an ultimate motive like original sin or ego inflation. As he climbed up the glaciers of Antarctica, he was optimistic that he would find an answer.

When his supplies had dwindled and could fit into his backpack, he burned the sled and slaughtered the dogs, cooking the meat to eat, sparing an affectionate black Labrador. He cached half for the return journey.

Robert Falcon Scott of the Arctic and his noble companions self-sacrificed heroically on the ice within a code of individualism. There were icy storms that lasted for days. The terrain was rugged and because Tom was solo, a slip could be fatal. He considered whether to go back and recruit companions, but because his health was above average, his prospects for survival would be better if he continued alone. He pushed on, encountering and overcoming terrible hardships.

Tom's progress was slow. When he became bogged by inconclusive arguments, he discarded sophistry and applied Occam's Razor to choose the most direct route. The black dog followed at a distance, fearing the fate of its companions. The way was marked by the remains of camps where explorers had abandoned their equipment and gone north along the Pacific seaboard, to places where self-interest evolved as utilitarianism or communism. These human social ideals have survived to today.

It was bitterly cold and the only life was a colony of seals and a rookery of emperor penguins.

Capitalist freedom was grounded on the bedrock of John Locke's empiricism, nourished by puritan zeal and sanctified by Darwin's theory of survival of the fittest. It had a mantra of self-interest. After individuals had promoted their kin's genes, they would combine with kin to fight an intruder, joining with strangers when it was in the group's self-interest.

He was shocked to find, preserved in an archive, correspondence between Roosevelt and Stalin in 1945, first at Yalta and then at Potsdam, indicating the two had conspired to escalate a mock confrontation with nuclear weapons. Nearby he found a 1962 agreement signed by Kruschev and Kennedy to stage a confrontation over the Russian's deployment of intercontinental ballistic missiles to Cuba. The evidence was heretical but appeared genuine.

Tom was amazed. The Cold War that had menaced the world for so long could be hypocritical posturing. The two sides were brandishing nuclear weapons to empower their autocratic governments and strike fear into the hearts of their citizenry. Missiles were being stockpiled in arsenals to give semblances of sovereign defences and to cynically stimulate industrial activity on both sides. The Cold War that had blighted the lives of millions was a pretended confrontation between two moral crusades.

'No evidence that a conspiracy had covertly united minds is likely to exist outside the leaders' heads,' he thought. *'These documents refute hostile intent and indicate conspiracy.'*

He needed more evidence. Risking discovery by security personnel, he followed the black dog underground. He came upon a radioactive fallout shelter, built as a safe retreat from nuclear winter on the surface. Lights were blazing and through an open door he could see canned food, equipment and electricity generators that could keep hundreds of people alive, the nucleus of a new society. He peeled off from a door and put in his backpack: 'Exit Code 27', written in Russian, Chinese and English.

Fearful of a patrol, he trekked back the way he had come. He had little desire to return to the Western world where, in the name of freedom, populations were enslaved in supplying the excesses of indulgent, conspicuous and addictive consumption. It was a world where the authorities denied people their needs for community and induced status anxiety to motivate them to consume products they would purchase with their earnings from working in missile factories.

Nor would he be better off if he returned to the East, where in the name of 'community', populations were motivated by fear to self-sacrifice, yoked to a concept of utilitarian equality and fairness that was impossible to provide. People here in the South were too individualistic and self-interested for their communities to have goals.

Tom realised that the impasse was not two incompatible natural philosophies in the West and East, as he had thought, but between two centralised superpower economies with vast military-industrial complexes that had grown out of control. Each was engaged in feverish industrial production, keeping their people enthralled with material consumption as a relief from perilous brinkmanship they had contrived.

He lay in a dark cave unable to decide what to do next, whether to give up and die there, or go on. He did not have the right to take his own life. He wanted to live and see Vicki and be there for a baby.

A month later, he was skin and bone. The world was false and it no longer had any attraction for him. When his hunger had overcome his revulsion from the cheesy smell of the black dog, he killed and ate it. He stumbled back along the watercourse, consuming food he had cached on the way in.

When he arrived home, he returned to the hospital day-care centre. He saw a psychiatrist regularly but he did not disclose to him the messianic delusions that were his only relief. His depression lifted and he returned to writing up his thesis.

Vicki visited him at home.

'Are you having any symptoms?'

'No,' he lied. A Messiah did not have symptoms.

'I know you are ill,' she said. 'Medication will not deal with the underlying causes. You need counselling.'

'Okay.'

Although he had failed to impress her with his heroic work, his bipolar expedition had succeeded in identifying the genesis of the Cold War and he was a hero to himself. He could cling to that, without seeking counselling.

He helped Ruth prepare their flat for the baby. The prospect no longer alarmed him. He redecorated several rooms and looked for paid employment.

CHAPTER 62
THEORY

'What are you working on?' Ruth asked him.

'Writing up for a MPhil.'

'What happened to the PhD?'

'My conspiracy hypothesis may not be testable. I am trying to frame it incontrovertibly by describing the Cold War as a symbiosis or mutualism between two otherwise incompatible systems of political economy.'

He sent an abstract to Professor Shapner and requested to discuss it with him.

'I am reluctant to tell you what I think of your conspiracy theory,' Shapner said at their meeting. 'I think you may not be well.'

'I'm fine.'

'Your judgement seems to be affected. Do you have any evidence of a conspiracy?'

'I have evidence of covert international collusion,' said Tom.

'Why do you say it is a conspiracy?'

'It betrays the public interest.'

'Interest in what: conflict?'

'No, people have a right to oppose their enemies. Secret dealing with the other side is morally corrupt.'

'What evidence do you have of secret dealing?'

Tom told him about the underground shelter and showed him the multilingual door label.

'Where was this underground shelter?' said Shapner.

'Antarctica.'

'How did you get there?'

Tom could only dimly remember. 'I travelled overland through Patagonia to Tierra del Fuego, and then across the ice with a dog team.'

'But the sea doesn't freeze over, even in winter. What ship were you on?'

'I have forgotten.'

'How long ago was this?'

'Several months.'

'When did you get back?'

'Last weekend.'

'But I saw you two months ago. You had been receiving treatment for a mental illness.'

'That's right.'

'Could this secret bunker be something you imagined? This label could have come from anywhere.'

'This may be the only place where the USA, USSR and China have a joint project.'

'The enterprise could be innocent,' said Shapner. 'Do you have any other evidence?'

Tom told him about the reports from Potsdam and the Cuban Missile Crisis.

'Your evidence is not direct observation,' said Shapner. 'You have inferred from documents that Stalin and Roosevelt were up to no good. You don't have the documents, do you? Could they have been forged? Could another explanation be possible? For example, could the leaders have been building trust as part of a negotiation?'

'It's a fine line. The provenance seems to be secret collusion, like a conspiracy.'

'Do you really think the missile transporters in Red Square, the fleets of nuclear subs, the loaded missile silos and the ICBM early warning system have all existed merely to keep the leaders in Moscow and Washington in power?' Shapner was incredulous, his voice shrill.

'Yes, I do.'

'That is ridiculous. Do you believe that the leaders on both sides are committed to nuclear confrontation as a stabilising force? Do you believe they are so enamoured of each other's potency they believe a secret mutualism, a duopoly, is the only way forward? Are they not antagonists in a zero sum conflict?'

'It is a prisoner's dilemma,' Tom said. 'If both sides confess to cooperating, their leaders would be out of office. If only one admits it, its government would fall. They are better off with a charade of mutual disparagement — a Punch and Judy show.'

Shapner leaned back and steepled his fingers.

'Tom, be sensible. The nationalism and xenophobia are real. Stalin's purges and McCarthy's witch-hunts were not contrived.'

'I believe they were.'

Professor Shapner shook his head, exasperated. 'When there are two possible explanations, we should use Occam's Razor and choose the simpler one. Our side opposes China and theirs opposes the USA. Do you accept that?'

'It is possible at some levels — but there is collusion at the top.'

'No!' He laid his hands flat on the table. 'The top leaders are not corrupt. I don't believe your conspiracy exists anywhere other than in your head, the same as your imaginary trip to the Antarctic. There is no cosy tête à tête as you suggest. A conspiracy is not credible. It may be fashionable to adopt Foucault's postmodern philosophy and infer power is applied by deception, but there is ample evidence to falsify it. The missiles lined up along both sides of the border can kill millions of people. They are evidence of a confrontation and it falsifies a conspiracy. Chinese, the USSR's and USA's behaviours are restrained by mutually assured destruction: a Mexican standoff. It is real.'

'Restraint may be by agreement, not fear.'

'Fear is more logical: if they did launch the missiles they would cease to deter and there would be a frenzy of retaliation with horrific destruction.'

'It is not whether we believe there is a conspiracy, or even whether the two sides believe there is a conspiracy. It is whether they are faking a conflict in which lives and money are being wasted.'

'Should we withdraw?'

'Not necessarily. We could want to take what is ours by force . . .'

'Ending the peace brought by the conspiracy . . .'

'Yes.'

'No!' Shapner said, thumping his fist on the desk. 'That is enough about conspiracy. You may not submit it as a doctoral thesis in this department!'

'Shapner is angry because he has lost the argument,' Tom thought.

'I'm sorry to be so negative when you are unwell,' the professor said, making an effort to speak calmly. 'I want you to write up showing that the evidence fits conflict better than it does conspiracy. It will help stem the cynicism. The possibility of a conspiracy being exposed and peace breaking out is obscure. Your theory of religion-led reconciliation is the most hopeful way forward. You will be able to submit it for the Master of Philosophy degree. Any questions?'

'What could refute a conspiracy?'

'Hmm. Outbreak of a nuclear war.'

Tom rolled his eyes. 'Then it will be too late.'

'There is no alternative,' Shapner said, palms upward. 'We must assume the conflict is real. A faked Cold War is a theoretical construct, refuted by the arms race and is only of academic interest. Your MPhil thesis must reject it. A PhD is out of the question. Close the door on your way out.'

CHAPTER 63
DUOPOLY

A month later, he met with Professor Shapner to review progress.

'As you instructed,' Tom said, 'I have presented data that refutes a conspiracy theory.'

'Good,' said the professor. 'That is practical, because there is no diplomatic process able to transition to peace, even if the Cold War is a sham. Capitalism and communism are incompatible and therefore friction is inevitable. It does not necessarily indicate hostility and the antipathy could be a smokescreen.'

'Shapner has changed his tune,' thought Tom. *'He isn't denying conspiracy — nor is he accepting it.'*

'Combat is unlikely,' Shapner said. 'The China, the USA and USSR can co-exist happily if they pretend to compete with each other at a border. The Berlin Wall was an emblematic frontier, like a tennis net marking location of game play.'

'What game is that?' asked Tom, reeling from Shapner's volte-face.

'The Cold War has the appearance of ferocity, to intimidate non-aligned countries into favourable trading relationships.'

'Because they want them as allies?'

'They need trade more than they need allies. The premise that the two sides are in zero sum Cold War competition is false,' said Shapner. 'It only appears to be winner-take-all. The reality is that the USA and China are in a symbiotic relationship that stabilises each other. They cannot admit to it because ordinary people are uncomfortable with ambiguity. They want to stay within our boundaries and despise the USSR from a distance. If there is collusion with the enemy, it has to be hidden.'

'So, in your view, another Cold War is necessary?'

'Not necessary . . . inevitable,' he said. 'What you call a 'conspiracy' is in fact bipartisan world government. Control is shared between two superpowers who posture as adversaries while covertly operating as a duopoly.'

'The American and Chinese publics would be surprised to learn that a new Cold War is a stable arrangement,' said Tom.

'It cannot end until one side capitulates.'

'My idea is that religion can bring the two sides together at the border,' Tom said.

'Hah,' said Shapner. 'Artificial intelligence could do it. Then they will go off to continue their pas de deux in some other arena. It is natural for the world order to come under duopoly control.'

'Does there have to be another mock military confrontation somewhere else?' asked Tom. 'Why not a less wasteful form of conflict, such as a trade war?'

'A trade war would be less violent, I agree,' said Shapner. 'But people could lose money. It would be better if religion brought rapprochement. Your religion theory may be accepted for a PhD if you re-enrol in Sociology or Psychology.'

'How long would it take?'

'To align your work with theirs — at least two years.'

'It's too long. I have a baby on the way. I need a job to get money.'

'Congratulations,' said Shapner. 'Write up for a MPhil and then get a job. You can develop your theory later.'

'We could be under a pile of rubble by then.'

Shapner shrugged as if there was nothing anyone could do to prevent it.

'You could take it to the British government,' he said. 'Try a Tory MP.'

Their meeting ended.

Tom submitted his thesis and was awarded a MPhil degree.

He met with his local member of Britain's parliament and told him his evidence of a conspiracy.

'Interesting,' he said. 'What would you like me to do?'

'The possibility of a new Cold War conspiracy needs to be considered at the highest level,' Tom said.

'The Prime Minister might want to deal with this secretly herself,' said the MP. 'I'll ask her.'

They met with the British Prime Minister over breakfast at the House of Commons' Terrace Cafeteria and Tom put to her his idea of using religion to bring the two sides together.

She sipped her orange juice and listened to his theory and solution.

'Your evidence of conspiracy would be denied in both Washington, Peking and Moscow, because it cynically denigrates the motives of the world's three most powerful nations,' she said. 'It is also diametrically opposed to the findings of your own research thesis. Why is that?'

'If I whitewash my findings like this, it could get us into trouble,' he thought. *'Too bad. World peace is a higher ethic.'*

'As you have indicated, Madame, a superpower conspiracy is not politically correct. My academic supervisors are suppressing the evidence of conspiracy. If your government made it public, would it be accepted?'

'It wouldn't do us any good,' said the PM. 'To win at the ballot box we need foreign military adventures against a common enemy. It doesn't have to be on a large scale. A fracas with China over Taiwan would be suitable.'

'Could Britain want to heroically heal this new Cold War rift?' *he thought. 'Like they did in the Falklands War?'*

'The confidence of the British public would be shaken by an accusation of collusion. Your idea about religion is more practical, but how could we get religions to focus their dissent near the East-West border, as you suggest?'

'Britain has brokered a religion-led reunification of Germany. Ever since Henry VIII's reformation, UK governments have used the Church of England as an instrument of state. The Church could send missionaries to East-West border areas. Other religions would follow. The USA's leaders could be okay with deploying religions for social appeasement between China and Russia. Intercession by religions could be accredited in their foreign policy. On the other side of the border, Russia could allow evangelists into East Germany and reinstate simmering religions, like the Orthodox Church.'

'Without the Cold War to worry about, the USA and USSR governments' domestic policies would be under fire at home.'

'Could the UK get the US and USSR to fight each other somewhere else,' Tom said, 'such as the Middle East?'

'Hmm. I like it,' said Thatcher. 'Are you suggesting we intrigue against the USSR, the Americans, or both?'

'Prime Minister, freedom of religion is a right, not an intrigue,' said Tom. 'British expatriates and agents can support cross-border re-unification with correspondence, visits, clerical conferences, escapes, breakouts and rescues. The churches can agitate for re-unification. The tension will cause cracks to open.'

'What should we do?'

'Could you propose strategic arms limitation talks as a humanitarian concern? The ICBM silos must be dismantled to prevent a nuclear Armageddon. The Americans and the Soviets could agree to restrict engagement to ground forces having only conventional weapons.'

'Won't the collusion be visible?'

'If they disengage slowly, it will look like a strategic withdrawal and they will be able to save face.'

'Shouldn't we stand with the Americans?'

'Ma'am, since the Cuban missile crisis, the Americans' posture has been less of a stand and more of a swagger,' Tom said. 'Despite the defeat in Vietnam, they are trigger happy and have dreams of an empire. They are in a confrontation in the Middle East and we should not let ourselves be drawn into it. An accident could ignite the Cold War with the Soviets. Britain's role should be to discourage animosity and create stability.'

Thatcher took a small mirror from her handbag and put on lipstick.

'Thank you, Dr Archer,' said the Prime Minister. 'Most interesting. I'll see what can be done.'

'It's Mister, Ma'am,' he said.

Her acceptance of his thesis allowed him to accept inflation of his qualification.

CHAPTER 64
NEW BEGINNINGS

A friend gave Tom a job in his petroleum consultancy in London.

While he had been ill, Ruth had run their household but she had not restored his equality when he resumed work. He confronted her and reclaimed his authority, bit by bit, until after several months they were back on an even footing.

'You can't go buying furniture without asking me,' he said. 'I live here too.'

'You know nothing about buying furniture.'

'You know nothing about buying cars, but I listened to your preferences.'

With reluctance, she conceded him his rights.

Ruth gave birth to a baby girl, Nicola. Tom was entranced and delighted. His life became centred on caring for a tiny person who relished his interaction. He loved being her father. Ruth shut him out from caring for the baby, claiming her expertise had precedence.

She became disaffected with London and a year later gave him an ultimatum.

'I am taking Nicola home to Canada,' she said. 'Would you sign this application for a visa?'

'I want to stay in London for a year or two. My new job is fabulous.'

'This is about my rights as a mother on behalf of our child,' she said. 'I am taking Nicola home whether you like it or not. If you won't sign, I'll apply for custody.'

She would too — she was that disagreeable. He would have to go to Canada with them or abdicate responsibility for his daughter. In a custody battle, her bond with the child would be rated stronger than his because she was the birth mother and had suckled Nicola. They would try to devalue his rights because he had been mentally ill but he was determined not to relinquish his baby to Ruth.

When he told Vicki of his dilemma, she was unsympathetic.

'Why don't you stand up to her? Do you think she would really go back to Canada without you?'

'Yes, she would. Our marriage isn't working for either of us.'

'Why don't you let her go?'

'A kid should have two parents.'

'You could be sacrificing your own happiness.'

He wondered if the sacrifice would be his by continuing with Ruth, or by declining to stay with Vicki. Her gaze was unfathomable. Nicola's happiness was his top priority. He accepted the move, returned to Canada, resumed work with Canoil and settled down in Calgary with his wife and daughter. They had been away five years.

During a truce, Ruth became pregnant again. She would be an 'elderly' mother and worried that the baby could be disabled. Again, her anxieties stressed Tom and he couldn't sleep. He was too stressed to work and admitted himself to a mental clinic. After resting for two weeks he went home.

He kept vigil with Ruth and was thrilled when she gave birth to Michael, a perfect boy. They brought him home from hospital to their newly built house. It was unfinished and Tom spent every spare moment plastering, concreting and painting.

Ruth complained.

'When are you going to carpet the bedroom?'

'When I've painted it,' he replied.

'When will that be?'

'I'm not sure. I must do the plastering first. I'm going as fast as I can.'

Ruth suffered postnatal depression, stressing Tom. He escaped to the paranoid world in which he was the Messiah and took refuge in the mental clinic. He had regular appointments with a psychiatrist, but never revealed this inner life, needing it as a bolt hole to escape from Ruth. After a couple of weeks there, he shouldered his bundle, went home and renovated the house.

A few years later they took their children on a visit to the UK. They went together to Vicki's house, an ancient manor melting into mossy gardens amid timeless Dorset woodlands. The Elizabethan timbering was infilled with red sandstone bricks around casement windows with small leaded panes. The thatched roof overhung snugly, with a weathercock on the chimney.

It bothered Tom that Vicki was still single. He wanted her to experience the joy children could bring. He loved the way his children trusted him and showed affection, with an arm around his leg, or a little hand reaching up for his. Vicki would understand why he could not leave them. He thought it might inspire her to have a child of her own. She glanced at his two tousle-headed children and then at Tom.

'You have done well for yourself,' Vicki said.

'I hope you find a man who wants children,' he said, 'who will give you a push in the right direction.'

Love was in his eyes.

Vicki laughed. 'I assume 'push' is a euphemism?'

He was embarrassed. 'No, I mean—'

'She knows what you mean,' interrupted Ruth. 'We should be going.'

Was it bad luck that he and Vicki had been out of phase with each other? Perhaps fate would bring them together.

At their home the house rang with children's laughter – but rarely Ruth's or his. They put the children's needs first.

Proust had written: *'Happy families are all alike; every unhappy family is unhappy in its own way.'*

His way did not include leaving Ruth.

'Our marriage is not failing,' he thought. *'We are on a life-raft and one day we will reach a pleasant shore.'*

There was stress and anxiety but he had to put up with it. Leaving Ruth with the kids was not an option. No Archer had ever divorced and he couldn't contemplate it. The only hope he had was to be with Vicki when his children had left home.

It was during a later visit that he asked Vicki, 'Have you found a man yet?'

'Several,' she answered, 'but none steady. I'm still looking.'

'Don't look any further. You can have me,' he thought.

But he was not free.

'He'll be a lucky guy when you find him,' he said.

He wondered why she was taking so long to find a man. Vicki had never said she had been waiting for him.

CHAPTER 65
REPRODUCTION

Vicki's solo status made Tom restless and like a bull wildebeest, he galloped frenetically around the herd as it migrated across the savannah. He locked horns with other bulls and tried to entice heifers and unmated cows into his harem.

Her childlessness was difficult for him to accept. It was tragic that she did not have children when she had such wonderful physical and mental attributes. She had not been short of suitors. He hoped that his prevarication had not stolen her child-bearing years. Perhaps she was unmarried and childless by choice.

He suspected that Vicki had taken responsibility for her own sexuality and was demanding equality with men. Her life was not much attuned to having a partner or a child. She was engrossed in her work and happy counselling children. Her memorial would be their gratitude and she did not need to parent a child for her own fulfilment or for posterity. She would have been loath to give up her job to have babies.

He supposed that Vicki liked children but not enough to have one of her own. It was like anyone not wanting to own a dog or a cat. She might not want decades of providing shelter, food and medical support, nor the possibility of lifelong enslavement if the child was disabled. Vicki was too detached, too cerebral, to be a mother. The serenity she had achieved would be torn up. Tom couldn't imagine her changing nappies; she was made for a more contemplative role.

She was reluctant to talk about her plans.

'Do you have a boyfriend yet?' he asked on a visit.

'Have I told you about Gossie?'

His jealousy welled up. This was a long-awaited development.

'No, I'm all ears!'

They had been shopping and when they arrived back at her place, he uncorked a bottle of wine and poured two glasses.

'Cheers!' They toasted each other.

'Now tell me about Gossie. What does he do?'

'He's a condom salesman.'

'Where?' Tom asked with steely control of his face.

'Africa, mainly. He sells them by the tonne to governments and they distribute them.'

'Does he get any opposition?'

'Yes, from Roman Catholics and Muslims.'

'How can they oppose condoms when they would solve the big problems: hunger, poverty and disease?'

'The people want them,' she said. 'Some government workers and agencies help distribute them.'

'Is he the one for you?'

'Maybe. You know how it is.'

'No. I don't. How is it?'

'Oh, Tom, you know. We overlap quite a bit — but we're independent.'

'Does he stay here?'

'Sometimes. He has his own place – he's not here much.'

'Does he want children?'

'His work is everything to him, like a missionary.'

'It's a good position to be in.'

She did not respond to his smirk.

There was something ironic about her being in a relationship with a contraceptive salesman, at a time when she could be raising children of her own. Perhaps Gossie was a smokescreen, to silence well-meaning friends who nagged her to get a man. The days had long gone when having children was a duty, to populate and prevent a human settlement perishing. Demand for cannon fodder had eased too. Even so, a woman without at least one child was incomplete in the eyes of many. Vicki and Gossie could tell critics that they were trying for a baby, when in fact they had their sights set on other things. She was an idealist and had a mission to help people. Tom could imagine them in a truck driving to deliver a shipping container full of condoms to impoverished Africans.

After another year, she said she and Gossie were over.

'What happened?' he asked.

She shrugged. 'I'm not sure.'

Was she hiding something? He couldn't tell. She was always tentative about relationships.

Regretfully he parted from Vicki to return to Canada. Although he had a good job with Canoil and a stylish house in beautiful surroundings, living with Ruth was lonely and stressful. She had no interest in his career and tried to prevent him bonding with his children.

'I'd like the children to help me build a cubby house,' he said.

'They have to tidy their rooms.'

She kept his children away from him.

He and Ruth were closest when they shared a bottle of red on the verandah. She had one glass and he drank the rest, in silence.

CHAPTER 66
RELOCATION REFUSAL

Tom knew that his transfer was a problem. He would be posted as manager to a remote oilfield, a day's drive from the city and Ruth would not want to go there.

'If she won't go, they will give up on me,' he thought. 'I need Ruth to accept that the change would have benefits and should reflect post modern manoeuvring that assumed power relationships existed. What he must do is present it now as metamodern liberation of their family unit, as a move that would free Ruth so that together they could move towards a general manager position. It made new assumptions about the interiority of his conditions of marriage.

Ruth was central to his promotion and she couldn't refuse. The company had scoped their interiority together and offered this transfer as a great opportunity. Conversely, he would need to comply or he couldn't expect further advance. The promotion assumed a balance between Ruth and him, in the service of the company. It made new demands where before there had been none.

The situation had to be considered with the new philosophy of metamodernism, with sincerity and the promotion as an irony. The metamodernism of the promotion lay in its own cause and effect, with the parts having their own agency and sovereignty, rather than the whole having an ontology on its own terms. The whole could not be broken down into parts. An interior view would not be popular and an interior daydream was not possible. Interior views had become unpopular and the tone had become ironic sincerity, replacing the ideals of egalite', liberte' and fraternite' from the French Revolution.

Tom wanted to become a manager, to be free of managerial favouritism and to be able to influence company policy-making. He competed with others and took the management aptitude test with other engineers at his level.

He asked an older engineer the purpose of the test.

'There are no right answers, only normality. It measures your propensity to run with the herd,' he said. 'Canoil wants its managers to correctly anticipate other's views.'

His responses must have been normal enough because they offered him a position as oilfield manager at Moose Jaw, Canada. The position was a first step on the management escalator.

'How would you like to live in Moose Jaw for a couple of years?' he asked Ruth at breakfast.

'I wouldn't.'

He told her about the position.

'This is my big chance to get into management. It will be good for all of us. We need a change from city living.'

'I won't go,' she snapped, setting a stack of hot pancakes in front of him.

'Why not?' he asked.

'Would I be able to work as a school health advisor in Moose Jaw?' she said. 'I think not. Will I live my life to advance your career? No way. What about me? Am I not a person, too?'

A wife of a Canoil manager was expected to promote her man's career. Engineers were paid enough that their partner need not work to maintain their family. He breathed in the steamy caramel aroma and reached for the maple syrup.

'Could you adapt your school health skills to other work?' he asked. 'There might be a job for you at Moose Jaw advising on education, family relationships, welfare or employment.'

She was holding a bowl of whipped cream as if she might throw it over him.

'No. We're not moving.'

Her glib defiance infuriated him.

'You married an engineer,' he said through his teeth. 'I have to go where I'm told.'

She spat back, 'And I am a school health advisor. I won't go where I can't get a job.'

She slammed a bowl of fried bacon on the table. He wrapped some in a pancake.

'Why can't you look after our kids for a couple of years?' He savoured the pancake. 'When you get a job, I'll take leave without pay and alternate with you. You'll like Moose Hills.'

'No,' she said, shaking her head.

She wept silently, leaning over the kitchen sink.

'You don't seem to like me anymore,' she said.

'I do like you,' he said automatically, pretending sincerity.

His appetite had gone. He scraped the rest of his breakfast into the bin and stalked out.

'Ruth won't go,' he told his boss. 'I have to stay with my kids.'

'Don't take no for an answer, Tom!' he said. 'Women nearly always oppose transfers to the sticks because they imagine inadequate schooling, or they cannot imagine living without hot and cold running doctors. My experience is that the man must insist and when she has lived there for a while, she comes to like it. Most women are naturally cautious and need encouragement to do something different. They think they need large shops, good hairdressers and sophisticated entertainments. They can't picture themselves happily dressed in thermals, jeans, lumber-jackets and muddy boots, enjoying country and western music. They would meet great people, learn to love it out there and come back better balanced. She doesn't know what's good for her.'

His views made it worse for Tom. He had hoped to persuade her but she wouldn't compromise. Her inarticulate opposition infuriated him.

His postmodern analysis of forces did not resolve anything. Ruth would not accept the need to balance their situations with each of them in a part, like a hammer handle separate from the hammer head, with the whole equipped for hammering. It was metamodernism, sincere irony that replaced the challenge **of** postmodern single truth, suggesting that knowledge, art and culture are created by people and can be interpreted in many ways.

Ruth said no to his metamodern interpretation.

'I'm not going to spend my life in some backwoods dump,' she said.

'It's not a dump, we wouldn't be there forever and we would be together. Not for more than three years,' he told her.

'I won't go.'

'Halfway between your zero years and the three I want is one and a half years,' he said. 'It is a reasonable compromise.'

'No, I will not go for one and a half years or, for any time at all. I have more keeping me here than you do.'

'It's true, you do have more 'inertia' than me,' he said. 'Inertia is when you keep on doing the same things over and over. We should compromise so there is equal sacrifice on both sides. What is the longest time you would go to Moose Hills for?'

'I told you: I'm not going at all. You can change jobs, but I can't change my friends and this move would lose them forever.'

'They can't be good friends. Let's say you have twice as much inertia opposing your movement as me. Inertia is like the weight on a seesaw. Our leverage is our inertia multiplied by our distances from the balance point of our compromise. In physics it's called balancing moments, when our leverages are equal.'

'Be reasonable,' he said. 'Consider the balancing forces and their duration. Suppose we compromise at one year. Because your inertia is double mine, your leverage would be two units of inertia, acting at one unit length from your compromise point. Giving two times one equals two units of balancing force. Mine would be one unit of inertia, times my compromise of two years less than I want, giving a moment of two units of balancing force also. Our moments would be equal. There would be equal fairness when you come for a year. With a compromise at one year, we would balance. Balancing is fair, isn't it?'

It was an engineer's argument. He wanted Ruth to visualise a seesaw, with her heavy inertia close to the pivot, opposed by his lesser inertia exerting leverage at the opposite end. Of course it made many assumptions. Ruth didn't understand the model and didn't ask for explanation.

Tom had hoped to persuade her. Her inarticulate opposition infuriated him. The two had tried to balance their incentives to transfer. Tom used a physics analogy that represented forces he and Ruth would face as if these would result from their psychological actions. The balance of their reactions would determine their advantages enabling them to decide what to do.

'No. I'm not moving,' she said.

He had to turn down the job offer. His boss reassigned him to less interesting work and Canoil forgot he existed. He was humiliated and his relations with Ruth were strained.

Canoil sidelined him as an oddball and his career stagnated. Then he applied for a job that he could commute to weekly, as Engineering Department Manager at Trapper Lake. The worst part was he only saw his children at weekends. He would not be there as they grew up, not for their triumphs, nor for their disasters. If he left Ruth altogether, it would be worse for the children. The transfer could save his bacon in the career stakes and he accepted it.

In his absence through the week, Ruth took over the children. He tried to have a say at weekends, but she upstaged his interaction with them. He was no longer needed and there was nothing he could do about it. Ruth didn't join him for a drink on the verandah anymore.

People sensed the conflict between them and stayed away.

These days he took a cask of red wine with him to the verandah. It was better company.

CHAPTER 67
EXPERIENCING OFFSPRING

Now she had passed 40, there was less possibility of Vicki having children with Tom and the tension between them eased. When he visited her, she told him how she was involved with her nieces and nephews. She had known them all their lives. Aunt Vicki counselled them on her couch, where they squirmed out their most secret thoughts. She did not tell them what they should be thinking, the way other adults did. She was like Julie Andrews in The *Sound of Music*, except instead of learning to sing, they were learning to think.

She asked her niece, 'When you look at yourself in a mirror, Carla, what do you think?'

'My hair is okay but my nose is ugly.'

'Why do you think that?'

'It is too big.'

'How do you know that?'

'The girls at school tease me.'

'What do you do?'

'I cry.'

'Why?'

'Because my nose is ugly.'

'Why aren't you crying now, then?'

'I don't know.'

'Could it be because your nose is okay?'

Vicki supplied ideas they needed help to realise. When the children's behaviour was inappropriate, she gently chided them to articulate their motives.

'Now, Simon. What are you doing?'

He was about to land a punch.

'I'm giving something to Charles.'

'Is it in your fist?'

'Yes, Aunt.'

'Show me.'

There was nothing in his fist.

'I can't see anything. You must have dropped it. You need to be more careful, don't you, Simon?'

'Yes, Aunt.'

Through her they realised that they could choose the type of person they wanted to be by their behaviour.

One day, Vicki returned from a country ramble with them, her hair in bangs, dressed in a mini-dress, black tights, an army greatcoat and gumboots. The children marched along with her, stride for stride, singing 'I Love to Go a-Wandering'.

Their fingers and mouths were stained with blackberries picked from hedges. They had found a thrush's nest with a clutch of perfectly proportioned, teardrop-shaped eggs, pastel-blue with brown flecks. She had told them the names of birds they saw and the names of trees they climbed.

When they were old enough, the children came up to London by train and stayed overnight in her townhouse. She took them to the theatre in the West End, to opera, to ballet, to museums and to art galleries. Her reward was their awe.

She was invited less often to dinner parties now, because she might lure away hosts' captive men. Her life now was with her brother's children, her counselling work, her gardening and holidays in Europe.

Although Tom didn't see Vicki often, it was with growing intimacy. They had a common interest in teenagers. He wished Vicki could live with him and help him with Nicola and Michael. The teenagers were troubled by their parents' rift. He wanted Vicki to be there to counsel them.

It seemed wrong to him that Vicki lived by herself. When he visited her one autumn, he helped in the orchard, gathering Granny Smiths into her apple barn. After filling several buckets each, Tom hunched over, with his knuckles dragging on the ground, whooping like a chimpanzee in *Planet of the Apes*.

'Hoo! Hoo! Hoohoohoo!'

Vicki replied in the same style, laughing. 'Hoo! Hoo! Hoohoo!'

They danced around each other crazily, leaping up and down. He grabbed her and they collapsed in a heap, with Vicki on top. They hadn't done rough and tumble together since they were undergraduates. He tried to kiss her.

'What about Ruth and the children?' she said.

He remembered his loyalty to his children and clambered to his feet, embarrassed.

They resumed filling buckets.

'These are bruised,' he said. 'They won't store for long. They need to be picked before they're ripe and handled gently.'

'Don't we all,' quipped Vicki, unsmiling. 'You had better go back to your family now.'

He thought she wanted commitment from him, but he could neither give it nor refuse it, only put it off until later. He would not be free to go to Vicki until Nicola and Michael left home. They needed both parents and Tom could not honourably leave them.

Vicki sometimes asked him about his work and his ideas.

'What do you think of Perestroika?' she asked. 'Has the Cold War ended the way you expected?'

'Not really. I proposed that the two sides could be brought together by religion.'

'Perhaps they have been. Gorbachev's new religion is capitalism.'

'It's true. The beliefs of Russians and Americans have converged.'

'Isn't that what you were trying to achieve, that the West and East had a faith in common?'

'Yes; Perestroika has brought a good result.'

'Was your theory used?'

'A little, maybe. They say a problem can't be solved until it has been described. Well, I did describe it. Maybe it helped reunify Germany.'

'Then you succeeded. You should get satisfaction from that.'

'The conspiracy has moved to the Middle East.'

'You and your conspiracies!'

He grieved for his aborted PhD. His contribution had not been recognised. He had only job satisfaction from his hard work clearing scientific underbrush and enabling the tall timber of socialism to be felled. His exposure of a conspiracy and proposal of a strategy to undermine it had been thankless.

He held her then, their bodies pressed together. She felt good to him and he ached to hold her the way he had when they first met, without restraint. He wanted to say to Vicki, 'It won't be long now until we're together', but rather than mislead her, he said nothing.

'What about Nicola and Michael?' she asked.

'They are doing fine.'

It was evasive but he had nothing else to offer. When he said goodbye, he caressed her face and kissed her on the cheeks and forehead.

Vicki pulled away and he left for the airport to go home.

CHAPTER 68
REFLECTING SUCCESS

In 1812, Michael Faraday was a humble bookbinder's apprentice in London. He attended the lectures of Sir Humphrey Davy, Professor of Chemistry, who was President of the Royal Society. In a series of lectures, he reported his team's discoveries. Faraday wrote down what he said and copied his diagrams. He typeset his notes, printed them, bound them into a 300-page book and presented it to Davy. Sir Humphrey was so impressed he appointed him Chemical Assistant at the Royal Institution.

Faraday invented many things: benzene, a chemical; the electric motor; the dynamo; the generator; a battery; electrolysis; electroplating; electro-refining of metals; nano-particles and colloids. He was offered presidency of the Royal Society, but turned it down and declined a knighthood, his reward being the utility of his discoveries.

Tom searched for someone like Sir Humphrey to sponsor his career. He read the profile of Ralph Gooder in Canoil's Annual Report.

Chairman of the Canoil board is Ralph Gooder. He graduated from Ottawa University in Environmental Science and was recruited by Canoil's Toronto oil refinery. He conducted successful experiments, reduced emission of pollutants and became manager of the refinery. He served as Chairman of the Canadian Petroleum Association and is on the government's National Environment Council, most recently as its Chairman.

Tom spent a week of his annual holiday in Toronto, collecting Gooder's public statements from the files of various organisations, from newspapers and from magazines. Gooder was a prolific speaker. Assembling a record of his life's work took up Tom's evenings and weekends for many months. He wrote away for copies of the minutes of provincial and local authority meetings where Gooder had spoken about Canoil projects and his speeches at special occasions, such as graduations, conferences and association dinners.

Back at Trapper Lake, he keyed Gooder's utterances into his computer. He compiled and edited the material, added an index, printed copies of the 300-page book on parchment and had them bound in leather covers embossed with gold lettering.

He went to Calgary and caught Gooder coming out of the boardroom. He was an imposing figure, tall with silver hair and a millionaire's suntan.

'Excuse me, Mr Gooder, Sir; I would like to give you this book.'

Gooder read the title aloud, *The Works of Ralph Gooder, Chairman of Canoil Limited.*

He looked inside, at the contents page. It was a timeline of his statements made in public over his long career.

'This is impressive,' he said, eyeing Tom with suspicion, 'and who might you be?'

'Tom Archer, Sir. I am Manager at Trapper Lake oilfield. I have put this together in my spare time.'

'Why did you do it?'

'I want to have a career like yours, Sir. I want to serve Canoil as a top manager, if my skills are good enough. Can you tell me how I can get advancement within Canoil from my position at Trapper Lake?'

'Hmm. You should ask that question to Don Walker. He's CEO. I'll talk to him.'

A few days later he was back at Trapper Lake when he received a phone call from the CEO.

'Archer, Don Walker here. Ralph has told me about you. How would you like to come over here to Toronto for a couple of years?'

'I would like that very much, Sir. What would I be doing?'

'Special projects. You won't have a set territory, but you will go into the divisions and deal with problems the board has identified – a sort of executive analyst. Your brains could help them.'

'It is a wonderful opportunity.'

'It's also very challenging. If it's too much for you, you will be able to return to Trapper Lake.'

'What if I succeed?'

'You could get a division GM position.'

'I will do my best, Sir.'

'Good morning, Tom.' Walker ended the call.

That evening, he told Ruth, Nicola and Michael about the opportunity.

'Will you get more money?' Ruth asked.

'A lot more. We can get a place near the city centre.'

'What will I do?' Ruth asked.

'You could get a job or you could organise dinner parties for government leaders, top executives and their partners.'

Ruth played her part socially but their lives were as separate as parenting of two young children would allow. He went several times alone to England by himself and visited Vicki. He told Ruth about his visits. Ruth resented him visiting Vicki but he felt no remorse. His view was that a marriage should be open to non-sexual friendships with either gender.

Vicki loved to counsel him. He reclined in a deep armchair as she sat over him, drawing out his truths as if she were an oracle. She had a gift for bringing his worries to the surface. She was an astute listener and he talked with her freely. Her questioning observed his innermost self. It was the first time anyone had taken this much interest in him.

'I don't know why I married Ruth. I must have been stupid.'

'You were in love.'

'Ruth didn't show her true colours until we were married.'

'Perhaps you let women push you around.'

'Hmm. Maybe.'

Vicki was empathetic and he told her about his disintegrating marriage. Later, when she didn't reply to his letters, he assumed she didn't want home-wrecking on her conscience.

CHAPTER 69
MODEL DISMISSAL

The 20 Canoil researchers at the conference in a Calgary hotel thought Tom was a boofhead from head office who had come to evaluate their work and do a purge. They revered his petroleum engineering expertise and feared they would not be able to pull the wool over his eyes.

He had worked at the laboratory and they knew him, either personally or by reputation, as one of their kind who had gone east. He was now loyal to the board in Toronto and had come back as a potential traitor. He could use his 'inside knowledge' to rip apart their projects. That morning he had cancelled one project, made major changes to two more and demanded detailed plans of several others.

They were in the conference room listening to him with faces upturned, despising him.

'It goes with the territory,' he thought.

'We'll break for lunch,' Tom said. 'I have booked tables in the dining room and I have an account at the bar. Order whatever you want.'

During lunch, he surreptitiously put away half a dozen Bacardis and Coke.

After lunch, they went back and the first presenter was Graham Antcliff, a researcher he had known for 15 years.

'My team's work is to come up with a design for miscible flooding,' Graham said, addressing the group. 'I want to convince Tom that our testing programme is useful.'

He held up a beaker containing pale greenish liquid.

'This is kerosene, which can be separated from crude oil at the wellhead by distillation. If we pump it back into the reservoir it will mix with the oil and 'dry-clean' the rock. It can get out most of the remaining oil, up to 70% of the original. We call the process 'miscible flooding'.'

'How do you get the solvent to go to where the crude oil is?' someone asked.

'We use fracturing to open up natural cracks,' he said. 'Injection through a natural crack is like an enema.'

There was laughter.

'The solvent flushes out the oil – like a laxative.'

More laughter.

'Anal retention is the main problem stopping this process being adopted. Although we discovered miscible flooding long ago in the 1960s, we still have piles of oil to get out.'

There were some smiles but no-one laughed aloud. With Tom present, they did not dare align themselves with Antcliff's criticism of Canoil's senior management.

Antcliff showed a couple of slides with his team's results.

'The best place to try this technology is at Bigeria's Panypo oilfield. The reservoir is an ancient reef, full of holes. The solvent can penetrate the rock easily and instead of getting the usual 30% we can flush out nearly all the oil.'

Alarm bells sounded in Tom's head and he interrupted. 'Have you told the Bigerians about this?'

'We have suggested a joint study to their Energy Minister. We haven't heard back yet.'

Tom glared at him. 'We don't know it will work yet, do we?'

Antcliff shook his head mutely.

'You should not have told them about it yet! Miscible flooding is a Canoil proprietary technology. Last year, it was agreed you would stop work on it until we had results from our pilot plant at Tundra. You have misled the Bigerians with pie in the sky. Correspondence outside this company must be cleared with senior management and you have contacted the Bigerian Government without authorisation. Canoil has delicate relations with Bigeria. The country is in the throes of a famine, with the possibility of civil war. We must be careful not to upset them.'

The audience was silent. Antcliff was looking at Tom, his face ashen.

'If you had spent your time sweeping the floor of the laboratory this past year it would have been of more value,' Tom said. 'Your work has been a waste of time because our pilot plant at Tundra has replaced the need for it. Their results are encouraging. I want the rest of the miscible flooding team to design a demonstration plant, to be constructed at Tundra as soon as possible.'

He turned to the lab manager. 'Trevor, I want to talk with you privately. The other presentations can be tomorrow. Good afternoon, gentlemen.'

He stalked out and the air could be cut with a knife. It was an aggressive display. Don had told him to be more relaxed, but today his interaction had been dictatorial and rigid. He had indicated Antcliff would be fired. He regretted that it had ended up this way, for he had known him for years as a friend and he didn't have many friends left. He had been blunt and a bully. Now he craved alcohol and was irritable.

He went straight to the office of Antcliff's boss, Trevor.

'I told him to stop but he took no notice,' Trevor said.

'The two of you have been disloyal. It would be best if you resign and leave this week. Would you inform Antcliff.'

Trevor was shocked. 'Can we appeal?'

'Yes, to the CEO.'

Don would back Tom. If he was to become Division General Manager, his orders had to be obeyed, even if they would hate him.

He went back to his hotel and opened a bottle of beer in his room. His feelings were in turmoil, his responsibilities weighing heavily on him. He longed to discuss them with Vicki, but the UK was seven hours ahead and she would be going to bed. He needed her with him, to be able to call on her common sense and people skills — to unburden himself. His work increasingly had to resolve human and ethical issues that were beyond his expertise. If only she would join him.

CHAPTER 70
HUNGER TREK

When he arrived back in his office in Toronto, Ralph's secretary showed Tom an article cut from *The Independent*.

BIGERIAN OIL: WHO GETS THE BENEFITS?

In northern Bigeria, Syrad Abdul Razak and her husband Abdi Shamarcke Razak are dejectedly surveying their land and home.

'My husband, we cannot stay here any longer,' she says.

Their house is one of five adobe and thatch dwellings in a cluster two kilometres above the rock formation of the Panypo oil reservoir. Each house has a hectare of bare earth. Inside is one room, with a mud fireplace, mud seats and a sleeping area. A month ago, the Razaks ate the last of their poultry, goats and corn. There is no food left and they have no seed to plant. For the past three days they have eaten flowers, berries and grass from the dry creek bed.

'Yes, it is time to go to the south,' replies Abdi. 'I have prayed and I believe we are meant to go. We will be able to live there. Allah is great.'

Hotu people have lived in the Panypo area for generations. Twenty years earlier, the national government, then Hotu, had granted to Canoil a licence to explore for and produce oil. They discovered it beneath the Razak's home.

The oil is in tiny holes in the rock, where it has reposed since it formed from vegetation in swamps when dinosaurs walked the earth. It squeezes into the well with a donkey pump nodding as it lifts it to the surface and out into a pipeline that passes by the Razak's house. The oil is gathered into a closed tank. Gas separates at the top and oil is pumped out from the layer beneath. Water drains from the bottom and is pumped back into the reservoir.

Syrad gathers her four small children together. She and her husband each carry a baby. Over their other shoulders are bundles containing cooking utensils and things they have been unable to sell for food. Stepping over the pipelines, they walk to the local village, Panypo. They hope there may be a handout of food, as there was several weeks ago.

Several international aid organisations have tents at Panypo. A truck bringing food was hijacked by a pro-Hotu militia, who took it to the rebel camp across the border in Zanabwe and exchanged it for guns and ammunition. Since then no food has been brought for the refugees.

As the Razak family nears the village, fleeing families flood on to the footpath and block it. People say the militia is burning houses and killing people. The Razaks detour around the village and begin to walk alongside the main road, going south to the oil port near Akar, the capital.

Gas and oil are flowing in pipelines beside the road.

The youngest child is weak with diarrhoea and unable to keep up. The Razak family is in trouble. They stop and shelter in a dry water culvert. They exchange all their possessions for a few handfuls of rice. The child dies in the night. They have no digging tool and without loose rocks to cover the body, they leave it for the jackals.

In the morning, a Fetani militia of eight men rides up on motorbikes. They brandish machine guns, round up the walkers and yell at them in Fetani to hand over their valuables, but the Razaks have none. The Fetanis become angry and start shooting the men. They make Abdi kneel. Syrad pleads and screams. They shoot Abdi in the back with machine guns. The children cling to her, sobbing silently. The babies sense their mother's distress but are too weak to cry. The soldiers shoot the remaining men. Then they roar off.

The gas pipeline has many illegal offtakes and the gas that remains is distributed to industries in Akar, the capital. Oil flows steadily in the other pipeline through a series of pumping stations to the oil port, Kosoto. By the time Syrad and the children have reached a quarter of the distance, the oil has run into one of several large storage tanks on the shore beside a tanker loading jetty guarded by the army.

All fat on Syrad's body has gone and hunger is consuming her muscles. Physically exhausted and her mind numb, Syrad lowers her almost dead baby to the ground and leaves it. She continues walking, forlornly. The remaining child tries to keep up. They pass families that have given up and sit under bushes, waiting to die.

Oil from the holding tank is pumped into an oil tanker. When it is full, tugs push it out into the seaway to sail for Canada on the other side of the world. The market value of the cargo of two million barrels, at US$40 per barrel is sufficient to buy enough rice, at $500 per tonne, to meet the dietary energy requirements of all 50 million Bigerians for a month. The oil can't be eaten but one tanker per month can buy rice to feed everyone. Every day they fill several tankers.

Syrad's milk has dried up and the second baby dies of starvation. She is too weak to dig and places the tiny body under a tree where the circling vultures might not see it but she knows that hyenas will find it. She walks slowly, holding the last of her four children by the hand. Swarms of flies cluster on the child's face but he knows instinctively not to complain and keeps up.

After crossing the Atlantic Ocean, the oil tanker slows down in the St Lawrence Seaway and slides through locks up to Montreal, where it discharges into tankage and is piped to the Sarnia oil refinery 500 kms away, near Toronto. Within a few days, they have refined it to gasoline for delivery to commuters' cars at gas stations. Many of them refill their cars weekly, paying by credit card. None of the money will reach the starving Hotus, nor the remainder of the Razak family.

When a truck stops for them, Syrad and the child stare, hollow-eyed. An aid worker helps them climb on. They take them to a refuge where they eat soup made from maize. They are taken in a truck to a camp a day's journey to the south.

Most of the commuters' fuel is consumed when their cars' engines idle in lines of traffic on the expressway going to and from work. Few of them carry passengers. They crawl forward competing with crowded city public buses. The oil from Bigeria fuels unwanted congestion and privileged wasteful lifestyles.

Canoil's Chairman, Ralph Gooder, has said: 'Our Canadian lifestyle depends on oil and an important part is supplied from Bigeria. We are bound by our contract to pay for the oil to the elected government. It would be illegal under Bigerian law to direct the money to the Hotu people. It is up to their political system to distribute the money. We employ local people in our operations in Bigeria and support local communities.'

Syrad and her remaining child wait in a refugee camp for conditions at home in Panypo to improve. A national election is scheduled in a year's time. Hotus could gain power and Syrad is hopeful that some of the oil money would flow back to the north of the country. Then they would be able to return to their homeland. It is the Hotus' turn to eat next.

Greg Castles for The Independent in Akar

The cutting had a note written at the top: '*Tom, this is a disgrace. Check for a fairer way of paying them. Talk to 'Shaver' Ronson in Ottawa. Ralph.*'

CHAPTER 71
DEMAND

Later that morning, Ralph Gooder called him into his office.

'Tom, nice job in Calgary,' he said with a smile. 'That Antcliff was a menace. I want you to go to Edmonton as GM of Exploration and Production. Think you can handle it?'

'Yes, no worries. Thank you, Sir.'

Tom was thrilled. He had hit the big time.

'I want you to help Don to sort out the situation with Bigeria. It could blow up in our faces.'

Ralph told him some personal interests of Canoil's top managers in Edmonton.

'Thank you. I look forward to working with them.'

'Good morning, Tom.'

He phoned Ruth and told her the news.

'I don't want to go to Edmonton. I want to go home to Calgary,' she said. 'I am losing touch with my family and friends.'

'It may not be for long. If I make the grade, the next step could be to CEO and we would live in Calgary.'

'About time too.'

Tom realised that nothing he did would ever please Ruth.

He phoned Manfred Brash, his friend at uni two decades earlier. He had recently complained to Tom that his job with an oil company in London was dull.

'Manfred, how would you like some excitement? How would you like to come to Edmonton as assistant to Canoil's GM Exploration and Production – me?'

Manfred congratulated him on his appointment.

'What kind of excitement?' he asked.

'Disputes with suppliers overseas; negotiations with governments worldwide; persuading our government to let us make more money. There's heaps to do.'

'I'll let you know,' he said.

Tom's priority task was to get up to speed on the Bigerian situation. Chairman Gooder seemed to want to bypass CEO Walker. Tom had to be careful not to be caught in the crossfire.

'What's happening?' he asked their manager at Kosoto on the phone.

'The government has banned the media from reporting famines,' he told him. 'They are opposing the Hotus, who are rebelling because of the famine, calling themselves the People's Party, led by Abdul Misoto. He trained with Al Qaida and is being supplied with food and munitions from Zanabwe. If he stops export of oil, the Fetani Government will be without funds and in trouble. The supply chain is fragile. It would be easy for the rebels to blow up the pipeline and the army is guarding it. They are also defending the port. Gunboats escort the tankers in and out. Pro-government militias are terrorising Hotu civilians to punish the rebels.'

Tom read a copy of the telex Don had received from the rebel leader.

To Donald Walker, CEO of Canoil,

I, Abdul Misoto, leader of the Hotus, demand that the government of Prime Minister Okonjo provide food relief to my people who are suffering famine. Unless food is provided, I will stop the production of oil from my people's land. Canoil must pay 50% of the money for oil produced from Hotu lands to our Bigerian People's Party (BPP), to be distributed to the Hotu people. Payment for oil shipped in July must be made to the BPP, Account No. 374844192 at the Commonwealth Bank in Zanabwe, by 31st August of this year.

Abdul Misoto
President
Bigerian People's Party

'This Misoto sounds dangerous,' Tom told the CEO. 'What are the Hotus like?'

'HOTU stands for Home Of The Underdogs,' said Walker. 'If a dog is repressed for too long, it will bite.'

'Can we condone extortion?' asked Tom.

'We should be even-handed,' Walker told him. 'If we hand over 50%, that is a bob each way on Okonjo to get back, or a Misoto coup.'

'I would prefer to sit on the fence,' Tom thought.

'Shouldn't Canoil back the winner?' he said.

'The Hotu demand for 50% is reasonable,' said Don. 'If they oust Okonjo, they will respect us.'

'An illegal demand is not reasonable,' Tom thought. *'Don will be on a collision course with the board.'*

'The board will want to know how to avoid a civil war,' Don said. 'But Okonjo has it coming and we should give it a push in the right direction.'

Don went off to a meeting of the board.

Tom phoned Vicki and told her of Misoto's demand.

'It's hard to know the right thing to do,' he said.

'I will discuss it with my group,' she said.

'Who are they?'

'We call ourselves Friends of Overseas Development, or FOOD.'

'What do you do?'

'We pressure international companies to act responsibly, such as to prevent famines. We have been trying to find out what Canoil is doing about the famine in Bigeria, apart from filling its tankers. What *are* you doing, for fuck's sake?'

She hadn't attacked Canoil before and he became defensive.

'Vicki, whatever we do has to be approved by Ottawa, because they licence us to import Bigerian oil,' he said. 'They send aid to famine victims but they see their responsibility as supplying Canadian motorists at the lowest possible price.'

'How humanitarian is that?'

'It's not, but that's the way our democracy works. Most Canadians neither know nor care about the famine in Bigeria.'

'That doesn't make it right to do nothing,' she said and ended the call.

Oil geopolitics were determined by the ambitions of the main players, especially the USA. Bigeria's oil was sold to the oil majors and to Canoil, at the world price for crude, as dictated by the US Department of Energy.

Is it the USA's ambition to dominate the world, or more than that? 'Tom thought. He was curious whether the USA would fill the vacuum after the Soviet collapse or whether a superpower conspiracy continued in the Middle East.

He could have met George H Bush out jogging when he was in Barcelona during the Olympic Games. Bush had his minders with him and was puffing at a pedestrian crossing.

'Are you running for office?' Tom asked him.

Bush smiled. 'Do you live here?'

'No. I live in Canada.'

'What is your work?'

'Petroleum engineer.'

'From England?'

'Yes, actually.'

'Hmm. What do you think the price of oil should be?' Bush asked him.

'That's less a matter of engineering and more a matter of the USA's ambitions.'

'We are creating a stable world,' said the President. 'The price has to stay low.'

The year before, the oil price had reached a new peak and the USA had launched Operation Desert Storm and driven Iraqi troops from Kuwait almost back to Baghdad. Many Americans had wanted them to go further, but when the oil price collapsed they had withdrawn.

'Your military has destabilised the Middle East,' said Tom. 'The Ruskies are hurting.'

'Good,' said Bush. 'They are too big for their boots. The USSR is the largest oil exporter after Saudi Arabia, we are holding down their income and they are about to disintegrate. Oil is a buyers' market and OPEC has to take the price we offer. The Arabs don't have enough clout to make us pay any more.'

'The US has taken on an Olympian role.'

'We are on top of the geopolitical games.'

'You have won the faked Cold War with Russia.'

'That is a cynical view, young man. The Cold War was real and America won because we were more prepared to fight. You British believe in reasoning, but history shows that might is right and that is what we Americans believe in. Brainpower alone is not enough to win — it takes passion and preparedness to use arms. When we have to, America fights. Now I must go to present some medals. Good morning.'

Bush strode away, flanked by his minders.

America won the faked Cold War because their philosophy of self-interest was taken up by the other side, 'he thought.

Tom's reverie ended and he turned back to the other threat to Canada's supply of oil, from Bigeria.

CHAPTER 72
DIVERSION

Next morning, Tom was in his office emptying his in-tray, for his move to Edmonton, when Ralph's secretary handed him a news report cut from the *Toronto Star*. He glanced at it, keeping her waiting.

BIGERIAN REBELS THREATEN CANOIL PRODUCTION

Rebel leader, Abdul Misoto, is demanding Canoil send to the Hotu people 50% of its payments for Bigerian oil. He wants the money to relieve a famine that is devastating the Hotus' homelands. Last year, 473 million barrels, 26% of Canoil's production, worth USD33 billion, was sourced from Bigeria. Government troops are protecting the pipeline and loading jetties but Misoto is threatening to stop the oil if his demand is not met.

Canoil CEO, Donald Walker, said, 'We buy oil under a contract between Canoil and the elected government of Bigeria. The contract includes a clause covering failure to make correct payment. If we pay the rebels, the Bigerian Government could stop supplying us. We are discussing alternatives with the Canadian Government.'
Matthew Eldridge, Business News

Tom asked her, 'Did Ralph say anything about this?'
'No. He sent a copy to Don with a note: 'There are no alternatives: pay as usual.'
'This is Don's show,' Tom thought. *'Maybe Ralph is pissed with him and is fielding me at backstop.'*

A week later in Edmonton, Manfred walked into Tom's office.

'Great to have you aboard, Manfred,' he said, shaking his hand.

'It's good to be here.'

They had lunch together. He filled him in on the situation in Bigeria.

'How did it get into the *Toronto Star*?' Manfred asked.

'It's a good story: 'Corrupt government lets its people starve'.'

'Did Don leak Misoto's demand?'

'I don't know who else would,' Tom said. 'Don wants to give Misoto half.'

'Would he go against Ottawa?'

'No,' Tom said. 'The PM would have one ball and Ralph the other.'

'Would they know where the leak came from?'

'The article implies Canoil is inhumane and self-serving,' said Tom. 'If Ralph suspected Don had leaked it, he would have some explaining.'

'Walker is in the hot seat. He could get burned and you could be pulled into the fire.'

Later that week, Walker telephoned him.

'I have just been in a board meeting. I told them my view of the situation in Bigeria. They don't see it my way.'

'How do they see it?'

'They said the board's allegiance is to Canadian shareholders and to customers, to keep the oil flowing,' Walker said. 'They want to continue paying the elected government, even if Okonjo sets himself up as dictator.'

'What do you think should happen?'

'I asked the board to agree to a compromise of 25% of the money to go to Misoto, but the vote went against me,' Don said.

'How did they leave it?'

'I'm fucked. Gooder told me afterwards, 'If you don't support Okonjo 100%, we will get someone else who will.' He could mean you, Tom. Would you do it?'

'Don could be warning me not to do the board's dirty work,' Tom thought. *'As CEO, he has to face the media and take the blame for the agony of the thousands of starving and dying Bigerians.'*

'I'm not sure,' he said.

'I am trying to get the board to behave responsibly,' Don said. 'No-one else is.'

'Don is fishing for me to declare my colours,' he thought. *'He may see me as a threat but I can't be loyal to him when he is out on a limb. I have to keep my options open.'*

'I can't see the board acting beyond self-interest. Maybe you will get what you want next time.'

'Fat chance,' the CEO said. 'Where do you think our Bigerian oil money ends up?'

'Not with the starving people, that's for sure.'

'A half goes into the Swiss bank accounts of Okonjo and his genocidal cabal.'

'You're kidding! How do they get away with it?'

'We pay the money directly into their accounts.'

'Holy shit.'

'It's confidential.'

'Can we stop it?'

'Damn right we can. We can divert the money from Switzerland to Akar.'

'Will it make any difference?'

'If I leak to the *Akar Daily* that Bigeria's national oil income is being rorted, Okonjo would have to distribute it.'

'Okonjo could shoot the messenger,' said Walker. 'We need to distance ourselves from him. We have to stop sending the money to Switzerland.'

'Do we have the account numbers?' asked Tom.

'Gooder refused to give them to me.'

'He might give them to me,' said Tom. 'I will say Ottawa wants to know details of who we are paying.'

Ralph gave Tom names and Swiss account numbers of the Bigerian ministers.

'These are Okonjo's cronies – senior ministers. At present, 50% goes into the government account in Akar and this mob takes the other 50% between them: Okonjo gets 20% and the other five get 6% each.'

'This information is dynamite,' Ralph said. 'It could start a civil war and cut off our oil supply. Be careful who you give it to.'

Tom phoned Vicki. 'This is confidential. Canoil pays half the Bigerian oil income into the private Swiss bank accounts of its government ministers.'

'My disclosure does not break confidence,' Tom thought. *'Without details it is only rumour.'*

'I suspected as much,' she replied. 'The thing is, how are you going to stop it?'

'Don is trying to get the money sent to the Hotus. He is going to leak to the Bigerian press the names of the ministers who get the money.'

'About bloody time,' she said.

CHAPTER 73
REJECTION

Tom was sorry to be firing him. He had known Graham since they joined Canoil together. His kids were still at university and he had a mortgage. He would find it difficult to get another job.

He dialled his number at the laboratory.

'Is that Graham Antcliff?'

'Yes.'

'Good morning, Graham. Tom Archer here. I expect Trevor has told you?'

'Yes,' he said. 'I have to resign – by Friday? You can't do that to me!'

'Graham, I have no choice. You have defied company policy.'

'Trevor was okay with it.'

'He said he told you several times to stop.'

'We would have lost good results.'

'You have passed sensitive company information to the Bigerians, in flagrant disregard of management policy.'

'We were teeing up a field trial. The Bigerians were keen.'

'Of course they were, but for their own benefit, not for Canoil's.'

'For needy people. If miscible flooding could produce more oil, they would get more money to relieve the famine!'

'It is a worthy ethic, but it wouldn't work and is morally wrong. It is not your job to take these matters into your own hands.'

'Am I being hypocritical?' Tom asked himself. *'Helping those starving people is ethically humane. Compassion is not limited by corporate boundaries. Should I be punishing a man for acting on his conscience to help deserving people?'*

'Don Walker and the board decide what we do. Not you; not me.'

'The board doesn't give a shit about Africans. All they care about is making profits for greedy shareholders and their own obscenely large salaries.'

Antcliff was right. Tom knew what to say next because he had said it before to other disgruntled staff.

'You do not have authority to give shareholders' money away. You can send the rebels as much of your severance pay as you want.'

'You nasty bastard. It will be a pleasure to stop working for you.'

'I'm sorry you feel like that, Graham. We used to see things the same way. Is there anything else we need to talk about?'

'You have changed. You used to have a heart. All you care about now is yourself.'

Was he doing bad things as a Canoil leader? People who wanted Canoil to bend with moral winds probably didn't have the full picture. There were structures in place to balance the different beliefs and competing interests. The system had always worked.

'Goodbye, Graham.'

'Go to hell.'

He would have Canoil help the famine victims, if possible. He wanted Canoil to be a good world citizen. He wanted Vicki to be proud of what he was doing. If he could get the CEO position, he would be able to do more good.

Manfred drove Tom to Edmonton airport for a flight to Ottawa to meet with Ronson. He needed a drink but he had to keep his wits about him to deal with the minister. He worried whether he would be able to persuade him to help the Hotus. These days his head was filled with anxieties, queueing up for his attention. Hardly anything was the way he wanted it. His choices were a crock of shit.

Their flight was delayed and they arrived late. Fortunately, Ronson was able to reschedule.

'There is nothing we can do,' he said. 'The famine is the Bigerians' problem. Canoil's payments are 40% of their GDP. The lion's share is being grabbed by Okonjo and his mates.'

'They are stealing food from the mouths of their own starving people.'

'We are sending food aid,' Ronson said.

'It is not getting there. The Fetanis are taking it. Okonjo is genociding the Hotus. There won't be enough of them left alive to win the next election. A coup is the only way Misoto can get fair treatment for the Hotus.'

'We can't go against Okonjo. We have to support his tribe as they slug it out with the Hotus. I sympathise with Don's point of view, but there is nothing we can do. He could take it up with the Foreign Office — but they won't bend.'

When Tom got back, he reported to Gooder.

'The Feds don't want to upset Okonjo,' he said.

'Quite right too,' the Chairman said. 'Try to talk some sense into Don.'

'Don is on a collision course with Ronson,' Tom thought.

He tried to reason with Walker, but the CEO was despondent. 'Canoil's money is being misappropriated and we are condoning it. I am haunted by the spectre of the Razak family's tragedy and the thousands of starving people. The board is making me compromise my humanitarian ideals.'

'Our Government is too.'

'Those fuckwits pretend the Canadian public doesn't care that Bigerians are starving. That's because they don't know what's going on. If they did they would care and we have a responsibility to act on their behalf.'

'The welfare of the Bigerian people is not the board's responsibility, Don,' Tom said.

'It is,' Walker said. His moral tone had become strident. 'My salary is not enough to compensate me for standing back while people die. I have to try and change the board's mind.'

Tom sympathised with him but he would not go against the board himself. He tried to forget the awfulness by burying himself in his work. Worrying about it made him hungry. These days he was always hungry. He sent out for some doughnuts. They were the English type, greasy balls of flour with jam inside and coated with sugar, the way he liked them.

'How are you?' Vicki asked on his next visit.

'Not too bad. I am drinking more though.'

'Is your anxiety building like it did during your PhD, when you became mentally ill?'

'I'm not going there again.'

'What are you doing about it?'

'I am trying to hold down my drinking.'

'Could your anxiety pop out somewhere else, as another bad habit?'

'Like what?'

'Is our relationship healthy, Tom?'

'Fucking hell, she is going to finish with me!' he thought.

'It is good for me,' he said. 'I love you. You make me happy.'

'You have a dependency problem caused by anxiety from childhood,' said Vicki. 'There is a condition called love addiction. You have to get over me, before it pulls you down.'

'How?'

'You need to think about others more.'

'How can I do that?'

'You need closure of your preoccupation with me. You need to move on.'

'How?'

'I know a psychotherapist in Calgary who could help you. I don't want a relationship with you until you are having effective treatment.'

'I am preoccupied with her because I need to close my short, which I will be able to do when I am free of responsibility for my family,' he thought.

'I will try to reduce my anxiety,' he said, 'but I want to be with you. What's wrong with that?'

'We are not getting anywhere,' Vicki said.

'It won't be for much longer. As soon as the kids are off my hands, I'll leave Ruth. I promise.'

She held his gaze as if remembering his earlier promises, then turned away.

CHAPTER 74
STATUS QUO

When Misoto's rebel army seized control in the north, Okonjo ordered his air force to put down the rebellion and they readied bombers at Akar airfield. An army division loyal to the Hotus surrounded the airfield, blocked the runways to stop the planes taking off and began shelling Okonjo's headquarters. He and his supporters fled to neighbouring Abyssia. Misoto took over in Akar, replacing the Fetani leaders with his own people and commenced sending relief to districts suffering famine.

Canoil's manager in Akar reported that army guards at the Panypo Oilfield fled from the rebels' attack. Ottawa arranged for an Air Canada 707 to divert en route from Cape Town to London, to evacuate all Canoil personnel from Bigeria.

The new government told Canoil to resume loading oil tankers, but a US government official in Washington phoned Walker and ordered: 'Refuse to load oil until Bigeria has a democratically elected government.'

The rebels lacked experience to organise an election and without export of oil, their money dried up.

'Without oil money, the rebels cannot succeed,' Walker said in a media conference. 'Misoto's government will crumble.'

Gasoline prices in Canada rose a little. Misoto's unpaid soldiers and followers became hungry and quit after 12 months. Dive bombers from a US carrier in the bay strafed and destroyed Misoto's air force and military tanks. There was no resistance when a dozen helicopter gunships filled with Okonjo's marines flew in from Abyssia and landed on the palace lawn.

Misoto was captured and killed; his followers dispersed. Okonjo moved back into the palace. He ordered repair of the oil wells at Panypo. Within a few days oil started flowing into tankers. Money flowed into the Bigerian treasury and into ministers' bank accounts. The famine continued.

Thwarted, Walker was disconsolate. Despite his humanitarian ideals, neither his board nor the Canadian Government had done anything to help the Hotus or oppose Okonjo. Hundreds of thousands of Hotus had died from starvation.

'I have lost faith in my employer and my country,' the CEO said.

'You did what you could,' Tom said. 'You couldn't have done more.'

CHAPTER 75
DRUNK

It was Friday and Tom lay awake at dawn with his mind on his next drink. Tonight he would get drunk and forget. He recalled his first drink when he was a teenager and yearned for the home-made blackberry wine he had made. It had seduced him and now he consumed Shiraz wine by the cask.

He still had a headache from last night's cask. With his head spinning, he had gone to bed early. He had become nauseous and thrown up in the ensuite sink. He remembered sitting on the toilet, at 2.15 am by his watch, in a cold sweat, retching and dozing off. Ruth awoke and put in her earplugs.

They still shared a bedroom but that was all.

He wanted to be with Vicki. His marriage was failing and he worried about Nicola and Michael. He couldn't remember when he had last had a conversation of more than a sentence or two with either of them.

After breakfast, he took Nicola to school on his way to work in Edmonton. He drove at the optimal speed for fuel efficiency, indicated by an instrument on the dashboard. He liked to be efficient: it was economical and conserved resources.

He asked Nicola about her school's play, wanting to have a conversation, but her responses were monosyllabic. They came off at Nicola's school 28.6 kilometres along the King Arthur Trail. He rejoined the traffic and crawled along Jasper Avenue into the city centre. At 102 Ave and 104 Street, he parked in the Canoil lot and took the lift up to his office, arriving 3 minutes and 35 seconds late. They knew he would still be there when they went home. He worked his way steadily through his in-tray, his brain on automatic, imagining what he would drink at lunchtime.

At mid-morning, desperate for a drink, he asked around if there was a farewell party or retirement lunch he could go to. A service company representative phoned and asked him to eat in a nearby restaurant. He left the office at 12.55 pm. He ordered a bottle of wine: his companion sipped a glass while Tom skolled the rest and another bottle too. He got back to the office exactly at 2.05 pm, five minutes late for his next meeting.

Afterwards, he slouched at his desk, micro-sleeping. A start jerked him upright. He glanced around to see if anyone was watching through the glass partition and to disguise his sudden movement, concealed it as opening a desk drawer.

At about 4.00 pm, his thoughts strayed to buying wine to drink at home. He imagined with relish the buzz he would get from gulping glasses of red. At about 5.05 pm, an hour before he planned to leave, he got a call from reception that Nicola was waiting for him in the foyer. She must have stayed late at school for something. He could leave work on time for a change. He collected her and together they took the lift down to his car.

'What have you been doing today, sweetie?'

'Play rehearsal.'

'How did you get on?'

She shrugged her shoulders. 'All right.'

'Are you enjoying being in the play?'

'Sometimes,' she said. 'Do you enjoy your job?'

He hadn't been asked that recently.

'Sometimes it's okay.'

He didn't want her to think he was unhappy. He imagined children would not want to grow up if their adults were unhappy. He wanted to say something positive to show that he was pleased with her, but he couldn't find words to begin.

She said chirpily, 'Do you want me to tell you about the American Civil War? We are doing it in history.'

'Yes. I would like that.'

She spoke with enthusiasm but he soon lost track. He was thinking about which wine to buy. His choice was between Tunley Red Claret and Vinolli Cabernet Shiraz. The cost per unit of alcohol for Tunley's was lower and therefore more attractive than Vinolli. It was lower in quality and he would drink less of it, which would be good. Wine was no longer an indulgence. It was shit.

He drove into a liquor store. Leaving Nicola in the car, he bought two four-litre casks of Tunley Red Claret. He had the check-out clerk put them in brown paper bags: drunks bought wine casks, whereas general managers were supposed to buy cases of champagne.

'Tell me more about the Civil War, please.'

'You don't listen. All you care about is drinking wine.'

Her innocence aggravated the shame of his drinking habit.

Her sharpness kept him from his usual micro-sleeping at the wheel. That morning, Ruth had prodded him awake and rolled him on to his side to reduce his snoring. He wasn't getting enough random-eye-movement sleep and had fallen asleep at the wheel several times earlier in the week. He woke up when his wheels jolted along the verge. It was only a matter of time until he caused a road accident. He had to drink less.

When they got home, he put his briefcase in the study and took the casks into the walk-in pantry. He polished a lead crystal wine goblet with a tea towel, filled it from the Tunley's cask and took a swig. Rinsing it around his mouth, he squirted the wine through gaps between his teeth onto his tongue. He gargled it as if it was mouthwash, feeling it splash over his soft palate. The alcohol started numbness at the nape of his neck and a familiar floating feeling low down at the back of his head in the cerebellum, where his sense of balance resided. He threw back three glasses in quick succession, a regular bottleful and the loss of feeling spread up into the occipital lobe. When he got up to refill his glass, he staggered and held on to the furniture.

He continued to refill his glass steadily from the cask and the alcohol anaesthetised his anxiety. He refilled his glass for the umpteenth time. It was taking more and more wine to forget the stress of work and relax.

Michael came in from football practice.

'Hi, Dad. Getting drunk, I see,' he said, as if commenting on the weather.

Tom winced. He was failing as a role model.

'Did you have a good day?'

'Are we still going to Zapulco?' Michael asked hopefully.

It was mid-semester, when he usually took them to Mexico for a week.

'Do you want to go?'

'Yes. Can Connie and Jamie come?'

'Did they ask their parents?'

'Yup. They're allowed.'

'Then, if your mother still wants to, we'll go.'

Tom felt hungry. His dinner was in the oven and Ruth was watching television. He ate it alone in the kitchen.

'Thanks for dinner, Ruth. Are you okay to go to Zapulco tomorrow?'

She thought for a full minute before replying, as if she was playing a chess move.

'Is Michael coming?'

'Yes, with two friends.'

'What time?'

'The usual: 7 am.'

'Is Nicola coming?'

'I'm not sure. I did say I was going to take her horse trekking on Sunday.'

'We can't leave her here by herself. Some of her friends are wild.'

'She has to come with us then. She can go horse riding later.'

'I'll tell her: you'd put her back up.'

Ruth's spin would be that he had demanded she go.

'What would I do without you?' he muttered, but she didn't hear. Nicola's wildness was her way of escaping from their unhappy home. He wished he could escape from it, too. So far it had taken a whole cask, or about 20 goblets, to make it tolerable.

Every Friday he drank himself stupid and thought about Vicki on the other side of the world. She had had maybe a dozen blokes by now. Richard had said she had a man living with her but it didn't last. Recently her boyfriends had become fewer. He was sad not to be with her.

He ate dinner, went back to the Tunley's and continued writing the report that Nicola had interrupted earlier. He started on the second cask. His eyes wouldn't focus and his stylish longhand had changed to untidy squiggles and crossings-out. The Tunley's had taken over his frontal and parietal lobes.

He went into the lounge for the TV news but the screen was so blurred and the sound so distant that he knew his De Broca's was shutting down.

'I am sick of politics,' Ruth said. 'I am not interested that today the Prime Minister met with the President of France.'

She looked at him as if he should say something but he could not remember what she had just said.

'Quite right,' he said, trying not to slur his words.

Ruth turned back to the news.

'What do you think about Camp David?' she said. 'George Bush and Boris Yeltsin have declared the Cold War is over!'

'It never started. It was a conspiracy.'

'They didn't say it was a conspiracy.'

'They wouldn't. It has shifted to the Middle East.'

'Does it bother you that the solution doesn't have your name on it, like Kissinger's?' Ruth asked.

She was sniping as usual.

'No. It is usual for university research to stay in the background.'

'It will be forgotten now,' she said, gloating.

She had always been dismissive of his research, as had others too. He remembered the jaundiced attitudes of Professor Shapner and his colleagues. The wine was helping him forget. He had a splitting headache and lay down in the bedroom.

Next morning, the six of them flew to Zapulco. Their apartment was by the beach and idyllic. The teenagers met others and circulated in party mode around the holiday homes of other Canadians, coming back for food, or for sleep.

While the kids were out, Ruth and Tom didn't talk to each other. He was spending more and more time working alone. He drank a lot, or puffed spliffs that he rolled from a brick of 'Acapulco Gold' bought in the village.

One afternoon they all went to the beach. He was unfit and overweight, wobbling across the seafront road in an alcoholic haze. The afternoon sea breeze was lifting dumpers. Body surfers were out in force.

'Dad, you are stoned,' said Nicola. 'You'll drown yourself.'

'I go better when I am slewed.'

The water was cold and took his breath away. He and Michael waded out, leaving Ruth and Nicola in knee-deep water near the beach. He tried to collect his senses. They dove under breaker after breaker.

Together he and Michael threshed down the face of a wave until it picked them up. Michael was in the corner of his eye as the surge carried them towards the beach. The water streamed out in a rip, taking him with it. He tried to swim back but was carried out beyond the breakers and he became exhausted. He floundered, panicked and coughed. Then Michael arrived and held his head up.

'Okay, Dad, take it easy. Get your breath. That's it.'

Michael brought him back to the beach, with Tom kicking a little to help. He sat on the sand, shattered and foolish. An adolescent had saved his drunken father.

'Thank you, son, you were wonderful,' he gasped.

Ruth showed no sympathy. 'Michael could have drowned. You had better stay out of the water when you are drunk.'

He was a liability now.

He realised his use of alcohol was irresponsible. When he was drunk, he felt sorry for himself and kept going until he was paralytic. It was taking more and more to get him drunk. If he went on like this, it could kill him.

He went to Europe regularly for Canoil. Sometimes he had time to visit Vicki. He hid his drinking from her and stayed sober, hiding that he was irritable. Vicki disapproved of drunkenness. If he was going to get back with her, he would have to bring his drinking under control.

When he had to leave, he hugged her close with his hands around her back and waist, pulling her up against him. He felt the softness of her hair and the shape of her ears. It was difficult to stop. He tried to kiss her but she pushed him away.

'What about Ruth?' she asked.

'The same.'

He couldn't expect Vicki to be sympathetic.

'It won't be long now,' he said.

CHAPTER 76
COMMITMENT

It was late one Saturday afternoon when his phone rang.

'Hello?'

'Tom, it's Vicki.'

It was unusual for her to call him.

'Are you okay?' he asked.

'Fine,' she said. 'There was something about Canoil on the BBC News — another famine in Bigeria, in the north. They said Canoil money is going to the government and they are not passing it on to people who live where the oil comes from. Is that true?'

'We can't control what they do with the money.'

'Those fuckers are totally corrupt. You have to make them feed the starving people.'

'We are in a legal contract with an elected government. There is nothing we can do.'

'The fucking government should be bombed. They would steal from their own mothers. For fuck's sake, find a way of getting help to those famine victims.'

'I have no authority to divert money.'

'What's your position in the company?'

'GM Exploration and Production.'

'Well there can't be many prats above you. Bend some ears and kick some asses.'

'It won't work.'

'You won't know until you have tried,' she said. 'I have to meet someone now. Goodbye.'

'Bye.'

Phew! Vicki had never been this wound up before. He wondered what had rattled her cage.

The following weekend, as he sat on the toilet retching, he realised he was in a very bad place with alcohol. He was determined to get to the top of Canoil and he would not let alcohol dependency get in his way. He resolved there and then to give up drinking. It would be difficult but he had given up smoking and it couldn't be worse than that. He was done with alcohol forever.

A few months later, Tom was in London and he called `on Vicki at home.

'How are you?' she asked.

'Good. I have quit drinking.'

'Oh, Tom! That's fantastic.'

'It hasn't been easy.'

'How did you do it?'

'When I want a drink, I have a coffee and throw myself into my work.'

'You must be feeling so much better. Be careful — you can overdo work too. If you can get rid of your anxiety, it should get easier. You have taken a very positive step forward.'

They talked about the situation in Bigeria. Vicki's group had picketed outside the Bigerian Embassy in London and because her home was isolated and down a dark Wiltshire lane, she was fearful of reprisal. She showed Tom her mechanical locks and electronic alarm system.

When he arrived on his next visit she was out. He found the key in its hiding place, disarmed the alarm, let himself in and brought in his suitcase from the rented car.

The sitting room had comfortable antique furnishings. The ceiling was crisscrossed by blackened hand-hewn oak beams and the outer walls were thick and irregular, with small windows and the room rather dark. He made tea and relaxed in the plush gloom.

An hour later, Vicki arrived. They hugged.

'I've missed you,' he said.

'It's fabulous to see you, Tom. I have arranged for our FOOD group to come around this evening to talk about the situation in Bigeria.'

'FOOD?'

'I told you, Friends Of Overseas Development.'

'I forgot. What kind of talk?'

'You can tell us what Canoil is doing.'

'We can't do anything about the famine. It is an internal matter for the Bigerian Government.'

'When people are starving, it's a matter of common humanity for everyone to help where they can,' she said sharply.

'How many are coming?'

'Only four. It's a subcommittee.'

'What do they know about Bigeria?'

'They know that Canoil is propping up a corrupt despot,' she said, accusing. 'They won't be friendly.'

Her group introduced themselves deferentially, unused to meeting a corporate chief from Canada.

'We have agreed that the Bigerian people need outside help to get organised for development,' Vicki said. 'What are Canoil going to do about that?'

'At present the oil money goes into the private Swiss bank accounts of Okonjo and his pals,' said Tom. 'We are trying to get it all paid into the government's account.'

'You don't have forever,' said Vicki. 'Get on with it. Those refugees are starving.'

'I have been working on Don Walker, our CEO. He wants to pay half to the Hotus. The board won't allow him. Ottawa has advised against breaking our terms of contract.'

'What if you did?'

'They could stop our oil.'

Vicki slammed her fist down on the stainless-steel draining board, making the china and cutlery bounce. 'For fuck's sake, what's wrong with you? Canadians piss oil away. They can go without some. Can't they see people are dying like flies over there?'

'Don is sticking his neck out, reminding them at every board meeting . . .'

Vicki hurled her wine glass at him and he ducked just in time. 'You have to make them see it is their responsibility. They are a fucking disgrace. We are going to picket your next board meeting. We have members in Toronto, you know.'

'It would be counter-productive,' he told her. 'The board are responsible to shareholders, not the public and especially not to a group acting illegally. Be patient. Don is providing board members with photos and statistics of deaths and they could come around.'

'It's too little and too late,' she spat the words. 'Tell your Don that we have had it with Canoil. We will stop buying Canoil products. Our membership is big in Canada and growing fast.'

'Getting upset won't solve it,' he said. 'What do you want us to do?'

She calmed down.

'We want you to stop buying Bigerian oil.'

'Canadians would have to pay more for their petrol and the starving people would get even less than they do now. If I keep my head down, the board may make me CEO. Then I should be able to get some of the money to the Hotus, but I can't promise anything.'

Vicki calmed down. 'Coffee, Tom?'

'Thanks.'

They chatted until the others left.

'I'm sorry I lost my temper,' Vicki said.

'Accepted. It must be upsetting to run into the narrow ethics of corporations.'

'I find it difficult to remain both resolute and calm,' said Vicki. 'Changing the minds of conservative board members takes more patience than I have.'

'Resolve runs on ego and it can get depleted. It could do you good to take a break.'

'Maybe not. Willpower is generated by struggling. You had to struggle to quit drinking. How long has it been now?'

'A year.'

'Do you feel any better for it?'

'Much better. I was poisoning myself.'
'You seem tense.'
'Drinking used to relax me.'
'What are you anxious about?'
'My life. Us.'
'What about us?'
'We're not happening the way I had hoped we would.'
'Me too. But you could do something about it.'
'Not while my kids still need me.'
'So what are you going to do about it?'
'Put my head down and work. It relaxes me.'
'You are eating more too, aren't you?'

It was true. Since he stopped drinking, his appetite had been insatiable. Inside him, a fat man was taking over his body. He pulled in his bulging tummy.

'I may have lost a bit of weight lately.'

It was wishful thinking.

As usual, Vicki recommended he get counselling. As usual, he did nothing about it. He was intent on his job and allowed his working hours and eating to be out of control.

CHAPTER 77
DISUNITY

His relationship with Ruth had deteriorated and become strained. He was like a plant trying to grow in her shade, unable to photosynthesise or gain nourishment. Part of his brain had withered and he was depressed. When he tried to meet Ruth's sexual needs, it was like a homage, lacking in passion, as if he was a vibrator. One day, after a particularly mechanical performance, he decided never to have sex with her again.

When she lay beside him expectantly, he turned away.

'What's the matter with you?' she demanded.

'I don't want to.'

'Is there someone else? Is it that Vicki in England?'

'No.'

Ruth was of the Silent Generation and expected him to do his duty. Something must be wrong with him.

'Are you ill?' Ruth asked at breakfast.

Nicola and Michael were there.

'No.'

'Are you impotent?'

'No.'

'Are you homosexual?'

'No.'

Nicola turned to him, eyes and mouth wide. 'Do you have a man friend, Dad?'

Michael stopped eating and looked at him.

'No,' Tom said. 'Your mother is making things up.'

'Why are you?' said Nicola, turning to her.

'Your father is being nasty to me and he won't tell me why!' Ruth flung a plate onto the tiled floor where it smashed. She burst into tears.

'Why are you doing it?' Nicola asked him.

'I am not doing anything. She wants me to do something I don't want to do.'

'What thing?'

'Use your imagination, Nicola,' he said.

'You won't have sex with her, will you? Why not?'

'I don't want to.'

'Why does he have to?' Nicola asked Ruth. 'Who says?'

Tom was silent and Ruth realised his refusal was unconditional.

'Is it that you don't like me anymore?' she asked.

'You are a Silent and I am a Boomer.'

'Those are American marketing classifications. What have they got to do with us?'

'Everything. Our lifestyles and psychologies are different. Silents are older, staid, quiet and stoical types who respect authority and do their duty. That's you to a tee. Boomers are younger, disrespect authority, deny duty, are hedonistic and self-centred.'

'Very self-centred,' she said nastily.

'We're chalk and cheese. It's your fault we're together. You lied about your age.'

'I did not lie.'

'You misled me!'

Absence of truthfulness in a person damned them in his eyes. Using a promise to gain his acceptance and then defaulting was unforgivable.

'Well, you misled me,' Ruth said. 'You kept me waiting for a year while you had a grand time in South America and kept me on a piece of string. Then you came back and dumped me! Why for God's sake couldn't you leave it at that, instead of trying to revive it?'

'Maybe I was desperate.'

'You told me you loved me,' she said.

'I did,' he said, 'but you didn't love me.'

They realised that what love there had been between them was dead. It was a heavy blow to both their self-esteems.

For Tom, giving up sex with Ruth was easier than giving up alcohol and smoking. It became a scarce-remembered pleasure of a past life. He was happier now that his disaffection was out in the open. He had self-respect. There was little in his life outside work.

He was emotionally involved with his job, like in a love relationship, soothing his anxiety with overworking and overeating. As he became more and more engrossed in running Canoil, his hours at work were increasing.

'My obsession with work is only temporary,' he thought. *'When I get on top, I'll ease off.'*

'You need to relax more,' his boss, CEO Donald Walker, told him. 'Go skiing or fishing or hunting. Join an association. Get your mind onto something else.'

It was advice he was unable to follow. He had hung up his rugby boots years ago and hadn't found another social group. There were clubs and associations, but like the self-deprecating Groucho, he wouldn't join any group that would have him as a member. He wasn't interested in solo outdoor activity.

He looked forward to going to Vicki. He was not yet sure that they were ideally suited but there was hope and he clung to it.

CHAPTER 78
CEO

One morning, Tom received a message to call Ralph Gooder in Toronto. His secretary put him straight through.

'Good morning, Tom. Don Walker has taken retirement due to a medical problem. I want you to take over as CEO. There is no-one in the country who knows more about the oil game than you. How do you feel about it?'

'Did Don have a medical problem or an ethical disorder?' he thought. *'Do they want me to do some dirty deed Don refused to do?'*

'Thank you for your confidence in me.'

He thought: *'I will not accept the job until I hear what the rest of the package is.'*

'Your technical skills are second to none,' said Gooder. 'Don says you have been under his wing with politicians. The other day I had a chat with Manfred Brash. He has a handle on dealing with the Government. Get him to check everything you send out.

'People need to believe that the rising price of gasoline is due to increasing production costs. We are putting our trust in you to persuade them. We're expecting great things from you. I know what you are capable of, Tom, and I am counting on you to be a moderate and reliable leader.'

'Moderate?' Tom thought. *'The word 'moderate' is to warn me that my workaholism is immoderate. Fuck that. I'll do as much work as I like.'*

He felt hungry.

'The board will meet in Calgary from now on,' said Gooder. 'Production is most important and Calgary is closest to the action. I want you to move there as soon as possible.'

When he told Ruth, she was happy to be returning to her home town. Nicola and Michael could transfer universities and continue living at home without disruption. When they finished their studies in the next year or two he would separate from Ruth. She would get half of everything.

His new job would be a continuous round of meetings. He wouldn't often get to the UK to see Vicki. Perhaps he could persuade Vicki to join him in Calgary. It would be expensive.

'What rewards are you offering?' he asked the Chairman.

'You'll get more than Don did,' Ralph said. 'The job is bigger now. McNabs have done an evaluation. You would get $15 million, plus $5 million in shares at issue price, depending on performance, plus the usual perks. What do you say?'

'Thank you, Ralph. I accept.'

They talked briefly about priorities. He understood Ralph's because he had studied his career.

'Congratulations, Tom,' Ralph said. 'I look forward to working with you.'

'*All Ralph cares about is serving shareholders' interests,*' he thought. '*He does not care about conserving oil and improving recovery efficiency. I will have to conceal my interest.*'

'I will do my best for Canoil, Sir.'

'Call me Ralph. I'd like you to go to Ottawa and talk with Picard, to make sure we're on the same page about the situation in Bigeria. Bob sent him some confusing messages.'

'I'll make arrangements.'

He had an extraordinary floating feeling. At last, it had happened: He was CEO of a corporation with 20,000 employees. He had worked all his career for this.

He got Caroline to call the Prime Minister's office. She arranged a brief meeting for the next day and told Ian to get the King Air ready to go to Ottawa. Manfred got clothes for Tom from home. He worked on at the office and Caroline brought coffee and biscuits. She told him that the CEO's car and driver were waiting in the basement to take him to the airport.

After a couple of hours he went down to the garage. A tall, powerfully built and fit-looking man, aged about 30, got out of the

CEO's armoured Lincoln Continental. His complexion was ruddy, as if he worked outdoors.

'My name is Thug, Sir,' he said, crushing Tom's hand painfully. 'I do security and driving. I'll look after you, Sir. Is that okay, Sir?'

'Did you say your name is Thug?'

'That's what they call me.'

'How did you come by that name?'

'It's really Tug, Sir,' he pronounced it carefully, through a gap in his teeth where there had been incisors. 'I worked on tugboats in Vancouver. My front teeth were knocked out in the army, playing rugby.'

With his broken nose and cauliflower ears, it was a good name.

Thug showed him the car's arsenal. A machine gun was clipped under the roof, a machine pistol below the dashboard and a handgun in the driver's side door pocket. He pulled out a canister, from under the driver's seat.

'The best defence is attack,' he said, lisping. 'This baby is tear gas. I can lob it or shoot it.'

Tom's girth made it difficult to do up the safety belt.

'My body is a disgrace,' he thought.

They set off for the airport.

Thug gave him a run-down on news and media reports. It was laced with gossip gleaned from other leaders' chauffeurs.

'CBC are on the rebels' side,' he said. 'There is a story on the radio that our board members are funding genocide in Bigeria.'

'Thanks for the tip, Thug. CBC are certainly biased. It is true that the Bigerian Government is prejudiced against the Hotus, but it may not be genocide. If we support the rebels, it could cause a civil war. That would be a blood bath.'

Thug drove him to the private terminal where Ian was waiting with the King Air, a twin turboprop. Manfred joined them with suitcases.

'See you in few days, Sir!' Thug said. 'Have a good trip.'

His meeting with the PM was brief.

'What's the problem?' Picard asked.

'Okonjo is pocketing the oil money and we are getting the blame for supporting a corrupt regime.'

'We can't do anything about that,' said Picard. 'Corruption is a part of life over there. It's not like theft — more like remuneration. Without it, their salaries aren't enough to meet the expectations of their extended families.'

'Can we redirect some of the oil money to the starving people?' Tom asked.

'We have committed 20 million in aid to the refugees,' the PM said. 'There is nothing more we can do.'

'What if there is genocide again, like seven years ago?' Tom asked.

'Internecine strife is the norm there. We just have to accept that Okonjo is a bully.'

'Someone usually catches up with a bully,' said Tom. 'Could someone take him out?'

'It didn't happen with Hitler and there were 22 attempts.'

'It happened with John Kennedy.'

'He was popular and their guard was down,' said the PM. 'Okonjo is unpopular and paranoid.'

'We must act,' said Tom. 'Resources diplomacy worked against Ian Smith and against Apartheid. Can we stop their oil exports again, like we did with Misoto?'

'No. It would wreck our domestic growth just before an election. It is out of the question.'

'Is there anything we can do?'

'You can do whatever you want, as long as you fulfil your contract with the Bigerian Government and keep the oil flowing.'

'What if we change who we pay the money to?'

'Hmm. . . I know who you are paying the money to and it stinks. If you change that you don't need to tell us. . . as long as you get receipts from the Bigerian Government. It has to look legal.'

'Would they take it to the International Court?'

'No fucking way,' said the PM. They laughed uproariously. He changed to serious. 'But if they complain in this country that Canoil is illegal, we could get egg on our face. We don't want that, do we?'

'No. Thank you, Prime Minister.'
'Under Canadian law, as long as you get a receipt from the Bigerian Government, you can pay the money to who you like.'
It was the U-turn he had been waiting for.

CHAPTER 79
SWISS ROLL

When Tom heard a car honk in the driveway he went outside. Nicola was sitting in her car flanked by suitcases and boxes of books. Ruth was there too, looking glum.

'Where are you going?' he asked Nicola.

'To Toronto, to do a PhD!'

'Congratulations! What in?'

'Psychology of leadership.'

'Interesting. I hope you'll let me know your ideas. How about a farewell party?'

'I hate long goodbyes. I would be sad.'

'Toronto is a long way. Where are you going to stay?'

'A friend in Regina is expecting me on the way.'

'Here's some cash. It's not much.'

He gave her a wad of cash from his wallet.

'Gee. Thanks, Dad.'

'Have you said goodbye to Michael?'

'Yeah. Don't let him get away with anything.'

She started the engine.

'I'll miss you.' Tom had a lump in his throat.

'Me too, Dad,' she said, her eyes moist.

He wiped away tears and she got out of the car and put her arms around him.

'I love you, Dad.'

She had lived with him all her life and now she was leaving, going far away, alone. She hugged Ruth, got in and drove off. They went inside.

'It's a good thing,' he said to Ruth. 'It had to happen one day.'

She said nothing, her head down.

It was Tom's last day in his Edmonton office before moving to Calgary.

'Would you get Okonjo's email address?' he asked Caroline, his secretary.

She sent it to him and he wrote an email.

Dear Prime Minister Emmanuel Okonjo,

'Our company is concerned about the welfare of victims of famine in Bigeria, especially those who live near the oil resources that supply Canoil. We believe that the local people should benefit by receiving a fair share of our payments to your government.

We affirm our responsibility to the Bigerian people, by redirecting to the credit of your government's account in Akar, our ongoing payments formerly made to you and your ministers' Swiss bank accounts. This is intended to bring transparency and fair distribution.

We will review the situation in three months' time. If the wellbeing of famine victims has not significantly improved from today, as reported by medical workers caring for refugees inside and outside Bigeria, we will devolve payment to government accounts at your nation's regional centres, in proportion to their population, within the terms of our contract with you.

Yours truly,

Tom Archer

CEO, Canoil Ltd

He asked Caroline to check it.

'That's telling the bastard,' she said.

'I am going to call it our 'Swiss Roll'.'

He sent a copy to Vicki and called her. It was late evening in the UK.

'Chief Executive Officer! Congratulations, Tom! You are stuck in Canada forever now.'

'I won't do it for long. It's a tough job.'

'How old are Nicola and Michael?'

'23 and 21. Nicola has just left home.'

'How did you feel about that?

'I was sad. Ruth and I have been fighting.'

'Her leaving was to be expected. You still have Michael with you. What is he doing now?'

'Honours; he'll be able to continue with a PhD in Calgary. We're going down there tomorrow.'

'How long will a PhD take him?' she said.

'A minimum of three years.'

'It's almost forever.'

'Why don't you come over here to live?'

'I've told you 100 times, I can't.'

She had to be close to her family in England. The alternative was for him to go over there. It was easy to imagine living with her in a loving relationship. It would be good to get back to a decent climate where he could jog and hike instead of being cooped up indoors all winter. His old university friends were in the UK and he could visit them at weekends. His termination agreement with Canoil had a condition not to take another job for a year. After that, he would be able to find something to do.

'When Michael finishes will you quit?'

'I could get fired before that.'

'I won't hold my breath.'

'I would come sooner, if I could but I can't walk out on my CEO position so soon.'

'So, I'm in second place again?'

His planning had lacked commitment to Vicki and they both knew it.

'I will come in a couple of years' time. I need to see our Bigerian strategy through first. Are you disappointed?'

'Of course not,' Vicki said, changing the subject. 'Your work is important to you. Do you think Okonjo will clean up his act?'

'He may try to hold out, but we won't let him get away with it.'

'*I've made it sound easy and definite but Okonjo is slippery,*' he thought. '*I could be wasting my time with Canoil and losing Vicki. If Okonjo won't do the right thing with the oil money, I could resign.*'

CHAPTER 80
WAITING FOR OKONJO

It was a happy diversion when Nicola and her boyfriend Scott arrived in Calgary from Toronto on a visit. Thug was away winter hiking and Ruth drove the Lincoln to the airport with Tom in the passenger seat.

They met Scott for the first time in the arrival lounge. He was tall and dark, with a slight stoop, reminding Tom of Wortham's vicar. They walked out to the car park together.

When Ruth sat in the driver's seat, Nicola asked, 'Been hitting the bottle, Dad?'

'No. I've quit.'

'Dad! Congratulations!'

'I drive because he might fall asleep,' Ruth said bitterly. 'He's hooked on work now. He works all the time.'

'Why are you working so hard, Dad?' Nicola asked.

'I enjoy it,' he said. 'Scott, tell us about your research.'

He designed artificial limbs for accident victims.

'Did Nicola tell you that I am an android?' Tom said.

'What do you mean?'

'Sometimes they call me Spock at work.'

'That is because you are so unfeeling,' said Ruth.

'My feelings are reciprocal,' he said. 'You scratch my back and I'll scratch yours.'

'I'm not a cat.'

'No?' he said, disbelieving. 'You are scratchy enough. Tell us about your research, Nicola.'

She was investigating the work habits of leaders of corporations. She quizzed Tom about his work at Canoil and the dilemma of who to pay the Bigerian oil money to.

'Can't you make Okonjo share out the money fairly?' she said.

He told her about the Swiss Roll.

'Awesome!'

'I heard last week some food aid had reached Panypo,' he said.

'Really! That's fantastic, Dad!'

'It's too early to call it a win.'

When they arrived at their apartment and the visitors had unpacked, Nicola came into his study where he was writing a report.

'Dad, how many hours per week are you working?'

'My job is 24/7. I get six hours of sleep a day.'

'They say a workaholic works for three reasons: because he has to do the job properly; because he can't leave it to anyone else; and because he has energy to spare.'

'It's all three with me.'

'Are your long hours hurting the people you love?'

When he didn't answer, Nicola said, 'Mum is very unhappy. You have acute workaholism. You should be in a clinic, chilling out.'

'I have quit smoking, quit alcohol and will quit overworking soon, so don't hassle me. It's under control. I am okay.'

He had also quit sex with her mother, but he didn't mention it.

'You are improving, but you are working far too hard and could kill yourself as well as innocent Bigerians!' she said. 'You need other things to get off on, besides work.'

'I have timeouts and drink coffee.'

She was too polite to mention his overeating.

'They're a start. It would be better if you reduced your working hours.'

'Okay, I'll cut back when I can.'

'I'll phone to see how you're doing.'

'Thanks, Nicola.'

They hugged and she rested her head on his chest as if she was listening to his heartbeat. He realised that she loved him and was worried about him.

He telephoned Vicki.

'Tom, how are you? When are you coming over?'

'Soon, I hope. I have had one problem after another. Drilling in the Arctic is a hassle. The oil in Bigeria is a headache. I miss you. Why don't you come over here for a few days?'

'I'm going to Spain with Anne next week.'

He had never heard of an Anne before. Vicki didn't suggest another time and he wondered if his relationship with her was intact. He told her about the food aid getting through.

'Well done, Tom!'

'It may not be true. I need to go there.'

'You are right to be sceptical. Bigerians lie when it suits them.'

'Have you been to Bigeria?' he asked her.

'No. I was going there once, but something came up.'

She didn't explain.

What is Vicki's interest in Bigeria? 'he wondered.

'Have a good trip,' she said.

'Bye.'

She ended the call.

He wished she was with him in Canada. Her independent viewpoint would help him in his job. One error of judgement could bring him down.

CHAPTER 81
DEVOLUTION

The alarm woke him at 4 am and Thug drove him to work, where he shaved and showered in the CEO's suite. Breakfast arrived from the café across the street: orange juice, pancakes, maple syrup and coffee. He sat at the breakfast bar, glancing through the morning papers. Next to the breakfast room there was a sitting room. Beyond was the boardroom and his office flanked by desks where Manfred and Caroline worked.

After breakfast, he went through as usual and started going through his inbox. Unlike other leaders who worked closely in teams, Tom performed solo.

'Groups are for posers and a waste of time,' he said.

He directed the corporation's firepower against its enemies from the cockpit of his desk, with weapons of producing, processing and marketing, activated by his phone calls and emails. He innovated and planned strategies without asking everyone's views. It was not a popular style. His work was under critical scrutiny of the board, who might at any time decide he was an impostor, compromised or flawed. To appease his anxiety demons, he overworked.

At 7 am, Manfred arrived.

'The board meeting is at 10 am,' he said.

Manfred helped him prepare an agenda, discussing each item. He was negotiating with indigenous people about a drilling site on the Arctic Northwest Shelf. Another matter was whether to drill an exploration well in waters claimed by the East Timor Government. Most bizarre, because the 'Canoil' brand would expire shortly, they had to come up with a new name to display at their petrol stations across Canada. The names proposed by Marketing were unsatisfactory. He and Manfred brainstormed together and came up with a new name: CANGAS. There were other problems to do with employee health, pay awards and pollution.

He went out to stretch his legs. When he looked in the bathroom mirror his face was worried. He was juggling too many problems. He had fumbled several and his portfolio was out of control.

'I solve problems by investigation,' he thought. *'I have too much to do to be able to investigate things properly.'*

Manfred came back. 'There is a bloke from the CBC outside, a journalist.'

'What does he want?'

'Your views on Okonjo rorting our oil payments.'

'Shit. Not that again. Our Swiss Roll should be bringing Okonjo into line.'

'That's what he wants to know.'

'We have no definite evidence that he is helping relieve the famine. It's too early for me to comment. Make an appointment in a day or two.'

He stood up and sketched on the whiteboard a diagram with his analysis of the risks of the situation in Bigeria. He listed the alternatives of 'do nothing', 'pay the rebels' and 'devolution'. For each alternative he estimated its cost, revenue potential and probability. After weighting for risks, the 'devolution' option had least expected cost. Sending of funds to the eight regions of Bigeria was the strategy Vicki's group had proposed six years previously. It had taken Canoil that long to learn not to give money to Okonjo.

He called the Energy Minister in Ottawa.

'Okonjo doesn't seem to have responded to our Swiss Roll. He may have rounded up the money we sent to Akar and be divvying it up with his buddies. We have been patient but now we are going to fix those greedy fuckers for good.'

He told him his plan.

'I didn't hear that,' said Ronson. 'It's a bad line. You're on your own with this.'

'Convenient,' Tom thought.

Tom checked his risk evaluation calculation on the whiteboard again. It made good sense. The analysis should have been prepared by his engineers but they lacked his acumen. Tom's risk analysis skills were the best in the company. He knew his intuition was messianic and technically unsound, but until he was found out, it would relieve the pressure on him.

The board members arrived and the Chairman began the meeting. The first motion was the mid-year financial report. They approved unanimously the dividend that Tom had worked hard to achieve.

While they ate sandwiches and drank fruit juice, Tom gave them a rundown on the situation in Bigeria. Walker had supplied lager, but Tom would not have the board deciding matters under the influence of alcohol. When he stopped it, there had been grumbling but Tom stuck to his guns.

'We need to be sober. We have to get the Bigerians to use the oil money for the public good, or the people will blame us and throw us out.'

'How are you going to do that?'

'We can devolve our payments to provincial bank accounts, requiring withdrawals to be counter-signed by bosses in each region. That should get transparency.'

'Are we able to do that under our contract?'

'It's not excluded. Ottawa will turn a blind eye. We will be putting Okonjo's ministers in a pincer. Credit and debit demands will bite on them from both sides.'

'What is the risk Okonjo will hit back at us?' a director asked.

'He needs us more than we . . .'

Tom was interrupted by a chant of 'Food For Oil!' outside.

'Gentlemen, that sounds like trouble,' he said. 'We had better make ourselves scarce. I adjourn this meeting until two days from now. I will let you know where.'

'Call me tonight after 10 pm,' Gooder told Tom as they descended the fire stairway.

They went down to the car park in the basement and left secretly.

At home, when he looked in the bathroom mirror, his face was haggard, with bags under his bloodshot eyes. He wondered what Gooder could want. He was apprehensive that he would ask him to resign. He might have detected that Tom was sleep-deprived and be concerned that his cognitive functioning was impaired. Stress was shafting him like a javelin up his arse. The pain was in his spine, his neck and his shoulders. He could hack the tough going but it was taking a terrible toll.

When Michael arrived home he was at his desk in his study.

'Are you okay, Dad?' he asked. 'You look like shit.'

It was Michael's way of being sympathetic and supportive.

'I didn't get much sleep last night and today has gone pear-shaped.'

He told him their manager in Akar had found no evidence that the Government was relieving the famine in the north. Their Swiss Roll had failed.

'I have some good news,' said Michael. 'Miscible flooding can get a lot more oil out from most oil fields.'

Michael's honours thesis was to study the potential of miscible flooding.

'Keep it to yourself for the moment,' Tom said. 'If governments get hold of it, they will use it as a stick to beat us with. Put it in your thesis.'

'I thought you would be interested.'

'I am interested, Michael, very. I am working on it.'

It was now 10 pm. He had been on the job for 17 hours. He called the Chairman.

'What is your proposal for Bigeria, Tom?' Ralph asked.

'Shit. Maybe he isn't going to approve my proposal,' he thought. *'Will this Bigerian nightmare never end?'*

'We should redirect the money to the regions.'

'Won't Okonjo grab it back for himself and his cronies?'

'If we can make the credits transparent, it will be difficult for him to rort the system.'

'It could work and the board will be okay with it. The shit will hit the fan in Bigeria, Bombay and Bogota but do it, Tom and good luck.'

'Thank you.'

Tom was relieved, but his reputation was on the line.

They talked about other business. Ralph okayed the 'CANGAS' name for their retail stations. Sometimes being CEO was sweet.

By the time Gooder was satisfied, it was midnight.

Tom emailed Canoil's treasury to implement The Pincer by cancelling further payments to the Bigerian ministers and dividing it between the eight regions in proportion to population.

He decided to stay overnight in the CEO's suite. He heated up a frozen dinner and ate it, watching the late news. Today he had made a difference. Vicki would be proud of him.

He realised he had not been to the UK since becoming CEO. A week ago he had tried to call her.

'Hello, Vicki. Tom here.'

'Oh, Tom. Look I can't talk just now. Can you write?'

'Okay. Bye.'

He emailed with his news, but she didn't reply. She rarely emailed. He would visit her soon. She could be peeved that he had not kept his promises but she would come around.

CHAPTER 82
YACHT HOPPER

Tom took another helping of steak and kidney pie. He was eating dinner with Michael, the first time he had been alone with him for a week. Tom was concerned he had crossed paths with him several times bringing home girls, when he should have been at uni.

'Michael, it's okay to have girlfriends, so long as they don't take your attention off your work. I want you to get your PhD done as soon as possible.'

'Why?'

'*His sense of entitlement is unrealistic,*' Tom thought.

'I want you to get a job and be independent, so I don't have to worry about you.'

'You don't need to worry about me, Dad. It's under control.'

'Is it self-control, or social control?' he asked querulously.

Michael went out, slamming the door. Tom regretted his sarcasm. His own PhD had folded under pressure, when he succumbed to a nervous breakdown. He would not let Michael suffer like that. He would scaffold him with a solid research project at Canoil.

'*It is not nepotism to create opportunities for my son and protect him,*' he thought. '*It's a perk of my job.*'

A few weeks later, the Archer family was in Zapulco for a week's holiday when Michael spoke to him with a different idea.

'I've decided to defer uni, Dad.'

'Why?'

'I'm not interested right now.'

'Where are you up to with your research, son?'

'I'm supposed to be doing a literature survey. It's boring. I need adventure. I have been offered a job on a yacht.'

'What job?'

'Deckhand and barman on a cruise to Hawaii and then back to the Pacific Islands for a year. When I get back, I'll be able to get into my project.'

'*Is my role as his carer extended?*' he thought, not letting his dismay show. '*Maybe he won't come back. I would be reprieved from supporting his PhD and could go to Vicki.*'

'It sounds lovely, for you. Will the uni let you defer?'

'They don't like it, but if I quit, they'll lose the sponsor's money. So, they have agreed to a deferral.'

Michael's plan was logical. He was experienced around yachts and could take care of himself. But it would fatally delay Tom's plan to go to Vicki.

'It seems your mind is made up then.'

He recalled his own travels in Latin America and hoped Michael would have as much fun as he did. Ruth opposed Michael going but she was overruled.

They went to the Zapulco yacht club to see Michael off. The yacht was a luxurious catamaran kitted out for heavy weather. Her owner, a French businessman, had sailed the Pacific Islands before. He showed them a machine gun and hand grenades.

'These are for negotiating with pirates,' he said.

There was one other crew member, the cook. She looked like she might eat Michael for breakfast.

Tom lay awake that night, worrying about all that could go wrong. He would keep a stash of cash available to pay a ransom. He set it against all the times that Michael had brought him joy.

It was at about this time that the feeling of impending disaster came upon him. He couldn't say what his premonition concerned, only that something dreadful was imminent. He was pumping adrenalin for freeze, fight or flight — whether from a natural disaster or a man-made one he didn't know. An earthquake, tsunami or volcanic eruption was unlikely because Calgary was situated well away from the east Pacific subduction zone. He concluded that his dread was of something else – like a road accident, a disease, or a terrorist bombing. His job exposed him to disgruntled people, including terrorists from countries where Canoil was active. He consulted Thug.

'I'll keep my eyes peeled,' he said. 'Pessimistic, paranoid and poised is the way we need to be.'

Even small movements startled Tom. He put first aid kits in his apartment, made an evacuation plan and stored cans of food in the garage.

CHAPTER 83
EDICT

Tom was having breakfast in his office, when Caroline brought him the latest *Inside Out* magazine, with an article marked by a Post-it in Manfred's writing: *'Tom: WTF?'*

CAN CANOIL FOLLIES IN BIGERIA CONTINUE?

President Okonjo is demanding Canoil, Canada's largest oil company, install more efficient oil production technology.

Bigerian oil production has been recovering since international oil companies lifted their embargo imposed after the coup 10 years ago by Hotu forces, led by General Misoto. The rebel government lasted for one year, until Misoto was killed and Fetanis, under Okonjo, regained control.

In a press release, Energy Minister Tinibu said, 'Primary oil production at the Panypo field will extract only 20% of the oil resource, leaving 80% in the ground. Water-flooding later will increase recovery up to 30%, but miscible flooding is a new technology that has potential to recover 90% of the resource. We require Canoil to adopt the new technique at the Panypo oil field. If they do not, their production leases will not be renewed.'

CEO of Canoil, Tom Archer, said, 'We have submitted a proposal to inject water at the Panypo field. We expect the government to renew our leases.'

Canoil has been testing miscible flooding technology in Canada with encouraging results.

Inside Out wants to know: How valid is the Bigerian Government's complaint? Why has Canoil not applied miscible flooding there? Is Canoil ripping off oil resources and

ruining oilfields because they can? What is delaying the new technology? At Inside Out, we are waiting for Canoil's response.
Walter Barnes, Staff Reporter, Politics and Business

Manfred's Post-it message continued: *'I am searching to find if they have any experience of miscible flooding, M.'*

Tom had read the article with mounting concern. The press release had been buried in his in-tray and he had somehow missed it. His CEO quote was out of context, from a talk he had given earlier in the year at a Canadian Petroleum Exploration conference. He would punish Barnes for dishonest reporting.

His first thought was that this was Bigeria's payback for The Pincer. He reread it slowly as he ate toast and marmalade.

Energy Minister Tinibu's comments showed familiarity with petroleum extraction technologies. On a hunch, he emailed Richard in London.

Hello Richard. Would you please supply full name, domicile and academic results of Vicki's erstwhile boyfriend, William. Thanks, Tom.

The next day, he received a reply:

William Tinibu, B.Sc. Hons, Eng 1969, M.Phil, Pet Eng, 1971. Living in Akar, Bigeria. Wanting his tips? Cheers, Richard.

His hunch was correct. Vicki's former heartthrob, William, was now Bigeria's Energy Minister. He could vaguely remember meeting him as a student in an earlier year at LUT. He had returned to Bigeria, leaving Vicki in the UK. Now he was a leader in a corrupt regime with a history of genocide.

Tom envied William that Vicki had loved him. Jealously, he compared his position with William's.

'Canoil's annual budget is larger than Bigeria's,' he thought.

Manfred came into his office. 'Miscible flooding might work at Panypo,' he said, 'but no-one is doing it anywhere else. The Bigerians only know what that bastard Antcliff told them, raising their expectations. None of our fields in Canada would be able to make money from it.'

'Michael thinks there is heaps of potential,' Tom said.

'It hasn't been demonstrated yet. We have not 'delayed', as *Inside Out* is suggesting. Could we persuade the Bigerians that miscible flooding is not yet ready for Panypo? If we show them our crappy test results from Tundra, it will pour cold water on their idea.'

'I can run with that.'

'Are you sure you are able to run?'

Manfred's quip stung but Tom knew he meant well and was warning him about his health. His belly was too big, hanging down over his belt. He must lose weight.

The phone interrupted them. It was Ralph Gooder. 'I have read the *Inside Out* shit. What's wrong with our water injection proposal?'

'Nothing. The Bigerians think it will leave too much oil in the ground, is all. Tinibu has seized on miscible flooding as a panacea. He sounds obsessive.'

'You have to persuade him that water injection is best practice.'

'I'll go to Bigeria,' Tom said. 'I'll be away most of the week.'

'Get back as soon as you can. We need you here.'

'If you fly Concorde,' Manfred said to Tom in his office, referring to his notes, 'you will gain two working days. You can leave JFK at the end of a day in New York, sleep for six hours on board and arrive in London in time for breakfast and a full day's work. You can have a night over there and the next morning be in Bigeria in time for a working lunch. On the way back, leaving Heathrow at 7 pm on Concorde, you can arrive in New York in the afternoon and be back in Calgary in time for a night at home.'

The phone rang. It was Ralph again. 'Picard called. He is worried that Okonjo will cut off our oil. He wants you in Ottawa pronto.'

'Tomorrow I am going to Bigeria.'

'Good. You can call in on Picard on the way.'
'Okay.'
Tom hung up.
His work as CEO was hemmed in on all sides. He was tired, working harder than ever, nearing exhaustion.
'Book our flights,' he said to Manfred. 'I'd like you to come with me as far as Ottawa. If there are two of us, Picard won't be as snotty.'

CHAPTER 84
PIQUE

Tom and Manfred were ushered into the Prime Minister's office. Charles Picard shook hands. Shaver Ronson showed them a newspaper headline: *'Threat to Oil Imports.*

'What have you done to upset the Bigerians, Mr Archer?' said the PM.

'We have started paying into their regional accounts instead of their ministers' pockets.'

'You seem to have pissed them off big time. Because they can't complain openly about you stopping their graft money, they have come up with this inefficiency shit. Is there any substance to it?'

'None whatsoever, Prime Minister.'

'They seem to think there is.'

'Miscible flooding is pie in the sky. It hasn't been demonstrated yet. Oil recovery at Panypo is not a problem. Our proposal for water injection is best practice.'

'To extricate yourselves, you must do what they want.'

'I won't have this weak-kneed bastard telling us what to do,' Tom thought. *'We will increase oil recovery but not until the technology has been demonstrated.'*

'It is not realistic,' Tom said, shaking his head.

'You mean *you* don't want to?' the PM exploded. 'That is not the point. Your inefficiency is a disgrace. The Bigerians have every right to complain. Your mentality is like farmers who 'slash and burn' the jungle. They strip nutrients from the soil in one patch of jungle after another and then leave the soil to regenerate. You do the same but the oil does not regenerate. What you leave in the ground is lost forever. It is not acceptable.'

Picard paused. Tom was silent, seeming to be listening. Ronson continued the harangue.

'When your returns dwindle, you cry poor, obtain tax concessions and look for a new territory to pillage. You leave behind reservoirs in which most of the oil has been locked away in rock pores by the very water you have injected to flush a little out. It is less like production and more like destruction.'

His tirade halted. He and Ronson glared at Tom.

'Canoil operates lawfully, Prime Minister,' Tom said mildly. 'We are committed to the conservation of Canada's oil resources. May I summarise Canoil's position in current legislation?'

He referred to the notes that Manfred had prepared for him.

'First, we are paying for leases that entitle us to extract unspecified amounts of minerals.

'Second, we have installed and maintained extraction facilities of our own choosing.

'Third, we sustain extraction in conformance with the government's criteria.

'Fourth, the percentage extracted is one of several sustainability criteria that we monitor.

'Fifth, the government may not renew the lease if the lessee does not extract sufficient oil. Canoil has never been notified by the government that our extraction of oil is insufficient.

'Sixth, and finally, leases do not preserve access to extract the remainder of the oil.

'Prime Minister, these are the rules and my company obeys them.'

Picard replied with disdain, 'The recoveries you are getting are pitiful. It is not acceptable to cream off oil resources that belong to the Canadian people. You have looted our oil to send high profits to shareholders in the United States.'

His voice had climbed and he was yelling.

An assistant brought in a tray with coffee and biscuits.

'What are you going to do about it?' he asked angrily.

The PM sat down with Ronson at the table and waved Tom and Manfred into the chairs.

'Prime Minister, our production operations have to be commercial,' Tom said patiently. 'Our strategy is to produce the most accessible oil first, as recompense for the high cost of exploration. Only one hole in 25 finds oil in commercial quantities.'

'You prefer to explore for new oilfields, rather than invest in efficient recovery from old fields, because dry exploration holes reduce your tax bill. Here is the choice you have: if you don't stop wasting oil, we will nationalise you and produce it ourselves.'

Tom leaned back in his chair.

'Over my dead body!' he thought.

'Prime Minister, nationalisation of Canada's oil industry would cause it to collapse. Oil investment cannot be run by a committee of bureaucrats. Investors must have control. The supply of risk capital for development would dry up.'

'We need efficiency not development,' Picard said.

'You make the rules, we make the profits,' said Tom, 'and we pay taxes.'

'The situation has changed,' Picard said, munching on a bagel. 'The world is running out of new oilfields and oil companies have to respect government priorities. What you are doing is not in the public interest and we are going to stop your wasteful ways.'

'Why pick on us?' Tom asked, through a mouthful of bagel. 'Why not regulate car manufacturers? Cars waste more oil than oil producers! The best efficiency a petrol car can get is about 20%. The 30% we get in production is not bad. We leave 70 of every 100 barrels underground. Of the 30 we take out, after refining it and transporting it to the pump, there are only 20 left. Of that, cars waste 80%. Only 4% of the initial oil is used for moving a car along the road. If your concern is inefficient energy use, you should require that car manufacturers invest in public transport systems. Ultimately, car drivers have only themselves to blame for the depletion of oil.'

'I grant you others are wasting energy too,' said Picard, 'but we have to make a start somewhere and that is to require efficient recovery of oil.'

'Voters want us to conserve oil,' said Ronson, 'before it runs out.'

Tom poured himself some coffee. 'Thanks to your government's tax incentives, we are able to sustain petroleum reserves by exploration.'

Picard got up. 'Archer, this is bullshit,' he said quietly. 'You are not going to fuck this nation on my watch, even if the legislation allows it. You are wasting oil willy-nilly and I am going to stop you doing that. You must install the best technology for the job. Is that clear?'

'We have been lawful —'

Picard raised his voice again.

'You may be lawful, but the Canadian people know you have not been acting responsibly. We will not licence you to produce oil or allow you access to the nation's oil resources if your recovery is lower than it could be. We require you to declare the efficiency you will get in advance. It will not be acceptable to install technology that merely creams off the most profitable oil.'

Tom's collar and tie were so tight they hurt.

'Prime Minister, Canoil will only invest in technology that returns profits.'

'Yes, of course. We will suspend royalties and taxes, until new investment in more efficient extraction is paid back.'

Tom's heart leapt. It was a deal-making concession.

He said evenly, 'Prime Minister, thank you for understanding our situation. I will have to consult with my colleagues and get back to you. They will be interested in your proposal. We would require your evaluation to be case-by-case, because some of our oilfields are too far gone to rescue.'

'Point taken, Archer. We will not force companies to lose money when they are willing to do what is reasonable. You do agree to increase recovery, don't you?'

'Yes, Prime Minister. I will seek my board's approval.'

'We expect to receive a detailed proposal for each oilfield. Then we can evaluate your efficiency and whether we will renew your production licences. Now, I have to go as I am expected in the House. Don't forget to give the Bigerians what they want!'

He shook hands all round and was gone.

CHAPTER 85
CANDID

A yell from the hotel forecourt awoke Tom.

'The police are coming!'

He stepped out onto his balcony on the 10th floor where he, Manfred and Thug were staying. A mob of reporters was gazing up at Thug, who was feeding an electrical cable, hand over hand, over the balcony rail, with something heavy hanging from it below. Looking down, Tom could see the soles of a pair of boots. A person was being lowered headfirst down the side of the building with electrical cable wound around his ankles. When he reached the ground, reporters untied him and he stood up.

'I want my camera,' he shouted up.

There was a movie camera on the balcony.

'Come and get it,' Thug called down.

The cameraman shook his head, 'Not likely, you fucking animal.'

'WTF are you doing?' Tom asked Thug.

'He was videoing you through the window. He abseiled down from the roof.'

'Don't antagonise the press any more than you have to.'

'They won't try that again.'

'Thank you, Thug.'

Tom went outside on the balcony. The reporters beckoned to him to face their cameras.

'Mr Archer, what is your comment on the news?'

'What news?'

A reporter held up a newspaper headline.

'I can't read it from here,' Tom said. 'Bring it up.'

It was a front-page story in the Ottawa Post. There was a photo of cars queuing at a petrol station.

CEO PROMISES OIL CHANGE

Prime Minister Charles Picard has notified oil companies that the government will regulate extraction technologies to reduce wastage of oil resources. To obtain a production licence, installation of an efficient secondary recovery system is required.

Oil producers want suspension of royalties and taxes on existing production to pay for their investment. Canoil CEO, Tom Archer said:

'Production of sub-economic resources requires a commercial incentive to develop and install more efficient technologies. Producers will consider each oil field on its merits.'

'No comment,' said a spokesperson for the Canadian Petroleum Exploration Association.

'The oil industry is expected to oppose government interference with what they see as their proprietary expertise. There is no way the oil majors are going to have some tin-pot provincial government telling them to install a new technology, even if a tax holiday is given away with it. If it doesn't work, they would lose. In their view governments govern; they don't engineer.'

Trent Camberwell, Staff Reporter

Tom clenched his teeth and swore. Trent had reported his meeting with the Prime Minister as a conflict. He would demand the *Ottawa Post* rescind the untrue statements.

'I deny ever saying that,' he told the clamouring journalists. 'This is faked news.'

'What is your response to the Prime Minister's announcement?'

'Sorry, no comment.'

He went in from the balcony. He passed the newspaper to Manfred, who was eating breakfast. Tom took a phone call from Gooder on speaker phone.

'I'm looking at the *Ottawa Post*,' Ralph said. 'What the fuck is this? Who do you think you are, cosying up to that megalomaniac?'

'I didn't agree to anything,' Tom said.

'Well, get back here pronto and repair the damage.'

'I will be in Bigeria. It is their threat that has set Picard off.'

'Sort it. I'll hold the fort here. The board want to know what the hell is going on.'

Gooder hung up.

'Ralph sounds ropeable,' said Manfred, munching a croissant.

'I would be too.'

'Were you really that compliant with Picard?'

'No. I said we needed incentives and he agreed to provide them, not that we would accept government interference. The *Ottawa Post's* story is shit but some of it will stick, even after we deny it. Picard knows what we agreed and that's all that matters.'

Gooder's anger made him anxious. He scooped jam into another croissant and tried to loosen his belt because it was cutting into him. It was on the last hole. He was a fat man and he knew Vicki would be repelled. He had to lose weight.

CHAPTER 86
REFLEX

Tom called Vicki from Ottawa but there was no answer. He hadn't heard from her since the last time he was in England. He wanted to visit her on his way to Bigeria.

It was early morning as he went through transit at JFK Airport, climbed the Concorde's boarding stairs and stooped to enter the tubular passenger compartment. In each row, there were only two seats either side of the central aisle. He crammed into one, claustrophobia gripping him momentarily, but he fought it and did up his seatbelt.

Air crew closed and bolted the hatch. An apron tractor pushed them out to the taxiway and the four Rollers leapt into life, whining like electric lawnmowers. With the awkwardness of a pelican unused to walking, they sashayed along the taxiway to the far end of the runway and waited, shuddering in gusts from aircraft landing nearby.

They trundled out to the centre of the runway, turned 90 degrees and teetered to a halt. Every metre of runway was needed and they powered up, shredding the air, dancing against the brakes. Tom was shaken by the thunderous torching of torrents of fuel a few metres away. They lunged forward and accelerated endlessly, until it seemed certain they would crash off the end of the runway, when suddenly the nose reared up impossibly high and they were in a steep climb. He felt like an astronaut. When the patchwork of blurred fields had receded to gingham in various greens, he relaxed his grip on the armrests.

In front of him, inlaid in the partition at the front of the passenger cabin, was a plate-sized dial with a needle that hovered on 1200 kilometres per hour. With a small jolt, they dropped off the sound barrier wave and the needle swung up to 2200 kilometres per hour.

After three uneventful hours, they glided into Heathrow and bustled to a standstill.

He called Vicki and drove down to her place. She had returned the previous day from a holiday in the sun. Her cheeks were tanned and she looked great. She went off to work and he drove to the local village, where he bought ingredients for dinner.

That evening, they stepped around each other in the small kitchen as they cooked roast duck à l'orange and vegetables. When they brushed against each other, her touch was electric. They ate by candlelight, savouring the succulent food. Vicki relaxed and they talked for hours.

As usual, he lay on her couch. He told her about Nicola's and Michael's studies and how both were interested in working in London when they finished.

'They can stay with me here,' she said.

'I would like that. I know you would take good care of them. I'll tell them.'

He talked and talked. Vicki threw in 'Uh-huh' or 'What did you do?' as if counselling a client.

'Is Okonjo still starving the Hotus?' she asked presently. She was in a better temper than on his last visit, when Canoil's inaction against the Bigerian Government's corruption had set her off.

'Yes, he is. Don was all fired up to send money to the Hotus, but the board wouldn't do it and he lost his job,' Tom said. 'My first move as CEO has been to do what I call 'The Pincer'.'

'What's that?'

'We have redirected our payments to the country's regions, to stop Okonjo and his ministers getting their hands on it. We are sending the money to local people.'

'Good move. You should have done it years ago. Is the money getting to the famine victims now?'

'We're not sure yet.'

He pulled her down beside him so they were lying full length beside each other, their bodies pressed together.

'Imagine this is Sidmouth Hall,' he said.

'No visitors after 10 pm,' she replied.

It was decades ago that they had met. There were a few small lines around her eyes. She was spicier, with stronger flavours and mellow edges. They spent the evening reminiscing.

Mustering his loyalty to his family, he said goodnight and went to the guest bedroom. It was on the other side of the staircase from her bedroom. He could hear her moving about and wished he was in her bed. There was a light knock on his door.

'Yes,' he called.

The door opened a crack.

'It's me. Is there anything you want?' she asked in a small voice. It seemed like an invitation and he was tempted.

'Who will know if I accept what I have waited for so long?' he thought. *'This is an opportunity to test the waters before I take the plunge.'*

But he wanted to be honourable. He had always been faithful to Ruth and his children. Should he betray their loyalties now?

He agonised. He had married Ruth for better or for worse, but it was not irredeemable. Was now the time to separate? His reflex was to be loyal — a prisoner of habit, in shackles.

'No, thanks.'

If he had been more prepared, he might have acted differently.

'Good night,' she said.

In the morning, Vicki was distant. He was confused, barely able to control his emotions. He wanted to do the right thing but he wasn't sure what it was. He asked Vicki if she would go with him once again to Salisbury Cathedral. He knelt in a pew beside her and tried to pray but he could not remember how. He thought how Vicki had given large parts of her life to others, caring first for her sick father and then for her aged mother. He wanted her to be happy.

They held hands as they walked down the cavernous aisle. He was overcome by emotions he didn't understand. When he squeezed her hand, she returned it, as if she understood his torment. With fingers entwined they strolled through the town.

'If we lived together, we could walk every day,' he said.

'How soon?' she asked.

'Michael should be back shortly. If he resumes his PhD, it could take three years.'

'It's a long time,' she said.

'I have to be there for him. The time will soon pass.'

'Maybe,' she said with a shrug as if it might not.

Tom sensed her patience would soon run out. When he said farewell, their lips touched briefly.

'Keep in touch,' Vicki said.

He left without getting any closer to her.

He was not looking forward to dealing with the Bigerians nor flying back to his loveless marriage. Philosopher Arthur Schopenhauer had investigated the meaning of life and concluded in 1860, just before he died, that 'human existence must be a kind of error'.

'Maybe it is an error, on average, but not in everything, for a single individual,' he thought. *'My difficulties will pass. It will be good.'*

CHAPTER 87
RIVALS

He sweltered at Akar airport. An assistant to Minister Tinibu met him in a black stretch limo. Tom's pants were too tight and when he sat he felt a stabbing pain in his balls. He envied African men who wore loose clothing, with colourful robes and kaftans, more comfortable in these hot conditions.

'I am looking forward to meeting the Minister,' he told the official. 'We were at the same university in England.'

'Were you together?'

'In different classes.'

'Petroleum engineering?'

'Yes.'

'You and the Minister have much in common.'

'Tell me, is Minister Tinibu married?'

'Yes, for many years.'

'Does he have any children?'

'Eighteen, I think.'

'It is many.'

'He is a big man. He has four wives.'

Tom understood why William Tinibu would not take Vicki home to Bigeria with him.

'He must be a very busy man.'

The aide laughed. They arrived at the oil ministry, a new steel and glass building. He was led up to Tinibu's office. The big man was almost as large as Tom. In Africa, fat indicated a fat wallet. He wore a white robe and sat behind a large mahogany desk, with the national flag draped down the wall behind him. They drank coffee and chatted about the nation's oil resources.

When Tom recalled their studies at LUT, he didn't mention Vicki. If he upset him, it could jeopardise their talks.

'My job is to direct Bigeria's oil production,' Tinibu said. 'Oil companies must install secondary recovery facilities.'

'We will if it is profitable,' Tom said.

'If you do not do it, you could lose your licences.'

'Canoil wants to increase oil recovery.'

'You must do it,' Tinibu said, grimacing, 'not just talk about it!'

Tom said quietly, 'It is too early for secondary recovery at Panypo. Primary is not yet finished.'

Tinibu's forefinger stabbed at him. 'That is your opinion. Mine is you must install secondary recovery technology now!'

This guy is coming from left field, he thought. *I'll humour him.*

'William,' he said, sitting forward, 'you are absolutely right. Too much oil remains underground. We are investigating ways to increase recovery. For example, we are testing the use of detergent in water-flooding.'

'Yes, yes, I know about that,' Tinibu said, drumming his fingers on his desk. 'I have heard that the detergent cleans out the oil but makes an emulsion that is too difficult to break. What other methods has Canoil considered?'

'We propose water flooding for the Panypo field.'

'It won't extract enough oil. Did you consider using miscible flooding?'

'Minister,' Tom asked curiously, 'how do you know about miscible flooding?'

William hesitated. They both knew Canoil's technology was proprietary and confidential.

'We have seen data from Silver Atoll,' he admitted slowly, sitting uncomfortably.

'Oh? Who showed you?'

Tinibu ignored Tom's question. Receiving stolen data was an offence in Canada.

'We believe it is a method that needs to be applied to all Bigeria's oilfields.'

'Was it Graham Antcliff?'

'The data appears to be authentic,' Tinibu said.

'Minister, Antcliff has left Canoil. He may have misled you. Miscible flooding worked at Silver Atoll but it may not work here. We are still testing it. If it is successful, we could build a demonstration plant at the Panypo field.'

'When would it be ready?'

'Our testing program at the Tundra Tar Sands pilot plant will take three years.'

'We need a plant to be built at Panypo now.'

An aide brought in tea and sandwiches. They chatted, comparing the weather in Akar with the weather in Liverpool. Tom mopped his brow with a handkerchief. The fatter you got, the more heat you had to lose. Unfortunately, as you gained weight, you had less surface area per kilogram to lose it. Losing heat was becoming more difficult and he could overheat. Sweat was running down Tom's forehead and into his eyes.

Tinibu's face glistened.

'We will have an election soon. We want to show voters that we are in control of what foreign oil companies are doing in Bigeria. Canoil must construct a demo plant now. If you delay, we will nationalise your operations. It will help us to win.'

Tom closed his folder with finality. 'Our board will say the investment is too risky.'

Tinibu shook his head. 'What will Canadian motorists do without Bigerian oil?' He looked out the window.

Tom stood up and walked to the door, then turned around.

'Minister, our board will not give in to threats. The global oil industry will unite behind us and you will not be able to sell your oil, to anyone.'

Tinibu stood up, large and heavy, leaning forward with his hands on the desk, as if he had planned this confrontation. 'Okonjo will be popular if he stops foreigners from wasting our oil.'

Tom smiled grimly. 'William, we want to play our part in increasing oil recovery, but our game goes beyond the next election. Ten years ago we supported Okonjo and he was able to topple Misoto. That embargo cost us dearly. We put our trust in Okonjo and he should trust us now to make the most of Bigeria's oil. He owes us.'

'*Have I overplayed my hand?*' Tom thought. '*If I report back that this dispute is intractable, the board will fire me.*'

Tinibu waved him back to his seat. 'Tom, Canoil has indeed made the most of it — for Canoil. You have done nicely for yourselves but wasted Bigeria's oil. That era has ended. You need to show your commitment to increasing oil recovery. You must set up a demonstration plant. What do you say?'

'Could Hotu people at Panypo blame Canoil for their empty bellies? A plant would be at risk of sabotage or hijacking.'

'Our army will protect it.'

'The situation with the Hotus is unstable. My board will not invest in a risky project. They will want your government to first relieve the famine.'

'We are addressing the problem. It is not your concern. By the way, the money you sent out to the regions has been returned to the government in Akar.'

'*Fuck!*' he thought. '*They have thwarted The Pincer. Our only leverage now is to withhold a demonstration plant.*'

He fought down his anger. 'The famine must be relieved before we will fund a demo plant.'

'I will pass your message to our Cabinet,' said Tinibu. 'We will wait until the end of the month for you to commence a plant, before we stop loading your tankers.'

'My board would want a written agreement,' said Tom.

'Thank you for coming,' William said, as they shook hands. 'A long-term relationship like ours is based on trust. When you make a commitment to increased recovery by commencing a plant, we will renew our commitment to your company.'

'*You snaky bastard!*' he thought. '*Your idea of trust is to exploit us to get your party re-elected. Vicki is fortunate to have escaped your corrupted grasp.*

William was a political heavyweight, devious and a con man. Unless Tom was careful, he would cheat Canoil. He used the handrail to walk down the stairs, unable to see past his belly where to put his feet. His feeling of imminent catastrophe was unnerving and he wanted to eat.

He felt unclean when he remembered that what he had done now clashed with what he had done earlier.

'I have been compromised badly,' he thought. *'I am now envoy for a development identical to the one that I fired Antcliffe for advancing. I fired him unfairly. I am a hypocrite.'*

On his way back to Canada, he visited Vicki.

'I met with William Tinibu in Bigeria the other day. Did you know he's their Energy Minister?'

Her face was indifferent.

'Oh, really? How did you get on with him,' she said.

'We agreed some things.'

He told her about his four wives and 18 children. She laughed with joyful vindication. It was better that she had never stood a chance.

'Canoil could go into an agreement with him.'

'Don't believe a thing he says,' she told him. 'He is only interested in promoting himself.'

'That's politics for you. What was he like when you knew him?'

'He was an honest engineer — politics changes people.'

'Would you like some payback for his cheating?'

'Thanks for the offer, but I don't want you to do anything to him. I am over what he did to me.'

'He has been taking money that belongs to the Hotus.'

'He's a cheat. I hope they punish him.'

They danced in her lounge to Bob Marley. Vicki was a good dancer, with her bare midriff and hips swinging sexily as she stepped backwards and forwards. The hypnotic rhythm and her erotic dancing were tantalising and they kissed briefly before she pulled away.

Later that evening he squeezed up the narrow staircase. Tired, he fell into a soft bed, with crisp white linen and a duvet so light he could barely feel it on him. He was happy to be close to Vicki. His marriage had stopped him going to her. He had hardly spoken to Ruth since Michael had gone away and his loyalty to her was costing him too much. He waited for Vicki to join him, but when she did not, he turned over and slept.

The next day he trekked back to Heathrow.

The Concorde hurtled down the runway at 400 kilometres per hour, climbed steeply, passed over Vicki's house and then levelled off at 0.95 Mach to prevent damage to buildings and livestock. They passed over Bristol and were well down the Severn estuary when a 'second take-off' pulled him back in his seat again and they accelerated up to cruise at Mach 2.

He arrived back at JFK in the afternoon and transferred to a subsonic plane that chased the lowering sun to land at Toronto in time for an evening meeting of the board.

The feeling of dread had stayed with him. Small movements at the corner of his eye startled him, readying him to freeze, flee or fight. Danger threatened but he had no idea what to expect.

CHAPTER 88
DEMONSTRATION

'Gentlemen,' said Chairman Ralph Gooder, addressing the board meeting, 'Tom is back from Bigeria. Oil Minister Tinibu will stop exporting to us unless we build a demonstration plant.'

'To demonstrate what?'

'Miscible flooding. It's a new process we are developing.'

'What would it cost?' asked a director.

'100 million and 20 million a year to operate,' Tom told him.

'Peanuts,' someone said.

'There could be additional costs,' Tom began. 'We don't have much experience with this type of technology.'

'Is it risky?'

'Yes. There could be teething problems.'

'If we have an accident, they could nationalise us,' said Gooder.

'It is on Hotu land and they could sabotage the plant,' said Tom.

The board members scanned the pages of Tinibu's proposal in silence.

Presently Gooder said, 'Canoil never obeys an illegal demand.'

'It is legal,' said Tom. 'They don't have to renew our licences.'

Gooder leaned back in his chair. 'This project does not meet our investment criteria.'

'If we refuse or delay, Tinibu will demonise us. We could be shut out permanently.'

'The technology could take years to work properly,' a board member said. 'High tech is a ball game we would rather not play.'

'It's not like a quantum change,' someone said. 'We can learn to add solvent to our game and win.'

'We should demand that they relieve the famine,' said Tom.

'We have already done that and Okonjo won't help the Hotus,' said Gooder. 'If we had an agreement, he would not honour it. He's got us over a barrel and we'll have to build the plant. Tom, you must be sure it is absolutely safe.'

'Okay.'

Gooder said, 'I want Tom and Manfred to go to New York and London to reassure United's shareholders that Picard's threat to revoke licences is merely a new variation on the old theme of 'oil company bashing'. The PM is trying to use the Bigerian situation as a lever to raise oil recovery in Canada.'

On his next visit with Vicki, she was rather off-hand and he wondered if he had failed a test of serious interest. Until now he had supposed that their relationship was like a lifeboat that one day would rescue them from solitude and carry them away to happiness together. They needed to test if their relationship would float as soon as possible.

'When Michael finishes, I will be free,' he said to her.

'How long will that be?'

'I don't know. A month ago he called from the Marshall Islands in the South Pacific, where he was living in a thatched hut with an earthen floor, catching fish and eating coconuts. He was with a girl.'

'A chip off the old block,' Vicki said. 'How long before he returns?'

'He originally planned to be away a year, so it could be another six months.'

'If he resumes his PhD, how long will it take?'

'At least two and a half years.'

'So it could be at least three years,' she said disconsolately. 'Anything could happen in that time.'

'If the right man comes along, Vicki could grab him,' Tom thought. *'She could get a good price.'*

When he was in London, he stayed with Richard.

'How are you getting on with Vicki?' Richard asked.

'Okay'

'Are you going to get together?'

'I hope so.'

'When?'
'I'm not sure.'
'What is it between you two? You are forever pussy-footing around each other.'
'It's difficult to arrange.'
'Perhaps you don't want her enough.'
'No, quite the opposite. I can't get her out of my mind.'
'Since when?'
'Since we did our deal. I feel committed to get her back.'
'Do I get first refusal?' said Richard, smiling.
'She wouldn't give you another burl, mate.'
'But your short is closed.'
'Undelivered. I could go long. She's available.'
'She won't have you now.'
'Au contraire — I am going to make it happen.'

CHAPTER 89
PRODIGAL

It was a Friday evening when the telephone rang. Tom got to it before Ruth.

'Hello?'

'Dad! It's me, Michael!'

They hadn't heard from him for three months.

'Michael! Are you okay? Where are you?'

'Vanuatu. I'm okay. How are you? I'm arriving back tomorrow at 3.10 pm.'

'Fantastic. I've so missed you.'

He was at the airport, standing with his legs wide apart, as if on a heaving deck, dispensing crushing hugs. He had been away a year in remote places, hopping yachts, adventuring and contending with brutal weather. He was six feet, slim and muscular with bulging biceps, a seafarer, in a stripy blue T-shirt, calf-length blue shorts with a rope belt, deck shoes and a kitbag over his shoulder. His fair skin was tanned dark, his hair was crew-cut and had gone yellow.

He was tired and he went to bed for almost 24 hours.

'How are you?' Tom asked when he got up.

'Not real good. I am riddled with tropical infections and parasites. I'll go to the doctor first thing on Monday.'

He had a bath. Tom got him a lager, with a brandy for Ruth and a ginger beer for himself. He wondered if the alcohol-fuelled yachtie social life had affected him. He hoped he had matured and would settle down now and concentrate on his research.

Michael called Nicola in Toronto.

'When can I meet Scott, Sis?' he asked her. 'No, I don't want to do any more travelling for a while. This mountain will not come to your Mohammed. Can you come over here?'

He was his ebullient self, interested in everyone and everything, guffawing at his own jokes.

'Did you find yourself, during your travels?' Tom asked him.

'I don't like catching my own food, nor preparing it from scratch, nor getting water from a well, nor shitting in a stinking hole in the ground. I guess I am too used to having it easy. Fast food is heaven.'

Ruth was uncharacteristically quiet. She seemed to have lost touch with him.

Later, Michael asked Tom: 'How's Mum?'

'The same.'

'The same good, or the same bad?'

'Baddish.'

While he had been gone, his relations with Ruth had deteriorated.

'Dad, would you tidy your study?' Michael said the next day. 'It's bothering Mum.'

'Everything bothers her.'

'Well, it's bothering me too. Your study needs tidying up. Would you do it, please?'

'Don't you get on my case. Tell your mother she is not to hide my stuff.'

'You shouldn't leave it around. You'll have to tell her yourself.'

'I live here, too, remember. I can leave my things where I want!'

He and Michael easily saw eye to eye. When he and Ruth pulled in opposite directions, Michael was assiduously neutral and tried to find common ground between them. His return brought them together a little. Tom tidied his study.

'Have you told the university you are back, Michael?' he asked at breakfast.

'Yeah. I met with the department head yesterday. They have transferred the Gatz money here for me.'

It was a foundation grant for research.

'For PhD work?'

'Yes. Continuing from where I left off.'

Tom understood the internal battles Michael would have to fight to keep going, when what he was doing would seem futile. From his own bad experience, he wanted to support him as he wrestled with abstract ideas and negative results. When a thing had never been done before, to do it was harder than most people could imagine. Like a trapeze stunt without a net, doing a PhD was dangerous and unnerving.

'I admire that you are picking up where you left off,' he told Michael. 'Working hard is not enough. There can be unforeseen difficulties that could cause you to fail: your understanding may be lacking or incorrect; or support could be withdrawn; or you could have bad luck. Only success is rewarded. You need as much help with your PhD as you can get. You have my full support.'

'Thanks, Dad,' Michael said, 'but you don't have to keep tabs on me. I can look after myself.'

'Would that it were true,' thought Tom. *'Michael's attitude is admirable but I am not taking any chances.'*

He wrote to Vicki.

1828 62 Ave
SE Calgary
AB T2C 0B5

October 15th

Dear Vicki,

Are you okay? It has been six months since my visit and I worry about you.

Last week Michael returned to us, a seasoned traveller. He has resumed his PhD studies and is making an effort. Time will tell if his adventures have settled him down.

Sadly, this puts a hold on me joining you. You know my reasons for wanting to stay with him until it is in the bag, which is likely to be at least two and a half years. I apologise for once again putting my obligations to family first. Time may seem to be slipping away from us, but this last delay will soon pass and then I will be free.

I hope your days are filled with wonder and grace. Your work absorbs you and because you are good at it, it brings you pleasure. I am working harder than ever and do most of the things I want to, except for being with you.

The window of my study overlooks a row of cherry trees, festooned in pink blossom. The extravagant display contrasts with my work, which is rather colourless, dull and laborious, until I think of you. The blossom is cheery with promise of new life to come.
An end is in sight.
I love you,
Tom

His sense of impending doom now intruded night and day but he refrained from mentioning it again to Vicki. Whatever it was, he would deal with it alone.

CHAPTER 90
SAFETY

Michael worked at the lab until the early hours, then came home and slept until noon. When he took a day off, his laughter rang through the apartment, alleviating his parents' doom and gloom. He took over the lounge, listening to music, flicking TV channels, debugging a math model on his laptop, making smart remarks on Facebook and chatting on Skype. His ability to multi-task was awesome.

He came home one day when Tom was having breakfast. He hadn't seen Michael all week and seized this opportunity to talk to him.

'Michael, are you still wanting a field project?'

'Yes – why?'

'How would you like to design a plant for a miscible flood?'

It was the technology Michael was researching.

'Where?'

'Bigeria — the Panypo oilfield.'

'How depleted is it?'

'Maybe 10%. Secondary hasn't started.'

'What size of plant?'

'Demonstration — 10,000 barrels per day.'

'Wow! Almost commercial. What would I do?'

'Design the safety systems.'

'What risks are there?'

'High pressures, high temperatures, material failures, unknown geology, human error, isolation, sabotage, hijacking, civil war.'

'Fucking hell. Is there a deadline?'

'It will start up next year — as soon as it's safe.'

'Is this a job?'

'Yes. The university would second you to Canoil who would cover your expenses. You would go over there for about six months.'

'That would be perfect! I can get data to test my model. I'll do it.' He gave Tom a hug. 'Thanks, Dad!'

Later that week, Michael joined Tom's meeting with the design team. There were engineers and drafting technicians.

'I've called you together today to consider our design brief and set our goals,' Tom said to them. 'Because my reputation is on the line, I'm going to lead this project myself.'

He read from an overhead projection:

'Our design will extract as much of the oil remaining in the Panypo reservoir as is profitable, by dissolving it in a solvent distilled from the oil, by bringing it to the surface, by separating the oil and by re-injecting the solvent into fractures made in the rock, all the while maintaining reservoir pressure. Safety is the highest priority.

'The plant is to be constructed in a minimum of time.'

'Do we use Canadian or Bigerian safety standards?' asked one of the draftsmen.

'Bigerian,' said Tom.

'Their safety standards are lower,' an engineer said. 'Is it ethical to benefit Canadians by doing tests that could harm people overseas? Pharmaceutical companies have been criticised for testing medical treatments on gullible and uncomplaining Africans.'

'It is ethical,' Tom said. 'Bigeria will gain a project that trains her people and brings economic betterment. We will manufacture and preassemble the hardware here. We can start construction at Panypo at the beginning of next year. Construction should then be finished by mid-year. Are there any other questions?'

He tore open a can of Coke and drank a mouthful.

'About safety, could there be spontaneous combustion?' someone asked.

'If oxygen gets past the pressurised air seals at the compressor bearings, a few percent could set off an explosion that rips the plant apart,' Michael answered. 'We will bleed off gas to keep the concentration down. If it rises above one percent, the plant will be shut down automatically.'

The others heard Michael with respect. He had made a good start. Late at night, unable to sleep, Tom sometimes found him poring over his laptop. They often talked about technical matters. When he brought a girl home, as he often did, he would introduce her to Tom. None of the girls lasted for long. Michael wasn't looking to settle down and he left a trail of broken hearts.

At the back of Tom's mind a presentiment of approaching disaster lurked, but he was helpless to do anything except wait and watch.

CHAPTER 91
TUG-O-WAR

As usual, he called her from Heathrow.

'Hello Vicki. I'm here, at the airport.'

'Tom! Are you coming down? Can you stay?'

'I'm flying to Bigeria early tomorrow morning.'

'Well, come anyway!'

He drove down to Salisbury and arrived as it was getting dark. He sipped ginger beer while she cooked. It had been several months since they were together.

'Have you put on weight?'

'Yes. My self-respect is in tatters. I am trying to diet.'

'It's a chicken and egg. You need self-respect to stop your eating, but eating stops you self-respecting. You have to break the vicious circle. Aren't you getting enough self-respect from your job?'

'No. When does a slave have self-respect?'

'When his master likes his work!'

'The board find me useful but being their tool doesn't bring self-repect.'

'I thought you liked being CEO?'

'I do, obsessively. But it is ruining me.'

'You are addicted to work because it soothes your anxiety. You are out of the alcoholic frypan and into the workaholic fire! Addiction transfer, they call it.'

'Which should I do first, reduce work or reduce food?'

'Could you get an easier job?'

'It would be less enjoyable.'

'Then you must diet.'

'It wouldn't work,' Tom said. 'When I stop dieting, I go back to the weight I was before.'

'Hmm. What you need is a change of attitude. You need to go on a permanent diet. If you don't, you will have a heart attack and it will be too late.'

She continued cutting up vegetables for dinner.

'I have fears and they're getting worse,' he said. 'It seems like something is going to happen.'

'Like what?'

'I don't know. Something bad.'

'You worry a lot, don't you?'

'Usually I can deal with worries. This time I don't know what to expect.'

'You are anxious and it is causing your addictions. Addicts are driven by anxiety.'

'What can I do?'

'Identify your anxiety and face it down. Don't reach for a substance to abuse yourself with. You have freed yourself from tobacco, alcohol and sex. If you can get your eating under control, you will be able to focus on reducing your workload.'

'I am always hungry and I always overwork.'

'You have to stop snacking, binge-eating and working long hours.'

It was a negative start to an evening that lacked romance. Tom thought that his fat was putting Vicki off and resolved to reduce his weight back to 80 kilograms as it had been five years earlier.

Before going to bed, he put his arms around her but she moved away.

'What about Ruth? And Nicola and Michael?' she said.

He was not sure whether she was reminding him not to desert them, or to be with her he had to do something about them. It was a classic Catch 22 situation. If he wanted her enough, he would have to desert his children. But if he deserted his children, she wouldn't want him.

'Does Vicki understand the pull on me of my children?' he thought. *'How they are stopping me going to her?'*

'Come and live with me in Canada.'

'My mother and family need me in England,' she said.

'Why don't you come back to live in the UK?' Vicki asked the next morning.

'I want to,' he said. 'I am being pulled by you, by family and by friends to come here. But I am pulled to stay in Canada by Michael, Nicola and Canoil. It is like a tug-o-war across the Atlantic. The UK would win, if I could be sure you wouldn't fizzle.'

'Me? Fizzle?'

'It has happened before.'

'When?'

'At least five times: at the May Ball; after the lie detector; when you went with Richard; when we went skiing in the Rockies; and Mission Figurehead. You pushed me away every time.'

'That was your fault,' said Vicki bitterly. 'You went wandering off, you horny sod!'

'Do you trust me now?'

'My expectations are dulled,' she said disconsolately. 'You always put your family first.'

It was true. He had no qualms in subordinating Vicki's wants to his family's needs. It was too late now to have a child with Vicki and his selfish genes gave Ruth's children priority. With Vicki there remained companionship and sex. It would be enough. He wanted to put Vicki first but he had to be free from Ruth.

'Goodnight,' he said.

If only Vicki and I were strangers again, before the lie detector,' he thought.

Early next morning he kissed her briefly goodbye.

'I hope to be with you permanently before long,' he said.

He would get together with Vicki soon, bugger the consequences.

CHAPTER 92
SPAGHETTI LAUNCH

Yesterday Michael had picked up his father from the airport and taken him to a hotel in Akar. He had caught up on his sleep and they had driven to Panypo where Michael had been setting up safety systems at the Canoil plant.

He drove Tom to a grandstand, erected for today's opening, in front of a 10-hectare tangle of pipes, towers and tanks. A distillation column trickled steam like Apollo on the launch pad, flanked by pressure vessels the size of buses. There were huge pumps coupled in trains, with multi-lane highways of pipelines between rows of oil wells, like a plantation of steel Christmas trees.

Tom climbed up into his seat with difficulty. God, he was unfit. He sat under a galvanised iron roof that creaked as puffs of cumulus took turns blocking the baking tropical sun. He mopped his brow with a handkerchief. Behind him, a dozen white-helmeted field engineers were talking quietly. On their right, 100 African workers with yellow helmets stood waiting under the shade of an awning, overlooking the plant they had constructed.

Michael came out of the control room opposite and walked over to Tom. He was slim, fit and brisk, reminding Tom of himself at that age.

'Is everything ready?' Tom asked.

'Yes.'

'How did the fracking go?'

'We pumped down several tankers of kerosene, but we had to go up to 6000 pounds.'

'Fucking hell,' said Tom. 'That's lethal. Are all the safety systems ready?'

'Yup. At the first sign of trouble she will shut down in seconds.'

'Good. Where is Tinibu?'

'He's usually late.'

Half an hour later, two motorcycle outriders bumped across the site under fluttering Bigerian flags, with a procession of government vehicles following. A white Land Rover stopped in front of the stand and Tinibu got out. He was wearing a white uniform with epaulets, lanyard, peaked hat and gold braid.

'Good morning, Minister,' Tom greeted him, shaking hands. 'Thank you for coming. When you are ready, we will sit in the stand.'

Tinibu followed him and sat with him.

'I knew you would come,' Tom said. 'Once an engineer, always an engineer.'

'Starting this plant is important to my country's future,' he said.

His aides filled the rest of the stand. Tom introduced him to Michael.

'The Minister was at Liverpool Uni,' Tom said. 'He is a petroleum engineer.'

'Your father and I have experiences in common,' William said, smirking.

'He is alluding to Vicki,' Tom thought, scowling. *'His bragging disrespects her.'*

'How will we know when oil is being produced?' Tinibu asked.

'See that tank?' Michael pointed. 'On the left end is a spinner with yellow and black stripes.'

'Are we ready?' Tom asked Michael.

'Yep,' he said, nodding.

'Minister, would you please go with Michael and press the button?'

Tinibu climbed down stiffly and went with Michael into the control room. A siren sounded and a handful of workers scurried out and joined the others under the awning.

The train of compressors began a strangled howl, with grainy squishing of liquid through small aperture holes. The noise increased to a shriek. They could see the steel pipes vibrating, the enormous internal pressure straightening out expansion loops, bending brackets holding them in place and bursting free from concrete supports.

'Bloody hell!' Tom thought. *'This is the most dangerous plant ever. If I order a shutdown, Tinubu would take away our licences. He wants this plant and we have to see it through.'*

Tinibu came back from the control room and took his seat.

They watched, mesmerised, as the spinner began turning and became a blur. With a roar, the pressure relief valve on top of the tallest distillation column blasted out a jet of colourless gas that shimmered in the light. A flare pit 100 metres away whooshed into flames as slugs of oil spurted from a steel pipe half a foot in diameter laid along the surface. The pipe kicked and began flailing wildly in a circle, lashing like a garden hose. It picked up speed, whirling around and whistling like a firework.

'Get down,' Tom yelled at the people in the stand.

The pipe whipped around and slashed in through one wall of the control room and out of the other side, slicing off the top of the building as cleanly as a knife through butter.

Michael was in there.

'He must be cut apart, crushed and dead,' Tom thought.

'Michael!' he yelled as he scrambled down and lumbered across, colliding with workers running in the opposite direction.

There was a sharp bang as the blow-out preventer on the wellhead drove blind rams in and severed the production tubing string. The pipe stopped flailing. Silence resounded, but the thunder of the discharge was still in his ears as he reached the wrecked control room and pounded on the door.

'Michael!' he shouted.

'Here,' said a small voice. Perhaps he imagined it.

The peace was short-lived. Suddenly, the wellhead hissed and increased to a thunderous roar. Tom flattened himself on the ground as the heavy valve assembly flipped back. Emerging from underground like a long thin Saturn launch vehicle, a kilometre of steel tubing accelerated upwards, jacketed in flame. It made a cluster high overhead like a clump of black spaghetti and fell down several hundred metres away in a cloud of dust. Fumes from the wellhead swept over him, his eyes wept and he lost consciousness.

CHAPTER 93
THRONE DISCOVERY

The ceiling spun down to a stop like a vinyl record on a turntable. Tom was flat on his back. He could not feel any pain and he was nauseous. He could see white walls, the top of a wardrobe, a glass-fronted cabinet and a doorway.

'I must be in hospital,' he thought. *'What happened? I remember the plant exploding. Perhaps I was gassed. Where is Michael? Is he alright?'*

He remembered hearing a voice from inside the wrecked control room, but nothing after that.

'Hello,' he called out.

'Here, Sir. How are you feeling?'

It was a nurse with a smiling face in a crisp white uniform.

'Where am I?'

'This is Botibo Hospital.'

'Is Michael, my son, here?'

'I'll check if he's been admitted.'

'Thank you.'

While she was gone, he rolled on to his side. He could see William Tinibu lying on his back in the next bed. He was either unconscious or sleeping.

Then a Caucasian woman walked in.

'Tom! How are you?'

It was Vicki. It seemed like a dream. He was delighted. She gave him a peck on the cheek. She must have come on a care mission. She had never shown such interest in him before.

He recovered his voice.

'What are you doing here, Vicki?'

'I heard there was an accident and that you were in hospital. So I came to see if you were alright.'

It was a long way to come, to a place where a single white woman was a novelty.

'Thank you. It was lovely of you to come. I don't know where Michael is. He could be dead.'

'He could be alive,' she said. 'What's happened to you?'

'I must have been gassed.'

Just then the nurse came back. She shook her head. 'Your son has not been admitted, Sir.'

'I'll check with the ambulances,' Vicki said, going out. She came back five minutes later.

'He wasn't with the others they brought here. Two workers are dead. Perhaps he was taken somewhere else.'

'If he was well, he would have been in contact.'

They were interrupted.

'Hello, Vicki. It's nice to see you.'

It was William's hoarse voice from the next bed. Vicki turned minimally towards him, as if to discourage his interaction.

'Hello, William. How are you?'

'I am okay. I have a headache and my wrist hurts. How have you been?'

'I have been perfectly white, thank you.'

Tinibu grimaced. She was not here to talk with him.

'Was Tom your boyfriend before me?'

'Tom and I have been friends for a long time, William,' Vicki said stiffly. 'They say you have been putting your countrymen's oil money into your Swiss bank account, leaving them to starve. Is it true?'

'Of course not. You know me better than that,' Tinibu shook his head vigorously.

'I know you are a liar and a cheat, William. I am going to look for Michael.'

She left.

'That one has a sharp tongue,' said William Tinibu.

'You seem to have offended her.'

Tom got down from the bed, in his hospital gown with bare buttocks, and walked along the corridor past the nurses' station. They did not look up. He went down to the crowded reception area, where he ran into Vicki going the other way.

'What are you doing, Tom?'

'Any news of Michael?'

'Nothing.'

'Come with me.'

He grabbed her arm and steered her towards the exit door.

'Where are we going?'

'To look for Michael.'

'But—'

'Sh—'

With all the dignity that his bare bottom could afford, they walked out of the main entrance and down the steps. He opened a taxi door for Vicki and climbed in the other side.

'Good afternoon, driver,' he said boldly.

'Yes, Sir.'

'Take us to Panypo Oilfield please.'

'To the accident place?' The driver was incredulous.

'That's right.'

He shook his head. 'I no go there.'

'Why not?'

'Too far.'

'How far?'

'Maybe two hours.'

'I will pay you to go there and come back. How much?'

'Five t'ousan zlotis.'

'Okay.'

'You have money? Show me, please.'

Tom turned to Vicki. 'Do you have any cash?'

'Only a little. Six hundred.'

He managed to get eye contact with the driver. 'I am the chief of Canoil. I will get money at Panypo. It is an emergency, to find my son.'

'It is true,' Vicki said grimly.

The driver gave the two foreign devils the benefit of the doubt.

'Okay, Chief.' He started the car.

'Quickly, man,' Tom said, as he spotted a nurse and two orderlies running down the hospital steps. They sped away.

It was just as well Tom's backside was well-padded, because the axle jarred under the car seat and it was like sitting on a farm tractor. After a while he went to sleep.

When he woke up with Vicki beside him, it seemed like a dream. Next she was poking him in the ribs.

'We have arrived.'

The Canoil office was a hut. He struggled to get out of the taxi. The receptionist did not have any money and the accident had disconnected the telephone. They could see a plume of black smoke in the distance.

Tom pointed to the smoke.

'Take us there,' he said to the taxi driver.

When they arrived, oil was sputtering from a wellhead and a creek was alight with a sooty flame. A group of natives sat under a tree. Hand in hand with Vicki, they ran past them to the decapitated control room and pounded on the jammed door.

'Michael,' Tom yelled.

There was no reply. They ran back to the group.

'Can someone help open the door?'

The assembly eyed his bare bottom with amusement.

'This man is a big chief. His son is in there,' Vicki said, pointing to the damaged building. She flexed a bicep. 'Is there a strong man who can open the door?'

A very large man, with a muscular body spilling out of his tank top, got to his feet and stomped along beside them. The sweat poured off Tom, whose thighs rubbed as he walked.

'Me Tom,' he said. 'This Vicki.'

'Me Aziz,' said the giant.

'Is Michael in there?' Tom asked when they reached the jammed door.

Aziz stopped.

'No, him not,' he shook his head and wagged his finger. 'Him at Chief house.'

'Him okay?'

Aziz grimaced and shook his head. 'Maybe deaded.' He rolled up his eyes.

Tom involuntarily sobbed.

'Can we see him?'

'Okay. We go.'

Aziz picked up the driver like a child and put him behind the wheel. He squeezed in the other side and the taxi sank onto its axles. They bumped along a track for a kilometre to a circle of dung and thatch dwellings. In the gaps between the buildings were thorn branches to deter lions. There was a communal house and a water well. The Chief's hut was of superior construction, with a galvanised iron roof and a portaloo outside.

Michael was lying inside.

'Michael!' Tom knelt and hugged him. 'How are you?'

'I'm better now but I can't stand up. It was the gas.'

'What happened?'

'I heard an explosion and dived under the table . . . something smashed through the roof . . . the door was jammed . . . I crawled through a hole at the back . . . there was gas . . . I fell into the portaloo . . . shut the door . . . don't remember . . . must have passed out.'

'How come the rescue party missed you?'

'I was lying jammed against the door and they couldn't open it.'

'Then what happened?'

'They came back to get the portaloo and found me. They brought me here.'

'Does the chief use the portaloo?'

'Yes. It's a status symbol, confessional and throne. He uses it for consultations.'

'Crikey. You were lucky they wanted it,' said Vicki.

'Yes. I was in the shit,' said Michael. 'Hello, who are you?'

Tom introduced her. 'Michael, this is Vicki. The last time she saw you, you were six years old.'

'Hi, Vicki,' he said. 'You haven't changed. Do you work with Dad?'

'No. We are old friends. We were at uni together.'

'Oh, I see,' he said. 'Were you his girlfriend?'

Vicki hesitated. 'We were just good friends.'

They chatted for a while.

'I need to sleep.'

They left him to snooze. It was hot and Tom's gown stuck to his back. After a tour of the village and meeting some of the people, the Chief's wife asked them in for lemonade. Michael revived and joined them.

'Thank you for saving my son,' Tom said to them. 'I would like to give you something to show my appreciation. Would you prefer a Land Rover or a Jeep?'

The Chief shook his head, embarrassed.

'No, we do not want.'

As they were leaving, his wife took Tom aside.

'We want a 10-seater people mover, please,' she said. 'For the villagers.'

Tom agreed.

The cabby drove a very full car back to the hospital. Tom obtained money from a bank and paid him. Tinibu and the others had been discharged.

Tinibu was staying at a hotel in the town. He had a broken wrist in plaster.

'It is fortunate I am not worse,' he said to Tom.

'I warned you that we should wait for the results of the pilot plant.'

Tinibu snorted. 'No. You fucked up.'

He turned to his offsider. 'Dismantle the demo plant. We will have to make do with water injection. I want oil flowing as soon as possible.'

He turned back to Tom and Michael.

'Get your sorry asses out of our country.'

'It will be a pleasure.'

They didn't speak to him again.

'If we leave now we can get to Akar in daylight,' Michael said and booked rooms at the Sofitel.

It was getting dark when they arrived and checked into separate rooms. Their plane would depart the next day. The three had dinner together and then Michael met a friend and went off for a drink. Vicki and Tom were alone at last.

CHAPTER 94
IMPORTUNATE OCCASION

Tom and Vicki strolled hand-in-hand into the Akar city centre at dusk. Businesses were closing and workers were homeward bound through emptying streets. On the way back to the hotel they passed through a park where scarlet petals from flame trees carpeted the ground, glowing in the artificial light. They tiptoed gingerly, savouring this time together they knew would be brief.

Tom looked at her and she smiled shyly. The wind blew her hair across her face and she pushed it back. In the Verandah Bar they sat apart from the other drinkers, their chairs side by side, overlooking the soft shapes and shadows of the garden. Leaves skittered and glittered in the moonlight.

He looked at the drinks menu. 'Would you like a cocktail? You can have a Martini, Singapore Sling, Daiquiri, Orgasm, Black Russian, Chapman —'

'An Orgasm sounds interesting,' she said with a twitch of a smile. 'What is it?'

'I haven't had one for ages,' he countered, reading from the menu. 'It's a mixture of Cointreau, Baileys and Irish Cream.'

'Perhaps I'll have one later,' she said. 'How about getting a bottle of champagne? Oh, but you don't drink.'

'No, but you have a glass.'

'I'd prefer an Orgasm.'

Tom ordered it, with a coffee for himself. When they brought the drinks, she linked her drinking arm through his.

'A penny for them,' she said, grinning.

'I was reflecting that I have wanted to have sex with you many times before but it has never happened.'

'What makes you think this time is any different?' she asked coyly. 'I am having an Orgasm by myself.'

'Ladies come first, but simultaneous orgasms are better,' he said, smiling.

'You are all talk,' Vicki laughed. 'Well, drink up then.'

By the time they finished their drinks, they were pushing their tongues into each other's mouths. They stood up and headed for the elevators, hand in hand. Vicki came to his room. He wrapped his arms around her. She felt soft and warm.

'Let's take off our clothes,' she said.

By the time he had hung up his suit and brushed his teeth, she was under the sheet.

'Come on!'

He put the light out and got in. It was a huge bed and after he found her they held each other close. As he ran his hands up her back, he marvelled at the firmness of her body and the smoothness of her skin. He was filled with apprehension that he would disappoint her and she would reject him again. He felt clumsy, awkward and inadequate. He had imagined making love to Vicki but he was tense and his body failed to rise to the occasion.

'Fucking hell,' he said. 'I'm out of action.'

'Tonight is your first night out of hospital. Could that be it?' she asked.

'It could be post-traumatic cock disorder,' he said. 'I have been waiting for you so long the mechanism has rusted up.'

'I'll bet you have worked it a few times, haven't you?'

'I mean my neurons are fibrillating. I have thought about you so much, I can't get started.'

'Perhaps you don't have enough feeling for me?'

'*The issue for me is trust, as it has been all along,*' he thought.

'No, the opposite,' he said. 'My feelings have been hurt so many times, my subconscious is refusing to be made vulnerable again. My mouse fears a trap and is too wary to grab the cheese.'

Vicki moved away from him. 'Don't you trust me? After I have flown halfway around the world for you?' She was indignant.

'I trust you, but I worry about your commitment. When a male and a female are capable of injuring each other, they have elaborate and protracted courting rituals. They expose themselves to each other with great care. If a mare kicks a stallion's testes, it can be the end of his life with the herd, so he waits until she wants him. A praying mantis may bite off her lover's head. A male has to be circumspect and make sure of his wicket before wielding his wedding tackle. Because I love you so much, I fear what you can do to me. I need more time with you, to get used to you. Then trust will happen.'

'I see. But we never do have much time together, do we?' She was forlorn.

'We will, before long; I promise you. I will leave Ruth, quit Canoil and move to England.'

'When?'

'As soon as possible.'

'Do you trust me enough to sleep together?'

'Yes of course. There's nowhere I'd rather be.'

'Goodnight then.'

'Goodnight, Vicki.'

They fitted together and slept.

He was up at 4 am as usual. He made himself coffee and sat quietly doing his paperwork until Vicki got up. They went down to breakfast together. She was distant.

'Are we okay?' he asked her.

'Yes, I think so,' she said. 'You are not exactly the warm cuddly type, are you? Your work must be very important for you to get up so early.'

'When I wake up my mind threshes around in circles and I am unable to get back to sleep. So I get up.'

'I thought you were going to reduce your working time?'

'I'm trying to.'

After breakfast, they packed and went to Akar Airport with Michael. Aboard, they lay back in recliners in first class. She seemed pensive.

'Can we talk about living together when I come over?' he asked.

He had long imagined this conversation and that she would be welcoming.

'What about it?' she replied yawning.

'I want our lives to overlap as much as possible,' he said. 'I want to be with you in every way I can.'

'What would we do? Apart from sex . . . if that becomes available?'

He ignored the jibe.

'You have a job,' he said. 'I'll get a job. Could we do things together at weekends?'

'Routine stuff, visiting people – like my family. Parties.'

'Could we go to a show in London?'

'That would be nice, once in a while.'

She didn't make any other suggestions. Discouraged, he fell silent. She went to sleep. When they reached Heathrow, they went through Immigration together, leaving Michael in the transit lounge. They collected her bag and took a lift to where she was parked. The concrete car park was oppressive.

As they hugged beside her car, they were both lost in their thoughts.

'Thank you for coming to look for me,' he said. 'It was kind and brave of you.'

'You can trust me,' she said.

She was not smiling.

A quick kiss and she got into her car and drove away into the distance.

He had become used to being with her and now she was gone.

He turned and walked back inside to where Michael was waiting. His life had taken an unexpected turn. He felt bruised but he had to keep putting one foot in front of the other. The sense of foreboding was there. He called Nicola to see if she was okay. She was fine.

On the flight to Calgary, Michael asked him about Vicki.

'Dad, what's your relationship with her?'

'She's a friend. I sometimes visit her when I am in England.'

There was a long pause.

'Are you going to leave Mum?'

'You shouldn't worry about that.'

'Why not?'

'We haven't talked about it. It is possible but not soon. Most marriages are uncertain underneath.'

'Okay.'

Michael went to sleep.

When he awoke, they talked together about the cause of the explosion.

'I don't know what went wrong,' Michael said. 'There could have been an explosion in the wellbore, or in the reservoir, or in both.'

'A movement in the rocks could have let in a bubble of high-pressure gas,' Tom said.

'It would have to be huge to pressure it up that much.'

'I agree. It doesn't seem possible.'

They tried to think of another explanation.

'The oxygen concentration wasn't high enough for spontaneous combustion,' said Michael.

'What about sulphur?' Tom exclaimed. 'Sulphur is an oxidant. Gas bores can get deposits of sulphurous compounds called mercaptans that decompose explosively.'

'But this is an oil well, right?'

'It produced gas for several years. Sulphur could have accumulated inside the production tubing.'

'The pressure and temperature were high enough for sulphur to oxidise the hot kero — KABOOM!' Michael said, causing passengers near them to look. 'Spontaneous combustion. I never thought of sulphur — I didn't have time to check every possibility.'

'We couldn't have foreseen it.'

Tom had been back in Canada a few days when the Canoil manager in Akar reported that oil production had resumed from the Panypo field.

'Okonjo has appointed a replacement for Tinibu,' he said.

'Good riddance,' Tom thought. *'It was wrong of him to insist we build the plant before we were ready.'*

Tom was glad to be back in his office, working quietly, preparing board papers. Now that the accident had faded from the news, he could relax but his growing apprehension of catastrophe kept him on edge.

Manfred showed him a media release from the Federal Government.

Ministry of Energy and Resources.
APPOINTMENT OF COMMISSION OF INQUIRY INTO
OIL RECOVERY

A Commission led by Dr Arnold Southwell, a consultant petroleum engineer, will investigate the cause of the recent explosion at Panypo Oilfield in Bigeria, in which two workers were killed.

The Commission will evaluate need for government control of investment in oil recovery technologies being tested by Canoil in Canada and overseas. It will consider efficiencies and safety of oil extraction technologies at Canadian oilfields.

'We have not achieved the improvement in efficiency the PM wanted,' Manfred said. 'He needs a fall guy, so he won't lose face.'
'Who?'
Tom shrugged. 'Me. Who else?'
'Why not Okonjo?'
'It may not be politically correct to blame a foreign head of government for an accident in their country.'
'Probably not.'
'Someone is going to be blamed and it looks like me.'

CHAPTER 95
COMPANY RETREAT

Ian was waiting at Calgary Airport, beside the King Air in his pilot's livery. Tom climbed into the co-pilot's seat with difficulty and started working his way down the pre-flight checklist. Ruth had the passenger cabin to herself. Ian had set it up with a couple of bunks, a bar for Ruth, snack foods and a coffee maker. Ian pulled up the stairs, bolted the door and got into the pilot's seat.

They were flying to the company's house at Montego Bay, Jamaica, for two weeks' holiday. They cruised down across the mid-western states, landing after eight hours at Memphis. Ian parked for refuelling and radioed for pizzas and fruit salad to be brought out from the terminal building. Tom added the price of the food to the docket for fuel and signed.

They rested their plates on the wing and stretched their legs as they watched the sun set. It was balmy. He smiled as he recalled freezing winters and cold wet summers in the distant Yorkshire Dales. He had been fortunate to rise to the top of a large corporation and have privileges including exclusive access to a plane and the company's mansion.

'I am going to try and get some sleep,' Ruth said.

'Me too,' said Tom.

'I hope you are not going to snore.'

'I'll sleep on my side.'

At midnight, an alarm woke him and he went forward to join Ian who had slept in the cockpit. Tom changed seats and piloted for the second half of the flight. He taxied out to the runway with the fuselage lights flashing and took off through a layer of stratus. To hurtle blindly through the night in command of so many different systems was a tonic of empowerment, an ego trip. He kept a steady vigil, periodically running checks. These hours would reach the total he needed for an instruments rating.

Dawn was coming up over the Gulf as they passed over the Bahamas and swung around Guantanamo, for the final leg into Montego Bay.

They touched down in a cloud of dust and slithered to a halt in front of the make-shift terminal building. Tom had called Garfield, their housekeeper, ahead from Memphis and he was there in the Land Rover. The Customs officer would come out to the house later.

They drove through the village, with its dirt floor dwellings and barefoot children. Some of the local people had invested in tourism and the local economy was buoyant. The oilmen's wealth caused some resentment but Tom didn't feel that his lifestyle was unfair or that he owed the locals anything. On the contrary, he envied them their simple and integrated lifestyle.

Ian had recounted a story that in Italy two peasants were labouring in a vineyard beside an autostrada, when a Ferrari drove past.

'Hey, Alberto, look!' said one. 'How beautiful is that?'

'I don't like it,' said the other. 'The price of that car is more than I will earn in my whole lifetime of hard work. It makes me feel very small.'

'Nonsense! Isn't it wonderful that a person can own such a thing!' exclaimed the other. 'One day perhaps your son or my daughter will own one. Think of the pleasure they will have!'

'Happiness does not require wealth,' he thought.

He was in a beautiful place and his work took second place to enjoying himself. The beach house faced a secluded lagoon with white sand shaded by coconut palms. Canoil held conferences of senior managers there. Garfield and his family maintained it and had their own small house behind.

He snorkelled over the reef in the day and went to house parties in the evenings. He imagined his colleagues in Canada would be shivering. It worried him that Ruth was so unhappy. People didn't usually persist with marriages when there was as little interaction as theirs. When they extended kindnesses to each other, such as drinks and snacks, they were habit, mere following of tradition. Tom and

Ruth were opponents and there were small conflagrations. Garfield tiptoed around as if in a minefield.

'Can I get you anything, Ruth?' Tom asked the next morning.

She shook her head without making eye contact, sipping from a glass. He seldom saw her without a drink in her hand. He would not let Ruth's brooding silences spoil his holiday. He wanted to enjoy his vacation and return to Calgary refreshed.

'Let's go sailing,' he said.

Canoilster was the company's 12-metre sloop moored at the yacht club. To her credit, Ruth had always crewed for him, usually under protest. It was their only surviving joint activity, apart from providing for their children.

'You go,' she said.

'You'll enjoy it,' he said. 'We will be in Grand Cayman in two days. I'll call Hans and see if we can stay at their place. We can split the mainbrace while you and Lottie go shopping.'

Ruth was thoughtful and replied slowly.

'Why do you need me to come?'

It was a tradition. The days when he and Ruth enjoyed being together were long past.

'It will be fun. Also, it will be safer if something goes wrong.'

'What could go wrong?'

'I could slip and fall overboard. I need you to help with the sails.'

'Are you going to put up that big one, like the one that nearly sank us at Zapulco?'

She never missed an opportunity to remind him of the spinnaker that had pulled them over in a squall. She helped to bail out and they recovered. Since then, whenever they heeled over in a breeze, Ruth was immobilised by fear. Running fast behind a kite was the apogee of his sailing pleasure and she was trying to thwart him.

He bit his lip.

'The spinnaker? Okay, I won't put it up, I promise.'

'And we won't be all tippy?'

'No, we'll be upright on a beam reach.'

'Could we hit a reef?

'Oh, come on. There's only deep water between here and Grand Cayman. With this wind, we'll be there in a couple of days.'

'Will it be rough?'

'No, like a millpond. The wind will be abeam both going and coming back; just a slow roll. No pounding into waves, I promise.'

'Will we be sailing at night?'

'The self-steering vane is very safe. It will be bliss under the stars.'

She paused and weighed it up. He could take Garfield if necessary.

'Okay,' she said reluctantly. 'I'll come, so long as I won't be stuck at the helm.'

'No, you won't. You'll have a great time.'

'When do we leave?'

'I'll give the Kings a call.'

Ruth liked the Kings. He telephoned them in Grand Cayman.

'They will have lunch for us when we arrive,' he told Ruth. 'I'll ask cookie for breakfast at 5.30.'

CHAPTER 96
HEADING OUT

At first light, Garfield's wife, Marjory, served up bacon, eggs and baked beans. Ruth wasn't hungry, as if her participation in the cruise would be minimal. Garfield drove them to the yacht club. He dragged the trolley with the dinghy down to the water, collected the outboard from a locker and attached it. Tom and Ruth got in and they motored out to the anchorage. It was almost low tide. *Canoilster* was in one of several parallel lines of yachts, swinging in a gusty breeze, jerking at the anchor chain.

They lifted their gear onto the transom and clambered aboard. Garfield went back with the dinghy. Ruth fed the mainsail leach into its track as Tom pulled it up with a halyard. They unfurled the jib from around its forestay. The sails flapped and fluttered, eager to work.

The scene was bathed in a peculiar early morning light. As he prepared *Canoilster* to sail out into the ocean, Tom felt as if something awful was about to happen and was more careful than usual.

He switched on the electric winch to draw in the anchor. Suddenly, from the bows he heard the machine-gun chatter of the chain links bouncing over the drive wheel teeth.

'Go forward and put the chain back,' he said to Ruth.

'Are you talking to me, or is there a dog on board?'

She always rejected his skipper's authority.

'Please, Ruth,' he said.

She had never re-engaged the chain before, but she had seen him do it. The mainsail had filled and was pushing them back into the moored yachts behind. He stayed at the helm to steer away from collision.

'Quick!' he said, 'before the chain tightens.'

Ruth moved cautiously, with fear and reluctance. She edged forward gingerly along starboard, holding on to the lifelines for balance. With difficulty, she lifted the anchor chain and reinserted it in the sprocket. Tom started the winch and drew in the chain. There was a jerk as the anchor broke free from the bottom and the bows swung across. Both sails filled on the wrong side and pulled them towards the parked yachts.

'Shit,' he said.

He needed to be on the other tack but they didn't have enough forward momentum to go about. The mainsail had filled and was blocking Ruth's return aft. She went back to the bows, pushed the bloated jib aside, stepped around the forestay and began to come aft along the port side. The boat was turning quickly with the wind behind them. To avoid collision, he would have to accept a jibe — the boom would swing across with abrupt force.

'Jibing!' he called.

Ruth had reached the shrouds and was edging past the cabin, holding on to the lifelines. There was a gust from the other side of the mainsail and it filled with a bang. The heavy boom began to swing to the other side, picking up speed.

'Get down!' he shouted.

Ruth crouched but not low enough. The boom gonged her on the side of the head. She squealed and pitched sideways over the port lifeline into the water. He ran forward. She had not come up. He dived in where she disappeared.

He swam underwater, trying to see her. On his second dive, he found her, grabbed her and hauled her to the surface.

She wasn't breathing. Treading water, he held her nose and mouth up above the surface and yelled for help. A few minutes later a small inflatable arrived. With Tom pushing, the boatman strove to pull her aboard, but they had nothing to brace themselves against. They gave up, held her arms over the side of the inflatable and set off with her body and legs trailing in the water. The tiny outboard pushed them slowly towards the closest land, a sandbank about 200 metres away.

When they reached the sandbank, several people waded in and helped drag Ruth ashore. She looked dead.

'Help turn her down the beach,' Tom said, hauling her around by her arms, face down.

He pumped her back. Water gushed out of her mouth, about a litre. She vomited and went into a fit of coughing. He rolled her onto her side to keep it out of her lungs. Then she began wailing, a long yell. She was delirious and he tried to quieten her, but when she saw him she yelled even louder. A small crowd had gathered and someone had a blanket that they put over her.

'The coastguard helicopter will be here in about 10 minutes,' someone said.

She lapsed into unconsciousness and lay still. When the helicopter arrived, they put her on a stretcher, loaded it in and took off in a flurry of sand.

He called Garfield who came in the dinghy and they moored *Canoilster*. He set off in the Land Rover for Kingston Hospital, where they had taken her. He hoped she was not badly injured. He was responsible for Ruth's condition and felt sorry for her. Events had been unfortunate but he should have been more careful.

CHAPTER 97
RECUPERATION

After a three-hour drive he arrived in the Jamaican capital and found Ruth lying on a trolley in a hospital corridor.

'How are you?' he asked her.

'Not good,' she replied. 'Not that anyone cares.'

'I'm very sorry that you were hurt. It was my fault and I'm to blame.'

They had checked her condition and were awaiting results of a scan.

He gave her the magazines and chocolates he had brought.

'Did you bring my nightie and sponge bag?'

'Shit! I forgot. Sorry.'

She wailed piteously and he went to buy the things she wanted.

'I should have gone forward myself,' he told Ruth when he got back. 'I thought I ought to stay at the wheel. It was a mistake. Please forgive me.'

She was too traumatised to talk and he was unable to relieve her anguish. She seemed fearful of him.

'We CAT-scanned her head, but didn't find anything,' the doctor said. 'Her breathing has recovered from the immersion. There is a cut on the side of her head, which I have stitched up.'

He asked Tom to recount exactly what had happened. He seemed suspicious that Tom wasn't telling the truth.

'Perhaps she has complained that I deliberately injured her and he is checking in case they should inform the police,' he thought.

'She is distressed,' the doctor said. 'We will keep her here under observation.'

Tom slept in a room for visitors.

Next day, she wouldn't go home and they allowed her to stay in the hospital. It seemed pointless waiting for her and Tom went back to the beach house. He telephoned the hospital several times but she wanted to stay there.

'I don't want to be with you,' she said. 'I want to be cared for.'

Unable to neglect his job any longer, he returned alone to Calgary.

After two weeks, the hospital said they would discharge her and he took the King Air down with two nurses and brought her back. She walked into their apartment, bent over with pain and lay in bed, complaining. He hired a nurse-housekeeper-cook to look after her, supervised by her doctor.

She was a demanding patient and would not turn over in bed or pick up a book without help. Her doctor reassured Tom that her injuries were psychological and it would take time for her self-confidence to return.

Ruth stayed in her room and life at home improved for Tom. He loved having the run of the apartment.

'This is my kitchen,' she had said when they moved in and he had tried to cook some kippers. 'Stay out of it.'

Now he enjoyed preparing foods he liked. When he left papers, books and other things lying around, they were still there when he went to get them. It was empowering and a foretaste of how good life could be without her.

Ruth was unpleasant. He left her in the care of the housekeeper and stayed in the CEO suite at the office, checking on her progress by telephone.

When he came home at weekends, he slept in a separate room but she complained his snoring stopped her from sleeping. It was a month before she got out of bed and went to visit Nicola and Scott in Toronto for a couple of weeks.

When she went, he realised that he would prefer to live without her. He hoped she would stay away for a long time.

CHAPTER 98
SEPARATE INTERSECTION

With Ruth away, Tom reduced his working hours and spent time relaxing at home. When she returned, she arranged for Michael to collect her from the airport.

Tom was reading in his study when she came in.

'Hello,' he said getting up. 'Welcome back!'

They had long since ceased hugging and kissing.

'Sit down,' Ruth said. 'This could be a shock.'

He wondered what was coming.

'You know how we're always pulling each other down?'

He didn't know. She had certainly been difficult to live with. Perhaps it was his passive resistance that she was referring to. He had never intentionally 'pulled her down'.

'What do you mean?'

'I'm leaving you,' she said, pausing for a reaction.

He thought: *'Oh, yeah. I've heard that before. It is a threat, to get her own way.'*

'Really?' he said, showing no emotion.

'I'll take my stuff and go this weekend. Okay?'

He shrugged.

He didn't believe her. They had been together for more than 30 years. People did not leave each other after so long without a compelling reason. He hadn't ever hit her. She had gone without sex from him for many years. What was new? It didn't seem likely she had met someone else. She must be upset by something and would get over it.

He went back to his novel.

On Sunday, Ruth started packing suitcases and boxes. He realised with a spike of elation that she was going. He would be free at last!

'Where will you go?' he asked her.

'Janet's place.'

Janet was her sister. He supposed she must be staying with her until she got a place of her own.

She lined up boxes and suitcases by the door. He was surprised that she was taking so little and leaving behind so much she had been fond of.

'Aren't you taking the mobile phone?' he asked.

'When a woman leaves the married home, she can take away only what she brought to the marriage and things she acquired in her own right.'

After 30 years with him, her personal belongings were few. They had pooled almost everything.

'Who will get what?' he asked her now.

'We will divide it equally at settlement,' she said.

'That seems fair.'

Without asking, she loaded her things into the new car they had bought jointly and drove away in it. It was the last time she bullied him.

When she was gone, his anxiety was acute. Sadness welled up within him and he was numb. This must be the disaster that had been looming. He had not expected to feel like this. His head felt about to explode. He had lived with her for so long that separation was traumatic for him. He alternated between feeling nauseous and browsing at the fridge. Unprepared for solitude, he wandered through the apartment, remembering times they had shared. Michael stayed home from work to be with him.

'Are you going to see her at Aunt Janet's?' Tom asked him as he was going out.

'No. She's on her way to Toronto.'

'Toronto? Where will she stay there?'

'George Watt has flown over and is driving back with her.'

'Who is George Watt?'

'He was her boyfriend at university.'

Tom was dumbfounded. Her departure without warning must have been carefully planned over a long period, possibly several years. Ruth's duplicity explained things that had puzzled him, such as her secrecy. He didn't know when George Watt had first adulterated their marriage.

'Was she seeing him when she visited Nicola and Scott?'

'I guess so.'

Whenever he visited Vicki, he had told Ruth. He had not slept with her, ever. It appeared Ruth had not reciprocated his loyalty and he felt cheated.

Deeper than his disdain, he grieved for Ruth. Loss of a spouse is rated as the second most traumatic of life's experiences, after loss of a child. He and Ruth had been together for half his time alive. Finding himself alone, he sometimes had to fight panic. But Michael was there too, also suffering from the break-up.

'It seems bad now, Dad,' Michael said, 'but it will soon seem like a change for the better.'

'Yours and Nicola's pasts are torn up,' Tom's voice was strangled. 'I have no-one with whom to share memories of your childhoods.'

'We were there, too,' Michael said. 'We'll still be with you, Dad.'

He gave him a hug and they cooked their evening meal together.

Over the next few weeks, Michael supported and counselled him as he regained the self-determination that had been sidelined when he married Ruth.

Parts of his cerebral cortex seemed to have atrophied and he could barely function on his own. He had lost a part of himself, like an amputation. Ruth had bought their supplies, cooked, cleaned, monopolised their mobile phone, navigated their car and decided social activities. He had to learn to use the phone and GPS. He was free to create a social life of his own.

He emailed Vicki, telling her he had separated from Ruth, but she did not reply. He imagined she did not want to communicate with him until he had a definite plan. He needed time to adjust to being single and to appraise alternatives. He wanted to be totally restored before he went to Vicki. To rush at Vicki in the state that Ruth had left him in could jeopardise the relationship he had waited for so long.

Michael was with him but he was isolated, without other family or friends in Calgary. Loneliness stalked him like a shadow. Their marriage had been an unsuccessful companion planting: she had blocked his light, over-shadowed him and stunted his growth. Now Ruth was gone, he could resume growing. He could mix with whomever he liked and have male and female friends. He learned to go for walks and see movies alone. His health improved and the paranoia and delusions that had lingered from his marriage disappeared.

'I used to believe I was the Messiah,' he confessed to Manfred. 'I was that crazy.'

It was strange to be revealing this secret part of his life after so long.

'You have been a bit strange at times,' said Manfred, 'as though you were getting instructions from someplace else.'

'It is behind me now. My illusions were a bolthole in my subconscious where I would go to get away from Ruth's avarice.'

'What did she want?' he asked.

'Control. She countered my careers, monopolised our children, concealed herself from me and treated me like I was second-rate. To offset her negativity, I created an alternative world where I was a hero. Now I don't need to escape from her anymore and can be myself.'

He took control of his life.

CHAPTER 99
REGENERATIVE AFFAIR

Ruth's departure re-awakened his sex hormones and he eyed every female he encountered as a potential partner. The naked midriffs and bare thighs of females slinking through Calgary's shopping malls stimulated lustful hankerings.

He was overweight and apprehensive of finally getting together with Vicki. He had been celibate since he had quit sex with Ruth many years before. Since his dismal performance with Vicki in Akar, she had not been receptive during his visits and he didn't know if a sexual relationship was still possible, or if they would only ever be friends now. If he could meet a suitable woman, he could resurrect skills that had atrophied with Ruth and prepare to be with Vicki.

Several single women in his apartment building followed him around, popping up unexpectedly to get his attention. They discovered he had a $20 million annual salary package. They valued him for what he earned, controlled and owned, rather than for any cultural interests he had that might coincide with theirs.

Michael found for him an online dating service called *Amour* and helped him enter profile data. His occupation was 'engineer'. He didn't have to wait long for a match. He met Helen. She was a zany woman, bohemian and spiritual, with whom he recaptured the existentialism of his hippy days.

He and Helen complemented each other: whereas he decided things by thinking, she was guided by her feelings. It was a formidable partnership. Together they campaigned to conserve public lands, fauna and flora, indigenous culture and heritage buildings. They participated in community meetings, went on protest marches, researched archives, wrote persuasive letters to government ministers, emailed media releases, built campaign websites, organised petitions and raised funds for humanitarian aid.

Their teamwork contrasted with his solo past and through her he met people from many walks of life. He had wanted their liaison to be brief but it was so good he was reluctant to break it off to go to Vicki.

'In my early years I was habitually anxious,' he said to Helen. 'People asked me what I was worried about.'

'What did you tell them?'

'I said I wasn't worried.'

'Was that true?'

'No. I was anxious to be doing worthwhile things — to be winning.'

'How did you feel?'

'I was strung up like a racehorse that frets and champs without ceasing. I wanted action. I was a daredevil who got attention by performing.'

'How did you manage your anxiety at uni?'

'I studied obsessively. And there were girls.'

'Did you have a relationship?'

'I did with Vicki.'

'What happened?'

'She put me on a lie detector.'

'Did she find out about you?'

'Yes, that I was crazy about her but had another girl.'

'What did she do?'

'She rejected me.'

'How did you feel?'

'I became obsessed with her.'

'The philosopher Lacan is reported to have said: '. . . *to be an obsessional means to find oneself caught in a mechanism, in a trap increasingly demanding and endless.*' Were you hooked, Tom?'

'Yes, I craved her attention.'

'Did you get her attention?'

'She kept me coming back.'

'Did she make increasing demands?'

'She started telling me how to do my job.'

'Did you do what she wanted?'

'When I could. But I resented it when she came on strong.'

'Are you over that now?'

'Getting there,' he said.

He and Helen played tennis, swam, did gym and walked. He slimmed down and regained fitness. Together they prepared food, did chores, visited friends, went to restaurants, enjoyed entertainments and attended cultural events. Helen's spiritual nature wrapped softly around his rigid purposefulness and she was not fazed by his antisocial behaviour. He had been lost in a lonely place and she brought him back to connect with her in the present, as he never had with Ruth. He was lucky to have Helen.

If he acquired Vicki in a long position, as he hoped, he could short Helen and be invulnerable in a straddle. People who expected him to brave a relationship without a back-up had never suffered as he had from Vicki in his final year at university. He would close the short on Helen as soon as possible, to avoid hurting her. She knew what he was like.

CHAPTER 100
WHISTLEBLOWER

The Commission into the Panypo disaster submitted its report and the government published its findings.

'They have damned Canoil,' said Manfred.

He read aloud. *'Canoil's judgement was unsound in that they constructed and tried to operate a demonstration plant before investigating all possible dangers.'*

'Bullshit,' said Tom. 'Danger couldn't be investigated because mercaptan explosion under those conditions was previously unknown.'

'Was it a chance occurrence, like an earthquake?'

'They won't allow that,' said Tom. 'As CEO, I'm responsible. They have set me up to resign.'

'Your judgement was sound,' Manfred said. 'You had to choose between the shutting down of oil imports from Bigeria or constructing a demonstration plant.'

'If I had refused to build the plant, I would have been blamed for an oil import crisis,' Tom said. 'Either way, they will make me the scapegoat.'

'Maybe you should have been more contrite in allaying the Prime Minister's concerns,' said Manfred. 'When he yelled at you about low oil recovery, you read him the rulebook. This is his payback. They are going to haul you over the coals.'

The Commissioner ordered Tom to attend a media conference. Later that morning he sat in a room filled with reporters and cameras.

Commissioner Southwell asked him, 'Mr Archer, do you agree with the Prime Minister's assertion that 'Oil companies are destroying this nation's oil resources?''

'Canoil obeys the resource extraction laws,' Tom said. 'The laws allow oil companies to extract first of all of the most profitable 30%

of oil. Doing that blocks forever getting out the other 70% and it is relegated to waste. Our shareholders want profits and don't care a fig about the wasting of resources. It is more profitable to find a new reservoir than to get more out of an old one. Within the past 50 years, Canada's oil resources have been pillaged. The government has only itself and its predecessors to blame. Their fiscal regimes have allowed destruction of Canada's national petroleum heritage.'

The room erupted, as people started yelling and the media scrambled to broadcast the sensational revelation. Tom's use of his corporate and technical authority to criticise the government was dramatic news. To end the uproar, the Chairman postponed the session.

Tom went back to his hotel room and emailed his resignation to Ralph. Before they could fire him, he would fall on his sword. His message crossed with one from Ralph informing him his CEO position was terminated for exceeding his authority. He had disrespected the government and put his opinions above the board's and shareholders' interests.

Reporters called, but he refused to see them. They would exploit the issue, seeking victims, without explaining to the public the failure of the government. Media were as much a part of the shameful scam as the politicians, board members, government bureaucrats and shareholders who had neglected the public good. He was sick of the lot of them. It felt good to be free.

Ralph issued a media release announcing Tom's resignation.

Media release
Toronto, July 1ˢᵗ

CANOIL CEO REPLACED

Tom Archer has stepped down as Chief Executive of Canoil. He is succeeded by Gary Ackman, formerly GM of Exploration and Production.

Canoil Chairman, Ralph Gooder, said: 'The Canoil board is saddened to lose Tom, who has improved the company's financial performance and contributed to development of civil society in Canada and overseas.

'We are fortunate to have Gary Ackman as his successor. He has worked in petroleum production in various countries and has made strong contributions to the efficiency of our operations.'

CEO Ackman said: 'I am honoured to be given the job of maintaining and enhancing Canoil's performance and reputation in Canada, as well as overseas. I have great admiration for Tom Archer and what he has achieved. I will endeavour to maintain Canoil's position as the nation's largest and most profitable oil company.'

Commenting on his decision to step down, Archer said, 'I greatly regret the recent disaster at Panypo Oilfield in Bigeria and the deaths of two African workers. As CEO at that time, I accept full responsibility. The tragedy there was compounded by drought and famine, unrelieved by Canoil's payments for oil to the Bigerian Government.

'I want to thank all the people I have worked with, for their loyalty to me and also the legions of Canoil's employees who have served the company with dedication while I was CEO.

'Company operations will be safe in Gary Ackman's hands. I have always found him to be a loyal and competent colleague. My decision to step down will enable Canoil to embark on new relationships within Canada, with Bigeria and elsewhere, bringing a fair return to investors from producing petroleum resources, from serving customers and from new opportunities.'

Tom's exposé didn't change anything.

'My criticism has rolled off the government and oil companies like water from a duck's back,' he told Michael. 'Attitudes are entrenched and will take decades to change. Oil companies will continue to waste oil condoned by governments.'

He forwarded to Ackman an email sent by Tinibu's successor requesting that Canoil pay to the Bigerian Government CDN$19 billion for loss of national income due to the Panypo disaster.

'You don't have to pay them anything,' Tom wrote to Ackman. 'Our contract with the Bigerians had a Force Majeure clause that the International Court must uphold, because our design followed best practices.'

Canoil was let off but Tom was blamed for allowing construction of a technology that had not been demonstrated.

Michael now had enough data for his PhD thesis. He gave Tom a copy of the discussion section to peruse. It listed various methods to eliminate the mercaptan hazard that was thought to have caused the explosion. He had recommended that another test of miscible flooding be done at Panypo.

Tom communicated Michael's conclusion to oil industry leaders and government technocrats across Canada. He arranged for Michael to discuss his study with Commission Chairman Southwell.

Michael submitted his thesis and it was accepted. He left to take up a post-doctoral position at a US university.

Tom was free to go to Vicki. He booked a return flight to England. If things worked out well with Vicki, he would move out of the apartment in Calgary and sell it. Although Nicola and Michael would be losing their family home in Calgary, they would be gaining a home in England.

He told Helen he was going on holiday and would visit his family in the Dales. She helped him pack and drove him to the airport. He would miss her. He felt bad about deceiving her. He had told her about Vicki but had not confided the true purpose of his visit, because if it fell through, he wanted to continue with her.

'You're going to see that Vicki, aren't you?' Helen asked him.

'No.'

It was a lie but he could not admit his purpose because she might tell him to fuck off. He had learned from a lie detector to conceal his duplicity. It had taken so long and so much anguish to reach this point that his deception was necessary in both their interests. Events were proceeding on automatic.

CHAPTER 101
SUBSTITUTE

A 'Fasten Seatbelt' gong sounds. The flight has passed quickly. Tom's new self is emerging from his chrysalis of memories, recalled in first-class comfort, his body and his psyche entering a new phase, preparing to couple with his soulmate on arrival.

He switches the screen to the pilot's view. The runway at Heathrow stretches ahead. Below, he glimpses England's carefully regimented housing estates, reposing wetly in the clouded half-light of morning drizzle. It is a sombre prospect, but today it does not dampen his ebullience at getting together at last with the love of his life.

With a thud and sickening bounce they touch down, reverse-thrust roars, flaps pop up and speed shakes away. His journey is at an end, a roulette is in spin and he is resigned to the fall of the ball.

On the moving walkway, he strides impatiently and joins the short line that gives preference to British passport holders. He declares nothing and wheels out through the sliding glass door to expectant faces. Vicki is not there — he hasn't told her he is coming. He goes to a quiet corner to phone. His hand is shaking; his mouth is dry and his heart is thumping.

'Hello?' she answers.

'Vicki, this is Tom. I'm at Heathrow.'

'Tom! How are you?'

'I'm fine. How are you? Can I come and see you?'

She pauses. Something has changed.

'Tom, I am married now – about three months ago.'

He is not expecting it. How can it be possible? Panic starts but he stops it. He didn't even know there was another man in her life. Why hadn't she told him?'

'Congratulations. Who is the lucky guy?'

He is sinking; talking to her buoys him up. His feelings are in turmoil: he feels hurt, possibly mortally wounded.

'Peter Huntley.'

He has never heard of him.

'Are you happy?'

'Yes, very,' she enthuses.

He feels foolish. Outbid. Gazumped. What does she matter to him now? Is there anything that still does matter? He wants to smash the phone on the ground and stamp on it.

'What does he do?'

'He's an engineer. He used to be in oil, in Canada.'

'He is like me — how weird is that?'

'Canadian?'

'English.'

'What uni?'

'Manchester.'

'A redbrick uni like mine,' he thinks. *'Has she stalked my kind? I could be flattered, but it is too late.'*

His instinct is to study the enemy.

'I would like to meet him.'

'Hmm. I don't know about that.'

'A quick visit. I can be there in half an hour?'

'Let me check with Peter.'

She is gone for several minutes. Tom still wants to be kind to her.

'The intruder will value her more and care for her better when he meets the other serious bidder.'

'Okay,' she says. 'You can come for tea.'

'Thank you. See you around 4 o'clock!'

'Bye.'

In a daze, he rents a car. When he drives onto the M4 there are five lanes, all with cars at high speed. He tries unsuccessfully to turn off the windscreen wipers. He is driving badly but he doesn't care: Vicki is taken. Sadness is in his mind, preventing him concentrating. He stays in the centre lane and turns the radio up so he can't hear horns blaring behind him.

He hurtles along the motorway like a bobsleigh down a luge. At her exit, the chute goes down a country lane between high hedges with ivied embankments where lived hedgehogs, badgers, foxes and rabbits, before cars killed them.

His reverie takes him across a welter of intersections, missing the turn to her place because he is distracted. He tries to backtrack but he can't find a gateway he can reverse into without getting stuck in the mud. On the verge of his dream, an abyss yawns, the danger too present and too real to ignore. He drives past her place, turns around, goes back and skids into her front yard. He is surprised to arrive and tries to recall what his purpose is there — or anywhere.

Vicki comes to the front door and they hug briefly.

Her man sticks out his hand as victors do to losers when they come off the playing field.

'Peter Huntley.'

'Tom Archer. How do you do. Congratulations on your marriage.'

They go inside. Peter and Tom sit in the breakfast room as Vicki makes tea. They recall some names of oil people they both know. Their careers have been similar. Nor is Peter much different to him physically.

Tom feels aggrieved that she has replaced him. She seems to have had her own love straddle and sold him down the river. He could hardly blame her for that — perhaps she had learned it from him.

His exchange with Peter ends from mutual lack of interest and Tom is relieved when Vicki pours the tea. She smiles and passes the chocolate biscuits.

'How have you been, Tom?' she says in her faltering, little-girl tongue-tied way.

'Okay. This is a surprise,' he says.

They both look at him, waiting.

'How long ago did you start seeing each other?' he asks Peter.

'Six years.' He says it defiantly, as if it is arguable.

Perhaps she had kept Peter on a piece of string too.

Tom's chances of getting Vicki now are miniscule.

'Peter's hobby is flying an aerobatic plane,' Vicki says with a laugh, reading Tom's mind. 'He could have an accident and kill himself.'

Tom nods, respecting fate.

They talk about her work, their holiday, then about Nicola and Michael. He tells them about his exit from Canoil. He is talking about someone else, the person he used to be. He is in shock, trying not to show his disorientation. He feels defeated and makes to leave.

'Where are you going?' she asks.

'I'll stay with Richard for a few days. Then I'll go to Larry's, Roger's and Jozef's.'

They are used to him turning up after visiting Vicki.

'Give them my regards,' she says.

A small hug with her and a handshake with Peter. He seems like a good guy. Vicki deserves to be happy with someone after being alone all these years.

'Bye for now.'

He calls Helen at home. He needs to rollover his straddle and maintain her in the long position. They chat and he feels better. Without her he would be abject.

CHAPTER 102
THE LONG AND SHORT

'Why didn't you tell me she was married?' he asks Richard the next day in London.

'I didn't know,' he says. 'I haven't been in touch with her lately. She didn't ask me to the wedding either.'

'Did you know about Peter?'

'I met him several years ago. Vicki often has guys hanging around. I didn't know she was serious.'

Her behaviour in not telling him is puzzling and he wonders if he is missing something. People sometimes inconvenience others unintentionally.

When he returns to Calgary, he confesses his duplicity to Helen. She is a psychologist and interprets his flight to Vicki as a personal betrayal but due to a pre-existing condition: in her eyes he is damaged.

'I'm sorry. It was a compulsion,' he said.

'How long have you had a crush on Vicki?' Helen asks him.

'Forever. Since final year at uni.'

'Do you mean you still have it?'

'Yes, but less strong now.'

'Does she reciprocate?'

'Not since she married Peter. Before that her responses were minimal.'

'Enough to sustain your obsession?'

'Yes.'

'Why?'

'Perhaps she wanted to help me by counselling me.'

'The way you persisted with so little encouragement was autistic,' Helen says. 'Vicki's responses were minimal but you kept phoning, writing and visiting.'

'Minimal was enough. It gave me hope. I couldn't stop.'

'What happened when you married Ruth?'

'It was a mistake from the beginning.'

'You had mental problems that went on and on.'

'Until Ruth left me. Then my delusion of being a Messiah disappeared like a mist in sunlight and never returned.'

'How come in all the time since you met, you and Vicki never got it together?'

'After the lie detector test, our relationship was like a time lapse movie. Our romance was composed from odd days far apart and a couple of weeks of holidays strung together, with years in between. The trust we needed for consummation had ended in the lie detector test. We never even got as far as a honeymoon.'

'Will you forget her now?'

He shrugs. 'I don't know.'

'Get over it or say goodbye.'

'Yes, Helen. I'll try.'

It isn't easy. She sends a Christmas card every year, from 'Vicki and Peter'. The card motif is usually a bird, resplendent and in colour. Her message could be that individuality is great, the consolatory message of a psychologist. He reciprocates with cards having two or three birds, in relationship together. He intends his cards to acknowledge the gender dimorphism that brought them together — and kept them apart when she had not followed the mating protocols he expected.

He thinks silently of Vicki's smile and it warms the cold places in his heart. When this occurs, he refrains from imagining he has a straddle, waiting to reacquire Vicki, when he will sell out Helen. Instead his thoughts turn to the love he feels for Helen and the absence of doubt he has in committing to her.

He remembers the philosopher Nietzsche's injunction, having faith a person is loveable makes exploration of a new relationship precarious. It can turn out right or wrong but being wrong and in love is better than being in doubt and without love.

He had been fortunate to be in love with Vicki but it is time to move on.

'If I give up on Vicki and depend on Helen,' he thinks, *'it would be fairer to her. I would be more vulnerable but maybe that's what real love is all about.'*

When Helen comes in, he goes to her and holds her, with eye contact.

'I'm over it Helen,' he says. 'I'm all yours.'

END

ACKNOWLEDGEMENTS

The author would like to thank the following for their contributions to *Short of Love* and its precursor, *Love Straddle* (2014).

Marilyn Higgins of Zeus Publications, Clive Dalkins (cover art), Zoe Lockley (editing)

Vesna McMaster for masterly literary editing

Gloria Webb for scientific editing

Ross Allen for continuous encouragement and ideas

Trina Beard for encouragement

Brad Ahern for literary critiquing and ideas

Roger and Jan Wooller for discussion of ideas

Kathleen Desmond for Liverpool and Beatles contexts

Donna Munro for assistance with covers and websites

Dianne Bishop for reading and feedback

Dr Zoe Knox for advising history of the Cold War

Dr Tessa Knox for African contexts

Bec Worrall and Ken for ideas and arguments

Kim Bishop for reading and feedback

Helga Parl for cover ideas and discussion

Councillor Nicole Johnstone for community updates

Uncle Albert Holt for inspiring rights of an indigenous people

Jessica White for reading and literary criticism

Colin Devine for advising Russian political contexts

Kenneth Wilkinson for Yorkshire Dales country

Andrea Appleton and Natalie Watson for their interest and encouragement

Lindsay Shepherd for philosophical point of view alternatives

Dr Bill Richards for advising on psychiatry

Dave & Joyce Keith: critiquing, petroleum industry advice and Canadian contexts

Dave & Judith Rurka, Ken Kolb, Jenny Perkins, Rommy Lis, Trevor Schragger, Maciej & Ewa Pomian, Peter & Dot Phillips, Alan & Pat Braithwaite, for friendly feedback and ideas

Adrian Harding for humour

Jude Mousley Osborne for her interest

Millie Brouwers for encouragement

Writers who provided advice and ideas: Francoise Pintat, Greg Lewis, Ian Lipke, Thea Biesheuval, Cally Jackson

Seville Writers Group for feedback and friendship: Nancy Cox-Millner, Robyn Martin, Alan Holzl, Denise Thomson, Jack Russell, Erica, Heather, Herlinde, Laura, Linda, Shirley, Faye, Carmel, Dan, Michelle, Tamara, Della, Carmela, Gloria

U3A Mind Stirrers students for stimulating ideas: Bruce Read, Lesley Brandis, Patricia Dickson, Judith Millington, Patricia Fitzgerald, David, Mary, Kerry, Stefania, Annette, Gary, Ray, Trish

U3A Philosophy students for perspectives and encouragement: Kevin Pearse, Dave Jones, Kathleen Taylor, Cathy Polities, Gaye Polities, Sandra Eatough, Carol, Chris Trehearn, Maggie, Annette, Margot

U3A Thinkers About Issues, Tutor Garth Sherman and students: Anne, Sue, Margaret, Pat, Ken, Len, Brian, Steve, John, Christina, Vivienne

Avid Reader Book Club with Fiona Stager for reader perspectives: Beverly, Colleen, Sonia, Alena, Zdena, Michael

Kurilpa Futures Group for public policy making: Phil Heywood, Helen Abrahams, Pam, Jan, Toby, John, Elizabeth, Peter, Steve, Patrice, Kate, Virginia, Belinda, Maeve, Steph, Ruth

QUMS for musical themes: Jago, Alex Wan, Thomas, Heike, Ian & Jane Clough, Andrea, Stephanie, Nelson, Andrew, Lauren, Zach, Alex, Diane Ho, Phaedra, Joshua, Grant, Marilyn

UQSPA for discussions of philosophy: Sam, David, Breite, Louis, Chris, Jack, Antimony

AUTHOR BIO

Martin Knox graduated as an engineer in the UK and worked in the petroleum industry in Canada. He married an Australian, had children and worked in mining. At age 40 he became a high school science teacher and wrote a textbook published by the Queensland Department of Education. He has been writing novels full-time since 2013: speculative, love, crime fiction, energy and satires. He is involved in public policy-making, proposing an underground railway for Brisbane and discussing climate science. He meets with writing and reading groups and studies philosophy. He writes letters, plays the guitar and does outdoor gym.